TEMPEST

Laura Parker

Zebra Books
Kensington Publishing Corp.
http://www.zebrabooks.com

For Chris; it's still you, babe.

ZEBRA BOOKS are published by

Kensington Publishing Corp.
850 Third Avenue
New York, NY 10022

First Printing: January, 1997
10 9 8 7 6 5 4 3 2 1

Printed in the United States of America

Part One

The Correspondents

"Be cautious then, young ladies; be wary how you engage. Be shy of loving frankly; never tell all you feel or (a better way still) feel very little."
    —*Vanity Fair,* William Makepeace Thackeray

One

Ireland, June 1, 1815

"You're absolutely certain? There can be no mistake? None at all?" The pleading note in the young woman's voice betrayed a desperation that was all too familiar to the old Gypsy woman who sat by her campfire.

"The truth is there, *Rawnie.*" The old woman nodded toward the blaze, setting the gold coins sewn into her head scarf tingling against her well-lined brow. "Titania sees the signs in the fire. It is so."

Kathleen Geraldine sighed dolefully. She had been sick three days running, her breakfast porridge never long in her stomach before it came back of its own volition. She had hoped the queasiness was the result of the deep sorrow she felt with the realization that her father lay dying. Now she knew it was a sign of her great foolishness.

I am with child!

For several moments the two women sat in silence, profiled by the blaze; the young Irish lass with hair the color of the flames dancing before her eyes and the tiny, hunchbacked figure in black with the white wisps of a billy goat's beard upon her chin.

Titania claimed to be two hundred years old. Nothing occurred in County Kildare that the old Gypsy did not know of and have an opinion about. Titania knew whose cows were sickening, whose hens were not laying, whose wife could not conceive. She was the most feared figure on the moor, and the only one with whom Kathleen dared share her secret.

"Ah, well, and there it is," Kathleen said after a moment.

The woman's black eyes caught and reflected back the red daggers of firelight. " 'Tis early days yet. I've potions that can free you of the burden."

Kathleen blushed, her cheeks turning the color of the rhododendron bushes blossoming along the roadways. "Oh, no, I've no need of Rom magic. I'll soon be wed, you see. To an Englishman. An aristocrat," she added reluctantly.

"An English, *Rawnie?*" The old woman eyed her with misgiving and not a little pity. Her voice was dry as dust and inflected with the strange cadence of her people. "What will the aristo say to the news you carry his child before you've borne his ring? You tell him. Then we see what need you have of Rom magic."

Annoyed, Kathleen pulled her shawl tighter against the bite of the wind and tossed her head. The gesture loosed her long curls that unraveled in the breeze. Most time she kept her "lamentable hair" covered. It was not, alas, the deep rich respectable claret inherited by her sisters, but of a fiery brightness crimped into a mass of sensuous corkscrews that brought her unwanted stares. It had brought her to the attention of the nobleman who'd gotten her with child.

"I've nae wish to bother his lordship when we're already affianced. Any day now Bonaparte's army will be bested and then he'll return covered in glory ready to wed me."

Though she did not reply, the woman's obsidian stare caused Kathleen to look around. "What is it, then?"

"You don't want him. It's written on your face, *Rawnie.*"

Suppressing a sigh, Kathleen nodded. "Is there no potion you can give me to cure an unromantic heart?"

Titania patted the pocket of her woolen skirt and then produced from it a small clay pipe. "Before the new moon is gone, you will have the cure for what ails you."

Kathleen stared into the flames. "Will you read my palm so that I may learn what the future holds for me?"

Titania grinned, her blackened gums showing where they clutched the pipe stem. "Have you not just said? Marriage to an English noble. Riches. Children. There is no Rom magic in proclaiming that. These things will be yours because you are what you are, *Rawnie.*"

Kathleen turned her face back toward the flames. She had accepted long ago that the ways of the Rom were indirect. Even their use of language conveyed the serendipity of life and chance. Maybe yes, maybe no. There were no absolutes like those that ruled the world of the *Gaje,* all that were non-Gypsy.

I am with child!

Kathleen breathed deeply, drawing the sharp, cold air as far inside her as possible, and shivered as it sliced into her lungs, a clean reality more easily accepted than the truth of her predicament.

Her father, the celebrated author and knighted Irish scholar Sir Rufus Geraldine, liked to claim he had a bit of Gypsy blood in his veins. He claimed ancestry, as well, with Ireland's great Celtic bards, whose prodigious storytelling talents once astonished and humbled even kings. A romantic tradition, indeed. Yet the indulgent and charming man had seen to it that his only living child had very little of the freedom he claimed as his birthright.

A widower since Kathleen's birth, Rufus Geraldine had asked of God only that she remain unwed to make comfortable his last years. This had satisfied everyone but Kathleen, who was not even consulted. And so she had remained at home unwed and uncourted. She cooked and cleaned and acted as her father's Fair Hand, making neat copies of his work before it was sent to Dublin or London to be published. No one seemed to notice that she felt left out and shut out of the world. Now he lay dying and her future—

"You stare at the flames too long, they make you mad, *Rawnie*."

Kathleen jumped at the sound of the woman's voice. Titania held an earthenware jug and two battered tin cups.

"For the cold," she said, and pulled the stopper from the jug. She poured a little of the brown liquid into the cups. "You drink."

Kathleen took a tentative sip. The drink was sweet and tart and smelled of the musky yeasts of fruity fermentation. She knew better than to ask what it was. Some sort of wild berry wine, she supposed. "It's good," she said with a smile.

Titania merely shrugged, her frail shoulders lifting for an instant the black wool of her heavy shawl as she squatted.

A few minutes passed with only the crackling of the fire and the low moan of the wind across the bog to keep them company.

Finally, Titania took her cup away. "Now what do you see in the flames, *Rawnie?*"

Kathleen stared until the compelling golden curtain of flame filled her view.

"Who do you see, *Rawnie?*"

Quinlan DeLacy.

Kathleen knew Titania had not spoken aloud, yet she heard the parched laughter echo in her thoughts. The thought crystallized on the cusp of that laughter.

Viscount Kearney. English aristocrat. Better known to his public as Quinlan DeLacy. Famous London playwright. And a poet.

Kathleen sighed as a single tear formed and ran down her right cheek. Though he could not know it, DeLacy was to blame for her present troubles.

September last, on her twenty-first birthday, which she had celebrated alone because her father was up in Dublin giving a paper at Trinity College, she could stand her solitude in silence no longer and had given in to a fit of weeping that had surprised even herself. Unaccustomed to self pity, she had done something even more remarkable. She had opened her da's best bottle of whiskey and drunk herself a toast and then another, until her tears ceased and she began reciting poetry to the farm cat from a slim volume recently sent her father by his publisher.

If only there had not been an etching of the poet's face on the flyleaf of the volume, she might never have succumbed to the flight of fantasy that gripped her that night.

Quinlan DeLacy. Even in pen sketch he seemed made of finer stuff than mere mortal flesh. The single color drawing of him was hand-tinted. It showed wide-set, misty green eyes gazing back at the observer. Dark, low-arched brows formed twin barriers, as if that dreamy gaze needed protection from the formidable high, wide forehead of the intellectual. A bold nose counterbalanced the sensitive mouth of a poet. Silky light brown hair spilled carelessly over his collar and draped softly as a girl's about his aristocratic head. He was the very image of the aristocratic dilettante. Byron's fairer cousin. Oh, but he was lovely!

No small wonder, then, that she, alone and destined to remain so, had fixated on his image. She had allowed herself to fall madly and hopelessly in love with a man whose portrait adorned a flyleaf! Because of that her life was ruined.

As the days wore on, she began to weave secret daydreams incorporating the most illusive and impossible of hopes. She felt as if she had taken a secret lover, one whom her da could not object to or frighten off.

She found more of his works among her father's collection. By reading and rereading every poem, essay, and play he had published, she could soon quote them by heart. Her love deepened and expanded. No longer was he a fair face but a kindred spirit. What power of feeling, what exquisite refinement of emotion he brought to each piece. With warmth and amused insight he wrote of a world where the clash of sensuality with sensibility often led to miscalculated alliances and broken hearts. It was as if he wrote directly to her own heart. She began to hold dialogues with him in her thoughts, wonderful witty exchanges on life and literature that drew them even closer.

"Foolish, foolish whims!" Kathleen murmured.

She might have been quite safe in her make-believe if the invitation to her English cousin's wedding last March had never arrived. Had she deserved no better than fate served her?

She had caught the eye of Errol Pettigrew, the Baron Lissey, the day of her arrival. What a Corinthian, all pomade and consequence, with silver eyes and raven hair that curled inward at his temples like Lucifer's own horns. That should have warned her, his similarity to Lucifer.

It was impossible to explain why she, always so sensible, listened to his flattery. Loneliness and madness, surely!

When he kissed her, she closed her eyes to pretend DeLacy held her. When the afternoon of the wedding he lured her away with wicked whispers and a bottle of champagne, to a deserted crofter's cottage, the romance of it made her even more daring.

Dazzled and dazed, she had allowed him to persuade her that their passion must be felt or die. He was a soldier returning to war. He could die. Did she not owe him proof of her constancy? Of course, he would marry her when—if—he returned.

She had not liked seduction. The kissing, yes, even a little of the caressing, at first. But then he had thrust and grunted against her, touching her in places she did not think men knew existed in women. The rest had been awkward, uncomfortable, painful, frightening, and ultimately disappointing.

Men were so different from women. He had enjoyed himself while she had . . . well, she had not. His actions had quite spoiled her lovely feelings and erased her picture of him as courtly perfection.

If she had not cried, she doubted he would ever have given her the ring he screwed off his finger and thrust at her. His proposal was not the most loverlike, interspersed as it was with "hell" and "bloody" and "confounded." She might even have refused him had she not been a little afraid of him.

Afraid? She was more afraid now.

I am with child.

She rose abruptly to her feet. "I must go home now."

Titania did not reply or try to stop her.

"Yes, Da. Good night, Da."

Kathleen shut the door to her father's room and then, thinking better of it, opened it just a fraction in case he might need her during the night. Her hand rested a moment longer on the door-knob.

She could not tell him. She had tried. Even before her visit to Titania she had tried to gather the nerve to tell him that she was affianced to a lord. Now she would have to follow up that admission with an even greater one, that she was with child by this Englishman. He was ill and frail. The shock just might kill him. She would have to manage matters herself.

She made her way quickly to the tiny sitting room of the cottage that served as her father's study and sat down at his desk. Reaching for a clean sheet of parchment with one hand, she dipped a quill in the ink with the other. Titania was right, she must inform the baron that she carried his child.

She stared at the pristine white sheet before her. What should she say? The signet ring with his family crest hung on a string beneath her bodice. The proof of his troth felt like the weight of doom as it lay cold and still against her flush skin.

Abruptly, she stroked the quill across the page, leaving a stream of ink in its wake. She did not want to be Baroness Lissey! She certainly did not want to wed a man she no longer liked.

But the choice had been taken away when she so foolishly dispensed with her virtue. There was the child to think of. She could not refuse him.

She reached for a second sheet and wrote quickly. When she was done, she folded and sealed it with wax and affixed the Geraldine stamp before she could change her mind.

She shoved away the morbid feeling that she was making a bargain with the devil. Misspent passion and misplaced trust, the situation contained all the ingredients of one of DeLacy's more wickedly satirical farces. She might have found amusement in the comparison if it had not been her own life.

Still, some dreams die hard. She carried to bed with her that night and read until her candle guttered a slim volume of poetry with the portrait of Quinlan DeLacy on its cover. It showed his profile tilted slightly upward, as if he were listening to the whispers of his muse.

Two

Quinlan DeLacy dozed in the shadow of the olive grove that sentineled the hillside overlooked by the Tuscan village of Montemerano. The moist pungency of dark earth and astringent odors of sun-baked ancient ruins tickled his nostrils. The droning of pollen-dusted bees in the nearby trellised roses serenaded his dreams.

The sun gradually shifted, slicing through his shade with light so white and pure, it could crack stone. When it lay heavily upon his face, paralyzing him with penetrating heat, the world pulsed red behind his closed lids, suffocating all desire to awaken . . . until fingers brushed his inner thigh.

He opened his eyes and saw beneath the shading brim of his straw hat a brilliant sky overhung by silver leaves trembling and rustling with the silky sound like that of a lady shedding her dressing gown.

He smiled. A dream, of course. He was alone. A pity. He would have welcomed the company.

Italy was a land of ancient legends, of fabled heroes and all-too-human gods, of pious miracles and earthy appetites, of beauty and blood, of rivalry and love. No surprise, then, that he should awaken to the passing sensation of a woman's touch.

As his sleepy lids slid shut, the lightest of touches again stroked near his groin, where his breeches were pulled taut by his spread legs.

He sat up, startled by the boldness of this curious, questing hand.

If you should love me not, let your answer be a steel-tipped arrow to pierce my too-full heart.

He knew the whispered words! He had written them.

He looked quickly about, intrigued. Yet, in searching from brightest light to deepest shadow, he could not catch sight of her. "Where are you, sweet lady?"

Spare me not that I may suffer least. I can endure despair but never constant hope.

More words from his pen! Was she an actress auditioning for a part in his new play? How novel her approach. And how swift of foot! She must crouch behind the low stone wall to his left.

He leaned back in his chair and dropped the rim of his low-crowned straw hat once more over his eyes, determined not to frighten her away. If she preferred him supine and dozing, he would accommodate her. "Come, lady. Do not be shy. Your awakening of me was a sweet stirring. Do I, perhaps, know you?"

You know. You know. In your heart.

"Do I, source of my dreams?" He opened his eyes, peering through the straw fretwork of his hat to see if she had reappeared. "Were we, perchance, lovers?"

You never love, you seducer!

He frowned, disappointed. He had not written those words. The phrase was too fatuous to convey the emotional extremes required for the stage. Yet he had heard the accusation as often as any handsome young gentleman was bound to. There were women in his life, there would be more, all left behind.

"Say not so, gentle creature," he chided in faint amusement. "I love only as a man can, urgently, fervently, and too rapturously for sanity's sake. Yet even the most foolish man will again have need of his wits. If I quit you, it was on reason's behalf. So then, let us forgive and forget."

Facile tongue! You are glib in your emotions and clever in your disdain. One day you shall regret it.

That voice, so lovely, so soul-stirring. Feeling convulsed

within him. Strong emotions startled him with the realization that he was close to tears. "If I have erred, it was with my head, not my heart."

The touch of unseen lips was startlingly cool upon his. *You corrupt me for your own purposes, but it is yourself you betray.*

He sat up, jerking his hat away from his face. Only a dazzling white brilliance greeted his too-sensitive eyes.

The faint brush of phantom fingers against his cheek sent tiny shivers along his skin. It was not a trick of the breeze. It still blew hotly, lifting the hair at his nape.

He felt confused, afraid. He must be dreaming. What else could explain this disconnection with reality?

He shut his eyes to steady his world. When he opened them again it was dark . . . except where she stood.

Tremulous as Botticelli's Venus arising from the foaming sea, she wavered at the edge of his vision like flame, a perfect sheer fantasy of womanhood dancing in a moonlit breeze.

So young, so fair. Good without effort, great without a foe!

Stunned by the accusation, he turned his head fully toward her, but she had disappeared.

A drop of chilling moisture struck Quinlan's cheek, arrowing across his skin as he jerked awake.

As he lifted his head, a second drop splattered against the hand that had pillowed his head. He glanced up and saw not the blue vault of a Tuscan sky, but the dark streaking of damp canvas.

This was not in Italy, but a rain-sodden tent, part of a British military encampment. He was not touring Italy seeking inspiration, but in Belgium preparing for battle.

There was no lady, no warmth, no love . . . only mud and discomfort and the certainty of renewed war.

He had been dreaming, the same dream that had visited him often during the last months. Was it his muse who taunted his sleep, or a bad conscience?

He laughed suddenly. The minx! At the last his fair dream had dared quote his literary rival, Byron, at him.

He glanced down at the portable campaign desk upon which he had fallen asleep. Scattered across it were the failed efforts of several hours' labor. He had been composing a letter. A splatter of rain ran through a few words, streaking them with blue-tinged tears. As he applied the blotter to the page, he reread it to discover that it was one of his better efforts.

Sweet Wife,

You are right to wonder at my silence, for it would seem to bear ominous tidings. Be assured, the fault is not yours, gentlest of hearts. The disquiet that burdened my soul and reduced me to silence is of my own making.

Tonight, as I prepare for battle, I feel the breath of mortality upon me and believe I shall not long be among the living. Let me then be quick to the purpose before my courage fails me.

Despite all evidence to the contrary, believe this to be true. In all my wretched life I have loved none but you!

Were I a wiser man, I would have spared you my hesitation. Were I a more generous man, I could have put your happiness ahead of mine. Were I a less selfish man, I should have bid you seek your happiness elsewhere. Yet, were I other than I am, I could not love you more.

Too brief our union! Too long the years of separation! Have I left it unsaid too long? Have I forfeited our chance for happiness? The possibility distracts me from all purpose, and I am ashamed. I beg you forgive the folly of a man too proud for his own good.

Do not be sad for me. Seek your full portion of happiness with another, dearest one, with my blessing. Yet believe: had I lived, you should not have regretted wedding me.

Your ever-faithful husband

When he had recopied it on dry foolscap, Quinlan leaned back in the canvas sling of his camp chair. A smile of satisfaction hovered about his well-shaped mouth. He had never before written declaration of love from a dying man.

If it had been part of a play or even a poem, he would have made the blandishments more intense and embellished the sentiments of imminent doom. Yet this was no mere theatrical effort. The letter was for a friend, Rafe Heallford.

The sporadic duty provided his regiment these last months had left him with a great deal of idle time and precious little inspiration for his imagination. It was quite by accident that he had found a diversion for his writing skill.

Several months earlier an officer with a wounded hand had asked him to write a letter for him to his wife. The officer had been too embarrassed to dictate his feelings, so, in the spirit of brotherhood, Quinlan had offered to compose the note for him. The fellow had been so pleased with the results that he had shown the missive around camp before posting it. Soon other soldiers, even friends, sought him out. Those with no facility with words deferred to his wording until he gained the sobriquet The Quill.

Though Quinlan could not agree with the morbid fears that had moved Rafe to have such a letter composed, Lady Heallford, whom he knew slightly, seemed to require his best effort. He had embroidered what little he knew of Rafe's very private feelings and his seven-year courtship with Lady Cordelia Lytham to give the letter its piquant urgency.

Quinlan carefully folded his latest effort in thirds and creased it. The exercise of supplying the words for others' feelings intrigued him. A playwright supplied speeches for actors. This was very different. He wooed with letters real women who often responded in kind, agreeing to engagements and offering declarations of love to men he suspected they might otherwise have spurned. Much like the legendary Cupid, he won hearts for others.

Quinlan smiled as he tucked the letter safely away. What came with such difficulty for others simply flowed from him with ease. How ironic that he should possess a particular mastery for penning love letters. For at thirty years of age he could claim—or disclaim—that he had never once succumbed to the very emotion he was so good at describing.

He shrugged in unconscious embarrassment. He could not explain it. He liked women, admired their beauty, and was easily seduced. That they could be roused to respond to him through the power of his words alone pleased and flattered him. But his heart? Ah, his heart. That repository of feeling had never been deeply touched.

So young, so fair, Good without effort, great without a foe!

Yes, the quote summed up his life neatly. For the past five years he had been one of London's premier playwrights. This success had given him a personal satisfaction that his peerage could not. But lately even that had begun to pall. Perhaps because it came too easily.

There was little in his life that had not come easily. What his position, youth, wealth, and attractiveness did not gain him, notoriety had. Not that he was complaining. When Boney was beat, he would return to London and to his life and doubtless wonder why he had bothered to risk his neck.

The onset of snoring caused him to glance over at the figure occupying his camp cot. Heavy black hair trailed out from under his army-issue blanket at one end, while a creamy thigh hitched up the covers midway, revealing a dimpled knee. She was one of the many Belgian ladies who had come out from the city to "entertain" the British officers. There was a little beauty but no special appeal about her, yet he did not begrudge her that. Mistresses were hard to come by in wartime.

He rose and approached the bed, a smile on a mouth so tenderly shaped that his current London mistress claimed it belonged on a woman. Ah, Violetta. Did she still think of him? Or had she, like he, found momentary solace elsewhere?

Most of the women who passed through his life were forgotten as soon as he left their beds. A few lingered in his mind for an hour or two. None haunted his memory for more than a few days. When the passion of tangled bedding and flushed perfumed skin was spent, he found himself no longer interested. When he was in need of intellectual stimulation he sought company distinctly unfemale, for women seldom held his interest when they conversed on ideas, possibilities, and theorems.

Was that his failing or theirs? Was he too fastidious? Too particular? Too critical? Did he expect too much? Was he too uncompromising to give his heart?

He released the suspenders of his overalls and shucked them. The woman stirred as he slipped into bed beside her and closed a hand over a warm breast. "Do you perchance know Chaucer, dear?"

She turned into his touch, her dark eyes instantly open, instantly aware, and instantly aroused. "Is he one of the Hessian majors, my lord?"

"No." He smiled ruefully. "I don't suppose you're familiar with Spenser or Dante, Keats or Sheridan?"

She frowned a moment, her strong features dissolving into a caricature worthy of Hogarth as she attempted the arduous task of thought. "I know a Keats, my lord. He owns the livery stables at Banderlez."

He chuckled and reached for the covers to shield them both from the chill damp of the night. "Never mind, sweet. You weren't fashioned for conversation."

As his bed partner's arm came around his waist and she began kissing a path down his chest toward his navel and then below, he sighed ruefully. He had never yet met the woman who could rouse his intellect and emotions as well as she could his loins.

Did such a woman exist?

"And where?" he muttered, eyelids drooping over lustful sea-green eyes as he allowed himself to be dissuaded from his thoughts by the wicked pleasure of his partner's mouth.

Three

London, June 16, 1815

The *ton* could speak of nothing else. The prevailing opinion was that the Rollerson half sisters' private presentation at St. James's Palace earlier in the week had been nothing less than a deliberate calculation to overshadow the expectations of every other lady making her curtsy before the Regent this Season.

While all other ladies had followed fashion's dictate by sprouting many more than the mandatory seven white ostrich feathers in their court headdresses, the Rollerson sisters had sufficed with the minimum. Other ladies wore festoons of pearls, swinging silk tassels, elaborate gewgaws and swags, diamond buckles and jeweled combs. The Rollerson girls were adorned only in garlands of fresh white roses onto whose petals diamonds had been glued to emulate dewdrops. Alongside their sleek plumage the other debutantes had resembled wind-ruffled pigeons.

This artifice of simplicity was all quite perverse, quite vexing, and—worst of all—quite successful. The Regent had spent twelve seconds conversing with Lord Rollerson's daughters while showing his boredom to all others. Alas, the quandary for women was now clear: Scorn the Rollersons or emulate them?

The only comfort mothers with eligible daughters could glean from the vexing matter was that the ten-day wonder of the Rollerson girls would be past by the time England's aristocratic officers returned from the continent, where they were, at that very moment, preparing to thrash the Corsican Terror, Napoleon.

Once Bonaparte's name was mentioned, conversation shifted at once into exclamations of affront and impatience. How dare he ruin a perfectly lovely June with rumors of war? Wellington would soon set him to rights!

That hope was shared by the Rollerson sisters, who occupied the conservatory of their father's Mayfair house. Surrounded by enormous pots of lacy ferns placed between the tall white columns, the *belles del'heure* were accompanied by their cousin and sponsor, Cordelia "Della" Heallford, the Countess of Cumberland.

As Della perused the solicitations to various routs, musical evenings, and soirees, she congratulated herself on the success of her daring innovations with the girls. She had, of course, heard the rumors. Such gossip made certain no fashion arbitrator of the *ton* would be satisfied until he or she had inspected the girls firsthand. Hence the flood of invitations.

"What a coup, my little darlings," she proclaimed as she laid aside the final invitation. "We've more than made up for our late start in the Season."

Clarette laid aside an invitation to a musical evening. "If only someone important were in town to witness our triumph."

Clarice offered the angelic smile that had so captivated the Regent days earlier. "Papa warned us that with the war, London would be bereft of its most eligible bachelors. He says we shall be paraded before green schoolboys and gouty elderly gentlemen."

"Things aren't at so wretched a decline," Della assured them. "The *ton* remains in town in hopes of being the first to hear the news of Boney's defeat. For that alone, I suppose, we must thank the Corsican!" she finished with a laugh.

Clarette looked up from the private missive she had begun to read. She was thinking of neither the Corsican nor war, except as they affected the author of her letter. Those thoughts colored her response. "How brave and fine of you to laugh, Cousin Della, when you must be suffering such dreadful anxieties." She reached for a lemon snap that exactly matched the yellow ribbon of her lavender morning dress. "If duty had snatched my husband away the day after our wedding, I should have wept continuously until his return."

"You must be glad, then, that you are not I," Della returned with a tolerant smile. "As my husband's absence amounts to more than four months, you should be quite soggy by now."

Far from been stricken by this gentle setdown, Clarette answered with the spirit of all her seventeen sheltered years. "How can you jest? The earl's orders to report to his regiment deprived you of your wedding trip to Italy. Lady Rutland remarked to Papa just yesterday at tea that the alacrity with which Lord Heallford obeyed his commander smacked of desertion."

A cloud of doubt sailed across Della's smiling face. She knew she was the subject of speculative gossip more censorious than Lady Rutland's, but was resolved not to be crestfallen by the reminder. "I'm not, I assure you, any different from dozens of other ladies whose husbands have gone to war. I expected nothing less of him."

Not at all convinced that any woman would willingly part from the man she truly adored, Clarette glanced down at the treasured letter lying open in her lap.

You alone have some inkling of the prodigious event which urges me to hasten back to London . . .

When she looked up again, her dark eyes had grown luminous with emotions that were not entirely pleasant. "I shall be quite selfish when I wed. My husband must remain by my side forever."

"Desist, sister," Clarice said with the gentle superiority of her nineteen years. "You will upset Cousin Della. It is our place to help her be brave."

"Oh, but she is brave!" Clarette gazed with admiration at Della. "It was quite gallant of you to agree, despite your own sorrow, to launch two country cousins on the town."

"Fiddle!" Della pronounced with a rich chuckle that had turned more heads than her husband's. "I'm much too vain to pass up any opportunity to wear pretty frocks in London. To wit, am I not quite the thing in my new spencer?"

She preened for her cousins' amusement, turning her shoulders this way and that so they could better appreciate the new fuller cut at the shoulders of her little red velvet jacket. When she dimpled, it was difficult to tell that she was Clarice's elder by six years. Indeed, she had been considered an Incomparable her first Season and might have remained so even now if she had not wed. Marriage gave her a respectability unattainable by mere age. "Truth to tell, I bear the burden of chaperon quite lightly."

Clarette answered with a note of doubt in her expressive voice, "Admit, you miss your husband terribly."

"Cousin Della is far too sensible to pine over an eventuality she cannot alter," Clarice offered in their cousin's defense. "Besides, gentlemen can be so taxing. One is ever at the effort to please with their favorite dishes, the correct amount of conversation, and the appropriate silences. All the while they spill their wine, trail crumbs on the tablecloth, and stammer awkwardly when they believe they are being most sincere. It's all rather tiresome."

"Only a beauty dares speak ill of a gentleman," Clarette remarked in faint envy.

Clarice's lovely face expressed a rare hint of contrariness. "I wish I were not beautiful. Gentlemen stricken with admiration quite forget how to behave. Gawking and stammering isn't in the least attractive. I prefer the company of my gallant Alfonse."

She lifted a bonbon from the tea tray and held it out to the liver-and-white-spotted spaniel puppy who lay sprawled at her feet. "Here, Alfonse. Come to your adoring girl."

Della smiled affectionately at her charges. She had taken on the task of introducing her seldom-seen cousins to London society with not a little trepidation. Bereft of their respective mothers at a very early age, the half sisters had been reared by a provincial aunt in Somerset. Thankfully, there was nothing gauche about either of them. All they required was a little town bronze.

Clarice, all rose and pearl fairness, possessed the classic beauty of a Grecian urn, the serenity of a church, the perfection of the finest porcelain. True, her tranquil beauty made it difficult to guess her thoughts or feelings, but, Della supposed, gentlemen would find the mystery an added attraction.

Clarette—plump, black-haired, and pansy-brown-eyed—seemed at first glance unremarkable. That impression vanished when she spoke. With a mind as bright as a gold sovereign and a spirit as lively as her sister's spaniel puppy, Clarette would prove a stimulating challenge to any gentleman who sought a spirited miss.

One thing seemed certain. The sisters would not attract or be attracted to the same sort of gentleman.

Clarette sighed deeply when she had finished her letter. "I believe I should like to be a man, for then I could behave just as I pleased. I would roam about on horseback, sword in hand, and test myself in battle." She rose to her feet, brandishing an imaginary weapon. "Then I should cut a wide swath through the impressionable wenches!"

"Whatever could have provoked such perverse speech?" Della asked with a small laugh.

"Perhaps it was Lieutenant Hockaday's latest letter," Clarice suggested with a sly glance at her sister.

"Would that be Lord Grafton's second son, the Honorable James Hockaday?" Della inquired when she noted Clarette's hectic color.

"Yes. A distant cousin on my mama's side," Clarice offered as she settled her puppy in the crook of her arm and covered him with one end of her paisley shawl. "Clarette has formed a tendresse for him."

"Oh, what stuff!" Clarette cast a murderous glance at Clarice. "We became famous friends last autumn when Papa invited

Cousin Jamie for shooting. As he has no sons of his own, Papa is quite fond of him."

Giving her sister an arch glance, Clarice said, "Since he returned to the continent, she has plied the captain ceaselessly with missives. Being a gentleman, he feels bound to respond."

Clarette bristled at this new implication that she was making a cake of herself. "You are simply pea green because he doesn't correspond with you!"

Intrigued by a situation she had not heard of before Della asked casually, "About what sorts of things do you and this young man correspond, dear?"

Clarette smiled smugly. "Oh, all sorts. Cousin Jamie pens wonderful tales of his adventures on the battlefield. He writes of deeds of great courage and duels of honor. Even accounts of the various mistresses Lord Pettigrew keeps."

"Clarette!" her two companions voiced in shocked unison.

Clarette shrugged and subsided onto her chair, almost as astonished as they by her revelation. She could not say what had provoked her rash speech. Her mother, who had died when she was nine, had explained away her daughter's provoking ways by saying that she was born with mischief as her shadow. According to her less indulgent Aunt Lucinda, impertinence was at fault.

"I had not supposed Cousin Jamie's letters contained such *malapropos*," Clarice said with a faintly superior tone. "I must tell Papa."

"You shall not!" Clarette rallied. "Else I will tell him that you ordered the puce taffeta cape after he forbade you to spend another pence on trinkets."

"Tale bearer!"

"Marplot!"

"Now, girls," Della interjected, seeing that her new position would provide challenges she had not anticipated. "This is the perfect opportunity for me to explain that now that you are in society, you will hear many things better ignored. Clarette," she said a little more severely, "I strongly caution you against repeating rumors about persons unknown to you."

"But we have met Lord Pettigrew," Clarette replied with perfect honesty. "He accompanied Cousin Jamie when he visited us in February on their way to your wedding. He's tall as a pike and dark as the devil with pale gray eyes that seem to see into one's very heart. I thought him quite dashing." Pinkening, she turned to draw her sister into the fray. "Tell her, Clarice."

"I did not like him," Clarice said with a shake of her elegant head. "He struck me as too forward and vain as a peacock."

Clarette rolled her eyes in an unladylike fashion. "You did not like him because he laughed at Celia Davenport's attempts to snare his interest. Cousin Jamie says Lord Pettigrew is a notorious wencher who has no time for green girls."

So much for her sermon on decorum, thought Della as a slight frown developed between her dark brows. She, too, had heard rumors of the baron's rakish reputation. "Yet," she mused aloud, "he went to great lengths to make himself unobjectionable to my Irish cousin who came to England for my wedding."

"Miss Kathleen Geraldine? Of course, you've mentioned her in your letters," Clarice replied. "Had you not expected that she would remain in England for the Season?"

Della nodded. "I had entertained hopes she might, but that was before her father became seriously ill."

"I should like to see Ireland." Clarette settled back in an elegant slouch that quite crushed her sash. "I'm told it's full of banshees and elves and pots of hidden gold. When I marry, I shall make my husband show me the world!"

"Who would marry you?" her sister questioned halfheartedly as she picked up another bonbon to feed Alfonse.

"Oh, won't you be surprised?" Clarette answered, and turned a shoulder away from her sister. Once more her gaze lowered to the letter she held.

You alone have some inkling of the prodigious event which urges me to hasten back to London. Be a puss! Don't reveal a word!

Clarette looked up quickly. Her cheeks flushed and her eyes brightened. "Why are men encouraged to think they know what is best while we women are repeatedly told we cannot judge such things?"

" 'Tis the way of the world," Clarice said philosophically.

"It is a very unfair world," Clarette murmured.

Della turned up her teacup to hide her smile. Clarette would need to school her features better if she hoped to get on in London. She had quite given away the depth of her interest in her cousin. Some further inkling told her the girl was not at all certain her affection was reciprocated.

That thought drained the smile from Della's lips. She knew only too well what it was to love and yet hide that yearning for fear it was not requited.

Desertion was an ugly word. It meant court-martial and death for a soldier in the time of war. But what did desertion mean for a wife of two days? Embarrassment, certainly, confusion, and anxiety. And whispers, so much innuendo and speculation!

Della set her cup aside with a force that jangled the saucer and drew the attention of her younger cousins. Embarrassed, she stood up. "Excuse me a moment. Sitting tires my back."

She moved quickly away from the girls toward the exotic plants emerging from chinoiserie pots at the far end of the conservatory. The colorful sprays of orchids balanced delicately on arching pale green stems were a recent acquisition from India by Lord Rollerson. She reached toward a creamy-white blossom the size and shape of a butterfly, and lightly stroked its satin surface.

Until recently she had been sheltered like these delicate blossoms from the harsher elements of life. Her family's prestige had made her position impregnable—until she wed. Becoming Lady Heallford had left her vulnerable, fair game for gossip, real and imagined.

She could not defend herself against the malicious whispers that attacked her as a fool to have chosen to marry over her father's objections, when four months of her husband's silence had left her with a desperation that bordered on silent hysteria.

She had inherited at eighteen a fortune rare for a woman, received from an eccentric maiden aunt who had wisely invested for years in English funds. Because the money was hers outright, she could ignore her father's pressure to marry elsewhere. In *tonnish* households throughout the realm, her independence was made to seem yet another example of why large sums should be kept out of the hands of inferior-brained women.

"You're squandering your brilliant chance on an indigent whose family is infamous for its spendthrift ways!" her father had declared even as he prepared to escort her down the aisle. "He'll wed you for your dowry and soon enough desert!"

She could not, would not, believe it. Not of Rafe.

When he had suddenly returned to London last February with warm embraces, heady kisses, and ardent expressions of desire, she believed it had all been worth it, even her father's anger and disappointment.

Della closed her eyes and willed herself into the moment of Rafe's proposal. All her years of yearning had crystallized that moment into an enduring memento she held under the protective bell jar of her love.

She could feel again the warmth of his cheek brushing hers, the tickle of his curling side whiskers, the scratch of his uniform through the sheer muslin of her gown, the drag of rough hands on her bare arms. He had not asked her. He had simply pulled her into his arms and offered her proof of his desire, the warm, engulfing kiss of a man tongue-tied by the very emotions that drove him. When she came out of his embrace, she had looked up into his dark, solemn eyes and whispered, "Yes!"

She had been much too happy to give any thought to the fact that after seven years of brief encounters followed by long separations, they were nearly strangers. After all, she had loved him, it seemed, all her life.

She had been exactly thirteen years old the first time she set eyes on Ralph Heallford, soon-to-be twelfth earl of Cumberland.

An active regiment of the 1st Royal Dragoons had been temporarily stationed in the village near her family's ancestral home. Her father regularly invited the officers to join the family on social occasions.

On one occasion the compliment of officers included a tall, slim nineteen-year-old with thick, dark hair, a hawkish nose, and deep-set amber eyes under heavy lids. He had recently returned to England from India with Arthur Wellesley (as the future duke was then known), where other noble sons of meager means had won their spurs.

With a severely handsome face that he had yet to fully grow into, he seemed upon first meeting to be the most serious person Della had ever met. He said little, just stood stiffly in the background as if a pike had been thrust down the back of his jacket. When he thought no one was watching, his expression reminded her of the forlorn puppy she had once taken too soon from its litter. That vulnerability had made her want to smooth the creases from his brow, then take his hand and lead him to a quiet corner so that he might recover his balance.

Though her father doubted the haughty young aristocrat enjoyed the informality of country ways, Rafe continued to visit with his fellow officers that autumn, enduring such childish pastimes as blind man's buff and the shadow game rabbit on the wall and eating mutton pies and apple tarts with his fingers.

One afternoon during a game of bob cherry, his lips, warm and dry, grazed hers. In that instant their eyes met and he smiled. The rare charm and grace and joyous beauty of that smile struck her to the marrow, and her young, inexperienced heart incandesced. This was the man she was destined to marry! He went away shortly thereafter, back to war and an uncertain future.

It was not until she made her debut in London that she discovered her desires and society's opinion were adamantly opposed. She learned that Lord Heallford was destitute, his earldom bankrupt. While it was common practice for second sons to join the army as a living, it was thought perverse that he, a peer, should do so. Only in times of great war did peers lend their prestige. Others hinted at the streak of melancholy that ran in the Heallford line. She must look elsewhere for a match.

But then Rafe returned to England that spring from the Indian frontier. He danced with her at Almack's, called often, and brought her little gifts such as a lovely French doll with a porcelain head and real hair the color of her own, an Indian fan of peacock feathers, and shadow puppets from the Far East. Harmless gifts for a girl, yet she was certain they represented more. The gifts said "I have thought of you while I was away."

The Season ended and he went back to his regiment, fighting the Peninsula War first in Portugal and then Spain. During his rare return visits during the following years he offered no promises, sought no favors, made no advances. And so she answered his reserved manner with cautious affection, and waited.

But it was hard. Once she reached the age of twenty-one, even her friends were eager to keep her abreast of rumors about herself. According to them, Lord Heallford had callously left her to dangle on the vine without the consolation of a ring or a vow. While the *ton* did not condemn a man for seeking to marry well, it did look askance upon one who would submit a lady to the humiliation of seven years of uncertainty.

When last February the banns were finally announced, the *ton* murmured darkly that only some new and dire circumstances must have forced Lord Heallford to submit to marriage. When he left England the day after the wedding, called away by duty, they withheld their pity for the bride, saying it was no more than she deserved for allowing herself to be duped.

Della gasped softly as the bloom snapped off and its crushed petals dropped into the palm of her hand.

Had she truly made an error in judgment? Had her father and all her friends been correct in their estimate of the man she had wed against every bit of advice to the contrary? Had she wed a man who wanted nothing more than the fortune her dowry brought him?

A shudder started deep within her. One night in Rafe's arms was much too brief. She knew his passion, but not his heart.

For weeks after, she told herself that the disruption of their wedding plans was a blow she could withstand. After all, he was one of Lord Wellington's most decorated officers. His country needed him. They were wed, nothing could change that.

But now that reports of a great battle were flying like gale winds, she could no longer contain her fears that something might happen that would change forever her hopes and dreams.

"Will this wretched fighting never cease?" Della whispered.

Then, catching herself brooding, she turned back to the room and moved rapidly toward her charges. She had taken action just a week before, having penned a rash note to Rafe. An ultimatum, actually. It bade him reply in kind or consider himself to be persona non grata to his own wife.

Della shivered in delicious fear. That should set Lord Heallford's back up. He would not let so direct a challenge pass unheeded, if only to wish her at the devil!

Feeling much better, she smiled warmly at her cousins. "Now then, have you chosen which invitations we shall accept?"

For the next hour they penned RSVPs to those they chose to accept and composed regrets to the others. The sun had lowered and cast the room in deep shadows by the time they were done.

Clarette, who had finished her correspondence first, surreptitiously opened the letter from Jamie Hockaday she had tucked away to reread the last lines.

Devil of a do expected in Belgium shortly. Once old Boney's given the rout, I will hie back to town to do the pretty for your father.

"I wonder what gentlemen speak of on an evening such as this?" she mused. "Do you suppose they think and speak of us?"

"No doubt they've better things to do," Clarice replied as she reached down to snuggle the puppy dozing in her lap.

"Oh, I hope not," whispered Della so softly, not even she was certain what she said.

Four

Brussels, June 17, 1815

"Bloody hell!" snarled Errol Pettigrew, the fifth Baron Lissey.

The letter he had been reading slipped from his trembling hand and settled on the dew cloth of his tent by his right boot tip. Even at a distance the brief lines penned in the remarkably precise hand were legible. As he stared at it, the phrase "with child" leapt again from the page.

> My dear baron,
>
> I am with child. This is no accusation against you. I have not forgotten you, nor your token. No one yet knows of our pledge. We can be married in Ireland in a manner that will not draw notice or comment. I await only your coming to post the banns.
>
> Yours,
> Kathleen

Errol smirked. Surely he had not been so alarmed by her tears that he had actually promised marriage?

He dimly remembered giving her, to pacify her, the heavy crested gold ring that had been a gift from his father upon reaching his majority. Her possession of his ring would be proof enough to some of his culpability. If he were not very clever, he might find himself leg-shackled behind the misadventure.

"Not possible!" he said, and kicked the letter from him.

The chit could not possibly be breeding with his seed. He had spent only one afternoon, a fairly uncomfortable one at that, with the sobbing virgin. It should not be possible that fate would so entangle his plans with this vexation. He had not even enjoyed the seduction, tempting as it had first seemed.

He glanced at the parchment that had landed a second time by his foot and snarled, "Bloody hell!"

What a crashing bore a February wedding in the Somerset countryside had turned out to be. If not for the sake of duty to one's fellow officers, he would never have agreed to be present.

Then the Irish lass appeared. The color of her hair had been enough to put him in rut before he ever spoke to her. The glorious red curls had lured him to her with the hope that they reflected the wanton nature of their owner.

A mocking smile rearranged his roguishly handsome, slightly dissipated face. Lantern light played along his severe features, turning his eyes into canyons and picking up red highlights from his black hair. He knew his faintly satanic mien both thrilled and frightened women. Some admitted that the source of their attraction to him lay in his wide pirate's smile. The more bold confessed it was the revealing cut of his skin-tight breeches.

He chuckled lewdly, remembering how her curious if innocent gaze had had him swelling in his trousers before they were even introduced. To be the object of rapt fascination was a novel sensation, even for him. Of course he had taken her. How could he not?

She had been remarkably unguarded for a gently bred girl. She had not protested his attempt to lure her away from family and friends. She had seemed almost eager to be in his arms. She had seemed equally eager to dispense with her virginity, until the moment of penetration. He could not be faulted for pressing the seduction. She had wanted to know how wicked he was. He had wrapped himself in her red-gold fleece and shown her!

"Breeding!" he voiced in contempt. An Irish scribbler's daughter!

He would not own the paternity. She could have bedded a dozen Irish farmers after he had shown her how it was done. Only now that she had come up breeding, she had thought to pin the deed on him, a titled Englishman.

"Not bloody likely!" He reached for his opium pipe, a taste for which he had developed during his years in India, but in doing so his eyes lit upon the saber he had been honing for the coming battle.

Only in the heat of conflict did he feel completely alive, thoroughly himself. The smell of powder and cries of battle gave his life a focus no other experience could match. The thrill of danger, the possibility of defeat, that is what he lived for.

While the battles of Quatre-Bras and Ligny had raged on about them these last days, his division had sat idle. Wellington was hoarding his limited cavalry to pit it directly against Napoleon when the moment came. The Second Dragoons, called the "Grays" because of the superb gray-coated horseflesh upon which they were mounted, were restless, eager, itching to fight. *He* was eager to fight.

He replaced the pipe. He would not drug his restlessness tonight. Tomorrow, oh, let it be tomorrow, he would fight!

He tugged at the gold lace peeking out beneath the cuff of his jacket. His gold-buttoned, fur-lined pelisse cost more than his saddle. Humility was not his hallmark. Nor was he accustomed to explaining himself—even to himself.

His gaze came unerringly back to the letter now bearing the muddy stamp of his boot heel. Clearly, he would have to do something. Could not leave it for her to publish her version abroad when she realized he would not marry her.

She might be poor, but she was well connected enough to be able to sustain her claim on him. She was a relation of Heallford's bride. A bit ticklish, that. One did not compromise a relation of one's fellow officers and expect it to pass unnoticed.

He would have to find a method to silence her until he could return and extract his ring from her. A cleverly veiled threat, perhaps. But what? And how?

A rakish smile lifted up one corner of his mouth. Of course! He'd apply to The Quill for help.

"Virgins are the worst!" he muttered.

Heated passions turned too quickly cold in the face of discomfort. The passion spent was not worth the trouble. He would never attempt one again. Yes, that would be his penance. He would never again seduce a virgin.

Quinlan had just begun to catch his breath when the flap of his tent was flung open and the gray overalls and red jacket of a dragoon officer appeared in the breach, streaming with rain.

"Lud! This drizzle will be the end of us. Oh, I do beg your pardon!" the invader remarked when he noticed Quinlan was completely nude and far from alone.

"Come for your letter, Jamie?"

"Righto! Only don't mean to intrude," Lieutenant James Hockaday answered, which was a highly inaccurate statement. The cherub-faced young man with golden curls often did just as he pleased even if it inconvenienced others. Because his actions were without malice, he was most often forgiven. In this instance he whipped off his pelisse and gave it a hard shake, prepared to stay awhile.

Seeing that the younger man had no care for the very pleasant interlude he had interrupted, Quinlan offered his bed partner a solicitous pat on her naked buttocks and shrugged. "Allow me a moment to dress."

As he sat up, his tent flap was flung back a second time and Errol Pettigrew strode in, looking as enraged as if he had discovered a company of French hussars bivouacked in the British encampment. Without greeting he strode over to the cot. "Out, Jezebel!"

He grabbed Quinlan's bed partner by the arm and tugged her upright, then scooped her dress from the floor and flung it at her. "Here's your finery. There's a full five hours before dawn. Find some other officer to scratch your itch."

Ignoring Errol, she turned toward Quinlan, her wide blue eyes in appeal. "What about my compensation?"

Quinlan plucked a coin from his trousers and tossed it to her. As she snatched it from the air, Errol laughed. "Would all slatterns were so easily satisfied."

Insulted by his words, she strolled provocatively to the exit before slipping on her dress, openly daring every man present to view and not want her.

"Haven't had a doxy turned out of my bed since I was seventeen and *Maman* sent my eldest brother to recover me from Miss Tilby's Salon," Quinlan offered when she was gone.

A smirk lifted Errol's upper lip, his humor seemingly restored by his efforts. "Seventeen? I'd passed through two mistresses by then."

"Some of us are less precocious than others," Quinlan said dryly. "Why are you here?"

"I just saved your wretched life. 'Tis a fact the first to fall in battle are those who go to face the enemy with their faucets wrung dry."

"How charmingly you put it," Quinlan remarked as he fastened his overalls.

Errol turned to eye the decanter standing on a small folding table in the opposite corner. "Captured French brandy? Excellent! We'll drink to the coming battle."

"If there's to be a battle, why was I not informed?" Jamie asked as the older man passed by him.

Errol shot the younger man a razor-sharp glance. "What are friends for if not to bring glad tidings?"

"You're in a singular mood," Quinlan remarked as he slicked his longish ash-brown hair back with both hands.

"There's cause enough." Errol helped himself to a healthy gulp of brandy, bypassing its flavor in favor of the liquor's bracing qualities. "Some sweet drab seeks to pin paternity on me."

"You've sired a child?"

Errol glared at Jamie as if he were the source of his displeasure. "Who among us hasn't?"

"I have not!" Jamie exclaimed.

The edges of Errol's smile could have etched glass. "You, dear boy, have scarcely graduated beyond diddling sheep."

The younger man flushed deeply. "I've lain with women, plenty of them. Ask Heallford."

Quinlan and Errol both raised questioning glances in the direction of Jamie's nod, to find Major Rafe Heallford, their superior, had entered the tent dressed in a well-worn uniform fashioned for battle more than style. Heallford had been in Brussels with Wellington for weeks. Without a word passing among them, every man present knew that his return meant battle was imminent.

Major Heallford lifted an imperious black eyebrow. "I cannot vouch for Hockaday's prowess." He raked rainwater off his dolman, adding, "Nor have I ever sired a bastard."

"Somehow I'm not surprised. You spend far too much time brooding." Errol turned to Quinlan with a broad pirate's smile. "But you, we've trolled the streets of Naples, Rome, and Paris together. Admit it, you can claim at least one by-blow."

Quinlan's gorgeous face retained its slightly bemused expression. "Sorry, but I'm not guilty of that specific crime."

The answer, Quinlan noted, seemed to reignite Errol's temper. "Don't come the parson with me, you sanctimonious lot! If you have no seed thriving, 'tis because you lack the zest."

"Then the child is yours," Jamie voiced with maddening politeness.

Errol snarled at the smiling man. "Am I to claim the offspring of every doxy who spread herself for my entertainment? I think not." He went back to pour himself another brandy.

"Suppose you've finished my letter," Jamie voiced hopefully to Quinlan, having found a comfortable perch on a trunk.

"As a matter of fact, yes," Quinlan answered, but his glance went to Rafe. "But I must conclude another matter first."

Mollified, Jamie occupied himself with an examination of his new sash. He was aware that he presented the indolent air of a young blood and might have easily been mistaken for one of the inexperienced nobles who had joined a local militia in order to wear a splendid uniform. Yet when needed, he snapped quickly into the role of one of the ablest officers in British uniform. Still, he had only one desire these days, and that was to get back to London as quickly as possible.

Only when Errol had drained his glass a second time did he notice Quinlan and Rafe with their heads together over a piece of parchment. "Here!" he cried as he quickly crossed the room. "Are those our new orders?"

Rafe's golden gaze came quickly around to repel the man. "No. It is a private matter."

The glint of hostility in Heallford's gaze sparked Errol's antagonistic nature. "Private, is it? Then it must be The Quill's latest work. Give us a recitation."

Rafe folded the paper without answering and placed it inside the open neck of his dolman.

The challenge was too much for Errol. Grinning his pirate's smile, he reached out to pluck the letter, but Rafe deflected his aim with a slashing movement of his hand.

"Ho! The man's offended," Errol crowed in mischief. "Come, hold him, Hockaday. I would know what secret Heallford's too stiff-necked to share. By God, I'll not be deprived of it!"

Rafe set his hand to his sword hilt. "Touch me and you will not have to wait upon the patience of an enemy's sword to draw your last breath." He spoke softly, but the threat of his challenge was the greater for its apparent coolness.

Errol still smiled as he drew his sword, but enmity glittered in his pale gaze. "I name 'now' the hour and 'here' the place!"

"Wellington would be hard put to make an example of you

in present circumstances," Quinlan offered casually as he moved to insert himself between the pair. "But if you must spill blood, do so out of my quarters. It runs with enough muck."

Errol snorted in derision as he continued to stare at Rafe. "Fair enough. I'll not preempt your fate. We all know you've seen visions of apocalypse." He smacked Rafe in the chest with the flat of his free hand, causing residual raindrops to fly from his dolman. "Keep your damn secrets. You are welcome to them!"

Rafe put his sword away, saying, "Occasionally even you go too far, Pettigrew."

"Where is *my* letter?" Jamie inquired, relieved to have the moment behind them. "I'll willingly recite it for all."

Quinlan reached into his desk drawer and then handed it to him.

With a infectious grin Jamie unfolded it and began reading aloud.

My dearest lady,

   Until now I have been like a stone in your presence, all feelings unspoken, all thoughts denied. I can abide in silence no longer. The very admiration that kept me mute now moves me to press upon you my suit by such means as are within my reach. Hear only the sentiments and scorn not the blank verse of this paper messenger. I must speak or burst!

   Kindest, gentlest lady, I offer you my hand and heart. Will you marry me?

   I beg you do not hesitate in your reply though it be the prerogative of every lady of sensibility to do so. Come, Sweetness, be as brave as your goodness and answer with the voice of your heart. Say, "Yes, Jamie, I will be yours!"

   Yet, if you mean to reject my appeal, do not spare me, tenderest of souls. Know that you wound only my aspirations—not my heart. As for my love for you, you can do it no harm. I claim the right to love you and to love constantly, forever.

Yours.

Jamie folded his letter with an accompanying smile of satisfaction. "If that don't turn her up sweet, there's no pleasing a lady. Thankee kindly, Quill."

"It's well done," Rafe agreed with a rare smile of amusement. "I wish you good fortune in your endeavor, Hockaday, though at four and twenty you seem a bit young to think of tying the knot."

"Agreed," Quinlan said. "But what can I say against this 'Love to which the gentle heart so quickly succumbs'? Though I should be remiss if I did not refer you to Dante's other observation, Hockaday. He said, 'O woe, how many sweet thoughts, what great desire, brought them to this miserable end!' "

Jamie laughed. "You cannot dissuade me. My mind and heart are set upon this course."

"Who's the chit?" Errol demanded with all the effrontery of an under informed parent. "You never mentioned her before."

"A gentleman don't divulge a lady's name till he knows her mind." He rocked back on his heels, well pleased with himself.

Errol turned quickly to Quinlan. "God rot the lovesick musings of callow youth. If you dare accept a real challenge, you may write a letter for me."

Quinlan laughed. "A love letter? To whom?"

Errol's expression hardened. "Nay, no love letter. A blistering epistle to the jade who would pass her by-blow off as mine."

"Then you were serious before," Rafe said, speaking aloud the genuine surprise of the other two.

"What of it?" Something dangerous moved in Errol's gaze as it again zeroed in on Heallford.

"Do you have one of her letters with you?" Quinlan prompted, to distract him.

Errol's gaze narrowed as he suspected a trap lay in the question. "What makes you think she wrote me?"

"Nothing in particular," Quinlan responded pleasantly. Now that he had drawn Pettigrew's wrath away from Rafe, he did not like any better having it directed at himself. "I merely ask so that I might learn if she is literate. If not, I shall take care to keep the words simple and the sentences short."

The thunder suddenly cleared from Errol's expression. "Then you will write the letter?"

Quinlan stared at his friend. "Is there such a woman?"

Calculation entered Errol's expression as he judged how best to win the sympathy yet not arouse the suspicion of his comrades. "She's a bold London baggage with a sweet mouth and a luscious body which she shares with whoever takes her fancy. Now that she's come a cropper, she seeks a pedigree for her bastard. You may tell the harlot in whatever words you choose that I will not own it. Tell her, further, that if she wags it about that the bastard she carries is mine, I'll publicly denounce her as an adventuress."

Quinlan shrugged. "That kind of bully threat doesn't require my services."

Errol wiped his mouth with the back of his hand. "Then dress it up with a ribbon but tell the slattern I rescind my offer of marriage."

"Marriage?" the three echoed.

"God rot the three of you!" Errol turned and strode out into the wet night, leaving his pelisse and dolman behind.

"Now, what do you suppose is wrong with him?" Jamie asked.

Rafe and Quinlan exchanged glances. "A belated onslaught of conscience?" Rafe suggested.

"Will you write it?" asked Jamie. "The letter to the slattern, I mean."

"I don't know." Quinlan picked up his quill. "Though he may be a devil with women, he is a friend."

"And the best officer of the lot," Rafe offered quietly.

Quinlan smiled slowly. "You are far too modest, Heallford. Still, I should like to put Errol's character on paper." He sketched an imaginary banner with a hand. "A study of the roué caught in contretemps."

"He won't thank you for it," Jamie said. "But what of the woman? Perhaps he did sire her child."

Quinlan lifted a brow "I'm not altogether convinced she exists. You've seen Errol when he was spoiling for a fight. Any provocation will serve."

"She exists," Rafe said quietly. "Pettigrew was sweating."

The three men shared a short silence. Errol Pettigrew never showed any sign of fear. Ever.

"I must away to post this." Jamie patted the letter tucked into his dolman. "I would know as quickly as possible whether happiness is to be mine."

Rafe gave the younger man a curious look. "It might be kinder to the lady if you waited until after the battle to post it."

"Never. Unlike you, I'm certain I will live."

"Ah, the bravado of youth," voiced Quinlan in mockery, for he saw the quick hurt come and go in Rafe's usually enigmatic gaze.

Jamie was undaunted. "In fact, I shall ride for Mont St. Jean in hopes of seeing my letter franked tonight. Will you ride with me, Heallford?"

Rafe shook his head. "But I bid you both a good night." He looked from one to the other with a grim face. "Until tomorrow."

An hour later Quinlan stared at the letter that flickered in and out of focus in the uncertain light of his guttering candle.

Despite reservations about penning a letter that would break an engagement to a woman with child, he had soothed his conscience with the possibility that no such woman existed. Or, if she did, then he might be doing her a favor by saving her from an unfortunate match with a man like the Baron Lissey.

As fine a soldier and drinking and whoring companion as any a man might want, Errol was nevertheless poor husband material. No woman, however loving, would long hold his interest, never mind his heart.

Quinlan lay the paper aside and rubbed his throbbing temples. Perhaps he was making too much of the matter. Women who lay with men who were not their husbands knew the risks. Who was he to take umbrage at the unfairness of it all?

Still, his artistic soul was moved enough by the plight of a supposed jilted bride.

He picked up the letter once more. He had written to this unknown woman as if she were his own mistress and he the infamous rake who was betraying her. Thinking to move her past the shock and shame of being jilted, he had deliberately chosen phrases that would provoke her anger. Such anger, he hoped, would buoy past her sorrow via righteous indignation. Was that a cowardly thing to do?

"Who's to say what lies in a woman's heart?" Quinlan murmured to the darkness as the candle suddenly snuffed itself.

Outside Rafe's tent the rain drizzled on, running in rivulets under his dew cloth, deepened into a morass of mud holes where his boots had passed and the weight of his few belongings sank in.

He flung an arm over his eyes as he lay on his cot, but he knew he would not sleep this night for it might well be the very last night of his life.

He did not know when the feeling first came over him that he would never return home. Perhaps it had been after Della's most recent letter. In it she begged him to answer, to give her some assurance of his feelings.

His feelings!

He did not know how other men loved. He knew only that for him his love for Della was a force so great that he feared it. A reasonable man, he had fought the astonishing emotion. He knew from the first he had no right to love so splendid a girl. Time only made things worse. As she grew from a girl into a woman, life put ever more obstacles in their path. When she turned eighteen, the year she made her curtsy at Whitehall and became an heiress, he thought he had lost her. So beautiful, so shining of soul, so courageous of heart, she might have won the love of any better man, a prince—even a king. And yet the dearest angelic creature had chosen him!

He was not immune, as his friends thought, to the gossip that had swirled about their courtship. He knew all London thought he had wanted Della only for her money. They would never believe that he wished her destitute. For then she would have believed without doubt that he loved her solely for herself.

But rumor had done its worst. He had known, even on the day they wed, that the doubts of others still plagued her. She had hidden it well, but he had felt her tension. Pride had kept him silent, convinced that his protestations of love would sound insincere after the fact of their vows. Then, too, if she had doubts about his feelings, should he not have been doubtful of hers?

Then on their wedding night she had offered him a pledge of her love with the sweetest gift of her body. Just looking at her made him ache so badly, he wanted to run roaring into the night. Those feelings made him reluctant even to touch her, afraid that the power of his need would bruise her. But she had not allowed that. He had discovered she was no china doll but a flesh and blood being with a passionate nature as real as his own. She was now his forever and always. No man could put asunder.

It was the moment of greatest happiness and humility of his life. Why had he not told her then how much he loved her? How could he have been such a coward?

The fault, the lack, was his. Quinlan's brilliant letter had caught his feelings exactly. If he had been wiser . . . more generous . . . less selfish . . . he would have wed her sooner or released her from his loving to let her find happiness elsewhere.

'Twas pride that delayed his pledge to her for seven long years. Jealous of her family's fortune and disdainful of his own disgraced house, he had let pride withhold his truest feelings from her. Now it was too late.

He suspected with the irrational presentiment that comes to

some men that he would never have a chance to say to her the only words that would give her serenity. He had brought her nothing but shame, doubt, and sorrow. Given the chance to begin again, he would make any sacrifice for her. Without regret. Because he loved her more than his own life.

He swore under his breath and swallowed back his unshed tears.

Part Two

The Correspondence

"Sir, more than kisses, letters mingle souls."
—Letters to several persons of honour,
to Sir Henry Wotton, John Donne

Five

London, July 15, 1815

Kathleen Geraldine held on to her seat atop the highway coach as it rounded a curve in the road, and prayed to the Blessed Virgin Mary and all the saints above to spare her worthless miserable life.

As she dug her elbow into the side of the corpulent pig farmer who kept pressing with unnecessary familiarity against her with every sway of the coach, she realized yet again that she was not as missish as she had thought she might be, considering her circumstances.

She was ruined, and her debaucher would never now rescue her. Lord Pettigrew, the Baron Lissey, had died at Waterloo. Shortly thereafter her father had died and, with him, her last hope for protection. Her unborn child, on the other hand, was quite well and thriving despite her first hopes.

She supposed, if she had been a truly repentant soul, she would have thrown herself into the Liffey and drowned. She was not the sort of girl to be overly concerned with her own survival, but she had other reasons for wanting to live just then. She was the repository of a life as yet totally innocent of the sinful nature of man. Therefore she was on her way to London to do what she must to protect the future of her child.

She had few illusions about her future, fewer hopes, and even fewer options. Already five months gone, she could no longer remain in her village without drawing the suspicious eye of her neighbors. She would not have it whispered behind her father's headstone that his youngest child had gone and gotten herself with child.

As the road jostled the passengers, she was all but swallowed by the bulk of the man next to her. She offered him a hostile glance from beneath her bonnet brim, but he merely winked at her.

Her father had said it was her coloring that made strangers bold. Today her flamboyantly red ringlets were tied back by a strip of blue gingham ribbon and hidden beneath her bonnet. Yet her bright red brows and thick, curly lashes and sprinkling of ginger spots across her nose could not be so disguised. Nor her eyes, the rare, clear green of a still lake under a spring sky.

She shifted her weary hips a fraction of an inch away from the pig farmer and set her gaze on the horizon of chimney pots that signaled the outskirts of London. Once the idea of visiting the great city had set her heart pounding in joy. Now a sour, queasy feeling enveloped her at the sight. Her hopes of living there as a respectable married woman were gone forever.

She could have forgiven Lord Pettigrew for dying. It was the way of all men. What she would never forgive was the letter that had arrived from him a few days after his reported death.

The virulent missive was tucked into her reticule. A more miserable exercise in dishonesty she could not imagine! The hand that penned it had not been quite steady, as if he had been drunk when he wrote it. But she doubted she would ever forget a line.

. . . *not my child . . . can in no way permit you to connect my name, my consequence . . . my generous nature opportuned upon by your treacherous wiles . . . no self-respecting woman would find herself so compromised . . . suspect to my regret other men must be in like favor with you . . . this revelation of your true character is a great disappointment . . .*

Indignation pumped through her anew. He blamed her for the seduction! After the shock wore off, she had decided that she disliked him more for spoiling her picture of him as a chevalier than for spoiling her virtue. She would rather her babe have had a dead hero than a cad for a father.

Ah, well, and was it not her own silly fault for thinking it would be otherwise?

As the coach swung out this time, the action should have carried the pig farmer's bulk away from her. However, he scooped an arm about her shoulder and squeezed her close so that the rancid stench of his clothing filled her nostrils.

"Have a care!" she shouted, and twisted away.

"Eeeyiaah!" He recoiled from her with a yelp of pain and grabbed his side just under the armpit. "I've been skewered! I'm bloody bleeding!"

Kathleen eyed him impassively. "Sure and now you're too braw a lad to be done in by a wee prink?" She held up her knitting needle for the other passengers to see.

The disclosure of her "weapon" produced guffaws of amusement from the men and knowing smiles from the other women sharing the top of the coach. The pig farmer snorted in affront, pulled his straw brim low over his eyes, and hunched away from her.

Satisfied that she would not be further accosted, Kathleen tucked her weapon away.

She had carried a bodkin under her shawl since she was five. The lanes and byways of Ireland were ever a dangerous place. Her father had explained to her that when men were deprived of honest ways of making a living, when they were forced to starve and watch their families do the same, those without hope became desperate, and desperation made some do what they would otherwise never have conceived of as possible.

She understood now the full implication of her father's words. She was doing what a few short months before would have been inconceivable to her. But the impossible had become a necessity.

She touched the package tied with a string that lay in her lap. Her future, and her babe's, depended upon her courage and her audacity. It was the highroad to London, or it would be the highway for her forever.

She did not regret the loss of her virtue as much as she lamented the thought of becoming a fallen woman. A deeper sigh escaped her. If she did not succeed in her plan, a life of prostitution might well claim her.

Strange how things worked out. Perhaps Father O'Donald was right and God was an Irishman. It would seem to take a being with an inordinate appreciation for the absurd to work out the retribution of one's sins so that the source of one's sinning might well become its just punishment.

July 18, 1815

Quinlan DeLacy eyed his publisher and producer with all the loathsome intensity he usually reserved for the physician's leech. "You do not like it?" he repeated softly.

"Don't like it doesn't begin to describe my feelings."

Horace P. Longstreet surged to his feet behind the desk in his office in Drury Lane, startling awake the fourteen-pound tabby cat that was dozing in a slat of sunlight at his owner's feet. "I abhor it! Despise it! Detest and—"

DeLacy had lifted a hand from the arm of the chair in which he sat, the action effectively silencing the man. His hand remained aloft a moment. As his fingers curled slowly, thin pink seams of healing scars appeared on the tightened skin of the knuckles that rose hard and knotty. Despite the implied threat of violence, DeLacy continued in an attitude of perfect ease in his chair.

"You will not produce my play?"

Horace eyed his client speculatively over the rims of his spectacles. A man of ruthless practicality in his business dealings, he considered the replies he might make, and rejected the first two as too honest for his health's sake. The third was scarcely less gracious. "It would ruin you."

"I see." DeLacy's features remained emotionless as his hand lowered to rest heavily on the chair arm.

"Hope you do, my lord." Horace stepped boldly from behind his desk, in appearance unflappable. "You must reconsider."

"If 'tis a mere matter of pacing, or phrasing . . ." DeLacy let the thought drift away.

"It ain't a matter of phrasing. It's a matter of subject."

Horace thumped the foolscap manuscript that scattered across his desk, a tribute to the swiftness with which he had skimmed and dismissed it. "What we've got here is a tragedy."

He judiciously omitted the observation that it wasn't even a good tragedy. "Plaguey poor drivel" would have been his verdict to any other author. But DeLacy had a reputation, a reputation that meant considerable attendance. As both publisher and producer, he was worth quite a fair amount when Lord Kearney's plays were running. It was in between engagements that his purse inevitably thinned. That was the case now. He was not about to run off his golden goose, yet he had to prevail against his lordship's new gnat-witted yearning to become a "serious" writer.

Men of DeLacy's ilk were thoroughbreds, a little wild, certainly high-strung. They needed to be given their heads most times, yet discipline must be maintained or else they would ruin themselves. He, Horace P. Longstreet, was the viscount's literary trainer.

"What does the public think of when they hear the name Quinlan DeLacy?" he asked rhetorically. "Why, they begin to smile. That's because they know DeLacy as the author of the finest comedies Drury Lane has seen these last five years. The Regent himself holds you in highest favor."

DeLacy dipped his head in acknowledgment of the praise.

Feeling progress was being made at last, Horace continued. "First there was *M'lady's Spaniel* followed by *The Baronet of Bow Street.*" He stretched his arms wide, as though they held a theater banner. "Then 1812 brought us both *A Rogue's Wedding* and *At Liberty, Madame,* my own personal favorite. However, who am I to quibble when I saw with my own eyes Lord Byron laugh aloud while attending a production of *The Failed Romantic* last spring."

He stopped short to cast a jaundiced eye on his scribbler. "That one could have earned us both a challenge. Instead, your pen aptly skewered both Byron and his detractors, earning his respect *and* making it your greatest success yet."

"The box office receipts were tolerable," DeLacy returned. "That is your measure of success, is it not?"

Horace knew better than to use the vulgar subject of money as an inducement to a nobleman, particularly one worth a fortune before he ever put quill to paper. Instead, he soothed his ego by stroking his new brocade waistcoat, an investment toward future earnings. " 'Pon my soul, don't know three authors together who can claim your equal. London audiences are tough nuts. Few playwrights escape a pelting. There'd be you and—and—"

"Sheridan," DeLacy offered in a bored tone.

"Never. Old stuff."

Horace looked away, allowing an expression of yearning to replace his showman's enthusiasm. "I suppose we could revive *M'Lady's Spaniel*. Five years. New faces in town. Not quite the cachet of launching a new DeLacy production, but—"

"I have said I will revise."

This time Horace could not hold back a retort. "It won't serve. The audience would lob sour oranges and worse at the stage before your tragic hero got off his first speech. They won't believe you penned such drivel."

DeLacy's storm-at-sea gaze lifted from a distracted perusal of the portly orange tabby batting the swinging tassel of his left boot. "You make it sound quite extraordinary that I should have achieved what little notoriety I have."

"Not at all . . . your lordship," Horace added as if it had just occurred to him whom he was addressing.

Horace had trod the boards in his youth until he realized that while applause was all well and good, money was the greater comfort. Backstage machinations, at which he excelled, were every bit as theatrical as what occurred after the curtain went up. The pay was better too.

"Come, my lord," he said in a tone designed to encourage confidences. "You may tell me what ails you. Are you dispirited by productions of your work which employs overwrought actors with underweight talents? You're right to think so. London is lousy with rouged actors and blowzy jades. Poxed ponces and doxies, the lot of them!"

Frowning, he wrapped one hand about his chin as he propped his elbow in the other. "I wasn't going to speak of this yet, didn't want to queer your muse. But now . . ." His bushy brows lifted to form caterpillar crescents above the rim of his lenses. "Here it is, then. I've got Kean all but signed for the lead in your autumn production."

The alert look that came into DeLacy's eyes told Horace he had struck the right chord at last. He lifted a hand toward the ceiling as if to cue it to crack open so that heaven's own light might shine down on them in beatific blessing. "Think of it! London's greatest actor spouting *your* words!"

Contrary to his expectations, DeLacy's handsome face did not bloom with a smile or even twitch with approval. "Kean is a tragedian. Would he not feel more at home in my drama?"

"A fish wouldn't feel at home in that dismal morass," Horace grumbled, and then harrumphed, pretending to clear his throat. It was time to take off the kid gloves.

He bent and snared his tabby under its sagging furry belly and hoisted the tangerine beast into his arms. "It's this way, my lord. My customers expect a comedy, and one way or the other I must deliver on their expectations." He paused to give added weight to his next words. "I cannot, will not, consider a drama of any kind from you until you have delivered me a DeLacy farce."

For the first time, DeLacy's face lost a little of its glamorous hauteur, and the expression of a more vulnerable man emerged, one who had seen too much and done things unthinkable.

"I have lost my way, Longstreet." He spoke with a gentle

simplicitly. "I can no longer write of trifles and the foibles of fools. I have seen such things . . ." His haunted gaze was utterly effective in disarming even his producer's mercenary soul. "Such things."

Now Horace understood truly the depths of his playwright's dilemma. So DeLacy's war experiences were behind this change of heart. Horace suspected it was nothing that could not be quickly cured by good wine and better whores. "You're not the only soul to suffer, my lord," he began carefully. "Half of London is in mourning. Yet we are the victors, and victors will have their celebrations. They want light and laughter and you're the man to give it to them. The public, *your* public, mustn't be let down."

Reaching out in a rare, uncalculated gesture, he lay a paternal hand on the younger man's shoulder and said in a kindly tone, "You're young, and young men are at their best when they are in love. Go and find yourself a lady."

The fatherly advice went amiss. DeLacy's expression altered. The mask of aristocratic enigma slipped back in place. "If that is your solution, then it would seem we have nothing further to discuss."

"So it would seem," Horace rejoined, allowing frustration to color the words.

DeLacy rose with effortless elegance from his chair, drawing the critical admiration of his producer, who would have paid a considerable amount to have the viscount trod the boards in one of his own productions. Impossible, of course. Unheard of. But what a superb masculine physique! The limp left by a leg wound was barely noticable, much less so than Byron's gimp. DeLacy was as handsome as Adonis, and his theatrical debut would have caused riots, packed the house for months, and sent Byron's brooding dark looks clean out of fashion.

Few actors successfully portrayed the aristocratic prerogative on stage. Edmund Kean had the gift. Kean! No DeLacy play . . . no Kean. Kean would sue! As for the Regent's reaction—without the Regent's backing, a Drury Lane producer might as well slit his own throat!

Horace took a step after his departing guest. His ultimatum now seemed a wild blunder. "If you entertain the mere suggestion of an idea for a comedy, my lord, I should be glad to hear it. Anytime."

The viscount did not bother to respond as he stepped through the door, the limp caused by his war wound a bit more pronounced than before.

"Artists!" Horace muttered as he methodically stroked orange fur. "High-fidgets and Bedlamites the lot of them!"

Kathleen had no time to prepare herself for the sheer splendor of the gentleman who stepped across the threshold of Horace P. Longstreet's office.

For three days she had been sitting in this ill-lit, unventilated anteway, and for three days she had missed the renowned producer and publisher. Today she was determined she would not be put off. She popped up from her chair as the door opened and thrust herself into the pathway of the gentleman who emerged, top hat pulled low as he prepared to barrel past her.

"I say, sir!"

He turned almost violently toward her and then paused.

Equally surprised, Kathleen stared back for she recognized the gentleman!

Six

His was an artist's face, fine-boned with chiseled features and boudoir-silk lips, framed by long ash-brown locks into which streaks of sunlight appeared to have been threaded. One might have thought the tender droop of dark lashes a curious balance for the purely masculine thrust of his angular jaw. But the air of the contemplative dilettante disappeared when she fully met his gaze. Sea green but with a tempest in their midst.

He stared at Kathleen a moment longer, the muscles in his jaw slackening as if he would speak. Then the muscles firmed. His fine mouth thinned into something less than a smile as he bowed his head a fraction, turned on his heel, and walked on.

"Quinlan DeLacy!"

The astonished whisper that escaped her caused his head to twitch back toward her for an instant. She caught sight of the tight curve of a bitter smile. He must think her a fan. If only he knew!

At that moment the door behind her opened again and a short man with bristling silver hair and spectacles spoke sharply. "Are you waiting for me, miss?"

"Aye—yes, sir. I am. She tossed one last look over her shoulder, but DeLacy was gone. She turned back to the man in the doorway. "Was that really—"

"Quinlan DeLacy? Yes, rot his temperamental soul! Beg your pardon, ma'am, but artists can be vexing." The man swung a hand toward the entrance to his office. "Come along, I'm a busy man."

Kathleen moved toward the office in a daze. *Quinlan De-Lacy!* She had actually seen, nearly spoken to the man she had adored for nearly a year! The realization was as swift and stunning as a thunderbolt. Her heart banged a heavy rhythm as odd feelings shifted within her so quickly, she had to grab the door latch for support.

Occupied by his own thoughts, Horace began pacing the cramped space before his desk. "Says his muse has deserted him," he muttered. "Says he wants to write drama!"

He glanced down at the orange ball of fur that was attempting to insinuate itself about his left ankle. "DeLacy's a satirist, a Chaucer of the Regent's England, a Swift for the *ton*. Now he would be Byron, pen tragedies full of strife and dying, laments and disasters. Rubbish!"

He looked up and paused suddenly to stare at Kathleen. "I say it cannot be done."

Skewered by his expectant gaze, Kathleen decided he must be awaiting her reply. She removed her hand from the latch and moved a little nearer. "Mr. Shakespeare wrote comedy and tragedy equally well."

The theatrical producer nodded once. "So he did. But you think DeLacy the Bard's equal? I do not!"

He pointed at the pages scattered across his desk. "See for yourself the offering of the playwright who would be a tragedian. Come. You may read it. Be my second opinion, an impartial judge." His eyes narrowed as she hesitated. "You *can* read?"

"Certainly," Kathleen replied, taking no offense in the question.

He scooped up a handful of pages and thrust them at her.

She was only half aware of the chair the producer drew up for her, so delighted was she to be handed DeLacy's work. She was among the first to read the latest lines to flow from her idol's pen! It was as thrilling as stumbling upon an ancient text never before deciphered—or at least it should have been.

After reading only a few lines, she began to frown. She bit her lip, her head giving little shakes of disbelief as the pages piled up in her lap while her host supplied her with new ones from the stack on his desk. When she reached the end of act one, she looked up with the bemused expression of one who has witnessed a disaster.

"Well?" Horace prompted. "What is your verdict?"

"It's—" She swallowed her reluctance. "It's quite bad."

"Exactly. Ex-*act*-ly!" He smiled like a man who had won a considerable bet. "Execrable! A plaguey poor exercise in self-pity lamentably executed. It won't draw crowds. 'Twill draw only flies!"

"You said such things to Lord Kearney?" she asked, too astonished to think to curb her own impertinent tongue.

"I did! Well, perhaps not in those exact words," Horace admitted. "Artists have tempers too."

Recalling the gentleman she had just passed in the hall, she could well believe that behind his lovely façade stood a temper capable of laying scourge to hell. It was there in those tempest-green eyes.

"Perhaps he could make a few adjustments?" she ventured to ask.

"Adjustments?" Horace repeated. "Other than the fact he should cut out the first act, eliminate the second, and burn the third, I can think of no other adjustments to be made."

"It's not that bad." Moved to defend the man she had admired to distraction, she added, "Lord Kearney is a brilliant writer. If his failings in this instance were pointed out—"

"He'd stomp out, leaving my office smelling of sulphur and brimstone. Which is what he has just done."

Kathleen glanced down at the text balanced on her knees. "I don't understand how so capable an author could fall so far."

"It's the war. DeLacy would go back to fight. I warned him of the risk to his talent. An artist must protect himself from as well as experience the world. Now he says he's seen things that make it impossible for him to laugh. That—" he pointed to the work—"is not drama. That is pathos. He is wounded and this is his blood. There is no skill in it, no calculation, no brilliance, only pain and sorrow and guilt. I cannot, will not, produce it!"

"And yet in places it is nearly like his other," Kathleen countered without realizing how she was challenging the judgment of the man whose good opinion she had come here to gain.

Struck by her temerity, Horace barked, "How so?"

"Did you not find the hero's encounter on the battlefield with the French hussar much like DeLacy's scene in *M'lady's Spaniel* where the curate must tell his benefactor that he is the sire of the benefactor's daughter's child?"

Horace's expression quickened. "You refer to the moment in act two when Lord Highbottom, who is suffering from a cold, holds his razor against the curate's throat and a sneeze nearly ends the poor fellow's life?"

Kathleen smiled. "Exactly. The soldier's actions in this text are similar. A French hussar has killed his best friend in the heat of battle. The hero is driven by revenge. Yet, if he kills the hussar in his sickbed, the deed will be no more than slaughter, for which he will be hanged. Perhaps if the hussar where a shade more philosophical about his own demise and the hero less tormented, the scene could be turned into a moment where the audience would smile through its tears."

Horace gazed at the strange young woman in threadbare clothing, wondering how such a sweet-faced chit could know so much about manipulating an audience's emotions. "Once I would have agreed. But this is DeLacy's third attempt to rectify the script, and the results are as you read them."

A chill overcame Kathleen. It had never occurred to her that talent could be lost, that brilliance could dim, that genius was as fragile as smoke. She had watched her father struggle with his books and seen how desperately lonely that struggle could be. But she had never known, even in his driest days, his abilities to fail completely. Only as he lay dying had his talent slipped behind the veil of mortality. Her fingers skimmed lightly over the bold script on the page. But this? This was the writing of a man who had given up.

She looked up from the miserable text. "Perhaps if I spoke with—"

The producer's laughter startled her and brought the flame of embarrassment to her cheeks. "You? Just who are you, miss?"

"I beg your pardon, sir. I'm Kathleen Geraldine, Rufus Geraldine's daughter." She picked up the parcel she had laid aside. "I have brought you his final text."

Wonder widened the publisher's gaze. "Let me have it, child. I may have need of a volume of light verse. I assume it is light verse?"

"Yes, sir." Kathleen did not quite meet his eye as she handed it to him while struggling to hold her shawl closed with her other.

Her action caught his eye. "I forget my manners. May I not take your wrap, Miss Geraldine? 'Tis lamentably warm."

"No, I won't be staying," she assured him as a traitorous bead of perspiration slipped from her bonnet onto her brow.

She rose quickly, only to snag her shawl on the chair arm. Even as she grabbed for it, the heavy wool mantle slipped from her shoulders, revealing her gown.

"Damn," she whispered, and bent to retrieve it, but a sudden sharp stitch in her side made her gasp and reach instead for the support of the chair arm.

With an agility to belie his years, Horace rounded his desk to come to her aid. "There now, Miss Geraldine. You've overset yourself. Allow me to assist you into your chair."

There was nothing else to do, Kathleen realized with a giddy sinking feeling that could be partially blamed on the fact that she had not eaten but once in the past twenty-four hours.

As she straightened, Horace gave her a thorough glance, prepared to enjoy the sight of her slim young body and generous bosom. Instead, he was startled by the swelling curve beneath the bosom of her high-waisted gown.

"My dear child, you're breeding!"

He had not meant to state the matter so baldly. His blunder was made clear by the bright red color that suffused her face. "Forgive me, ma'am. I should congratulate you." He reached down and picked up her shawl to offer it to her. "I did not know you were married."

Kathleen hesitated as she arranged her shawl to hide her protruding stomach. The truth could drown her, but she was already weighted by so many stones of misfortune, what was the truth compared to that? She lifted her chin. "You've not heard I'm wed, sir, because I'm not."

Horace watched the rosy hue in her face deepen before it receded and quickly revised several opinions of her, not all to her discredit. "I see."

"Most certainly you do." She turned to pick up her parcel. She would leave before she was kicked out.

"And where do you think you are going?"

The question halted Kathleen in her tracks. Where did she think she was going? Where, indeed? Had she thought? No, she had not. She had depended upon success. Depended upon it!

She never cried. Oh, she had shed a few tears over her father's grave as any loving daughter might. But she was not given to fits of self-pity or feminine hysteria or melancholia. She had faced dry-eyed the reality that she carried a child. She had crossed the Irish Sea in solemn determination. She would not give in to tears. She vigorously ignored the sneaky droplets coursing down her cheeks.

"The father is, of course, a blackguard who seduced then abandoned you." Horace suspected she would not recognize the mockery behind his words.

Indeed, she did not. When she turned back to him, her face was composed, if one ignored the clear tracks on her cheeks. "He is dead, a hero at Waterloo."

"Indeed." Horace leaned back against his desk with arms crossed. In the past month he had heard this story from any number of breeding actresses, singers, and opera dancers draped in black. Their true loves had conveniently died "at Waterloo." By his reckoning, there would be a bastard born for every man who had fallen in that conflict. For all he knew, the girl before him might even be telling the truth. That did not matter. She was pregnant without benefit of a ring or a husband. Any way one turned it, she carried a bastard.

He had liked Rufus Geraldine. Never met the daughter, but knew she was an indispensable part of her father's work. His "darlin' Fair Hand" Geraldine had called the child who copied his efforts in a neat, legible script.

He was accustomed to sizing up the weaknesses of young women in desperate circumstances. To judge by her attire and thin face, she had little if any money. Too bad London had a sufficient number of Fair Hands. She would find no work here.

Something akin to pity twinged his middle, but he squashed the emotion. He was a practical man, clever and subtle, full of craft and wile. Sentimentality never touched him. More likely, the annoying pang was a result of the grilled oysters with bacon he had had for breakfast. Still, he might do her some good and make a little money into the bargain.

He relieved her of her parcel and then waved her back toward the chair with an impatient hand. "You have come this far to see me, the least I can do is tell you if it was worth the effort."

She brightened. "You will read it while I wait?"

He glanced at her over his spectacles. "You are so impatient to be gone? You've someplace to go? Lodgings, perchance?"

She tugged her shawl tighter. "No, sir."

"I thought not."

He walked over to his sideboard and poured two glasses of canary, the larger portion for himself. "Drink this. You look peaked." He glanced about, spied a tin of Scottish shortbread, and opened it. "Take two," he directed her.

When he decided she was suitably occupied, he resumed his seat behind his desk and began to read. Charming as the text proved to be, he did not miss it when she reached out to take a portion of DeLacy's work from his desk and begin to read again.

Half an hour later he looked up, more puzzled than disappointed. "Why did your father choose the subject of a fool's journey for his last book of verse?"

"Well, now," she began with a trace of Irish inflection and the first smile he had seen. It quite changed her pleasant face into a fetching one. "My father was thinking of our homeland. The fool is Ireland. He's rather like Parsifal. The fool with the uncanny luck to delve into the muck yet come up smelling like a rose, don't you see?"

Horace saw a great deal more than she supposed. "You're amazingly well read for a young woman."

"My father—"

"To be sure. Your father." He slapped her father's text down on his desktop. "Your father never wrote this. It ain't in the least like his work. Who did write it?"

Lie! the voice of self-preservation cried. "I did," honesty made her answer.

Her answer stunned him, but only for an instant. "What did you hope to gain by the hoax?"

"A little money, sir, for myself and the babe. Father always said I had a talent for mimicry. Now that he's gone, I'd no other way to make a living. His writing was all that kept us fed. Our cottage was deeded to him through a benefactor for his lifetime."

Horace eyed her with the jaundiced eye of a man who had dealt with far too many desperate women. She was attractive, if one liked the Irish-milkmaid sort, but not the sort to storm London as a temptress of the demimonde. Nor was she the sort to make a popular writer. No Jane Austen, her stinging wit reminded him more of— "How well do you know Lord Kearney's works?"

"I know every play by heart!" Kathleen responded with great daring. " 'Tis like you thought them yourself, only you know you couldn't have. That's his talent, don't you see? I could mimic his style if you wish."

"Mimic his—"

Madness struck, sudden inspiration so concentrated that Horace's eyes crossed.

Staggered, by the audacity of the scheme scintillating in his thoughts, he chuckled. He wouldn't dare! DeLacy would call him out! No, hire thugs who would use him as bait for the Thames's fish. And yet . . .

He had promised the Regent a DeLacy comedy in the autumn. He had signed promissary notes based on the income DeLacy's play was certain to bring him. Without a DeLacy play he would face ruin, or worse, be sentenced to King's Bench Prison for debt! Unless—

The mercenary heart that made him a success began to beat in its most manipulating rhythm as he turned back to her. "Tell me what you would do with Lord Kearney's text?"

Caught unprepared, Kathleen regarded him with astonishment.

"Don't come the mummer with me now, child. You were well and full of opinion before."

Mystified by his request, she nonetheless repeated her earlier observations. "Well, sir, if the hero were an innocent at the onset, a bungler or naive soul, then his transformation into hero on the battlefield would be more ironic. A sense of the absurdity of life would infect the entire play."

The gleam in the producer's eye turned suspiciously golden as guineas. "So you believe you could mimic DeLacy's style?"

She frowned. "I can't honestly say. I've never actually done it." But the idea took instant root in her imagination. "I should like to attempt it."

"Clever girl!" he said quickly. "I want you to write the scene you described about the hero and the hussar. Remove yourself to the desk just there." He pointed to the secretary next to the window at the far end of the room. "You will find ink and quill, and fresh paper in the drawer."

Never a fool, Kathleen shook her head. "No, not until you explain why I should."

Unaccustomed to young women who brooked his desires, Horace rose to his inconsiderable height and leaned across his desk.

"I've need of a young woman of your special talents. To that end I'm prepared to offer you a small sum for your trouble."

"What will I have to do for it?" Kathleen rallied. "I'll not lie with you, not for that and twice as much."

Horace straightened away from the pugnacious expression on that winsome face and wondered fleetingly why it had not occurred to him to consider making the offer. Still, her talent was rare compared to any mistress's. "I'm not offering you a slip on the shoulder, chit. I'm asking you to rewrite Lord Kearney's play. Of course, no one must ever know. No one."

"You're not out to cheat him?"

Horace smirked. "Hardly."

But the suspicion once raised would not leave Kathleen's mind. "No, I won't do it."

"You won't?" Veins popped out on his forehead. "Did you not come to me bold as brass to sell counterfeit work?"

"That was different," she answered primly. "Father gave it his blessing. Lord Kearney's work is another matter. I won't be party to outright deception. My scruples—"

"Your scruples be damned! Where do you think you will end if you refuse me? You should thank providence that you possess a talent I'm willing to offer good coin for."

He saw his words fall like bricks against the glass shell of her self-esteem. Her lips quivered and her hands flexed into fists. His conscience tweaked him again, but he told himself that if she were wise, she would come out of this scheme with a tidy sum and a future she did not probably deserve. But De-Lacy . . . DeLacy worried him. Thoughts of the Thames again drifted through his mind. He did not know how to swim. Detested fish.

He picked up his cat and began massaging its bright orange

fur. He would suggest his noble playwright take a sabbatical abroad to heal his spirit, somewhere isolated and distant. With luck, DeLacy might remain out of London until spring. More than enough time to produce a play without the knowledge of the man who would get the credit for it. But first things first.

He suddenly brushed the cat off his lap, unable to fathom why he had picked up the shedding creature in the first place, and looked at the white-faced girl rooted to her chair. "Well, my dear. Which will it be?"

Kathleen had never thought more quickly in her life. She had sworn to herself she would do whatever she must to provide for her child. If she must stoop to sinning, then defrauding a playwright held infinitely more appeal than prostitution. "Do I have a choice, sir? Yet I would have something in return."

Horace's gaze narrowed. "More than I've offered. What?"

Kathleen steeled herself, for her needs had not changed. "Enough money to leave England and Ireland forever."

Horace answered slowly, wondering what bats had taken flight in her belfry. Not blackmail, surely? "Forever is a long time."

"I will do your dirty work," she went on as if he had not spoken, "but when I'm done I must away to have my child in peace. I shall seek a warm climate for the babe's sake. Do you promise to help me?"

"Certainly." Promises were as easy as lies.

To his amazement, she reached across his desk, plucked his quill from its perch, and then offered it to him. "You will write down the exact amount you're offering me and sign it."

He recoiled. "We've no need of a contract, surely?"

She smiled sweetly. "I've naught to lose, sir, and you have all to gain by our bargain."

Horace recognized stubbornness when he saw it. "How do I know I can trust you?"

"Trust, sir? And aren't we both in need of the trust of the other to survive?"

"You drive a hard bargain for a gently bred girl." He offered her a begrudging smile and then began to write. "It might prove cheaper to marry you, if I weren't already wed."

"I take that as a compliment, sir."

"So you should!"

Seven

"Huzzah"

Jamie Hockaday's whoop startled every servant in Lady Elberta Ormsby's Belgravia house. They would have been further unsettled had they witnessed him enthusiastically kiss the invitation that was the cause of his exuberant vocal display. The invitation was for an informal dinner *en famille* with Lord Rollerson's family. He knew it could well be the most important social event of his life.

Moments later the door to the servants' stairs opened on the second floor and the lieutenant plunged down the flight. Taking the steps two at a time, he ran smack into the newly hired tweeny who was climbing those stairs with a nose-high pile of fresh linen. Luckily, the lieutenant's agility was not much hampered by having his left arm in a sling. He caught her by the shoulder with his good hand and thereby prevented what might have been a tragedy had she toppled over backward.

Once on the main floor, Jamie paused at the breakfast sideboard to fill a plate with several slices of toast, a dozen rashers of bacon, grilled kidneys, and shirred eggs. Throughout his breakfast he kept glancing at the invitation he had laid by his plate. And each time he smiled.

He had not received one word from the Rollerson household since his wounds at Waterloo landed him for a month in a Brussels hospital, not even from Clarette. He had come to look forward to her letters. Remarkably, they were as entertaining and informative as any gazette, and often more amusing. He had assumed, when he heard nothing, that Clarice was keeping her own counsel until his return. Quite right of her. No lady published abroad her intentions to wed a man who had not first publicly declared himself.

To announce his return to London, he had left his calling card at the Rollersons' Mayfair residence for three days running but had not found them at home. In the meanwhile he had occupied himself with putting his business affairs in order and selling his commission. He glanced again at the card and grinned. With the supreme confidence of youth, he expected Clarice would accept him.

Minutes later, as he pushed back from the fortifying meal, Lady Ormsby sailed in under the full rigging of mourning, her husband being but five months deceased.

"What the devil are you about, sir, to be jostling maids on the servants' stairs?" she inquired in her vibrant contralto that easily penetrated her black veil. "I will not have my girls interfered with." She pounded the tip of her alabaster cane, an affectation rather than necessity, on the parquet floor. "Whore in other quarters, young sir!"

"Hello, Auntie," Jamie greeted her, unoffended by her frank speech. She was a product of the Georgian age. Profanity and irreverence held equal fascination for her when she was of a mood. He bounded around the table toward her even as the footman pulled out a chair for her. "In a dash, Auntie. Ta-ta!"

"Hold to, young sir." Swinging her cane up and across the space between the table and the sideboard, she effectively cut off his line of retreat. "Have you forgotten your promise to accompany me to call on Lady Fairweather?"

Jamie paused, a quick frown forming then clearing on his brow. " 'Fraid I had. Sorry to disappoint. Can't help it. Make it up. There's a promise."

Lady Ormsby gazed up into his face framed by golden waves that foamed into curls at his temples, and suppressed a very unwidowlike sigh. She knew him for what he was, a handsome scamp occupied entirely by his own pleasures, as most young men were want to be. Upon his majority of five-and-twenty years, he would inherit her late husband's portion of the Ormsby entailment, as the gentleman had died without issue. Duty not blood bound them, yet she tolerated her nephew's unannounced arrivals and abrupt departures at her home as a demonstration of their genuine affection for each other.

"I won't ask where your spend your evenings. Nor will I ask why you are prepared to treat an elderly woman in this shabby way." She fluttered her lashes shamelessly. "You will, however, wish to repent your desertion."

"Sorry. Can't accommodate, Auntie." A thoughtful guest, Jamie took over the butler's task of arranging the lady's chair as she seated herself. "Must see my tailor. My bootmaker. My haberdasher. Send flowers! A thousand things!"

Lady Ormsby threw back her veil the better to study him. A lively woman of diverse interests, she found the dictates of a widow's mourning severely confining. Consequently, she took advantage of every bit of intrigue that swept through her doors. On this occasion she noted that her nephew's expression contained barely suppressed emotions which flushed his cheeks.

"Do I detect the application for a lady's favor in these preparations?"

"It won't serve to quiz me," he answered cheerfully. "Not till I've news to tell."

Her interest sharpened on this turn of phrase. "Good news, I imagine?"

Instead of answering, he bent swiftly and kissed her rice-powdered cheek.

Her color rose instantly behind the impression of his lips. It puffed up her consequence considerably to have a decorated officer from Waterloo beneath her roof.

"You are mightily pleased with yourself today," she said, as she gave the sling cradling his bandaged arm a gentle pat.

Jamie merely smiled. He had Clarice to thank for his mood. No doubt she had engineered the invitation he had received. If

she accepted him, he would ask DeLacy to be his groomsman.
Then there would be a wedding to plan, a home to be purchased,
soon a nursery to set up—

"Do you suffer a bout of the colic?"

Jamie looked up to find his aunt eyeing him through her
lorgnette. She continued to employ the trappings of an earlier
age. For instance, though elaborate hairdos were two decades
out of fashion, she wore towering gray curls that Jamie referred
to behind her back as her "moldy shepherdess" coiffure.

"Haven't seen quite so vile an expression on your face since
you climbed a tree in your father's orchard and ate all the green
apples you could hold." She chuckled. "Never heard such
moaning and groaning. And your eyes kept rolling back in your
head."

Jamie colored to his cheekbones. "You may quiz me all you
like. I shan't be put out of temper today." He made her a quite
clever bow. "But you must excuse me."

She allowed him to pass, though she would have preferred
his company a little longer. "Wear cream and caviar, my boy."

"I beg your pardon?" Jamie paused short of the open doorway to turn toward her.

"Now that you're cashiered out of the army and cannot dazzle
feminine hearts with your uniform, it will pay to appear a touch
more somber than one's mood." She applied her lorgnette to a
study of him once again. "I should gather by the look of you
that you're about to choose a daffodil waistcoat figured in vines
of turquoise and puce."

"Nothing so fashionable," Jamie declaimed, though he had
had in mind one made of rose satin embroidered with gold
clocks.

"Black and white, 'tis the combination worthy of a hero. And
clawhammer tails on your evening coat. The lady will not be
able to gainsay against you. Believe it!"

* * *

"Why are you so plain?" Clarette complained to her image reflected in the looking glass.

She wore an elegantly cut gown of sea green with elbow-length sleeves decorated in the new French fashion of tucks and bows. The bodice, so shallow and tight as to make the most of her modest bosom, was held in place by a deep pink sash passed high under her breasts and tied in a banded bow in back. A garland of pink silk roses circled the lower skirt midway between horizonal rows of tucked ruching. Long kid gloves and a single white feather in her heavy, sleek dark hair, piled high in a simple chignon, completed her ensemble. In spite of her complaint about her face, she had felt a spurt of satisfaction with the display, until her gaze strayed to her sister.

A vision in a high-waisted gown of pale pink sarcenet, Clarice possessed sloping ivory shoulders that rose above the stiff lace ruff edging the back of her draped bodice. This neckline displayed to perfection the ripe golden ringlets twining along the arching length of her long, slender neck. A tortoiseshell comb decorated with gilded lace was tucked into the topknot of her chignon. If a more elegant creature walked the earth, Clarette could not imagine her.

"You're so beautiful," Clarette whispered without resentment. She might as well resent a flower in the garden. One could hope for betterment, improvement. Clarice was proof that perfection was born, not achieved. Yet it was a bitter recognition. "I should have been drowned at birth like an unwanted kitten," she pronounced in resignation.

"Nonsense. We are as alike as not." Clarice leaned close, bringing her exquisite face next to her sister's more prosaic one. "The chin is the same, as is the angle of cheekbone. Something similar, too, at the brow line."

Clarette stared at the faces side by side and wondered at Clarice's extraordinary charity. The clash of gold and raven-wing hair coloring, cream and buttermilk complexions, lily and mushroom figures, was too much for her sense of the absurd.

"The something similar between us is our youth, dear sister. It is a miracle Papa claims both of us!"

A cloud of doubt sailed across Clarice's serene expression, only to be chased away by a thought. "I know!"

She straightened and placed her hands on Clarette's shoulders to force her to turn around. "We shall have a portrait done to prove how alike we are. We shall have it commissioned for Papa's birthday. I shall wear rose and you will wear white. What a pretty picture we shall make. We'll call it 'Rose Red and Snow White.' "

"Rather, 'Rose of May and Stark Mad in White Muslin,' " Clarette suggested dourly.

Clarice shook her head. "I had expected you to be in the best of moods tonight. After all, we will be dining with our heroic cousin, Lieutenant Hockaday. Papa says it was very smart of him to send each of us a bouquet. Shows he's become a gentleman of consequence. I know! I shall pluck a bud to tuck in my hair to show my appreciation. I'll be right back."

As her sister sailed out, Clarette glanced again at her reflection. Her complexion was now alarmingly flushed. Pansy-brown eyes brimmed with a terror no one else in her household shared. But how could they? Not even her dear, sweet papa knew precisely what to expect this night.

Clarette turned away from her betraying image.

"It's not my fault!" She had in actual fact done nothing at all . . . except remain silent in her speculation that the last letter she had received from Jamie was not meant for her at all.

A proposal of marriage!

She had read it twice—oh, the glory of it!—before it occurred to her to wonder if there had been some mistake. But no, no one could expect her to believe anything other than her most fervent hope had come true . . . except herself.

She knew Jamie was infatuated with Clarice, yet it was *she* who wrote him faithfully and *she* he answered. Surely he could have altered in his feelings during the last months for she had poured all her love into every letter without actually revealing those feelings. He might have been swayed by her devotion, her steadfastness, her sheer will to have him love her. Oh, but what if she were wrong?

Of course, she had plied Clarice for months with questions about Jamie, giving her every opportunity to express her true feelings toward him. But Clarice had always been strangely reticent in her feelings, especially those related to gentlemen. While she had, when pressed, expressed a "cousinly affection for Cousin Jamie," she would admit to no sentiment "above the average" in the matter.

Even so, Clarette mused, she felt like a traitor. She would not have stood in the way of her sister's true happiness, but she was less ethical when it came to the gentleman's. Jamie must be made to see he should love her—because she loved him.

"Oh, but I shall be ill," she murmured to the room, and clutched at her bosom, where something frantic was trying to escape. That something frantic, she finally realized, was her heart.

What would Jamie, her dear, sweet, lovely Jamie, do if she were wrong? When he learned what she had done? Would he draw his regimental sword and drive it clean through her middle?

A yelp of terror erupted from her, much like one her vivid imagination suggested she would issue under the influence of a sword's thrust. And then she sank gracefully to the floor, clutching an imaginary if vividly bloody wound.

She lay a moment on the Turkish carpet, staring up at the ormolu medallion on the ceiling as she tried to imagine her own demise. Death would be no more than she deserved. Yet she doubted her father would approve of an angry relation stabbing even his plain daughter in his drawing room. Still, her papa might send her into exile if he decided she had done wrong. It would be no more than she deserved, to be banished forever from seeing Jamie again. Oh, but she was wretchedly unhappy!

If only Cousin Della had remained, she might have had someone to confide in, someone who understood what it was to love with patience and tolerance and total belief in the devotion of one's chosen love.

Clarette bit her lip. She had never seen anyone faint away before. It was quite shocking. After hearing the news that her husband had died at Waterloo, Della had simply slid silently to the floor.

It had taken several frantic minutes to revive her while footmen and maids ran hither and fro and Lord Rollerson was summoned home from his club. For three long days Della had lain in her bed with her face turned to the wall, not eating or speaking to anyone. When she emerged from her room on the fourth day, she was dressed in black, her veil so heavy her features were obscured. She announced that she was retiring to the country to await word that the Horse Guards were mistaken, that her husband was not, after all, dead.

Next to that, Clarette realized with sympathy, her own problems should seem insignificant. They were, except that her insignificant problems were the only things that mattered in her small, insignificant life.

She struggled to her feet, aware that it would send the household into an uproar if she were discovered supine on the carpet. She yanked her shirts into line and smoothed away a stubborn crease. After all the weeks of waiting and hoping and holding on to a secret that had nearly burst from her a dozen times a day, she must not allow her thoughts to fret her nerves to fiddlesticks. Worry would ruin her adequate complexion, and there was little enough to recommend her at the best of times. Therefore, she would *not* dwell any longer on the coming hours.

Now that she thought about it, no real harm had been done. If Lieutenant Hockaday were so mistaken about the direction in which his feelings lay, he could say for so himself this every night!

Yet, if she were right . . .

Clarette hid her disappointment behind a pleasant face as the former Lieutenant James Hockaday entered the Rollerson drawing room dressed in black and white evening wear. A thousand times she had pictured his return and how he would look arrayed in the brilliant red uniform of his rank. She had chosen to wear green to complement the scarlet of his coat. There could be only one explanation for the change. He had sold his commission, as many were doing now that the threat of war was over. His splendid scarlet plumage was lost forever.

Gazing at the tall, elegant man, she became uncertain of herself in his company for the first time. This new Jamie, the fellow in somber black and cream and silver, this gentleman was not unpleasant to look at, but he was different.

Dismayed by her own shallowness, she watched as he paused to greet her father; Mr. Poole, the family solicitor; and Lord Giles, her father's oldest friend. His golden hair was longer than before, side-parted and brushed in rolling waves across his head to end in a foam of curls at either side. There was something else. Of course, he was bearing his left arm in a sling.

"Poor, dear Jamie," she murmured with heartfelt compassion. Why had he not informed her?

As she spoke, her father turned and brought Jamie with him toward the group of ladies that consisted of two elderly aunts, Clarice, and herself.

"Here now, ladies," Lord Rollerson began heartily, "greet our guest of honor. The Honorable Mr. Hockaday, hero of Waterloo."

"Cousin Jamie! How delightful to see you again," Clarice said warmly, and moved gracefully forward with her gloved hand extended to him.

Clarette watched closely as Jamie brought her sister's hand for the briefest of moments to his lips. If she were wrong about Jamie's or her sister's feelings, this moment should betray it.

"Dearest cousin! You've no idea—" He broke off, cheeks mantled with emotion, and stepped back from her to execute a formal bow.

"Oh, you were wounded!"

Clarette watched in growing alarm as Clarice's exquisite features pleated in distress. Then she touched his sling, drawing her sister's eyes to the contrast of her slim, pale hand resting against black satin. Clarette held her breath as Clarice leaned close, gazing up at him with infinite compassion in her blue eyes. "Does it pain you very much?"

"Don't hurt a bit," he quickly answered. "Just wear it to show off."

Clarette doubted anyone else noticed that the tips of Jamie's ears had turned pink. So much for her hopes that his infatuation with her sister was utterly at an end. Jealousy and guilt and dread squeezed her middle.

Clarice smiled. "I find your forbearance honorable, sir. But then, you've not greeted your greatest fan." She turned to draw Clarette to her side. "My sister positively dotes on you."

Clarette wanted very much at that moment to kick her sister, but the damage was done. She knew she was blushing that dreadful shade her aunt called "hectic rose."

"Hello, Mr. Hockaday," she said stiffly when he moved to stand before her. She did not offer him her hand as her sister had done. If he touched her, she was certain she would burst into tears.

"Hello, Puss."

The pet name drew her gaze up to meet the glorious blue of his. It struck her anew with the enormity of what she had done.

Jamie winked at her and fingered the heroic medal pinned to his lapel. "Told you I'd make you proud. Hero of Waterloo. Are you duly impressed?"

"The fact that you nurse a wound puffs up your consequence quite enough," Clarette replied, choosing impertinence as her only line of defense against the onslaught of her feelings. "But tell us. However did you convince Lord Wellington to allow you to vanquish Monsieur Bonaparte's army single-handedly?"

Her father gasped, but Jamie laughed. "Still the same sly Puss," he said, and bent to kiss her cheek, chuckles gusting the breath that fanned across her skin. "I see I must keep my wits at the ready when I converse with you."

A fit of giddiness infected her as his lips grazed her cheek.

The sensation was not unlike one she had experienced when she once fell out of a pear tree onto her head while attempting to pluck a fruit too far out of reach.

He kissed me! her heart sang. Her head warned that she was once again attempting to overreach herself. Still, there was nothing to do but brazen out the evening.

At that moment the butler announced that dinner was being served. As she had been much too nervous to consume a bite during the day, the announcement came as a relief to Clarette. The condemned would eat a hearty meal.

She saw Jamie turn to Clarice, but her father, bless him, was just taking his elder daughter's arm. Without missing a beat, Jamie turned to her.

"Allow me, Puss," he said warmly. He took her hand and folded it into the crook of his arm. He even squeezed her fingertips before releasing them.

It was the polished gesture of a libertine, Clarette decided as they joined the procession into dinner. It was the kind of thing Cousin Della had warned her against during their first ball. Della had said even the best society included accomplished libertines, hardened roués, and remorseless reprobates eager to take advantage of unguarded innocence. The Jamie she remembered had not been so adept a rakehell. Where had he learned this new manner of charming ladies? In France, no doubt. Or, perhaps, as a result of his association with poor, dead Baron Lissey.

Then, as they passed through the portal of the dining room, he glanced down at her and smiled a charming, boyish smile of masculine vitality that made her wonder why she had ever considered a uniform an essential element of his attraction.

All through dinner Clarette silently observed the new self-confidence that showed in Jamie's manner of speaking and his expressions when he listened to another. He was attentive without being toady to her father, engaging without being overbearing, opinionated without passion, and generally unobjectionable as only the fully at ease can be. The teasing of a young man on holiday was gone. The man who had assumed his place was still charming but equally formidable, and even more handsome in his maturity. He was all and much more than she remembered, and it quite frightened her.

As she watched and listened, she became more and more daunted by the knowledge that she had imposed upon his generous nature by continuing their acquaintance through letters. Had she met him as he was now, she was not at all certain she would have dared to write to him. Love him, certainly. That was an action requiring the cooperation of one. Correspondence required two.

Near the end of the third remove, after taking wine with her father, two elderly aunts, both gentlemen, and Clarice, Jamie looked across the table at Clarette with his glass lifted and a meaningful glance of salutation.

Shocked to suddenly be the center of his attention, she grasped her glass, lifted it too briefly to minister to his vanity, then occupied herself with staring into its claret depths while pretending to drink until he looked away.

What would happen when he learned what she had done? Suddenly she was exceedingly grateful that he was not possessed of his lovely uniform with its requisite ornamental sword.

After a moment she glanced down the long table to where Clarice sat opposite her father at the foot of the table. She was conversing with Mr. Poole, perfectly composed, perfectly at ease. Several times she had spied her sister gazing at Jamie. Yet she could not be certain that anything more than cousinly affection shone in Clarice's gaze.

After several more courses, Lord Rollerson gave Clarice the signal and she stood up to lead the ladies into the drawing room, where dessert was being laid, while the gentlemen remained to circulate port and cigars.

When the ladies were seated and served, Clarice said thoughtfully, "Hasn't Cousin Jamie matured?"

"I find him much the same as last we saw him; sweet, pleasant, immature," Clarette answered waspishly as she stuck her fork in her chocolate cream.

"I think he's grown quite handsome," Clarice said with a reproachful glance at her sister. "And so dashing!"

Clarette gnawed furiously on her lower lip to keep from saying something quite shocking. Nine months earlier Clarice had dismissed Jamie as a "sweet boy." Now she called him handsome and, worse, dashing!

"I wonder how long they shall be?" she murmured, feeling like a traitor awaiting execution. She set the chocolate cream, her favorite sweet, away untouched.

"Have a port, dear boy." Lord Rollerson poured for them, generously filling two Flemish-crystal goblets filigreed in gold. "I trust you don't object that I drew you away from the others."

"Not at all." Jamie took up a post by the library fireplace with the negligent grace of a man who knew his worth. "I'd hoped for a private word with you, my lord."

Rollerson nodded. "But first things first. A good port deserves respect. Take your leisure."

Jamie observed his hoped-to-be father-in-law over the rim of his glass. The older man's pate was bare to midline, where a shock of thick white hair sprouted and fanned like combed cotton over his ears and collar. His face was the round, jolly kind that made small children smile and elderly ladies feel at ease. A little stout, he managed a dignified presence that was at once reassuring and suitably imposing.

When passed a glass, Jamie lifted it in salute before taking a sip. He had always liked Rollerson. He did not subscribe to the waggish opinion that the gentleman was somewhat careless when it came to wives, having buried three of them in less than a dozen years. Bad luck or pestilence had carried away each of them. Still, it could not be denied that several ladies since had shied away from the honor of becoming the fourth Lady Rollerson. He, on the other hand, was most eager to join the family.

After several minutes of idle conversation, Rollerson set his drained glass aside and reached for his pipe. "Always been fond of you, Hockaday. Your father and I were down to Cambridge together. Didn't know him well but liked the looks of him. Real bottom. Would seem you're of the same stock. Decorated warrior. Good show."

"Thank you." Jamie felt his heart swell in his chest as he finished his port. He had been debating during dinner the merits of disclosing his budget to the viscount. He would rather have had a private word with Clarice first, to judge her feelings.

Oh, but she was more beautiful than even his doting memory recalled. How tenderly she had gazed at him at the table. Surely there had been consent written in the appeal of her soft azure gaze. And here was her father, tossing him a posy of compliments. He would broach the subject of marriage at once.

Before he could assemble the words, Rollerson spoke again. "I don't make complements to swell your head, sir. As the father of young ladies, I would see them settled as happily as circumstance permits."

His eyes twinkled as he saw the younger man's jaw drop. "Did you think the girl wouldn't inform me of your offer, sir?"

Jamie felt a strong inclination to flee, where moments before he was prepared to charge ahead. "Didn't know precisely what to expect."

"You would seem to have *some* aspirations." The older man regarded him with amusement. "So then, tell me of your present condition and future prospects."

Jamie happily did so, having prepared a short speech for this express purpose.

"These Italian vineyards," Rollerson questioned at the back of Jamie's rendition. "They are profitable?"

"Quite, so I'm told." This produced a heavy frown from his lordship, which made Jamie hasten to add, "I can't say with any certainty, as they have yet to come into my hands. They will do so at the end of the year."

"You must, when the time comes, go there to take a measure

of things." Rollerson began pacing, the habit of a man who found city life confining. "A gentleman's lands are his livelihood. I'm never long from Somerset. Doesn't do to leave land in the hands or estate agents. Crooks, the lot of them. Foreigners are the worst. Can't help it. Bred into them with mother's milk."

"Your advice is much appreciated," Jamie answered pleasantly, though he knew from his aunt that the family holdings in Italy were the best run of all the Ormsby properties. It was English land agents whose tactics had forced her to hire solicitors in order to protect her assets from them.

"Yes, you must go to Italy." Rollerson paused to wink at his guest. "Clarette will like that."

"Clarette?" Jamie echoed in mystification "Whyever should Clarette's opinion matter?"

Rollerson smiled. "Is it to be that way with you, sir? You care not for the good opinion of your wife?"

"You mean Lady Clarice," Jamie suggested with a smile bordering on jubilation.

It was not answered in kind. Rollerson's frowned. "I mean Clarette. After all, it is to her that you proposed."

"Upon my word! I never— How could you possibly—" Jamie ground to a halt, overwhelmed by an onslaught of emotion that he could not adequately express. One thought came clear in his mind. Something was wrong, terribly wrong!

Eight

His head awhirl with more than Lord Rollerson's finest port, Jamie straightened away from the mantel to his full height. "I begin to think, my lord, that an error has been made."

"Has it indeed?" was Rollerson's indignant reply.

He looked up into the face of the young man, who topped him by some five inches. While youth had the advantage of height he had the advantage of girth and years and position. "Did you or did you not, sir, write to my daughter a proposal of marriage?"

Acutely embarrassed by a confusion he could not yet work out, Jamie chose the mannerly approach. "Yes, I did."

"Were you not sincere?"

"Most certainly I was." He clapped his right hand across his left breast in the region on his heart. "Upon my honor."

Rollerson's side whiskers twitched. "Then you are prepared to stand by your word?"

Jamie saw a trap opening at his feet. "My lord, I believe an error has been made."

"Then you seem to have made it. Clarette informed me of the contents of your missive some four weeks ago."

Did she?" Jamie murmured, beginning to see the imprint of a feminine hand in the knotted skein of his plans. Clarette—clever, sly prankster that she was—was quizzing him! No doubt she was holding her sides in mirth, just waiting for the opportunity to jump out and cry, "Lark! Lark!" But to choose such a matter as a source of jest! The girl was too old for childish antics. "May I inquire, my lord, as to whether you have actually seen my letter?"

Rollerson's gaze narrowed, aware now that the young man before him was seeking a hole in the net he had sprung over himself. "What are you suggesting, sir?"

"Only that there is necessarily some mistake." Jamie paused to reconnoiter. One could not very well impugn the veracity of one daughter while hoping for permission to marry the other. "Not that Clarette is not a perfectly nice young lady," he added.

"Enterprising of you to notice." Rollerson continued to scrutinize the younger man. "Most young jackanapes refer to the superficiality of Lady Clarice's beauty. Which is not to say her sweetness is not bone deep. But Clarette is like spiced wine, tart at the first taste but a thoroughly warming experience that can quickly become habit-forming." He nodded. "That's my Clarette, young sir."

Jamie was not certain it was appropriate to compare a gently reared young lady to stimulating spirits, but as her own father chose to draw the parallel, he could not every well naysay it.

"Perhaps if my letter were sent for, the matter might come round." He smiled the smile that had made every lady at dinner, married or not, wish he were seeking her hand. "Once you have seen my declaration with your own eyes, you shall understand all."

Rollerson's expression would no longer have encouraged a child's confidence. It certainly did nothing to embolden Jamie's. "Are you telling me the wrong sister received your letter?"

"I'd as lief believe it as not," Jamie replied simply.

Rollerson strode over to the bellpull beside the fireplace and gave the tapestry ribbon a vicious yank. Almost before he released, it the doors were opened by the butler. The expectant look on the retainer's face suggested that the servant had been expecting a summons.

"Send for Ladies Clarice and Clarette. I would have them join us. Clarette is to bring Mr. Hockaday's letter. At once!"

The bombastic tone of his lordship quite erased the butler's kindly expression, and he was gone in a trice.

"I shall judge matters when they arrive," Lord Rollerson said moodily. "Would you care for more port?"

"Indeed. Awfully good of you to hear me out."

Jamie assumed a second, less easy but still confident stance by the mantel. Once that minx Clarette confessed, they would all laugh together over the matter. Unless Lord Rollerson did not share his amusement.

Doubt furrowed his brow as he glanced at the stern-faced older man. Though she had embarrassed him, he hoped Clarette would not be made to suffer for it. Usually, he appreciated her sense of humor and the absurd. But, really!

The gentlemen had each consumed two glasses of port before the doors reopened and the Rollerson daughters appeared. Lady Clarice, shining as ever, sailed in on feet that did not quite seem to touch the ground. Beside her, Clarette's steps faltered. Her complexion was infused with the greenish tinge of her gown, making it seem as if she had been stricken by illness.

"Clarette!" her father began without any pretense to niceties. "Do you have Mr. Hockaday's proposal?"

"Proposal?" came the faint echo in Clarice's lovely voice.

"Didn't you know?" Jamie asked with a start of surprise.

Ignoring both of them, Clarette swallowed and said, "Yes, Papa."

It took her only a few seconds to produce it from the lacework reticule tied to her wrist, but it seemed like hours to the other occupants of the room. Only when she had delivered it into her father's hand did she slant a cautious glance at Jamie, who stood stiff as a cinder block by the fireplace, his gaze fixed on Clarice.

Lord Rollerson unfolded the letter, produced his monocle, and peered closely at all sides of the missive before grunting and thrusting it toward Jamie. "Read here for yourself, young sir, in your own hand, your words."

"Yes, gladly." Jamie took the paper eagerly, concerned not

with the text but the address. What he saw drained the color anew from his handsome face.

The letter was addressed to *Miss Clari- Mewson* a water stain having erased several letters.

"Clar—Clarice—Clarette!" he pronounced in profound understanding. "No wonder the confusion. Yet it is easily amended." So eager was he to right this wrong that he stepped toward Clarice with the purpose of handing her the correspondence.

Sensing his intention, Rollerson interposed himself in the younger man's path. "This will not serve, sir! It was a simple assumption to believe that smeared ink or no, this letter was meant for Clarette."

"It was not," Jamie maintained.

Rollerson held firm. "You never before corresponded with Clarice. Am I not correct, daughter?"

" 'Tis so, Papa," Clarice answered in mellifluous tones that intensified Jamie's adoring gaze. She smiled at him with much the same piteous sympathy Helen of Troy must have shown her smitten abductors. "I don't understand what has occurred, Papa. Yet, I don't believe Mr. Hockaday to be anything other than sincere."

"That remains to be seen." Rollerson's mutter drew all gazes back to him. "Sir, have you not some dozen and more times been free with your missives to Clarette?"

"Yes, Papa," Clarette answered, though the question had not been proposed to her. To her disappointment, Jamie did not even glance her way.

His attention was on the man he must convince of this great error. "They were, I assure you, of the most harmless variety. I'm certain Clarette will agree that I've never given her cause to expect anything of a romantic nature in our friendship."

"So say *you*." Rollerson scowled and pulled at his lower lip. *"I* call frequent correspondence with a young lady a bit coming for any but a most particular sort of relationship. Yet when I saw how things were between you last winter, I reasoned it was harmless enough."

James nodded, feeling on solid ground at last. "As early as last winter, sir, my affection was fixed."

"So I thought. So I *clearly* thought." Rollerson glanced at his younger child, who had hung her head in a most wretched fashion. His brows shot up. Was it possible Hockaday told the truth? He began pacing anew, his jaw working up and down as he chewed over the possibilities.

Hockaday did not seem a brazen liar, nor yet a nincompoop. Yet he had to be either or both to expect a father to allow him to bait and then switch his daughters' affections.

He could not forget how Clarette had looked the night she had come to his study with Hockaday's letter in her trembling hand. She had been lit with a glow that had utterly changed her face from acceptability to genuine prettiness.

His little Clarette was in love. He knew it before she spoke. Then her news. She could scarcely speak the words. Young Jamie Hockaday, nice, steady lad, had chosen her. He had been afraid the young man's calf love for Clarice the previous winter had blinded him to Clarette's obvious affection for him. Happily, it seemed he was wrong.

Rollerson glanced again at his two daughters. Clarice could marry whenever and whomever she chose. But his little Clarie, bless her good heart, she would not find love so easily. She loved Hockaday. And, truth to tell, the lad had led her on with his letters, however kindly meant. If his proposal had reached the wrong sister, it had been a most telling sort of mistake. The one thing he could not gauge were Clarice's feelings. Was she, too, enthralled with Mr. Hockaday?.

He stopped pacing. " 'Tis a devilish tangle!"

"I don't see it so, my lord," Jamie replied at once, having spent the short silence in equally deep thought.

He moved quickly toward Clarette and took her by the shoulders, his warm fingers pressing insistently into her bare skin above her neckline. "Tell your father that he is mistaken, Clarette. You know the truth."

Clarette looked up into his stricken blue gaze and shame swamped her. She had covertly glanced at him a hundred times tonight and was each time astonished by the enormity of her feelings for him. Her heart pumped out a tattoo of adoration and longing as she felt the pressure of his hands and the strange intensity between them. But she could not ignore the source of his tension. He was on tenterhooks waiting for her answer.

"I think it would be lovely if Jamie were to marry Clarette," Clarice said in the fragment of silence.

That casual remark silenced Clarette's truth.

Rollerson stopped pulling his lip to smile. "I quite agree. That is why the banns are set to be posted in the morning."

"What banns?" Jamie and Clarette cried out simultaneously as they both turned toward her father.

"You can't mean *my* engagement?" Clarette whispered.

"Yours and Hockaday's," Rollerson confirmed.

Jamie went pale as a flounder. "See here! You cannot post banns. I will refuse to acknowledge them!"

"You will not dare!" The roar was so unlike Lord Rollerson that both his daughters quailed before it and Jamie's color rushed back into his face.

He lifted a finger of accusation and pointed it straight at the young man. "I'm not to be trifled with, sir! Neither are the affections of my daughters. I have your offer in writing. My daughter has given her consent. It would seemed to have required only the formality of this evening to make things a certainty. But all that is nothing compared to your sudden cowardice."

"My coward—" Once more Jamie felt his emotions carrying away his power of speech.

He glanced from the choleric countenance of his accuser to Clarice, who stood pale and slim as a beeswax taper, to Clarette, who was twisting her skirt with her fingers. *Why do you not speak?* he wanted to cry at her, but suspected her father would physically attack him if he dared so much.

Clarette was not unaware of his thoughts. She felt a wild, absurd desire to fling herself at his feet and beg his forgiveness. But the words would not come nor would the confession. She would rather he hate her than cede to her the tepid bonds of friendship.

Under the heavy weight of Jamie's accusatory gaze she moved to stand before her father. "Papa, perhaps Mr. Hockaday and I should speak together." She glanced sideways at Jamie. "Alone."

The heavy weather lifted from Rollerson's expression. He had begun to think his daughter no longer wanted the fellow. She had not put up much of a fight so far." Demmed fine idea!" He raked Jamie with a less friendly gaze. "Young bloods are all alike! It's tally-ho and forward into the teeth of hell on the battlefield. But it's lift tail and run at the first sighting of leg shackles!"

The reckless bravery that had made him formidable in battle rose in Jamie's blood. He took a menacing step toward his tormentor. "My lord, I cannot allow you to further impugn my—"

Clarette grabbed his sleeve and tugged hard. "Come with me!"

"I was about to challenge him! Clarice's own father! What madness!" Jamie bent forward and dropped his head into his hands.

Clarette stared shamelessly at the strong masculine fingers clasping his handsome brow and murmured, "What a tangle!"

They sat side by side on one of the pair of settees that faced each other in the hallway outside the library doors, alone but certainly not secluded. Yet now that she could, at last, speak privately with him, his proximity and their isolation were almost too much for her.

His shoulder had brushed hers when he moved. If she chose,

she could lean just a little nearer and repeat the action. She had only to shift her foot an inch to bring her slipper against the side of his boot. This must be what it feels like, she thought, to glimpse heaven through the barred gates of hell. If only he would say something kind to her.

Jamie abruptly sat up, his composure somewhat restored. The dregs of his anger he served up for Clarette. "I should have suspected you would meddle in things! But steal another's correspondence? That is beyond enough! How *could* you play tricks on me tonight, Puss?"

"Don't fly at me!" Clarette replied. Resentment that he had nothing kinder to say to her evaporated her shyness. "I stole nothing. The letter was delivered to me. You've seen it. You could not expect me to know it was for Clarice."

"You are right, of course." He turned on her a lopsided smile that restored her bruised feelings a little. Once the stern lines vanished from his face, he seemed more like the man she adored. "You must have thought I'd taken leave of my senses."

Only in the most delightful fashion, she longed to answer. She said, "You will admit you never wrote to Clarice, not once."

He sighed, his expression dejected once more. "That is because I could never think of anything to say to her."

She bridled at this excuse. "You could have written to her all what you wrote to me."

"Don't be daft. A man can't tell the lady he adores about how he fought an infestation of lice by dosing himself with kerosene."

"I suppose not." Her expression became a match for his. "One tells such things only to inconsequential, ill-favored cousins."

He glanced at her. "You're not inconsequential, Puss. I know you meant no harm. You alone know of my adoration, devotion, and undying love for your sister."

The sentiment phrased thusly did not further endear him to her. "You did pen rather vile odes to her eyes, but never once did you say you hoped to *marry* her."

He favored her with a heart-melting smile. "What else could I have meant?"

"I don't know, precisely," she temporized, more interested in watching his mouth form words. His voice was so lovely. *He* was so lovely. She would die if she lost him.

As she shifted away to keep their shoulders from accidentally brushing together a second time, his attention focused on her for the first time. "As for your looks, they are quite nice." His appealing blue gaze swept over her gown, pausing long enough to appreciate for the first time how she filled out the bodice. "Why, you've become quite a taking little thing."

Clarette's heart turned over in her chest. Yet she knew that whatever appeal she might have possessed at the beginning of the evening had long since been worn away by the fits of guilt and anxiety of the past two hours. "You are making fun of me."

He grinned at her. "Never! Now that you're out, you must receive complements daily."

She regarded him skeptically. Gentlemen of Jamie's consequence would afford to hand out Spanish coin to ill-favored sisters. She would be a fool to believe his flattery. "I shall be six and eighty before the gentlemen think to look past Clarice to me."

His smile soured. "Do very many fellows look at her?"

Her voice grew wistful. "They look, and sigh and flock and follow her about like a gaggle of geese. We are mobbed at every function. That is, *she* is mobbed. I am sought after only by such fellows as would have me push forward their suits with her."

"Gosh!" The light of battle leapt into his gaze. "I knew I was right to make my offer early. I feared, once Clarice made her debut, some town toff might supersede me in her affections."

Clarette just refrained from pointing out that as far as she knew, Clarice had no affections for him that could be supplanted. She had just seconded their alliance.

He reached for her hand and gave it a tiny squeeze. "She does love me a little, doesn't she?"

Clarette could have slapped his handsome face. How could he ask her of all people such a question? She longed to rail at him, to scream, *Clarice cares nothing for you! 'Tis I who love you! 'Tis I who would make you happiest!*

Instead, she withdrew her hand and said primly, "I haven't sought to force my sister's confidence in the matter of her feelings toward you."

He looked hurt. "Did you tell her nothing of the things I confessed to you?"

"You swore me to silence," she reminded him coolly.

"I suppose I did." He sighed and sunk his chin into the palm of his hand, elbow resting on a knee. "Devil of a coil!"

She adopted his thoughtful pose though it was unladylike. "I never expected Papa to post banns without your consent," she admitted after a moment.

He stiffened at the reminder, his knee accidentally jostling hers. "I will demand a retraction!"

Greatly daring, she reached out and brushed his sleeve with the lightest of touches. "If you cry off now, Papa will never again allow you inside our door. I shouldn't think you will be allowed to even contact any of our household." Her fingers curled into the fabric of his sleeve. "All shall be lost forever!"

The sorrow in her voice was real enough to stir his emotions. "You are right. But I must do something."

Marry me, she longed to whisper as she held his blue gaze. Yet even she was beginning to realize that he would have to come to desire her, even a little, before he could be convinced of the idea. And that would require time.

"I've an Idea." Her infectious smile often surprised those who thought of her as plain just as her Ideas often alarmed those who had experience with previous ones. "We shall tell Papa that we agree to the engagement." She hurried on as she saw mutiny rising in his eyes. "It's not the same as agreeing to wed. Many couples become engaged and yet never actually marry."

"What good would that do?"

"It would give Papa a chance to calm himself. Then, after a while, we might break it off."

His skeptical expression remained. "That doesn't seem as if it would improve my standing with your father."

"Perhaps not." She looked away from his eager gaze.

He reached out and lay his hand over hers, which were folded in her lap. "If you can think of a plan that will accomplish that, I will kiss you."

Clarette looked up, her eyes betraying her thoughts. "You may kiss me first."

His golden brows shot up in amusement. "Aren't you the forward miss!" He squeezed her fingertips before releasing them. Now tell me your idea and let's see if we can bring this disaster to a standstill."

Disappointment tugged at her mouth, but Clarette soldiered on. "When we go back into the library I shall tell Papa that we have mended our lover's quarrel. You can say you balked owing to a sudden onset of nerves."

Jamie shook his head emphatically. "I never have nerves!"

She ignored him. "I will then say that while I've accepted your proposal, I see now that it's quite unfeeling of me to think of marrying until Clarice's prospects are established. She is, after all, the elder. Therefore, we will remain engaged until Clarice has affixed a suitor."

He balked. "But *I* mean to be Clarice's suitor."

"You know that and *I* know that," she said a little crossly. "But Papa mustn't know that until his temper is restored."

"How long do you suppose that will take?"

She crossed the fingers of her left hand within the folds of her skirt. "Six months, perhaps even a year."

His eagerness evaporated. "Clarice will not last the Season on the marriage market. An earl or marquess or even a duke will ask for her hand, and your father will give his consent."

"That is a possibility." *Fervently to be hoped for,* she added in her thoughts. She wished Clarice well with any gentleman other than Jamie.

Again he shook his head. "Your idea will not serve. I must find a way to be constantly near her, to protect her from unwelcome advances from libertines."

"If you were engaged to me, our house would be constantly open to you," she replied, dangling the idea like bait. "Why, you'd be expected to accompany me—us—everywhere."

"I don't know." Doubt puckered his face. "But I see now that I cannot withdraw from this engagement to you in good order without ruining all possibility of a future with Clarice. She would rightly think me a bounder for rejecting her sister."

"But that's it!" Clarette cried as the final piece of the scheme fell into place in her mind. "You shan't need to reject me. I shall reject you!"

"You will? Why?" he asked suspiciously.

"Because I shall fall in love with someone else."

"You'd toss me over for another?" Laughter accompanied his inquiry.

She bristled. "Do you think no one else would have me because you do not want me?"

He looked instantly contrite. "I did not mean that at all, Puss. But, yes, I see it! You must find a new suitor, in as little as a few weeks—"

"Or months," she interjected.

"You can then cry off our engagement and I shall be free to seek Clarice's hand, my honor unbesmirched. What a sound plan!"

Clarette was not altogether convinced that he would give it his best effort. "If we are to be believed, you must first appear to be genuinely enamored of me. After your protestations tonight, Papa will see right through our scheme unless it is so convincing, even we begin to believe ourselves in love."

"That is a truth worth repeating," he conceded. "I had not known before tonight that your father possessed such a temper. But answer this, Puss. Why would you think that I had asked for *your* hand? Dashed loose-screw notion, that."

Clarette looked away from him again, feeling as if he had set his boot heel on her heart. Poor organ, it was taking quite a trouncing this evening.

"It was an honest mistake," she said in a very small smothered voice. "After all, I am not likely to receive many proposals of marriage. I merely sought to take advantage of the first to come my way."

He gathered her chin in his fingers and brought her face back to his so that his gaze met hers. "Then your feelings . . . you aren't seriously . . . you don't love me?"

She met the wonder of his adorable gaze. "I do love you . . . as a girl loves her brother, her cousins, with genuine affection." *And desperation,* her heart whispered as her lids fell to shield the whole truth in her eyes.

"Very well." He released her chin and stood up. "We shall go forth with this charade. But only to save your father disgrace and only if you are certain it will do you no harm."

She stood up and attempted to smile, but felt instead the push of tears. She took his hand and clasped it tightly for reassurance. Oh, how she loved him! How could he not know it?

"As long as you are beside me, Jamie, I cannot be hurt."

He stood up abruptly. "Very well. Let's get this charade under way."

It occurred to her much later, as she lay in her bed staring at the strip of stars visible between the gap in her drawn curtains, that she might have set herself up for the most exquisite torture imaginable.

Nine

London, August 15, 1815

"What wretched business is this!" Jamie's expression eloquently reflected his distaste of squalor before it was masked by the scented handkerchief he pressed to his nostrils.

"What the devil are you doing here?" Quinlan's greeting was matched by a scowl of displeasure. He stood arms akimbo in the doorway of the tumbledown flat he had recently rented amid the bustling alleyways of knavery and villainy in a corner of London called Lambeth.

"Is that any way to greet a fellow?" Jamie questioned behind the barrier of his kerchief as he stepped past his friend into the room.

Quinlan shifted his gaze meaningfully from his guest to his open doorway. "I don't recall extending any invitations."

"I can see why."

The lintel was so low, Jamie had to duck. The ceiling was not much higher. The smell of the privy was strong. Though it was balmy outside, the air held a chill which a narrow slat of sunlight from the small window did not dispel. A ladderback chair pulled up before a writing table covered with papers, kerosene lamp, and small cot spread with a blanket took up nearly all the floor space of the tiny room. The only trappings of an aristocrat spilled from the beautifully hand-tooled trunk of Cordovan leather with silver hinges that lay open next to the bed.

Within it lay clean shirts, folded stocks, and even a frock coat of deep blue superfine.

Jamie turned back to DeLacy. "You look knocked into horsenails, Quill. Haven't taken up Pettigrew's nasty habit of the hookah, have you?"

"No." In rolled sleeves and open-throated shirt, rough chamois breeches and dust-dimmed work boots, Viscount Kearney looked more like a pieman than a peer, which was exactly the way he wanted it.

"Does this self-inflicted punishment have a cause? *I say!*" Jamie sidestepped in alarm. "Is that a rat creeping in the far corner?"

"Most likely," Quinlan answered, and moved with a slight limp toward the table, where he began sorting scattered papers.

"Your valet was tight as a clam about your direction. Good man and all that. I was quite put out. Set Simpkin to follow him. Eventually he came here. To deliver those, I suppose." Jamie indicated the fresh clothing. "None too soon, I'd say."

Quinlan smirked as a whiff of Hockaday's perfume reached him. Since his return to London, the former lieutenant had reverted to the role of fop. His frock coat was pea green, while his waistcoat was daffodil yellow. Lace foamed at his throat and wrists, and white silk brocade formed the sling for his arm. With his blond curls and choir-boy visage it was sometimes difficult to remember he had ever faced death at Waterloo.

Jamie frowned, his attention snared by a new shadow creeping along the baseboard. "Don't imagine Violetta finds your pied à terre to her liking."

"She and I are finished."

This news returned Jamie's full attention to his host. "You've given the most sought-after woman in London her congé?"

Quinlan smiled thinly. "Exactly."

"Has some maggoty cheese turned your brain? What exactly is behind this—this—" He swung an arm to indicate the room. "And don't say 'tis the war, because I was there and *I* ain't holed up in a rat's nest behind the fact."

Quinlan seldom talked about his work, yet he knew Hockaday would not go away without some explanation. "I'm writing."

"Writing? You're living among lunatics, housebreakers, and thieves!"

"One must know the villainy of deprivation if one is to write about it."

"Doing it a bit brown, I say." Jamie cast a cautious glance toward the now-empty corner. "What say we repair to a more convivial place? My club in St. James's, for instance."

Quinlan moved to lean an elbow upon the window's high sill. "This place is no worse than the Belgian hovels we commandeered during the war."

"Perhaps," Jamie admitted. "Yet to see such wretchedness and filth existing in the very heart of London gives one pause."

"Exactly!" Quinlan turned from the window. "Did you know there is a custom in London where unwanted children are 'laid in the streets' to be picked up by any who want them? Foundling hospitals, orphan asylums, and charity schools cannot begin to accommodate them all. Chimney sweeps take them up in great numbers where they are forced to work—" He stopped himself. " 'Tis this hardship of life which I seek to put upon the stage."

"Why?"

Quinlan mastered his earlier passion before saying, "So that society may know the shocking lives of those less fortunate."

Jamie's handsome brow puckered. "I'd as lief not experience it. Certainly wouldn't shell out good coin for it. Mark me, I'm a most unexceptional patron in matters of public taste."

"So said Longstreet when he refused my latest play."

"Ah-ha! This is an artist's fit of pique."

Quinlan glared. "What would you know about the artistic temperament?"

"Nothing. Next to nothing," Jamie amended. "Have a cousin who's forever scribbling sonnets. Takes to brooding with a vengeance when he can't make a rhythm. Damn silliness over a word or two, I say. Still, what do I know? Ain't a poet, am I?"

Quinlan did not bother to answer that rhetorical question. He had never known Jamie to be long concerned with things that didn't affect him personally. In fact, he doubted want of his company had brought Hockaday there. "One supposes you have a reason for this visit?"

"Well, yes." Jamie's face brightened with appreciation for this segué into his own concerns. Then, as the conditions of his life flooded back upon him, his smile slid away. "I need your help. 'Tis been a month and I'm still misengaged."

Quinlan shrugged. "You put yourself under the hatches by agreeing to court one sister while in love with the other."

"Too true." Jamie helped himself to the ladderback chair after giving it a wipe with his handkerchief. "Who knew wooing the wrong lady would be half so painful?"

Sympathy entered Quinlan's expression. "Is the chit that much of a millstone?"

"Clarette? Not a bit of one. She's sweet as gooseberry tart. Well, most times." In the defense of the complete truth, Jamie added, "She does have a temper. Was cross as cats after I beat her in a canter through Rotten Row yesterday morning. Still, she never cuts up a man's consequence as most ladies are apt to do when one is late, or forgets her nosegay, or prefers to spend his evenings in the card room instead of the ballroom."

"She allows you uninterrupted hours in the card room without quarrel afterward? Marry her at once! You'll not do better!"

"Don't roast me. I'm in a most wretched state." Jamie's pleasing face reflected his misery. "Clarette says she has explained things to Clarice for me, so she knows my true feelings, but I cannot be certain she understood, because I can never find a private moment with her."

Quinlan offered a skeptical lift of one brow. "Why not?"

"Her father," Jamie pronounced like a sentence of doom. "He eyes me like a piece of suspect beef. A duenna wouldn't be half so watchful. Not that his presence deters a man, let me tell you!" His cheeks mantled with fury. "It's above enough. Fellows tripping over one another to do Clarice the least favor.

They argue over who will collect her wrap or fetch her a cup of raffia. Last night our opera box overflowed with beaus. Their prattle drowned out the soprano."

"I heard she was not especially good," Quinlan offered by way of consolation.

Jamie's scowl deepened. "Tonight the Everharts are hosting an end-of-season ball and I must be put through the pain of watching Clarice on the arms of other men all evening long."

"Then why attend?"

"To give Clarette the chance to land other fish."

"Ah, yes, *that* plan." Quinlan eyed his guest with a little more interest. "Again, who's idea was this?"

"Clarette's, of course." Brought back to humor by the thought, Jamie smiled. "Brilliant girl, really. Level-headed, nerves like a man's. Don't know as I'd have fared half so well with her father if it hadn't been for her quick thinking. Still, she's not the sort one develops a mad tendre for. Don't know why her father couldn't see that."

"Fathers tend to cherish what suitors do not," Quinlan suggested as his thoughtful gray-green gaze remained on his friend. "If she is all you say, won't you feel a twinge when another gentleman makes off with your 'gooseberry tart'?"

Jamie laughed. "Any fellow who'll have her will receive my blessing, which brings me to the point of my visit." He leaned forward earnestly. "I need a favor, Quill. Come tonight and sweep her off her feet."

Quinlan started. "Miss Clarette Rollerson?"

"No, Lady Clarice. I can't dance with her more than twice of an evening without drawing her father's scowl. Yet he leaves the field free for that gaggle of nodcocks who flock about her. That's where you come in. You must occupy her exclusively this evening. Gentlemen will scatter like mice once you've made your interest in her known." The mention of rodents caused Jamie to glance once again at the shadowy corner.

Quinlan lounged back on one elbow, his green eyes shaded by lowered lids. "You do me too much credit."

"Not a bit. If you show a marked interest in a very eligible young lady, the gossips will have put it about by morning that you're looking to set up your nursery. No gentleman will dare go near Clarice for weeks after for fear you'll confront them. By then I'm bound to have brought things around."

"How do you propose I square myself with her father?"

"Lord Rollerson? He'll be delighted to have a serious contender take the field," Jamie lamented.

"Quite right." Then *he* would be under the hatches with Rollerson when the man realized he had no interest in his daughter.

Quinlan smiled suddenly, the mischief in the grin so apparent that any man less preoccupied with his own affairs than Jamie would have been alarmed. He was not the least interested in a green schoolroom miss, no matter her beauty, but Jamie's tangled love affair had in it more than a few elements of farce. And that deserved a closer inspection. "I'll do it."

A smile of supreme relief bowed out of Jamie's cheeks. "Knew I could count on you. There's just this," he added, his face reflecting his new concern. "I know you shall find it difficult once you've met her, but you are not on any account to fall in love with Lady Clarice."

"Of course."

"That is no answer!"

Amused, Quinlan threw up both hands in protest. "I can promise faithfully that I will not fall in love with your lady."

Jamie remained skeptical. "Is your heart otherwise occupied?"

Quinlan sighed in exasperation. "No. I do not fall in love."

This response drew laughter. "But of course you do! You write of little else."

"That's precisely the reason." Quinlan pinched the bridge of his nose between ink-stained fingers and briefly shut his eyes. When they opened, the placid green irises had shifted color like the ocean on a stormy day to pale gray veined by lightning bolts of weariness. "It's my detachment from the emotion that allows me to manipulate that emotion in others as persuasively as a puppeteer at his strings. Prevarication is a playwright's stock-in-trade."

Doubt furrowed Jamie's brow. "You've never been in love? Never once?"

Quinlan's chuckle was as cynical as it was irreverent. "Not since I discovered that the desire to bed a female doesn't mean that I should want in any other way to continue an acquaintance."

A blasphemy could not have shocked Jamie more. "If, indeed, you are serious," he said after a moment, "then you'd do well to remedy this failing in yourself. Love is the finest emotion a man may know."

Quinlan would not be drawn by this earnest soul. "Thankee, no! I prefer to forgo the humiliating perplexities and freakish conduct of men who claim to have fallen in love. Now, if that's all, I've work to do."

But Jamie was far from willing to forgo a topic so dear to his heart. "Come now. Every man's susceptible to love. Even Pettigrew."

Quinlan glanced at his seated guest. "Errol?"

Jamie suspected the cause of Quinlan's surprise. "No need to dissemble. Worked it out on my own. He wouldn't have been so adamant about disowning a bastard if he weren't certain it was his. Why? Because he was confident in the constancy of the lady's affections! Fear for his freedom prompted him to have you write that disavowal. Surprised when you agreed to do it. Then I realized he must be in earnest. He franked it, you know."

Quinlan frowned. "No, I didn't. Are you certain?"

"Saw him give it to a foot soldier before the engagement began."

Quinlan's brows lowered like thunderclouds. "To whom did he send it?"

"You ask me?" Jamie laughed. "You know Pettigrew's views on me. I had supposed he'd confided the truth to you."

Quinlan shook his head so that fine, gilded, light brown hair swept his collar.

"Ah, then, the puzzle continues." Jamie pulled at his lower lip. "He'd not have wasted tuppence to spurn a slattern or unprotected woman. She's so eligible that Pettigrew knew he'd find himself leg-shackled behind the seduction. So why, one wonders, when he had scores of willing women, would he make promises to an unwed lady, seduce her, and then shab off? Unless . . ." He deliberately drew out the suspense, hugely enjoying himself. "It was all prompted by love!"

Quinlan slumped against the support post nearest him and let that possibility sink in but then rejected it. "What is the point of this exercise? Errol is dead. Even if there were a lady— and I have my doubts—Errol threw her over despite his feelings. 'Tis no pretty advertisement for love. And if *you* are an example of love's victim, I absolve myself of the emotion altogether."

As the youngest member of his set, Jamie was too accustomed to his friends' setdowns to take offense. "What of Rafe? He loved long and well."

"What of Rafe, indeed?" Quinlan said so softly, Jamie barely heard him.

A brooding silence of their own making settled over them.

After several seconds, Jamie licked his lips. "Quill, did you go through with it?"

Quinlan's face darkened with anger, though it was not directed at his companion. His anger was inner-directed. He had planned half a dozen times to make the journey to see Rafe's widow. If he had not written the letter he now carried, he would not be in this position. Nothing less than cowardly reluctance had made him delay so long. "I haven't gone yet, but you've prompted me to act. There's nothing for it," he said heavily. "I gave my word. I will leave in the morning."

"I'll go with you."

Quinlan cast a speculative glance at the younger man. Hockaday seldom allowed anything to stand in the way of his own concerns. "Didn't imagine you would be persuaded to leave London under any circumstances now that you're near your true love."

"Neither did I," Jamie allowed in perfect honesty. His boyishly handsome face sobered under the mildly critical gaze of his friend. "Look here, you weren't the only one to hear Rafe's last request. A promise to a friend is as good as a sworn oath."

Quinlan hesitated only a moment. Jamie might be a dandy at heart, but his was a good heart all the same. Who better to accompany him on this thankless task than Rafe's other surviving companion in arms? "Agreed."

Jamie rose to his feet. "Shall I come for you tonight?"

"No." Quinlan slung a companionable arm about his friend's shoulders, but it was a ruse to steer him toward the door. "I've plans. I'll meet you there."

"Don't be late. No, fashionably tardy is good." Jamie nodded. "Make an entrance. Be sure the fellows take notice."

"Haven't required a lesson in social behavior in some time," Quinlan said shortly as he opened the door and none too gently pushed his friend into the breach. "Until tonight."

Ten

It was an oppressive night though not especially warm. A gray, soot-choked fog held the city in thrall, weaving in and out of trees and around lampposts like wisps of coal-dusted spiderwebs. As hansom cabs made their lackadaisical way through the streets, the clip-clop of horses' hooves echoed in the mist, sounding first deceptively far away, then ominously near.

Quinlan shut the brass carriage lamp as a safeguard against being recognized by any of the shadows passing on foot through the darkness.

For the same reason, he had taken the precaution of traveling in a public conveyance when his own carriage would have been much more comfortable and pleasant-smelling. The crest on the door, liveried driver and footmen, plumed horses, flash of harness brass, and tinkle of silver bells that were the trademarks of aristocratic conveyances would have alerted everyone in the lane that he was passing by. The last thing he wanted was word of his arrival to precede him to Longstreet's office.

The day before, when he had delivered the outline of his latest effort, Longstreet had not only not invited him into his private office but had barred him from the door. He had murmured something about a prior engagement.

Then that morning Longstreet had sent around a rejection letter describing Quinlan's new idea to be maudlin, melodramatic, and wholly unacceptable. It was a "flight of fancy" to which his talents were not suited. In order that Quinlan might "clear your mind of these whims of glory," he suggested he retire from London life to court his muse in the country . . . another country . . . for at least six months!

Quinlan cursed under his breath. The note was enough to prompt the suspicions of a nun at her prayers. Longstreet was hiding something from him.

"Bloody well certain of it!" he muttered.

The question was, what? He meant to find out that night.

The thought of ambush put his every sense on alert and set his pulse throbbing ever so slightly up-tempo. His lips rose at the corners. It felt good. He felt alive.

An odd melancholia had settled over him during the two months since Waterloo. That ennui had driven out every creative impulse. He often slept badly, yet lately he had found himself needing a good excuse to rise from his bed. The Allied losses in that Belgian farmer's field were history, nearly 22,000 men dead and wounded. But for every man who had been a participant, those numbers were counted in individual painful losses.

After most battles, officers rallied their men with cries of "Who's dead?" After Waterloo, they had inquired more fearfully, "Who's alive?"

Quinlan shifted on his seat. The answer had been that while he lived, two of his best friends were lost.

Rather than wait for the damning memories to steal upon him as dreams, which they too often did, he conjured to mind the dreaded reminiscences in the dank confines of the hackney.

The pitched battle in the farmlands near the Belgian hamlet of Waterloo was hours old. It was later said that for the high commands of both sides, stationed on elevated ground, the shifting scenes of battle could be observed as a classic match of two brilliant strategists. But for the men in the thick of it, the mist-infused breaths of thousands of men and horses combined with the pall of black smoke from cannon and musket fire had long since merged to obliterate the sky. That deadly pall concealed both enemy and foe.

The onslaught of thunderous cannonade that signaled the French infantry advance across the valley toward La Haye Sainte in the early afternoon was so volcanic in sound and vibration that the English defenders momentarily had been forced to take refuge in farm buildings. Still, the British quickly rallied and answered the French assault. The infantry's attack was followed by a full cavalry charge.

Caught up in the fever of a battle that could yet go either way, Quinlan had ridden with his fellow "Grays" forward across the fog-shrouded valley toward the enemy, impelled by a shared exhilarating heroism that he had never before felt. That bravery ultimately betrayed them.

Choking on battle smoke that blurred his vision and deafened by repeated cannonades, Quinlan deemed it a miracle when he finally heard Rafe's calls for retreat and wheeled his horse about. Through the shifting mists he saw that they had galloped deep into French-held territory. If the enemy noticed, they would be cut off. Ironically, the French infantry seemed to realize their luck at the same moment that Englishmen discovered their peril and rushed the confused cavalrymen.

The confusion, the battle cries of blood lust and pain, his terror and desperate will to survive—these remembered sensations and more washed over Quinlan in the quiet confines of the hackney until he could once more smell the acrid odor of gunpowder and feel the bloodied mud slipping beneath his feet.

Swinging his saber in desperate defense of himself and his horse, he neither heard nor saw the cannonball that exploded in the midst of his men. The force of the blast lifted them from the saddle and tossed them onto the backs of the advancing French infantry. Panicked by injury and confusion, horses and men flayed in the mud. Cursing roundly, he scrambled for footing in the mired earth and glanced about for signs of his friends. The French were closing in fast.

Rafe shouted in warning to him an instant before a French lancer's bayonet sliced deep into the taut muscles of his left thigh. As his knees buckled beneath him, he stiffened in anticipation of the next lunge that would finish him off.

It never came.

Errol was there, grinning through his smoke-blackened face like some demon let loose from hell as he drove his saber through the French soldier's middle. "Never say I didn't do you a favor! I—"

The statement was never finished.

The earth bucked and heaved a second time as the deafening sound of cannon shot slammed with physical force against them.

This time he felt no pain, not even when he struck the ground. He did not expect as his eyes fell shut to ever open them again.

The shouts of the advancing columns mingled with the screams of the wounded. Men in blue coats scrambled over enemy bodies. A soldier stepped on his wounded leg. Yet the excruciating pain could not rouse him to movement.

Seconds passed, then minutes. The sounds of fighting moved away from them. . . .

Someone bent over him, rifled in his coat for coins, and then passed on. . . .

It grew dark. Around him, men lay in the mud groaning and crying. Snatches of French, English, and German prayers mingled piteously. . . .

He strained to listen for the sound of familiar voices. Rafe's. Errol's. Jamie's . . .

Morning. British soldiers scouting for the wounded brought him to a makeshift field hospital. He would live.

Errol lay dead, his face blackened by a musket blast at close range. All that remained for identification was the silly yellow silk scarf he had tied around his upper arm, a token from a Belgium whore. . . .

Jamie, miraculously alive, was relatively unharmed. The broken arm would mend. . . .

Only Rafe's fate remained in doubt. . . .

Quinlan ran a trembling hand over his face, clammy now with perspiration. He did not want to remember, but he could not forget. In a farmhouse where wounded French cuirassiers had taken shelter he found Rafe . . . three days later.

A captured French cavalry officer led him to the back of the stable and pointed to the last stall. In hay blackened by blood lay a man in the muddied and gored uniform of the 2nd Dragoons. Part of a hussar's dolman had been wrapped around the man's right arm. Though his face was draped in a blood-soaked cloth, Quinlan recognized the locket showing through the opening in his shirt. This was Rafe.

He moved forward into the stall, dropped to his knees in the hay, and lifted the face cloth. "God in heaven!"

His eyes misted with tears he did not think he had left to shed. The right side of Rafe's face was gashed open from brow to jawline by a saber slash. He was not even certain Rafe was alive, until his one good eye opened, vividly golden in his ravaged face. "Quill?"

"Who else? Didn't think I'd leave you?" He touched his friend gently. "Rest easy, Rafe. We're here to take you home."

"No!" Rafe's voice was muffled by pain. "Leave me—to die." With his good hand he fumbled under his shirt until he retrieved a bloodstained letter. He held it out with an unsteady hand. "Give this . . . Della."

Quinlan recognized his own handwriting. "But you aren't—"

"I . . . cannot live. Not like this." Rafe lips cracked and bled as he spoke. "I do not . . . want to. But I may . . . tarry. Never tell her. 'Tis kinder." His good eye welled with moisture. "Swear . . . on your honor."

"I—I so swear."

"You could do me . . . another service. A quick thrust . . . beneath my ribs."

"Faith!"

Rafe turned away. "Then leave me . . . to die . . . in my own way."

"In his own way."

Quinlan dragged his hand heavily down his face. Rafe had not died that night, or the next, or the next.

He had not known until then that there were ways of dying that did not require placing the corpse in the ground. Strange how life demands to survive in spite of damage, despite even the will of the creature involved.

Two months had passed, yet the letter remained in his possession. Rafe would curse him if he knew. He had made a promise that he did not know how to keep, or even if he should.

He reached for the silver flask tucked into his waistcoat and took a swallow of the oldest French brandy money could smuggle. The fiery warmth of it flooded his discriminating palate with satisfying results, yet it did nothing to mitigate his dilemma. That could be resolved only by going to visit Rafe's widow.

Strange that he should have been spared when, unlike men like Rafe and Jamie or even Errol, he had had nothing and no one waiting for him upon his return. A mistress did not qualify in his mind as a genuine attachment. If he had stuck his spoon in the wall, Violetta would have replaced him with another in less time than it took a Flemish tatter to complete a square of lace. She had not even resisted his efforts to throw her over once she was satisfied that it was not for another woman. In the end, all that he had to come back to was the adoration of a public eager for his next play.

Quinlan tapped the fingers of his right hand on his knee in agitated impatience. His next project. He had no next project. All he had was the as-yet-unfounded suspicion that his producer was hiding something from him.

Quite without willing it, a memory had recalled itself. The day before, in the instant before Longstreet's inner door had closed, he had glimpsed a woman sitting with her back to him. He frowned as he forced the memory to completion. Ah, yes! What had arrested his attention was the color of the tresses that had erupted from beneath her rather shabby bonnet. Her riotous red curls were the most flamboyant he had ever seen.

Who was she? An actress? Longstreet's newest paramour? Neither possibility explained why Longstreet should have sought to hide her. A man with a braggart's heart, the producer was usually eager to flaunt his latest light o' love. Curious, indeed.

He smiled absently. He had never had a lover with red hair. To be wrapped in hair so vibrant it sang against the skin . . .

The unexpected frisson of sexual desire that sped through Quinlan had an unusual effect. It recalled to him his purpose.

His brows knit into a single slash above his aquiline nose. Perhaps he had been too hasty in sending Violetta away. Beautiful women of a particular inclination had their uses. But he was not seeking a new mistress at the moment. He was set upon ferreting out his producer's scheme!

Letting the window down with a bang and a bump, he glanced searchingly out. He knew the area well. Longstreet's office was in the middle of the next block.

"Down here!" he cried suddenly to the cabbie. Moments later he was on foot, a purposeful stride on long legs carrying him toward his destination.

The outer door to Longstreet's office was unlocked. The treasures of a publisher/producer were not the kind to interest pickpockets and cutpurses. Yet once inside, he was annoyed to discover a faint luminescent glow filtering down the narrow hall. It had as its source the inner office.

Mouthing a curse, he slowed his step. He had not expected to find anyone there at this hour. He moved closer. Was Longstreet entertaining, or had he underestimated the temptations for a thief?

He felt a second's hesitation. London thieves were notoriously bold, as likely to slit a man's throat as beg his pardon. The thought inexplicably peaked his anticipation.

He reached into his right Hessian boot and withdrew the stiletto he carried whenever he went out. The only sounds he heard the instant he opened the door were the deep whirring of a sleeping cat and the faint scratch of quill on parchment

Kathleen Geraldine was in deep deliberation, head bent, shoulders hunched protectively over the work before her. The pot of tea by her elbow had long since been consumed. The thick slice of bread and wedge of Yorkshire cheddar that had comprised her supper was reduced to a few crumbs. Her spine ached from the unforgivable pressure of the wooden-bottomed chair. Her eyes smarted from straining through her lenses against the unreliable light provided by the oil lamp. Her head pounded from concentration. Still, she had no time to waste. Every day she remained in the city was a day she came closer to being recognized, and that would mean disaster.

Just yesterday she had spied a friend of Errol Pettigrew's, Mr. Hockaday, in Fleet Street while on an errand. Thankfully, the young gentleman whom she had met at her cousin's wedding had not noticed her. If he had, he might have noticed her condition as well, and that would have led to the matter sooner or later reaching the ears of her cousin Della Heallford. The incident just went to prove her suspicion that not even a city as large as London was a safe haven for her. It was imperative that she finish the final draft of her play, collect her money, and leave England.

She paused to scratch her chin with the tip of the quill, eyes half closing with fatigue. As they did so, her mind drifted off to the place where it dwelt more and more these past weeks, to Lord Kearney.

In order to help her compose her play, she made up an imaginary game where she and he sat and talked for hours about his work. The ridiculousness of the game did not faze her. At least she was cured of her romantic notions about him.

And so she dreamed freely, allowing herself to believe that if she were his equal, he would have found her observations on his latest work fascinating and thus sought her out at every opportunity to discuss them. They would have shared a platonic relationship in which lust and attraction had no part.

It was all nonsense, of course. She would never even see him again unless it happened that, as with Mr. Hockaday, they passed in the street.

"And even a cat may gaze upon a king," she murmured to the occupant of her lap. She scratched between the ears of Longstreet's portly tabby, who had all but taken up residence there in her lap for the long hours she sat and worked. Her lap was shortening with every day, but the feline did not seem to mind.

The soft click indicating the lift of the door latch warned her of an intruder. With a shock two parts alarm and one part pleasure, she glanced up into the arrested expression of the very last man she ever expected to meet face-to-face.

As he paused on the threshold, her startled brain absorbed a dozen useless details. He was even handsomer than her memory or any artist's talent had recorded, and every bit as elegant. His formal dress included black satin knee breeches with diamond buckles, a white silk waistcoat figured in silver embroidery, and a ruby stickpin in his cravat.

Belatedly, she noticed the more salient cues to his appearance. His chiseled features were taut where muscle bunched beneath the skin. And there was a stiletto clutched in his right hand. The gentle hero of her dreams was in reality a very angry man!

"You!"

At the sound of his voice she nearly bounded to her feet to flee but thought better of it. The wicked, rapier-thin blade and the piercing intensity of his gray-green stare were fairly convincing evidence that he was in no mood to be challenged.

Instinctively she wrapped one protective hand around her swelling belly. The work in which she was engaged, if not outright illegal, was a deception of vast proportions against this very man. Her wits were her only defense. Jesus, Joseph, and Mary, she prayed, let that be enough!

She gave him her brightest, brassiest smile.

"Good evening, Lord Kearney."

Eleven

Quinlan's aggressive gaze took in the office at a glance before it came pointedly back to the sole occupant of the room. He had expected to startle an intruder. What he had not expected was that the occupant would startle him.

What struck him was the intensity of expression in her eyes. It held all the abashed fright of a woman caught flagrante delicto. He felt her tremorous anticipation like the brush of electromagnetic sparks against his skin. As rousing as a secret caress, it startled him with its sensual implications.

Because he seldom forgot a face, he knew who she was. This was the woman he had nearly overrun in the hallway of this very place a month earlier.

The lamp on the desk beside her abruptly flared as a knot in the cheap wick caught fire, diverting his attention to the hair loosed about her shoulders. Its color was so thoroughly red that even yellow lamplight could not dim its vibrancy. He recognized that hair as well. This was also the woman Longstreet had tried to keep secret from him the day before!

A sardonic smile curved the edges of his lips. Here at last was a lightning rod for his suspicions.

He bowed slightly, a deceptively charming smile stretching his fine, wide mouth. "Good evening, my dear.

"Good evening, my lord," she answered softly.

Her whisper assaulted Quinlan's senses anew. Something in it was both exotic and familiar. He stared at her in deepening curiosity. Black-framed pince-nez balanced near the end of her nose gave her a bookish appearance though the gaze meeting his above them was a clear celadon green. Her hair and eyes were made all the more vivid by her complexion, which was the color of buttermilk into which a few summer strawberries had been crushed.

A pretty face but not to his usual taste, which was for slim, dark beauties. But no matter. He had felt the flattering intensity of her admiration the day they collided in the hallway. It was there now though banked by caution. He would use it to his advantage.

"I fear you've the better of me, Miss—"

"Oh, I do not doubt it," she answered in a voice that was melodic yet matter-of-fact. "Everyone knows the great playwright Quinlan DeLacy." Her gaze moved slowly from his face to his right hand. "Were you after stabbing someone, my lord?"

Quinlan looked down, surprised that he still held the stiletto. "I heard a noise and thought it might be a burglar."

"And you would be a thief-taker, my lord?"

He glanced up sharply, certain he heard mockery in her voice. The frank openness of her stare had vanished. She gazed back at him, mild as any owl, through her spectacles. "You're Irish," he said, as the thought occurred to him.

"Aye." A hint of a smile played on her lips. "But that is not a crime, my lord."

"Just so." He slipped the offending weapon back into his boot, saying, "I take it Longstreet is not with you."

"As you see, my lord."

She was as careful with her words as a pauper with her pennies, he noted. Perhaps Longstreet had warned her against him. "May I enter?"

Her soft mouth tightened. " 'Twould seem you've done so already, my lord."

Her pert answers annoyed him as well as her repeated pointed emphasis on the words "my lord." Dressed in a gown of figured lawn topped by a spencer of rough brown cloth, she exhibited

the prim demeanor of a parson's daughter. But no pious clergyman's child would have trafficked with Longstreet, nor, he
surmised, possess hair so seductively red.

"Shall I leave the door ajar," he said politely. "I'd not have
your reputation suffer were we discovered together."

"As it pleases you," Kathleen answered softly, and relaxed a
fraction. It did not seem he intended mayhem, after all. Yet his
lovely smile elicited only trepidation. There was something in
it like the sting of a wasp. No artist had ever captured that. But
it served now as a warning.

Bitter experience with Lord Pettigrew had taught her that the
manners of the nobility were not born out of consideration for
others. This Lord Kearney was no figment of her imagination
to be manipulated at her bidding. He was a genuine nobleman
and he would behave as it pleased him.

When Quinlan had propped the door open, he turned and came
toward her, pausing only when the width of the desk separated
them. He bent slightly forward and extended his hand. " 'Tis
time we were properly introduced. I am Viscount Kearney. But
you may call me DeLacy. And you are—"

"One of many an Irish lass forced to leave her homeland in
order to earn her own way."

Her hands remained primly in her lap, yet Quinlan gained
the impression that she was secretly laughing at him. Twice now
she had neatly sidestepped his attempt to learn her name. "Will
you not be more forthcoming, Miss—"

"You must forgive me, my lord, for not offering you the
curtsy due a gentleman of your august personage." Definitely
there was mockery in her tone. She reached into her lap and
lifted into her arms a huge orange muff, which he recognized
as Longstreet's corpulent tabby when the feline opened one topaz eye to regard him balefully. " 'Tis that my person is otherwise occupied."

"I envy the puss his position."

Bracing a hand on the desktop, Quinlan leaned across to
scrabble his fingers through the feline's thick, feather-soft fur

pressed against the full swell of the brown-clothed bosom. He
let his gaze linger deliberately on the neckline of that rough
fabric. " 'Tis some time since I lay so snugly in a pretty
woman's lap."

He saw faint color flow into her cheeks. The trace of pink
shaded even her freckles with embarrassment. The effect was
charming. He had never met a London actress who could be
put so easily to the blush. As for harlots, he would sooner bloom
than they react with genuine embarrassment. Who was this im-
pudent colleen with an expression at once guarded and touch-
ingly vulnerable? And why had she given herself over into the
callous confidence of a fellow like Longstreet?

"I seldom approve of Longstreet's taste in actresses," he continued in a winning tone as he anchored a hip on the edge of
the desk. "Had we not met like this, I would never have thought
to cast you in the part of royalty."

He reached out and whipped the spectacles from her nose.
Her lips parted in inaudible surprise. Good. He was making
progress. Really, she was too easy prey for a rake of his experience. "No woman since Queen Bess has been able to carry
off regal imperialism while sporting curls that put the sunset to
shame. Yet, there was something of the duchess in your carriage,
the obdurate set of your jaw which says you value yourself
above the common mode. If you can act, I'll write a part for
you myself."

Before he considered why he would do such a thing, he
reached across and plucked the tabby from her arms, dragging
the backs of his fingers softly against the plush of her bosom.
"So, you are a particular friend of Longstreet's?"

"Not that particular."

Kathleen moved back from his much-too-personal touch as
her heart gave a nervous start. Lord Pettigrew had been equally
forward in his speech and too free with his hands, assuring her
that it was her appeal alone that drove him beyond the bounds
of propriety. Heady stuff for a poor Irish lass. But she was no
longer ignorant of where such flattery led. Lord DeLacy might

wear lace cuffs, but the gleam in his eye was as dangerous as the wicked point of his stiletto.

Yet, some dreams die hard. Inconsequentially, she noted that his smile lacked the bitter edge of Pettigrew's and that his lips were nicer.

She tucked the thought away, certain she was in control of her feelings. "Is there something you'd be wanting here, my lord?"

The warming expression in his eyes warned her. "I would trade places with the tabby you embraced so warmly." He stroked the cat's fur with such sensual languor that Kathleen felt as if he touched her.

Ashamed of her thoughts, she looked away. Oh, yes, he was very compelling with his seductive glances and outrageous comments. She would have several new impressions of him to add to her repertoire of daydreams.

"Come, there's no need to play the shy maid with me." Tawny hair shifted like silk tassels across his shoulders as he leaned in more confidently toward her. "No doubt the reason Long-street seeks to shield you from me is that he is afraid I shall steal you for myself." His lids lowered, lashes drooping as he said, "Your manner need not be reticent to entice my interest. In fact, I'd prefer if it weren't. Be your own delicious self and, I assure you, you will have my full and appreciative attention."

Kathleen refused the appeal in those romantic eyes. If she were a lady, she would have had the right to slap his face for insulting her in such a manner. Because she was not, she re-treated behind the only defense left her, her pride.

"You're presumptuous, my lord. And I've done nothing to deserve it."

"What do you deserve, my sweet?" He reached out to touch the irresistible fiery curl trembling against the cushion of her left breast.

She lifted a hand of protest, pushing his away. "No, my lord. You may not."

"May not?" Quinlan smiled, amused. The novelty of rejection was new to him. Quite new.

She held her head high and her back rigidly straight, trying, he supposed, to appear worldly. Alas, with her pink lips puckered in disapproval and her sea-green eyes bright with indignation, she succeeded only in looking vulnerable and childlike. He had been wrong to think her plain or even average. She was adorable. And that redoubled his interest.

He folded his fingers around the back of the hand she held up in protest and rubbed his thumb sensuously across the well of her palm. "Are you then so certain of Longstreet? It might be wiser to set your snare for more lofty game. For instance, I could see to it that you received a part in the next production at the Drury Lane Theatre.

"You mistake the matter, my lord," she answered politely, but her eyes said she remained insulted. "I'm no actress. I'm employed by Mr. Longstreet as a Fair Hand."

"I see."

What he saw was that her green gaze, tucked between thick golden lashes, was even more arousing up close. The slight dull ache in his loins was more than the reflex of a man who had gone too long without a woman. It was the resurgence of genuine desire, something he had not felt in months. He had been propositioned repeatedly on the street these last weeks, but felt no desire or hesitation in refusing. Now, however, because of a pair of green eyes simply gazing at him, he could scarcely keep from reaching out to embrace the young woman no more than an arm's length away. The soft contours of her brow and chin begged to be kissed. The full curve of lower lip deserved the salute of a man's licking caress. Lust surged and heated his blood until he felt afire. Oh, yes, he wanted to touch and stroke and wrap himself in her glorious hair.

As the viscount's gaze reflected his thoughts with alarming intensity, Kathleen felt for the first time how very vulnerable and quite alone she was. He would understand *she* was no partridge for *his* snare. "Is there something missing in your inspection, my lord? Perhaps you'd care to count my teeth?"

Quinlan chuckled. So much for his seductive powers. She had an uncanny ability to cut up his consequence. Why, he could almost believe that she was as innocent as she appeared, that she was, indeed, only Longstreet's employee. Following his thoughts, his gaze lowered to inspect the page she had been so intent upon when he entered.

Kathleen moved a hand to cover the middle of the page, smearing the ink as it did so. She saw his gaze follow her actions, move away, and then swerve back.

Holy Mother of God, don't be letting him discover what I'm about! she silently prayed, and then wondered if it was a sin to pray that her deceit not be discovered. *For the unborn babe's sake,* she added.

Unfortunately for her prayers, Quinlan had seen enough to recognize the text was a play. His brows contracted to form a slash over his aquiline nose as he set the cat aside. "Whose work do you copy?"

"I'm not at liberty to say, my lord." In desperation she splayed the fingers of both hands across the text, though they were too small to completely cover it.

Realizing that he might, however inadvertently, have stumbled upon the subject of his quest, Quinlan smiled again. "Now what," he began silkily, "do you suppose I can do to change your mind?"

In answer to his own question, he reached into his pocket and pulled out a few gold coins. He let them tinkle in his hand. "Surely we can come to some understanding?"

"We can," Kathleen answered quickly as a flush flared up in her cheeks. "It's that I cannot be bought!"

Anger struck flame in her green gaze like sunlight striking the depths of an emerald. It did not surprise him that she would react with anger, only that it was genuine. Her rejection left no room for compromise.

He rose and pocketed the coins. "I meant no insult, my dear."

Despite her better judgment, the appeal in his smile acted like tonic on Kathleen's frayed nerves. " 'Tis I who should beg your pardon, my lord. 'Twas only my weariness speaking." She reached up and rubbed her aching forehead, leaving behind a smudge of ink over her right brow.

Her momentary release of the text was all Quinlan needed. He reached over and snatched the text from the desk.

Kathleen shot to her feet, forgetting everything but those damning pages. "Give that back, my lord!"

"All in good time." Not even bothering to look at her, Quinlan backed a few feet away from the desk as he scanned the smeared words. A few lines were enough to give away that it was a play, a comedy, in fact. No wonder Longstreet did not want him to know about it. This was the work of a talented hand. His own replacement, perchance?

"Give me that!" Her hand struck through the sheet of foolscap he held, tearing it in half.

"What the devil!"

Without compunction for her actions, she yanked the torn paper from his grasp, then backed abruptly away, looking frightened yet resolute. "I am sorry I had to do that, my lord, but you had no right! No right at all!"

Enraged to be chastised by a mere girl, Quinlan eyed the five-foot young woman before him with all the daunting hauteur with which six centuries of noble lineage had provided him. The cold gray sea of anger in his gaze was now a tempest. "I don't care for your method of attempting to teach me manners, my girl. Let's see if you will approve of mine!"

A less burdened mortal would have quailed before his advance, but Kathleen's rage was spurred by the frightful desperation of her own situation. Resentment flushed and tingled her skin as she held her ground, for suddenly he seemed the cause of all her misery. She had been a fool to allow her feelings to be swayed by a pretty face! If not for her misplaced feelings for this man, she would never have been beguiled by Lord Pettigrew!

Yet, when DeLacy drew close enough to grab her, her courage failed. With a squeal of fright she turned and lurched away.

Quinlan noted in passing that when he lunged at her she did not move as quickly as he had expected and he caught her easily. Grasping her from behind, he then turned her around in her arms.

"No! No! Don't touch me!" Using all her strength, Kathleen kicked out at him, twisting and pulling to break free of his grip on her upper arms.

But Quinlan's anger, once aroused, was not easily tempered. He brought her effortlessly up against his chest, tightening his embrace until she could scarcely breathe. Then he grabbed a handful of her curls, exulting in the vibrant feel of them. Just as he expected, the sensation of sliding his fingers through them was shockingly sensual. He held her immobile with a long arm clamped across her back, luxuriating in the feel of the woman pressed against him.

"So, you don't like my treatment of you?" he taunted as she squirmed against him. "Then you'd best remember it the next time you're tempted to cross me. Do you understand?"

When she did not reply, he forced her head back until she was staring up at him with tear-swamped eyes. She made a frightened sound, a pleading little moan that begged him to release her.

That tiny sound caught at the ragged edge of his humanity, pulling him back from the brink of cruelty. Discomforted, he looked away, but his gaze moved no farther than her mouth. Her lips were parted, trembling, drawing his pity by their defenseless softness. He felt compelled to shield that exposed vulnerability, but his hands were caught in the tangle of her fiery curls. Instead, he bent his head and placed his mouth over the delicate contours of hers.

Her lips parted a fraction more in surprise at his touch, her shuddering breath slipping over his tongue. The action sent pleasure streaking through him and made him want to offer her a measure of it in return.

His kiss was not so much a shock as a divination for Kathleen. For months she had been daydreaming of what it would be like to be embraced by Quinlan DeLacy. When Lord Pettigrew had taken her in his arms, she had pretended it was this man. It was pleasant enough, but even in her ignorance she found it less compelling than she expected. Now here she was in DeLacy's embrace, as real as any miracle was ever likely to be for her.

His mouth moved sensuously on hers, sending startling streaks of pleasure though her middle to tense in sweet aching in her womb. This sensation of desire was utterly new and *enlarging* to her understanding. She was shockingly, achingly alive. No doubt, a tiny part of her mind whispered, he was a decadent, villainous, heartless seducer. But at that moment she could no more tear herself from his embrace than sail to the moon.

Perhaps, if things were different, if they had met . . .

She sighed and despaired, for it was all too late! Too late. Much too late!

Aware only of her acquiescence, Quinlan continued his exploration of her mouth, drinking in the tantalizing, enchanting, mesmerizing taste of her. He had almost forgotten what it was to simply want a woman with a pure burning desire that had in it no calculation but its own fulfillment.

He wanted her. Wanted to go on kissing her, to undress and kiss every bit of her sweet womanly body, to lose himself in the moist, dark warmth of her secret places. He wanted to drag her with him into the hot oblivion of desire and then make her cry out his name so that when he came it would be the only sound in the world.

He reached for her hips to draw her in closer, only to be struck in some less occupied region of his mind by the fact that she did not fit as snugly against him as he might have expected. In fact, there was a barrier, a very solid, rounded barrier preventing him from pressing his blatant arousal against the apex of her thighs. She had not seemed large, certainly not overweight. And yet . . .

His hand moved from kneading her derriere, up over her hip, and down across the unexpected roundness of her belly. He jerked it back in astonishment. A second later he released her with a force that left her stumbling backward even as he drew away.

"Madame, you are with child!" he declared in accusation.

She stared at him for a moment, her eyes so wide they seemed about to spill over. Then she shivered, closed her eyes, and said, " 'Tis not so much a surprise to me as to your lordship."

Quinlan found her presence of mind remarkable, considering that he still trembled from barely contained desire. "It may be of no moment to you, my dear, but you might have warned me."

At the back of his speech, Kathleen looked up, struck with shame by what had occurred. The horror of her actions washed over her. She had nearly been seduced a second time by the unwitting author of her original fall! What was the matter with her? Was she mad? Or merely a sinful, lustful creature ready to kick her legs in the air for any fine face?

She stared at him a moment longer, one hand brushing away the memory of his kiss with her fingertips. He looked nearly as dazed as she felt. But, of course, that was impossible. He must be accustomed to seducing any silly female who found his face and money too much to resist.

That last thought made her straighten as if to prove he had not bested her. "No harm done," she said bravely.

The blithe words did not distract him a second time. Quinlan had searched her left hand for a ring and found it bare. Of course, his wit inserted into his astonishment, she must be accustomed to such treatment, as she was breeding to show for it. Even so, he felt contrition for his behavior toward her. He was not a man who forced himself on women. In fact, he had never before done so.

Yet, as he formed an apology, an ugly suspicion entered his head. "Is the babe Longstreet's?"

In shocked amazement she looked at him for the first time. "It is not!"

"Thank providence," he murmured. The world did not need another of Longstreet's looks or disposition.

As she moved slowly yet gracefully toward the desk, he regarded her from beneath the sweep of his lashes. The formation of a slight frown on her brow as she lowered herself into the chair caused him to wonder if he had hurt her. He had never touched a pregnant woman before. He wondered why it had not dampened his very blatant arousal.

Chagrin, mortification, and wretched embarrassment vied with his inclination to burst out in laughter at his own conceit. The moment of theatrics was over. He would simply state his need.

"Tell me whose play you are copying and I will leave you in peace, madame."

Kathleen looked up into his impassive expression, feeling sick with anxiety. Maybe she was no more than a wanton with the devil's own sign on her. But she was also a young woman whose dreams had suffered a nasty collapse.

Lord DeLacy was no knight errant. If he discovered what she had been doing this night, he would not care a whit for her or her babe's future. He would have her tossed in Newgate and the key thrown away. There she would languish until she and her babe perished. How could she have feelings for so wicked a man? Oh, she hated him, really hated him!

Appalled by her own behavior and more devastated by his than she would allow him to suspect, she scrambled madly about in her thoughts for the appropriate words with which to salvage the situation. She found them in an attitude of humility she was far from feeling.

She bowed her head to make the words easier to utter. "You have every right to be vexed with me, my lord. I've been less than gracious and provoked you, surely. But I cannot say whose words they are."

"Cannot or will not?"

In spite of her trepidation, Kathleen bristled at his imperious tone. Just as well, she was not looking at him. "That's no way to address a poor, weary soul who was minding her own business till you came here. 'Tis doing my job, I am, and with little or no thanks for it, to be sure."

Quinlan had already noticed that her speech had a more pronounced lilt when her emotions were heightened. This time the words fairly sang with Celtic fervor. "Blarney!"

Her head jerked up at his tone. "Even if you are simply copying text for Longstreet, you must know the author."

He took several intimidating steps toward her, as if he expected the barrier of the desk to simply vanish when he reached it. "If you wish to be left in peace, you will tell me what I want to know."

"I don't like bullying," she responded, her chin rounded in stubbornness. "I'd expected better of you."

Taken aback, he asked, "Why should you expect anything of me?"

She sniffed suspiciously as if trying to prevent the escape of a tear. "Because you don't like bullies either."

His brows shot up. "How would you know that?"

"You wrote a play about it, now, didn't you?"

"You know my work?" Quinlan could not contain his surprise.

She nodded. "In *M'lady's Spaniel* the young page was bullied something fierce by the duchess's retainer. You wrote it for comedic effect, but I get a wee lump in my throat whenever I come to the scene where the retainer takes his cane to the page when the lad would warn his mistress of the plot he's discovered against her. Three great whacks he gives the poor soul, knocking him to ground. Yet he takes the blows and finds a way to warn her anyway."

She smiled at some inner thought only she was privy to. "I always laugh when, in the last scene, the duchess takes the very same cane and strikes the retainer before casting him out."

She lifted eyes full of genuine emotion to his. "There's been a time when I'd have liked to do the same."

Quinlan did not doubt that this was one of those times. He

felt chastised just looking into her tear-drenched gaze. "You have my apologies, madame."

This was something Kathleen had not expected, that he, a nobleman, would apologize to her, a commoner. Was it genuine or another tactic? "I accept," she said simply.

Quinlan racked his brain for another approach, for he had no intention of leaving before he learned all he could. Yet he was equally eager to get away from this strange young woman as soon as possible. Every glance reminded him of his abominable behavior toward—and his abiding desire for—her. "The fellow whose work you copy is not half bad."

She started. "What?"

"I said the author has a way with words."

Kathleen smiled in spite of herself. Unsolicited praise from him was more than she could accept in silence. After all, a celebrated writer was praising her work! "Do you truly think so, my lord?"

He stroked his chin. "Perhaps if I were allowed to read more . . ." The arch look that came into her expression bade him abandon the enterprise. There were other ways of finding out who the elusive playwright was now that he knew there was such a person. "As I was saying, the voice is good, the rhythm passable. I should like to share a glass of port with the fellow, hear his opinions. I imagine he has much to say."

"Why would you suppose that?" she asked in great daring.

"Because 'tis obvious he has studied his craft. His talent is not as great as some, of course."

"No, of course not," she agreed quickly to shield her own feelings. "Sheridan was better, Goldsmith, Voltaire, Racine, and, of course, yourself."

Quinlan acknowledged this kudo with a slight bow. "You are well read for a Fair Hand. Who is your favorite playwright?"

She did not hesitate. "You are, my lord."

Quinlan felt the unanticipated sting of chagrin enter his cheeks. He was flattered, grossly, unexpectedly so. Strangely, he knew she had not said that to appease him. She meant it despite his actions of the last minutes. "Thank you."

"You're welcome."

Kathleen held her breath as he continued to regard her. He nearly spoke again, and she felt an answering desire to speak herself. He wanted to know more and she wanted so badly to tell him, oh, a dozen things!

But he did not speak and she knew why. What useful conversation could she, a mere Fair Hand and woman, have to offer a celebrated author and peer of the realm? She resented the fact that she did not share his surpassing beauty and lofty pedigree, for then she would have had the right to tell him how his words moved her and disclosed more about his private thoughts than he might ever suspect.

But Quinlan was beyond the subtle pressure of curiosity. The instinctive need in him to regroup and reseal his composure was stronger than ever. He needed to be away from her and from the tumultuous needs thumping inside him.

He turned away and strode purposefully to the door.

Because he did not want her to think he was deserting the field, though in truth he was, he paused and turned to offer her the sketchiest of bows. "Good night, madame."

Kathleen sat in perfect amazement as he offered her this symbol of gentlemanly curtsy. "Good night, my lord."

The moment he was gone she collapsed in relief on the desktop. Never before in her life had she behaved so erratically. It seemed these last months that she had become a complete stranger to herself, not knowing what to expect from moment to moment.

She reached around to press a hand into the small of her back to relieve the twinge at the base of her spine. Oh, what she would not give for a back rub like those her father had given her to relieve the spasms that plagued her after she had taken a tumble from a cart a few years before.

As she ground the heel of her palm into her lower back, she pictured the viscount's hands as he held her text. He had large, attractive hands, clever hands, as her aunt Rose would say. She suspected his strong fingers would know just where to find the kinks along her spine and know how to rub and knead deep into her aching muscles with warming strength.

The thought of Lord Kearney's hands on her naked back brought a warm flush to her skin. What on earth was she thinking?

She had made a proper fool of herself in believing that any gentleman would look favorably upon a woman with means as modest as hers. No matter that she liked Lord Kearney's voice, found his touch warm and his kisses infinitely thrilling. He was not for the likes of her.

Kathleen shook her head in silent denial. She must have been mad, quite mad, to have believed herself in love with him. She would never again look at his portrait with admiration, and never ever dream with devy-eyed wonder of what it would be like to gain his admiration.

Except, how could she not think of him when she was attempting with a desperation bordering on hysteria to emulate him on paper in both thought and style? Now she carried the added burden of the pleasure of his kiss to taunt and keep her guilty company through the rest of this long night and, she suspected, a string of future ones.

"I must finish my work and be gone!" she whispered furiously to the tabby who jumped onto her lap.

She picked up her quill. As she did so ink ran out of its damaged stylus and ran down her fingers and onto the stack of completed work. In a fit of temper she tossed it aside, folded her arms on the desk, bent her head over them, and wept shamelessly all the tears she had been holding back for six long, harried, and harrowing months.

Beyond the door, Quinlan had paused, equally deep in reflection. What he had done that night passed all bounds of propriety. Ordinarily this would not have bothered him, for society's proprieties more often than not were mere conveniences skewed to serve the needs of the advantaged.

But tonight he had stepped beyond his own personal code, and that was another matter entirely.

Never had desire for a woman betrayed his self-possession. Despite every reason and thought of sanity, the urgent beat of lust in his blood had not vanished. He could still feel her lips clinging damply to his, feel the pressure of her hand slip up the column of his neck to curve shyly about his nape. He was rigid with need for a woman ripe with another man's child. The knowledge shamed and inflamed him. He turned away from the door into the street, his hands forming fists.

It came to him more slowly that he had enjoyed their joist of a conversation as much as the taste of her lips. That in itself was a novelty. If she were not pregnant, most likely unwed, and employed by one of the most unscrupulous men in the theater, he might have sought her out again. But he knew what society would make of that! In every way that mattered—money, breeding, even looks and style—she was as far beneath him as the earth to the stars. Association with him could only ruin whatever reputation she managed to maintain. Lud! Rumor might even put it about that her babe was his!

More than halfway home he recalled that his presence was anticipated at a ball. Moreover, he was expected to pay gentlemanly court to a lovely innocent creature whom society would consider his perfect mate. If only they knew! He was in rut for a wild redheaded vixen. The absurdity of the thought made him laugh aloud.

Twelve

"You wish me to what?" Jamie whispered in astonishment.

"Make love to me," came his partner's hushed reply.

"Absolutely not!"

Minutes before, Clarette had persuaded him to quit the Everharts' ballroom for the garden by complaining of a headache caused by the heated crush of guests. He himself had been perspiring and welcomed the suggestion. However, now that they were at the far end of the moonlit garden, away from the dozen other couples who had sought the same relief, he began to question whether he had made a tactical error in secluding them.

"I don't see that it's so very much to ask," Clarette whispered, her pale face as softly rounded as the moon shining upon it. "It's not as if you have never made passionate love to a lady before."

Jamie felt himself blush, though it did not show in the handsome profile he turned toward the slant of lunar light. "That is not a fit subject for a lady of your tender years."

"What a prude you've become!" she rejoined teasingly. "You wrote ever so more frankly to me than you speak now." She glanced again toward the back of the house and then took a step toward him so that her nose was on a level with the diamond stickpin that decorated his cravat. "I liked your letters better."

"I wish those letters at the devil!" Jamie muttered, for those letters contributed to his present predicament.

He took a step back from her, but she reached for his hand

to keep him from making a complete escape. "We are supposed to be engaged, Jamie. It is permissible to kiss me."

"I will not! If your father should suspect I've compromised your virtue in any manner, he will demand we wed immediately."

"A few kisses won't compromise my virtue," she answered crossly. "As to that, Papa has commented more than once that for a fiancé, you are remarkably undemonstrative."

"He has?" This was an entirely unexpected criticism. "Undemonstrative? In what way?"

Clarette stepped closer to him, hoping he might notice the daring décolletage of her apple-green gown. She had had to bribe her modiste to cut the bodice to its scandalous four-inch depth and then hide the results from her father and sister until they reached the ball. "Papa remarked only this morning that you never even hold my hand."

He glanced down at their interlocked fingers. "I'm holding it now."

"You are not. I'm holding yours." She squeezed his fingers to emphasize the fact. " 'Tis ever my prompting that brings it about. You might at least be seen gazing at me as if you were deeply infatuated."

He shrugged. "I don't wish to distress Clarice with sham public gestures to her sister."

"What of my feelings?" Clarette bit her lip. She had spent the day orchestrating very carefully in her mind how the next moments should play out. She had promised herself that she would not chastise him no matter his reluctance, but now her feelings were hurt.

"How do you think it seems to others when you spend no more than five minutes in my company on any evening? The only time you sit near me is at the opera. Otherwise, you keep a greater distance than any brother would. Several of my friends have remarked upon it."

"I don't see that it's any of their business."

"Very well. Then how do you expect me to snare the interest

of another gentleman when it is so patently obvious to all that my own fiancé cares not a whit for me!"

"What fustian! Who would dare think— Oh, you aren't puckering up, are you?" Jamie inquired uncertainly when she pulled her hand free and turned away from him.

When she did not respond, he stepped closer and lightly touched her shoulder. "There's a good girl. Don't go nabbing the bib."

Clarette lowered a hand from suspiciously dry eyes and turned back to him. "Don't what?"

"Don't cry," Jamie translated. Having spend a better portion of his afternoon at Tattersall's selecting a new mare for his aunt, he had inadvertently picked up several cant phrases from the stable hands. "You're in the mops, that's all."

"I am not!" But there was a suspicious wobble in her voice.

After a month of hoping otherwise, it was now obvious that Jamie would not come to love her of his own volition. He was besotted by Clarice. Yet she believed that if only they could be alone together, he just might find himself at least liking her.

She turned fully to him. "Don't you want the masquerade to succeed? I have been watching the marriage market these last weeks and studied the stratagems of gentlemen. They want most what the other one has. Do you think Clarice is pursued solely out of love? I do not. I believe a full half of her suitors are simply vying against their friends to see who is the better swain. If that is so, then she is little more than a pretty prize in a contest for and about men. I have no wiles, no beauty, no talents to lure the gentlemen to vie for me. Yet, if you were seen to be over the boughs for me, gentlemen might suppose that I possessed some allurement equal to beauty."

"What could that possibly be?" Jamie responded without thought for how his words might wound.

Clarette bristled. "Oh, I suppose I could be thought to possess a rather wild nature." She twitched her shoulders, an action that caused one puffed sleeve to slip from her shoulder and reveal even more of her amply displayed bodice.

"Don't!" He reached out and hustled her errant sleeve back up onto the chaste ledge of her shoulder. "Such conduct will only encourage scoundrels."

"Why do you care whom I encourage?" she asked petulantly. "After all, you would have me off your hands sooner than later."

"Unfair, Puss! Of course I care how you fare."

"Then you must help me," she encouraged as she lifted her face to his. "Make wild, passionate advances to me."

"No!" To soften the rebuff, he reached across the darkness to squeeze her shoulder. "I'd feel foolish. We're friends."

"That is just the trouble," she whispered, and cast her eyes toward the fountain hissing quietly behind them.

A little distance away, hushed voices could be heard among the hedges. Smothered laughter drifted in on the breeze, as did the music from the ballroom. The lush decadence of summer's last roses nodded on the nearby trellis, and the peppery sweetness of the Sweet William tucked among flagstones scented the air with the perfume of romance.

She inhaled deeply and set her purpose anew. This was the perfect place, the perfect night for a tryst. Jamie must be made to see that.

"Clarette?" he said uncertainly.

The sound of her name in his deep, hushed voice sent an arrow of anticipation through her. As she turned back to him, she unleashed the breath she had been holding in expectation that the glory of the night had worked its magic on him.

She lifted her face to his, leaned slightly toward him, and closed her eyes. "Kiss me, Jamie!"

As he hesitated, the sound of a nearby voice caught his attention, and he started to turn his head away.

Determined not to let the moment pass, she rose on tiptoe to cup his cheek and turn his face back to hers. "I don't ask for myself, Jamie. I'm thinking of the good of our scheme. Please, kiss me just once," she whispered.

Jamie was not accustomed to taking romantic direction from inexperienced young ladies. Yet, he was a man, a man thwarted by passions he could not direct elsewhere. The temptation offered by her sweetly pursed lips coupled with his certainty that she was too young and ignorant to know the danger in the temptation she offered prompted him to act.

"Oh, very well. But let's do it properly."

When she launched herself at him, hands reaching out for him, he balked. "There's no need to crush one's clothing," he began, as if giving a lesson in decorum.

With gentle insistence he set her back on her feet and then lifted her hands from where they clutched his coat sleeves. "Now then. Follow my lead." He stepped back two paces and slipped his almost-healed arm from the sling. "Come here. Slowly."

As he opened his arms to her, Clarette stared up at the moon-spangled face of the man she adored and suffered the first pangs of guilt since the night she had engineered their engagement. Would she be struck by a heavenly bolt for daring to kiss a man who was sworn in spirit to her sister?

"What? Are you now the shy one?"

He moved forward. Strong hands embraced her upper arms, and then a warm searching mouth lowered gently over hers. She heard someone—was it her?—sigh.

Almost before it began, it was over.

To have the pleasure snatched away so precipitously brought tears to her eyes, and she almost stamped her foot.

"Well?" he prompted with a smile. "What do you say?"

"It was . . . nice."

"Nice? That's all?"

"Admit it. It wasn't your best effort."

"You little devil. What would you know about kissing?"

"More than you might suppose," she lied. She did not look directly at him as she said, "For instance, you did not bother to take me into your arms."

"Very well. Let's try again, shall we?"

This time his strong arms went around her shoulders as his lips, firm with purpose, stroked her unformed mouth, making her smile. For a moment it seemed that this was all he would offer her. Then his lips parted slightly as he deepened the pressure, causing her mouth to open and expose the full tenderness of her lips. The effect was thrilling. His hands spread across her back and waist, molding her against his harder frame.

Reaching for the anchor of his hard shoulders, she clung to him with all the ardor of her youth. Immediately she was falling, drifting, spinning like a leaf toward the stream of desire.

But Jamie was not finished with his lesson in the sensual art of the kiss. Not his best effort! He would show her good effort! He ran his hands lightly up and down her back, rousing as well as soothing the trembling restlessness coursing through her. Then he opened his mouth and plied hers with lips and tongue and every nuance of expertise in his arsenal of seduction.

A tidal onslaught of delight raced in against Clarette's senses, clashing and doubling and spewing drowning waves of joy as frightening as they were pleasurable. So this was desire!

"Oh, my!" she gasped when he finally lifted his mouth from hers. Overwhelmed by her emotions, she dropped her head weakly against his chest.

"I say!" Jamie echoed in a state of astonishment as great as her own. It was not as if he had never felt passion before. He had, and often enough to understand the difference between pleasant stimulation and the rare jolt of pure desire kissing Clarette had brought him. What shocked him was that his chaste little friend had been responsible for it.

After a moment he bent his head tenderly over hers and kissed her hair. "Are you all right, Puss?"

As she lifted her head, he cupped her cheek, astonished by the heat in it. "Oh, Jamie, it was wonderful!"

"Then shall we try again?" he asked hopefully.

"Oh, yes!" Ever willing to learn a new lesson thoroughly, she gamely went into his arms and hungrily applied all her concentration of body and mind to the exercise.

* * *

Clarice Rollerson was everything Hockaday had claimed: a vision to quicken any green boy's heart and make a man of experience clutch protectively at his own. Gowned in a shade of wild rose, she was as delightful as spring's first rosebud. Her dewy skin was made to be viewed by candlelight. In its glow her golden head shone like raw silk. Odes were composed to necks like hers, poems offered to the tilt of so proud a head, protestations of affection prompted by the curve of such a shy smile. More than one confirmed bachelor had lost both sense and heart at the sight of ethereal beauty such as hers, only to awaken to reality in his marriage bed.

As Quinlan led her through the third set of dances, he almost felt sorry for the jealous young gentlemen following her every movement like timid mice who had spotted a block of cheese. He was the tomcat chosen to hold them at bay. Though Hockaday had cause to worry on other accounts, the child was entirely safe from him. Pretty young ladies of impeccable manners and exquisite sensibilities had long ceased to interest him.

Several times earlier he had attempted to lure her into conversation, but she had been so quiet thus far, he might have been steering a shadow across the floor. Luckily, his healing leg gave him no trouble that evening. But it was a burden to dance so often. Still, he supposed, he was obliged to entertain his partner.

"I find London suffocating this time of year, Lady Clarice. Don't you agree?"

"Oh, no," she answered with charming enthusiasm. "I shall be loath to leave." She looked up at him with a rapt attention he found faintly pleasing, then spoiled it by saying, "Papa says the best society began leaving town when Parliament adjourned August twelfth. He says we shall be labeled unfashionable if we are not gone by the end of the month."

"And so you shall be. You'll miss grouse season. You do hunt?"

She smiled. "No, my lord."

"You might call me Quinlan," he murmured with head bent

daringly close to hers. No callow youth would have attempted such a flirtatious maneuver on first acquaintance. The room was bound to take note of it. Ah, the things he did in the name of friendship. "After all, we have been introduced."

Any lady with a heart in her would have answered him saucily or served him a setdown for his want of propriety. She merely blushed a deeper shade than her gown as she whispered, "Please, do not tease me."

He drew back in mock affront. "Tease you? I was but agreeing with your father that you must not be allowed to wither in the town heat." He offered her a rake's smile. "Grouse are not the only thing in season of a country weekend."

Confusion entered her lovely face, rendering it a trifle blank. "I do not take your meaning, my lord."

Behind a bland expression, he doubted that this was true and pressed the flirtation. "Country matters are the same in town, my lady."

She lowered her gaze to his cravat. "Young ladies must seem poor goods to a gentleman of your vast experience and tastes."

He looked down at her a little severely, determined to push her over the provincial hedgerow of her prim breeding. "What could you possibly know about the tastes of a man of my vast experience?"

She looked first doubtful then perplexed. "Why, nothing."

All at once he understood. The girl was as lovely as a peacock but as green as grass. Forsaking conversation, he directed her into a turn and curtsy, thus ending the set.

Perchance his judgment of her was a bit harsh, he decided as he led her toward her chair. At least she did not mince and giggle or affect a lisp like the first and second chits he had danced with. He glanced down into the limpid blue eyes gazing up at him and wondered if her beauty would be enough to keep Hockaday content the next score or more years. Perhaps. Continued acquaintance with London's rakes and dandies and libertines would soon dispel her ignorance of how to conduct a flirtation. In a few years her shell of sophistication would pass in most circles for high intelligence.

That thought depressed him.

He lifted his head to scan the dance floor. Where the deuce was Hockaday? He had done his duty of a evening. Yet he could not find among the couples on the floor either Hockaday or the pleasingly plump little minx in the daringly cut apple-green gown. He suspected she had slipped it past her father's eye. He would have fired the modiste who allowed a daughter of his to purchase a garment fit for a member of the demimonde.

Daughter? He must be wool-gathering.

Directing his thoughts to the other end of the female spectrum, he decided that he should like to see Longstreet's Fair Hand gowned in apple green. The color would provide a dramatic setting for the cascade of her red hair. The only thing he would enjoy more would be helping her out of it.

His musings must have been reflected in his expression, for he realized two nearby matrons were staring at him with great censure in their hawklike gazes. No doubt they suspected him of dishonorable designs on his companion. If only they knew!

He was relieved when he saw Lord Rollerson making a beeline toward them. Expecting to be warned off for his pointed attentions, he had taken leave of Clarice by the time her father reached them.

Instead of chastising him, Lord Rollerson greeted him warmly. "Good to see you, Kearney. I'm looking for Clarette and Hockaday. Have you seen them?"

"I believe they are in the garden," Clarice said quickly, then blushed when her reply drew Quinlan's inquiring glance.

"The garden?" Lord Rollerson's expression gave an inkling to his thoughts. "We'll just see about that!"

"Clarette! Is that you, child?"

That voice of authority was enough to break the embracing

couple guiltily apart, when an instant before neither had thought to ever let the other go.

"Lord Rollerson!" Jamie exclaimed, and hastily pushed Clarette back to arm's length. His contrite glance went from her father to Clarice, who, on Quinlan's arm, stood staring at him with a quizzical expression on her face.

"I—it's not," he stammered, only to feel Clarette's hand clutch his sleeve. Abashed, he took a hasty step back from her as though she had suddenly grown a second head.

"I should—must apologize. Can't think what I was doing." He reached up and began massaging his forehead. "Mistake. Yes. Just so. Mistake. Terribly sorry."

No one sought to answer that rambling statement.

Clarette threw him a pained glance, all her lovely feelings squelched by his ungallant desertion, but he did not notice. He was staring at Clarice again, as if she were the only other being in the Garden of Eden.

Yet Clarette had seen her father's face and hoped against hope that she had, after all, accomplished her goal for the evening.

Rollerson bent a hard eye on the pair. What he had seen quite alarmed him. If they had been truly in love, he would have welcomed this display of mutual attraction. But he had not been fooled by Hockaday's unpersuasive attempt to enact the embarrassed suitor. Just as he had not been entirely convinced of the young man's sudden turnabout in agreeing to an engagement to Clarette. The young jackanapes gave himself away with his every glance in Clarice's direction. His children might think him a fool, but he was an *old* fool, and that made him wiser in the ways of the world than they.

"It's time to go home, Clarette. Come along at once."

"Yes, Papa!" she cried with false gaiety as she hurried toward him.

"I'm disappointed, child. You do yourself little credit with such conduct," he said quietly when she reached him.

She grasped his arm firmly in both of hers. Her cheeks were burning, yet very little of it was caused by shame, and only some of it by anger. "Oh, Papa, do not scold. I am so happy," she whispered, and hid her hot face in his sleeve. "Jamie's the most wonderful man in the world."

"I don't doubt you should think so," he muttered. "It's time we had a serious chat, Clarette. You and I, in my library, after breakfast."

"Yes, Papa," she answered, too distracted by the memory of Jamie's kiss to heed the warning in her father's tone.

Jamie had kissed her! It was as if a star had dropped on her. He had felt it too. She had seen the revelation of desire on his face the instant before her father's appearance broke them apart. If only he would remember that later, when Clarice was not there to confuse him.

Rollerson glanced at his other child, who was staring at Hockaday with suspiciously wide eyes. "Clarice. Attend me." He offered her his free arm. Only then did he look again at the two young men in their midst. "Good night, gentlemen," he said with a finality of a door banging shut.

When the Rollersons were out of hearing, Quinlan clapped Jamie heartily on the back. "Changed your mind about your preference for gooseberry tart?"

Jamie jerked with surprise. "Certainly not! We were only pretending. Did it for Rollerson's benefit."

Quinlan's laughter was rude. "Seem to be taking your role rather seriously. You're still drooling, dear boy."

Jamie blushed The truth was he was not at all certain what had occurred, but things had definitely gotten far out of hand. In another minute he might have pulled Clarette into the concealing bushes and well, who knew? The fact that an untried girl had sparked in him a lust quite unlike any he had ever before felt made no sense to him. The spontaneous meeting and igniting had quite unsettled him.

He smiled rather too broadly at Quinlan. "Fooled even you, did we? Rare girl, that Clarette."

Quinlan kept his thoughts to himself. Jamie must be willfully blind not to see what any nodcock could observe upon scant acquaintance with the pair. Clarette Rollerson was as much in love with Jamie as he was with her sister.

Quinlan smirked. A less moral man might have placed a tidy bet in the books at White's on the outcome.

Jamie turned back toward the house. "I need a drink! You too?"

Quinlan nodded. "Yes, but not here. Let's retire to a corner tavern in Lambeth I know for a bobstick of geneva."

"What's that?" Jamie questioned suspiciously as Quinlan slung a companionable arm about his shoulders.

"A cousin of Blue Ruin. Holland gin that has been flavored with juniper berries.

"Is it safe?"

"Absolutely not!" Quinlan grinned wickedly. "We may end up stark staring blind. Why else would a man drink it?"

Thirteen

Northumberland, September 1, 1815

The trip from London north had been long and arduous. Late August was a fair month in the borderland with its windy peaks, sprawling moors, and deep forests. Here myriad lively streams ran through valleys and gorges like so many threads of silver, hiding the flicker of shy brown trout. Exhilarating and expansive, the country welcomed the traveler in need of respite from the rollicking, cosseted life to the south.

But the purpose behind this journey was not one to imbue the spirit or refresh the soul. The Viscount Kearney and the Honorable James Hockaday had come north to pay their respects to Lord Heallford's widow.

That knowledge had not prevented Jamie from launching unprompted into another of his many soliloquies on his favorite subject: Lady Clarice Rollerson. Many times during the tedious journey he had held forth in rapture on his as yet unattainable love. It did not matter a whit that Quinlan did not feel constrained by social custom to occasionally nod politely and say, "Oh, really?" or "How nice."

For his own part, Quinlan made a few notes on his lap desk, letting Jamie, who sat opposite him, ramble because it was better than putting up with the younger man's restless tapping and humming and drumming when he was silent.

When he realized he was being ignored yet again, Jamie

sighed and glanced out the window. In the distance a lonely gray-stoned fortress rose in the apron of a hill. Recognizing it from a previous visit as their destination, he reached across and slipped the quill from Quinlan's moving hand. "That's enough of that! There's Heallford Hall just ahead."

Quinlan slumped against the cushions of the traveling coach, too weary to take umbrage at this high-handed tactic. "Remember your part. Be yourself and no more."

"You don't trust me?" Jamie inquired in an offended tone.

Quinlan's smile was bitter. "In this I don't even trust myself."

Though never one to worry when he could find distraction of any kind, Jamie could no longer ignore what now loomed before them. "Can you go through with it, Quill?"

"I can." The resolute expression on Quinlan's face was one that two short months before had given confidence to men facing certain death.

Jamie had lived through the consequences of battle and was less ready this time to simply obey. "Still, to—well, lie and rob—"

"There's no treachery in my actions," Quinlan countered flatly. "I act an oath sworn to a friend."

"Call it what you will," Jamie countered in fresh doubt. "The result is that we're about to defraud a friend's wife."

"Call it what you will, if that eases your conscience," Quinlan parroted, and then reached forward and snatched back his quill. "Now, if that's all."

Jamie began plucking imaginary lint off his coat sleeve, a sure sign that he was far from at ease. "Harris knows his part?"

Quinlan regarded his companion sharply. He had questioned more than once on the journey north his decision to allow Hockaday to accompany him. The plea that he needed an excuse to escape from the Rollersons for a time should, perhaps, not have weighed heavily with him. "Remember your duty to Rafe. You need not know the particulars of my part. So then your conscience will remain clear on at least one point."

Jamie muttered something all but inaudible about his conscience. "Yet, about the letter—"

"Damn the letter."

Though Quinlan did not raise his voice, the travel coach seemed to reverberate with the violence of the declaration. He slammed his lap desk closed and set it angrily aside.

He shifted his glance out the window, his jaw set against an inward struggle. Not for the first time he wished he had never set pen to paper for any of his friends. But what was done was done. Only a coward did not do his duty because it pained him.

Lady Cordelia's guests were shocked by their first sight of her. The smiling, dimpled lady of memory had vanished. Above her black mourning robes her once-glowing complexion was alarmingly pale. The spark had left her bluebell eyes. Her once-lush figure had wasted to willowy slenderness. Even her dark, heavy hair was covered by a black veil, as if to keep its beauty a secret. Still, she approached them with a quick, youthful step and held out her hands to Quinlan, who met her halfway across the morning room into which the butler had shown them.

He clasped her cool, slim fingers. "Countess, I hope you are well."

"Well enough, Lord Kearney." She smiled, but it was a ghost of the generous welcome he had always received from her when, in Rafe's company, he had visited her. "I've been expecting you since your letter arrived nearly a month ago. How good of you to bring Mr. Hockaday as well." She nodded at Jamie. "Rafe's friends are always welcome."

Quinlan noted that she had not hesitated to speak Rafe's name, and felt a fresh prick of guilt over the duty he had come to perform.

"Do excuse me for not greeting you in more formal surroundings, but I must continue to work while we converse."

She moved back to the table in the morning room, where fresh-cut flowers were laid out on paper. "I've just been pre-

aring these rosebuds for Lord Heallford. One must act quickly
 order to preserve them. I don't know if either of you gentle-
en are aware of Rafe's fondness for roses."

"I am," Jamie volunteered a shade too cheerfully. "He col-
cted several varieties to ship home while we were in Spain."

Della nodded. "We planted two of them in the garden here
uring the week of our wedding." She glanced at Quinlan. "We
ere so sorry that duty kept you from the ceremony."

"So was I." For a moment their gazes met, and each felt the
ther's loss.

"By all means, Lady Heallford, allow us to help," Jamie of-
red as he surveyed the process.

"How kind of you. Oh, no, don't touch the bud, Mr.
ockaday. It will spoil. Let me show you how."

She moved with the quick, easy movements of one familiar
ith her task. "First tie a piece of thread around the stem of
ose. Then carefully dip the cut end into melted sealing wax."
he stuck her forefinger in the pot set upon a tripod and candle
 test its warmth. "The wax must not be too hot or it will
amage the stem. Now then, Lord Kearney, if you will be good
nough to place Mr. Hockaday's dipped rose in a paper cone."

"Of course." Quinlan regarded her thoughtfully as he
rapped the rose in paper. "As a child I helped my mother
repare buds from her garden. She put them away to use as a
reat at Christmas. A bit of summer laid by."

"I hope these will not need to be kept that long." She favored
im with a shining expression that transformed for a moment her
adness. "I preserve them merely against an early frost. Rafe's
irthday is in October, and I would not want him to think I was a
eglectful wife. He has already missed so many of the glories of
ummer. This way I can preserve a little of it for his return."

"His return!" Jamie began in some alarm. "You cannot mean
hat—"

"I think," Quinlan cut in strongly with a warning hand
ropped heavily on Jamie's shoulder, "Mr. Hockaday fails to
nderstand the subtler forms of a lady's grieving." He searched

Della's upturned face for any signs of distress. "I have heard that you still entertain hopes of Lord Heallford's remains being returned to his native soil. The roses will make a pretty memorial."

Her blue eyes turned a shade more emotional than before. "You understand with more subtlety than I imply, Lord Kearney. I do not preserve flowers for Rafe's grave." She flushed. "They will be a welcome-home, for, you see, I do not believe that Lord Heallford is dead."

Quinlan gave a sharp shake of his head when he saw that Jamie was about to speak again. "May I ask on what you base your belief, Countess?"

She turned away from him back to her work. "I have heard many Belgian peasants took soldiers home with them to nurse back to health. Just last week Lady Carroll's son was restored to her. It's been claimed a miracle."

It occurred to Quinlan as he noticed how her hands shook that she might not be emotionally well. But delusions would not heal her troubled spirit. As gently as possible he proceeded to dash her hopes.

"Mr. Carroll's case was different from Lord Heallford's. Carroll's physical wounds were slight. He went wanting in the wits and wandered far from the fields of battle into France itself. His facility with the French language was so good that the peasants who found him assumed he was a French soldier and so he was sent to Paris. It was only by the merest chance that he was recognized on the street by an English officer of his own regiment."

Della went on working, her eyes averted. "Yes, well, perhaps Rafe suffers a similar fate."

Quinlan lay the lightest touch of his hand across her wrists to still her actions. "I would not depend upon it, Countess."

She turned on him quickly, her expression suffused with anger that flamed in her cheeks. "Would you have me rescind all hope?"

"I would beg you yield to the truth, however distressing.

"That Rafe is dead?" she questioned in challenge.

"Yes, difficult as the thought must be for you."

"Did you see him . . . after the battle?"

Quinlan gave a quick nod, but his gaze no longer held hers to strict accounting as before.

She seemed to sense some hesitation in him because she caught at his coat sleeve as she stepped closer to observe his expression. "Was he dead? Did you witness that too?"

For the same reasons that kept him from making this call for weeks, Quinlan found he could not lie outright to her. "Madame, he was as good as dead when I last set eyes on him. He was badly wounded. He had no other desire than to die."

Her eyes filled with silent tears. "Because he was suffering so?"

"Yes."

"Tell me how he looked."

"No, madame!" He stepped back from her, removing her touch from his sleeve. "I've spent too many days and nights attempting to dislodge those memories and others. I will not burden a lady with them."

She reached out again, her hand chill upon his now-flushed face. "What you must have seen, dear friend!"

Guilt flogged Quinlan. This was obscene, what he had come to do. Yet he had sworn an oath. It was Rafe's wish.

She removed her hand from his face as a sad secret smile flickered in her expression. "For a time—after—I thought I might be with child, a consolation, don't you see? But, alas, it was impossible. The doctor said it was only my nerves. Silly, really. I suppose I'm better a widow without a child. Still, I did so hope . . ."

She bit her lip and gave her head a tight little shake. "I apologize. You must think *me* wandering in my wits to speak of such things."

Quinlan resisted the impulse of a further gesture of comfort. He had no right, no right at all, to attempt to assuage the pain he was deliberately causing her. "Rafe thought himself the most fortunate of men because you were his wife."

"Did he?" She moved away from him at last, every line of her posture one of grief held in strict check. "I cannot abide the thought that he is gone." Her voice was husky and tight, the words barely escaping. "We had so little time. If we'd had even a few years together, the loss might not seem so keen. I would have memories—years of remembrances—for comfort. But there is so little. A few days, a wedding, and then he was gone. 'Tis too little."

Churning emotions made her turn once more toward Quinlan, and he saw the ravages of tears on her cheeks. "Rafe cannot be dead. I won't believe it!"

This was the moment. Quinlan pulled the battered letter from his coat pocket. "I don't wish to distress you further, Lady Cordelia, but I have a letter for you."

He saw her eyes widen as she noticed it. The paper was filthy, spattered with dried mud and blood and water marked. He had scotched the impulse to recopy it for her because it had laid next to Rafe's heart. "From Rafe?"

When he nodded, she snatched it from him with both hands. Her complexion paled further as she recognized her name written in Rafe's hand. She sent a fearful gaze toward Quinlan, then turned and ran out of the room without a backward glance.

"What do you think?"

Quinlan jerked about at the question, having for the moment completely forgotten Jamie's presence. "That she will now grieve."

Jamie licked his lips nervously. "Are you certain we've done right? I mean, dash it all! You heard her. The lady could be suffering from a disordered brain."

"As you suffer from a loose clapper," Quinlan said in terse tones. " 'Tis what Rafe wished. How could we do any different?"

"I don't know." Jamie looked as miserable as Quinlan felt. "Only I do know it don't serve! Havey-cavey, that's what it is!"

"Then go back to London and forget you were here. I've decided to cross the border into Scotland."

"For the hunting?"

Quinlan shot him a dark look. "For the solitude."

They were both startled when a minute later Lady Heallford suddenly reappeared, her face gleaming with spent tears. Yet she was smiling the old charming smile that had been missing before from her lovely face. She walked right up to Quinlan and laid a hand on his coat front.

"Thank you. Thank you! You have no idea—" She choked on emotion but continued to smile. "It means everything!" Her eyes filled with tears again, but they did not spill. "I am so ashamed, Lord Kearney. My last letter to Rafe was filled with accusation and ill feeling. I thought he must hate me. But here is proof otherwise. I can scarcely believe it. That Rafe should have written such words to me!"

This time need moved Quinlan beyond his self-imposed reserve and he moved to stand close beside her. Though he did not touch her, he offered his handkerchief. "You are much too severe with yourself, lady. Rafe spoke of you only in the fondest terms."

"He would." she nodded to herself as she wiped her eyes. "He was more generous to me than I ever deserved. It was only with himself that he was too severe. He never saw that I could love him for himself alone. He wanted to be able to offer me everything. I wanted only him."

She shook her head as if to scatter unhappy thoughts. "Yet there is something queer in it." She looked down at the letter she held. "Only my name is in Rafe's hand."

When she looked up, Quinlan found himself the focus of her considerable concentration. "Did you write this?"

Looking down into her trusting gaze, Quinlan teetered on the edge of a lie, but he knew she would find him out. "I did."

She stiffened, doubt edging aside tearful joy in her expression. "Why?"

"Because Major Heallford had jammed his thumb while reassembling a rifle," Jamie offered with a false note of urgency that made both parties turn his way. "Right thumb," he added, and offered a demonstration by wriggling his own.

"I see." She held Quinlan's gaze doggedly, as if she could read more than he intended in its expression. Bleak misery had replaced her earlier joy. "Rafe always said you were prodigiously clever. I own I envied your friendship."

"Any ape can entertain his fellows," Quinlan said with self-mockery. "You brought him what joy of life he knew."

"Perhaps."

A feeling of helpless rage surged through Quinlan. He should have thought to disguise his style to save her this embarrassment. Better yet, he should never have agreed to write the accursed letter!

Most of the women he had written to for soldiers were illiterate or nearly so. They had cared nothing for handwriting or the author, were grateful only for word from their men. In many cases the local curate would have read the letters to them. Yet, he should have known Rafe's wife would recognize her husband's hand. Now she believed that her husband had shared with another his most intimate feelings for his wife.

She looked down and touched the delicately edged band of gold circling the third finger of her left hand. "Life was not kind to us, Lord Heallford. We were due much more happiness than was our portion."

"At least you had a portion, Countess."

She glanced over at the half-full box of stored roses. "Still," one can yet hope for a miracle, isn't that so?"

"Miracles are by their very nature unexpected," Quinlan answered carefully. "You therefore cannot expect them."

She again surveyed his face as if it were a map to be read. Yet her own was more easily perceived. Hope and doubt vied for control of her quivering mouth and too-full eyes. "Tell me. Is this letter of your devising, or did my husband dictate it to you?"

He was more embarrassed by the question than he expected,

but what was another lie next to his larger transgression against her? "The words were his."

"Truly?" Hope won out, flushing her too-pale cheeks a pretty blush rose.

"Truly." Quinlan's silent sigh was that of a thief who had escaped the eye of the night watchman. "Now Mr. Hockaday and I will leave you to your task."

He turned away, then paused as if something had just occurred to him. "I have only one small request."

"For Rafe's friend, anything."

Quinlan did not look at her, but studied the rose pattern in the carpet. "I would like to spend a little time in Rafe's room, looking through his things. He borrowed a few items from me, and I should like to have them back, if that wouldn't distress you."

"By all means, take whatever you like. I'm afraid you'll find his personal things in disarray, just as they were shipped here from the continent." She paused to clear her throat of a suspicious roughness. "I had many plans to restore my husband's ancestral home. Rafe deplored the way his family had let it run to ruin. But now . . . I don't know what I shall do. Perhaps you can advise me, Lord Kearney."

Quinlan looked up at her quickly, a hint of shame staining his cheeks. "Perhaps you should finish your roses first."

She smiled as if she understood more than his words implied. "Very sensible advice, my lord. Now, if you will excuse me, Henley will show you to your rooms."

After an early supper eaten in near silence and minus the company of their hostess, Quinlan retired to one bedroom while Jamie repaired to another. Unlike Jamie, he had things to do before he slept.

As he lay back, still fully dressed, against the bed bolsters, waiting for the house to settle for the night, he felt a familiar trepidation of spirit. His conversation with Rafe's wife had nudged awake his conscience.

He had long ago learned that the most accomplished liars were those who kept their lies brief. His wish to visit Rafe's room was not questioned because it seemed unimportant in the aftermath of a tumultuous interview. He really was beginning to wonder what sort of duplicity he was *not* capable of.

Rafe was not dead. Yet, because of a letter he had composed in a moment of supreme self-indulgence, the lovely young woman who was Rafe's wife was now condemned to live a lie in widow's weeds.

That was a secret he did not know how to keep, or even if he should.

The familiar black sting of guilt swarmed about him. He had no right to interfere. He had given Lady Heallford the letter. Better he should not have written it. But he had written it, had delivered it, and made matters infinitely more complicated.

Annoyed with himself, he rose and went to pull a sheaf of papers from his traveling bag. When he could not sleep his only recourse was work. He might not be able to work out his friends' troubles, but theatrics he understood. A play followed rules and logic, rewarding the good and punishing the bad, demanding a balance that real life too often did not.

In life the best of intentions often went horribly amiss. His sense of duty to a friend who claimed as motive love for his wife left him no way to repair the needless damage done to the feelings of a lady he much admired. Where was the balance in that?

He reached for a quill and then brushed the feathery end slowly across his slightly parted lips. He had never felt more compelled to—nor less like—minding his own business. He smiled suddenly. Why start now?

He sat a long time on the Sheraton chair set before a matching writing desk and simply stared into the middle distance. Yet he was not thinking of his play. The matter he was contemplating required a stretch of imagination he had seldom brought to bear on a mere plot.

A full hour passed before he thumbed open the hinged silver lid of the crystal inkwell on the desk and dipped his pen.

He wrote quickly, making many errors and scratching them out until he had the text he sought. Then he practiced disguising his handwriting. Finally, when half a candle was used, he sat back and surveyed his creation.

It might just work, if . . .

He was in luck. The trunk containing Rafe's effects stood in the center of the floor, where the servants had been ordered to leave it undisturbed. Most likely Lady Heallford planned to unpack it herself. The thought of a countess wishing to perform that small domestic task out of love made him feel doubly culpable as he loosed the latch. Once lifted, the lid revealed all Rafe's belongings. There was very little else to add.

He went about his task quickly, adding to the trunk Rafe's requests of Lady Cordelia's miniature portrait from the mantel, several volumes of poetry from the shelves, and a packet of letters from the niche to which he had been directed.

In addition, he took several jeweled stickpins, shirts and stocks, shoes, coats, and a valuable gold snuff box to encourage the belief that a theft had occurred. He even broke a small pane of glass near the latch of a window with a hearth brick wrapped in cloth. Only then did he open the communicating room to the valet's closet to let in a guest Lady Heallford did not know she housed.

"Is that it, then, m'lord?" The thin little man with homely features who entered was dressed in dark, nondescript clothing.

"It is, Harris. Your booty is there."

Harris followed the direction of Quinlan's finger to the trunk and nodded. "Good as pinched, it is."

"Yes, well, I never count chicks in their shells." Quinlan lifted a finger to his lips. "Have a care. Nothing must be lost or broken."

"Righto, m'lord." Harris touched his cap respectfully before whispering, "Leave it to 'arris. Always at the ready to do a swell a service."

Quinlan waited until the man had hoisted the heavy trunk onto his back before speaking again. "Wait until the hall clock strikes twice before attempting to leave the house." He glared at the man. "Take nothing else. And leave no trace."

"No need to sit on thorns, m'lord. 'Arris ain't the sort to pinch on the parson's side."

Quinlan understood enough of the man's flash to concede the point. "You will seek out and deliver the trunk to a Mr. Sexton in the maritime offices at Greenwich. He will supply the second half of your payment. Let nothing detain you."

"All's bowman, m'lord!" The man huffed and wheezed as he scraped through the narrow doorway back into the closet.

Quinlan smiled at a job well done.

Tomorrow or the next day Lady Heallford would discover that her husband's trunk was missing. A few days later she would begin receiving missives containing clues as to her husband's whereabouts. What she did after that was her business.

He had not betrayed Rafe by telling his wife the truth. Yet if the countess were the woman he supposed her to be, she would take up the challenge in this tantalizing dispatch. What came after that would be up to her . . . and Rafe.

He did not believe in love, but they did. It would be interesting to see how far and to what lengths love would drive two people. Mere loyalty had driven him from his peace of mind.

One thing was certain. What he had done here this night had made it impossible for him to simply go back to London and pretend to his friends that Rafe was dead and his wife a widow.

An expression of faint amusement lifted his features. He scarcely recognized his own character after the business of the last weeks. Today alone, loyalty had driven him to lie and steal from his hostess. A week earlier, suspicion had driven him to break into Longstreet's office. Pride had driven him to accost a poor soul who was minding her own business. And, in a rare moment of lapsed willpower, he had let lust drive him to molest a young woman with child.

The recall made Quinlan sigh. A week after their meeting he had not forgotten the young woman with flame-colored hair, a novelty in his experience. Impossibly pretty when kissed to distraction, she occupied his thoughts, he had determined, precisely because she had retained her wit at such a moment. And more, they had actually begun an intelligent conversation because she was well versed in his field. Something, too, in her eyes, so clear a green, he was fascinated to find he could read every emotion reflected there. Fine-minded innocence wrapped in a siren's provocation. 'Twas practically a sin they had met when he was in least humor for a new mistress and she, in a delicate condition, was least able to assume the role.

Alas, he would take Longstreet's advice, well meant or otherwise, and seek solitude in Scotland. Although he still suspected Longstreet of duplicity, he had come to the realization on the journey north that it was of no moment.

Maybe when spring came he would have rediscovered his humor and his talent. However misguided, his efforts for his friends had been driven by the desire to abet their pursuit of love.

As an idle afterthought that followed him back into the comfort of his bed, he wondered what, if it ever came to him, love might drive him to do.

Part Three

Courage

"I will not let thee go.
Ends all our month-long love in this?
Can it be summed up so,
Quit in a single kiss?"
—*I Will Not Let Thee Go,* Robert Bridges

Fourteen

Italy, November 1815

On a clear day the view from the coastal harbor at Porto Venere to the isolated villas perched on sheer cliffs above was breathtaking. Travelers often found the jagged outlines of mountain peaks and precipices rising above the deep blue waters unspeakably grand. Byron had written his *Corsair* upon the rocks at the extreme end of the promontory. But on a stormy day, winds whipped up those rocky ridges, making a journey treacherous.

Ensconced in the depths of a heavy barrel-shaped barouche that appeared to be at least half a century old, Lady Cordelia Heallford clung to the balance strap with the fast disappearing hope that they would, at any moment, arrive at their destination. Far below them and lost to sight by mist and the encroaching darkness, the roaring sea frothed and hissed like a fabled sea monster loosed from the deep.

A sudden gust carried the slithering sea's white curl unusually high upon the rocks, lashing at the coach with a fury that threatened to sweep it from the road and tumble it into the sea below. The vehicle rocked and swayed wildly. The hinges shrieked and the horses snorted and whinnied in protest.

"Ooh, my lady! I fear we've done ourselves a terrible wrong. 'Tis no place for God-fearing folk!" exclaimed Sarah Dixby, Countess Heallford's new companion.

"Please be silent!" Della retorted, her patience whittled away by their ordeal. "It cannot be much farther."

"It's been an hour, my lady," Sarah replied, not at all daunted by her new mistress's temper. "That demon of a driver assured us we were only minutes away from our destination!"

"So he did," Della murmured. In three brief weeks she had become quite fond of this short-pudding of a woman with small features crammed together in the center of her full-moon face. A clergyman's indigent spinster daughter of middle years, Sarah had shown remarkable aplomb in very trying situations far from her vicarage in Umbria.

Though much disheartened, she struggled to summon a smile for Sarah. "What is a little weather compared to the great adventure we are having?"

"I'd as lief the adventure were not so great, my lady."

When the coach seemed to gain its balance once more, Della sank back against the moldy squabs, only to straighten again immediately as a loose spring dug into her back. Shuddering in distaste, she rearranged one of her tapestry traveling bags over it before settling again. Her buttocks could attest to the fact that there was little else of sprung comfort in the contraption in which they traveled.

From the very beginning of this secret enterprise, nothing had gone as she had hoped. After an interminable voyage upon churning gray seas, the ship's captain had promised that once on land, the much-heralded sunny Italian Mediterranean coast would unfold it secrets. Instead, the stormy autumn weather had followed them ashore, wreaking havoc upon what was supposed to have been an easy drive to their destination.

Not one to readily believe in such things, she could not help but wonder if the weather was an ill omen for what lay ahead.

Had she been sent on a fool's errand, tricked like a moonraker's daughter into a search for something that could not be? Or was it only her own stubborn pride that would not allow her to believe what everyone else did?

Della fretted the dark curl hanging free from her bonnet by

her right ear. Despite every bit of evidence to the contrary, she still believed, deep down where good sense and reason held no sway, that Rafe was alive.

She glanced at Sarah, who, amazingly enough, had closed her eyes, and then opened her reticule to withdraw the letters that had prompted her reckless journey.

By coincidence or fate, this adventure had begun on the very day she had steeled herself to confront Rate's belongings and put them away for good. The visit by Lord Kearney and Mr. Hockaday a few days before had convinced her mind to accept what her heart could not: Rafe was gone and his last letter must be her comfort.

The trunk had disappeared. The discovery surprised but did not alarm her. She decided at once that Lord Kearney had taken it. He had requested a memento. He had been so kind to her that she could not begrudge him, yet she would have liked to have kept some item that had been with Rafe's at the end, even if it was only his comb.

Then she had noticed that a windowpane had been smashed. Further inspection of the room had led to the discovery that several other items, some quite valuable, were missing as well. Most significant, a small framed miniature of herself. It had been Rafe's favorite portrait of her. She was left to ponder a new possibility, that she had been robbed!

The first letter arrived while she sat writing to Lord Kearney to ask if he had taken the trunk. The letter was addressed simply to Heallford Hall. Because it did not contain a return address or salutation, she had read it with half a mind. Strangely, though written, not printed, it read like an advertisement: "Expatriate and former English officer seeks the services of an English gentlewoman to act as nurse and companion. Inquire for details."

She had laughed and tossed it away, thinking it must be a mistake. She was a countess, not a poor relation in need of employment!

The very next week she received another, and a third the

following week, worded exactly the same. She was astonished, then annoyed, by the persistence of the writer. Inquire for details indeed! Had there been a return address, she would have written to inform the person of his mistake.

She had ignored the subsequent weekly notices through the end of September, until the tantalizing weight of one made her open it. To her shock, out slid the missing framed miniature of herself. How had it come into the hands of her unknown correspondent?

Furious that some unknown person would torment her in this way, she had ripped the letter to shreds. But after a restless night during which she had had a horrifying dream in which Rafe was not dead but being held prisoner in a medieval dungeon, she had awakened at dawn, pieced the letter together, and reread it carefully.

Della opened the letter, which had been pasted together like a puzzle onto another sheet. Biting her lip, she ran her fingers over the curling edges. It was worded like the others but with this addition: "Master speaks Greek, Italian, and German. Lady seeking to fill position must be of stout heart. Villa located on Italian coast. Send inquiry in care of Professor Giorgiolani, Naples."

Rereading it, it still seemed full of the clues she had overlooked upon first perusal. Rafe spoke Greek, Italian, and German. She had never thought herself courageous, but Rafe had said in a rare moment of emotion that her stalwart refusal to submit to her father's opinions against him had touched him deeply. They had planned a wedding journey to Italy. Could it be, was it possible, that Rafe was alive and the letters were clues to that fact?

For three days she had deliberated over what to do. She considered going down to London to see Lord Kearney, yet he had not replied to her month-old inquiry about the trunk. Perhaps he was connected to this mystery. But no, she would hire an investigator, someone from Bow Street, to look into the matter. She was a widow of considerable means. Unscrupulous villains might have stolen the trunk as a stratagem to lure her into danger. Yet the longer she thought about it, the more certain her first conviction seemed. Rafe was alive and seeking her out through this mysterious method.

Yet who would believe her? Who would believe that Lord Heallford was in such extreme circumstances that this was the only way he could contact her? Exactly no one.

Her friends and family would think she was mad. The authorities would listen, then wink behind her back and say grief had made her as unreliable as a new-hatched booby. She could not reasonably say she would blame them. Yet she felt, oh, how she felt like the tumultuous beating of her own heart, the abiding presence of Rafe in this world. He needed her. She would go to him, but she could trust no one else with the secret.

Della turned to the final page of her correspondence, to the letter that was responsible for her trip to Italy. It was from Professor Giorgiolani of Naples. She smiled, noting it was addressed to Miss Kathleen Geraldine, for she had written to him using her cousin's name and giving herself, Countess Heallford, as her own reference. The familiar names were meant as a sign to Rafe that she understood his enigmatic summons. It was an acceptance and gave as the location of her new position a villa near Porto Venere.

The carriage slammed into a rut, nearly launching Della into her companion's lap. As the women exclaimed in unison, the wheels flung up new spatters of soft mud to obscure windows that the driving rains had washed to dingy usefulness.

"Another such as that, my lady, and we shall lose an axle!" Sarah cried over the keening of the wind.

Della nodded absently. Another such as that and they might find themselves tumbling over the edge of the cliff into the sea. If it came about that Rafe was dead and she was little more than mad, it would not matter. Perhaps it did not matter even now.

She leaned her forearm against her brow. The gallant courage that Rafe admired in her was tiring. If they did not soon reach their destination, it would desert her altogether.

The abrupt lurch of the coach to the left did not impress Della with its significance until they began bumping over cobblestones. "We've turned off the main road," she declared in relief. "Paving must mean we're entering a town."

"If this not be our destination, my lady," Sarah said quickly, "I beg you insist the driver find us lodging for the night. Perhaps by morning the weather will have cleared."

The carriage swung wide again, this time to the right, and then they heard the crack of the coachman's whip as he bawled orders to his team to stop. Seconds later the coach came to a sudden halt before an archway shrouded in mist.

The driver was as precipitous in setting them down, baggage and all, at the main archway door, as he had been in dispatching himself from their presence. He had scarcely bothered to assure them that this was the place they sought. It seemed as if he did not want to linger in the vicinity.

As she waited for someone to come in answer to Sarah's repeated pulls on the bell, Della could understand why. The spot was as austere and forbidding as an abandoned monastery.

For the few seconds it took her eyes to adjust to the faint light of dusk, other sensations took precedence. The chill of the stonework penetrated her senses, followed by the dank odor of mossy stone and the hollow sounds of dripping rain. Gradually she realized that they stood beneath a covered arcade formed by a series of archways held up by black marble columns that marched away into the distant gloom, giving her the impression of having entered a catacomb.

"What sort of place be this, my lady?" whispered Sarah after several silent minutes.

"I don't know," Della answered in equally hushed tones. "An old church, perhaps, or a nunnery."

"No fit place for a lady, if you ask me."

"I'm certain we shall be seen to perfectly well once Lord Heallford has been informed of our arrival," Della answered.

"Yes, my lady," Sarah murmured, but her concerns switched from fear for her own safety to worry over the well-being of her mistress. Each new glimpse of Lady Heallford's face, framed in clusters of dark sausage ringlets inside a deep bonnet brim, drew Sarah's apprehensive gaze and troubled her mind. Her mistress was too pale, her blue eyes so prominent as to overburden on this occasion the delicate balance of her wide cheekbones and generous mouth.

The reason for the journey had not been fully explained to her until they were far from the shores of England. It would be nothing short of a miracle if Lord Heallford were, indeed, alive and living under this roof. Yet, if he were not, she did not know how her young mistress would survive the blow.

Della had begun to entertain the uneasy feeling that the villa might be uninhabited, when out of the darkness at the far end of the piazza a squat figure appeared carrying a torch. After a moment Della distinguished the features of a grim-faced woman whose head and upper body were covered in a heavy black wool shawl. The woman paused before Della but made no effort to address the two.

Della stepped forward with a slight nod of greeting. *"Buona sera,* my good woman. I am La—" No, she wanted to keep her surprise for Rafe. "I'm Miss Geraldine, and this is my companion, Mrs. Dixby. I've come in answer to the advertisement from the *signore* who resides here. The English gentleman," she added for emphasis when the woman did not respond.

"No English here," the woman said after a moment, and moved to turn away.

"No, wait!" Della's alarm forced the woman to turn back. "Is this not the Villa de Toscana?" The woman nodded once, reluctantly. "Certainly your master received a letter from Professor Giorgiolani informing him to expect me."

The woman merely sniffed, though whether it was from contempt for her question or a lack of her understanding of English, Della did not know.

Determined not to be outdone by this new estimate of things, she continued in her own rusty schoolroom Italian. "I wish you to present me to your master, the *signore,* of this place."

"He is *villeggiatura*. He sees no one," the woman answered in thickly accented English.

"So, you do speak English!" Della murmured. Hungry and aching in every bone from the bruising ride, she was in no mood to coddle recalcitrant servants. She stepped toward the woman and said bruskly, "Let's let your master decide. Lead the way."

"The *signore* sees no one," the woman reiterated firmly.

"You will announce me!" Della burst out in a fury of over-stimulated nerves. "I command you to!"

The woman's black eyes reflected balefully the light of her torch, but she said only, "Be it on your head, *signora*. I did try to warn you."

With those ungracious words ringing in her ears, Della fell in behind the woman to follow her down the narrow hallway lit only by the torch which the servant carried high above her head.

Della's stomach did a pirouette. She was about to face Rafe! What would he say? How should she act? Should she be haughty and aloof? wait for him to make an explanation? Or would his rare smile of joy send her headlong into his arms?

She had dressed with particular care that morning, wanting to arrive looking her best. But her traveling costume, a pelisse gown of Sardinian blue velvet bound with ermine, was horridly crushed from the drive, and her bonnet was damp from the rain. She knew it was vain to consider such things important, but she had hoped to dazzle and move Rafe to a display of emotion.

Nettles of doubt raked her courage. What if he did not react with joy when he found her on his doorstep? What if it were he who remained aloof while she dissolved into protestations of love?

She had come to suspect his melancholic nature might be responsible for the freakish turn of mind that had led him to allow her to believe that he was dead, when perhaps he was only brooding. Well, if that were true, it was a horrible trick to play on her, and she meant to make certain that he made considerable amends before she forgave him.

But she would forgive him, forgive him anything if he would take her in his arms and whisper the words she had only read in his letter.

The stones beneath their heels rang and echoed down the tunnellike hallway. The sunny Italian villas of lore and her imagination were a far cry from this dim and dismal dungeon. They turned into several equally narrow halls, each more dark than the one before, until Della was not at all certain she could have found her way back to the entrance unaided. She would demand that Rafe take her away from there after the rains ceased.

Finally the woman halted before an arched doorway closed by a set of heavy doors with gothic hinges and a knob in each center. She pushed them open without even a knock. The vast low-ceilinged room beyond lay in deep shadows relieved at one end only by the yellow flames wavering behind a black wrought iron grill of a hearth. The billowing heat exhaled the smell of the sickroom.

The musky sourness halted Della at the threshold. She clenched her hands as a shiver shook her. This was something she had not expected. She was afraid of illness, had been ever since a noxious fever had swept through her home when she was no more than eight years old. In the space of three brief days, disease had snatched away her mother, her two sisters, and her nanny. Ever after, the smell of a sickroom had made her weak with fear.

"What is it, my lady?" Sarah whispered behind her.

"Nothing, nothing at all," Della answered with more confidence than she felt.

She quickly dug out a scented handkerchief and pressed it to her nose, breathing deeply of attar of roses to displace the rancid odor of the air as she made herself step inside.

Flanked by the firelight's pale glow, a hulking silhouette of indistinct relief occupied a low-backed chair. The hunched figure in the chair was certainly not Rafe, she told herself sternly. He had a proud posture that was as natural as it was imposing. This person, who was obviously ailing, must be his Italian host. The thought emboldened her faltering spirit, yet she was disappointed. She had not wanted their first meeting to occur before strangers. Now there was another person to be considered.

The servant woman moved toward the fireplace, her steps slow and deliberate so as not to startle, and then she spoke in a rapid whisper of Italian too low for Della to hear.

The figure in the chair made a sudden move, as if it were a shadow that had gained independence of its source. "No!"

The word was not shouted, but the surly temperament with which it was uttered pricked Della's spine.

The woman retreated quickly back toward Della, waving her arms in a gesture of dismissal. "He will not see you, *signora!* You go now! I say so!"

A faint flush of anger warmed Della's cheeks. Not since leaving the nursery had she been so summarily dismissed, and never in her life by a mere domestic. The slight prompted her to forget her fear of the sickroom.

"Step aside. I can speak for myself." Moving past the startled woman with a sweep of her hand, she crossed the floor in purposeful strides. She didn't know what the woman had told her master, but she had come too far to be put off.

She paused only when the radiant heat from the fire forced her to. The intensity of it at six paces made her eyes water and her cheeks sting. More profoundly disturbing was the fact that the person huddled in the depths of the chair stationed much closer was wrapped in blankets. Only his left hand in which he clutched a wine bottle was free. This mute outline of a stranger was not at all encouraging.

"Signore?" Della whispered as her courage threatened once again to desert her.

The figure did not answer or move or even indicate that he

heard her. The continued silence relieved only by the soft hiss of the fire was unnerving.

Sarah moved up behind her. "Mayhap we should wait to make our presence known in the morning, my lady."

"Certainly not!" Della retorted. She had come much too far and endured too many unspeakably difficult months to reach this moment. She had no other place to go nor any way to get there even if she had. Whoever this was shrouded in wool and silence would be her host at least for the night.

She said distinctly in Italian, "I regret the need to disturb your peace, *signore,* but I have come very far to find my husband. Am I right to believe that you are responsible for the letters I've received?"

He moved so quickly, she had only begun to cringe in alarm, when the bottle he loosed struck the grate and shattered, showering the fire in spirits, which flared and sizzled as the blaze devoured the alcohol.

"Come away, my lady. He's drunk!" Sarah whispered urgently as she tugged at her mistress's arm.

Shaken, Della turned to the Italian servant who was smiling at her malevolently. "Is he intoxicated?"

The woman shrugged. "He seldom speaks except to order more wine."

"And you have no better sense than to give it to him," Della said in disgust. The poor man was clearly badly served by his menials.

The woman shrugged. "He is the master."

Della supposed that was explanation enough even for an English servant. But she was not a domestic.

In an attempt to reach through his stupor she spoke again in Italian, using her best lady-of-the-manor voice. "I was assured by Professor Giorgiolani that you would know the gentleman I seek. His name is Lord Heallford, he is the Earl of Cumberland. I am his wife, Lady Cordelia Heallford." She waited five heartbeats for a response to her half-truth. "You might at least have the courtesy to look at me when I address you, *signore.*"

"Leave me."

Surprised to hear the shroud speak, even in Italian, Della stepped a little closer. "What say you?"

"Leave me! Get out! Go *away!*" The final syllable careened up the scale as he lunged from his chair. His voluminous coverings sailed out on either side of his tall frame like the unfolding wings of a carrion bird as he swung around to face her. The countenance he presented to her in the hideously flickering play of light and shadows had no features. He had no face!

"Merciful heaven!" Frozen by the apparition, Della stared at him in unconcealed revulsion as he lurched blindly toward her.

He paused a few feet from her, head cocked as if listening for the sound of her breathing or the thump of her heart. "Who are you?" he rasped out. "What do you want here?"

But Della was no longer capable of speech.

His right arm came up as though he meant to shake his fist at her, but the arm ended in a swathed stump.

"Della?" he questioned in an incredulous voice.

"No!" she cried in childish defense. How could he know her name? Unless he recognized her voice!

For one nightmare of a moment Della remained rooted to the floor as his arm swung out, brushing a scrap of ragged linen dressing across her cheek. It felt like the touch of the grave, and she whimpered, "Please don't."

"Della?" he whispered even more softly.

The blood seemed to freeze in her veins. Was this Rafe? No! This could not be her husband. Dear Lord! she prayed fervently, this fiendish creature must not be her wedded spouse!

At that moment a resinous log exploded in the fireplace, sending a monstrous, mishapen shadow leaping across the stuccoed wall behind him. She heard her own scream of fright in surprise, but it unlocked her rigid muscles and she reeled away.

She heard Sarah's cry of "Oh, my lady!"

The dark room was suddenly much too warm. Her limbs

seemed to melt like jelly. Her breath constricted in her throat. She saw the open doorway and with it the path to safety. She set a foot in that direction, but instead she was sinking, falling down through the dubious, unbounded darkness.

Fifteen

Della. Here. Seeking him!

No. He must not even acknowledge the reality.

He was more drunk than he had been three hours before, when his uninvited guests invaded his self-imposed exile. The stupor sometimes helped him to forget, and there was so much he wanted to forget.

His hand flexed, crushing the bit of lace and dimity tangled about his fingers. He had forgotten he held it. The crest embroidered in the corner was unmistakably a rose, the Heallford family emblem. He brought it to his nose and inhaled deeply.

Roses. Della always smelled of roses.

If he had not trod on the handkerchief, he would not have known his guest dropped it in her flight from his presence. She had fled because he had shown himself to her. If she thought his bandages hideous, then how much more repulsive would she find what lay beneath them.

Ugly. Deformed. Monstrous.

He smiled absently. The words no longer invoked pangs of remorse. He had put away his humanity with his feelings. He could afford to do no less. He did not need eyes to know how he appeared. The reaction of others had helped him understand that his ruined countenance was the stuff of nightmares. His missing right hand earned him the label "cripple."

No wife deserved a blind, lame, and grotesquely scarred shell for a husband. Certainly not his exquisitely beautiful Della. He had spared her, and himself. And that was as it should be.

He could not even see her!

The loss of his right eye had affected the vision in his left. Doctors at the hospital in Genoa the previous July had told him that the condition might be temporary but he had never again tested the eye, kept it covered. He did not want to see himself. The daily sight of his ugliness would disturb his emotionless existence. He could scarcely dress and feed himself. Those were reminders enough of his deficiencies.

The urge to raise an arm to protect himself from the French hussar's saber stroke had been instinctive. It had cost him a hand and an eye. Had his arm not taken the brunt of the blow, the saber slash would have taken his head instead. A clean, honorable death. Why had he thought at the last second to cheat the very fate he was expecting?

She must never know.

He had wanted to live, to be with her.

But no more. He had no wants, no needs, no desires but the taste of wine. Rafe Heallford had bled his last in a Belgian farmer's barn. *He* was no more than a ghost with a pulse.

He heard the chime of the clock by his bedside and sighed. He was restless. He often prowled the house when the shroud of night gave him, for a few hours, an equality with the rest of the world. Even a ghost was allowed to haunt his dwelling place.

The room smelled of roses.

He stood by her bed. It did not matter that he could not see her. He felt her presence as he did the subtle beating of his own heart.

She had fainted at his feet. He would have scooped her up into his arms had he not feared she would awaken in his embrace more shocked than before. Servants had carried her away and brought her there.

Ah, yes, he caught the sound of her breath. The shivery sighing invaded his thoughts, stirring to life forgotten memory.

He stretched out his hand, knowing instinctively where she lay. He did not touch her. He did not need to. The warmth of her skin rose up to meet his palm, stimulating nerve endings that raced a rare, tingling pleasure up his arm. So warm, so alive, so real.

Della had found him!

He picked up a strand of her hair, running it carefully through his fingers like a merchant testing silk thread. He remembered the full weight of her hair in his hands on their wedding night. He did not need eyes to recall the contrast of its deep coffee color against the cream of her skin.

He bent and brushed the tip of the curl slowly over his lips.

Della, who smelled of roses.

Too much. He shivered and released the curl. He was feeling too much after too long. She was bringing it back, the memory and the pain.

Yet his hand moved back to her, skimming her cheek so lightly she did not stir. For an instant at her jawline a pulse leapt under his fingers and the throb was answered in his loins.

He snatched his hand away.

Foolish, dangerous, impossible. He had not felt the push of desire since . . . since . . .

She came toward their marriage bed wearing only two sheer panels of white silk tied with ribbons at the shoulders and on either side at her waist. Candlelight made the garment all but transparent as she approached on the shy tread of silent feet.

His heart stopped. He could not swallow, could scarcely breathe. The trembling thrust of her breasts, dusky nipples imprinted in the sheer cloth, the indentation of her navel, slight swell of stomach, and the tantalizing shadow at the apex of her slim thighs all vied for his delighted attention.

She paused just out of arm's reach, as if doubtful of her welcome. Her dark gaze searched his face as her unbound hair undulated down her back in waves that seemed to have a life of their own. "Are you pleased, my husband?" she inquired when he did not speak.

My husband. Lord, how he liked the sound of that!

"I am," he answered shortly, embarrassed by his lack of adequate response.

He longed to tell her that she was beautiful, the most exquisite being he had ever beheld, beyond his best dreams and more than he deserved. But he had never possessed the facile words of a rake. Nor would he repeat to his bride the banalities men used with their mistresses. No, better he should say nothing than insult her by the comparison. In fact, he had come here to say very different things to her.

Still fully dressed, he had come to explain that he must leave her—again.

He had brought with him the official order from the Horse Guards to report without delay to his regiment in Paris. It had come by mounted messenger while he bade the last of their wedding guests good night.

"You are strangely silent." She smiled in encouragement but her hands moved forward and laced fingers together where the deepest shadow hid the mound of her femininity. "I begin to suspect that you are . . . unimpressed."

"Madame, you mistake my awe. I have something to tell—to show you."

"I rather hoped you might." Her provocative laughter held a whisper of bashful coquetry. "But you are still dressed." Her gaze strayed toward the folded-down expanse of the bed on which he sat. "Shall I call your valet?"

"No."

He could not tear his gaze from the gentle rise and fall of her unbound breasts. Silk and candlelight shadows teased him mercilessly. Her scent, at once subtle and potent, wafted sensually about him like an evening breeze from a rose garden.

"Hear me, please, Della. I've been back scarce five days. We are all but strangers. You need time to—to be certain."

She shook her head, her long, dark hair shifting and drifting forward onto her shoulders. "I am certain I wish to be your wife. What else is there?"

"There are other considerations."

"Do tell me, husband," she murmured, drawing a fraction closer so that he could see the welcoming smile in her warm eyes.

He crushed the order in his hand. How unfair that on this, their wedding day, he should have to deny himself the miracle of her. For he would not bed and abandon her in the same evening. It would be more unfair to her.

Looking into her inviting gaze, he could not forget the hint of doubt that had shaded her eyes as she marched up the aisle on her father's arm. He had not heard the words they exchanged moments before in the vestibule, but her father's opposition to the marriage was openly known. He would not betray the courage she had shown in marrying by consummating the vows between them and then departing before she had time to trust in his love.

Oh, but it would be the most difficult thing he had ever done in his life.

"Am I being too forward?" She made a helpless little gesture with her hands. "I've no practice at the art of wifery."

"Lady, you need only be yourself," he answered on the ragged edge of his control. He felt drawn across the sharp edge of a blade. One wrong move and he would be done for. Yet how could he refuse her? The perfume on her skin intoxicated him. She intoxicated him.

"Then, I think," she began teasingly as she stepped up to him, stepped right between his spread knees, "that your wife should like you to kiss her."

She looked at him with her bashful, eager, brave heart in her eyes, and he knew she was all he would ever want of this life.

Just one kiss, he thought. He would leave her after one kiss.

He lifted his head as she leaned down to him, one hand falling lightly on his shoulder, and captured her soft lips with his and tasted paradise.

One kiss. So easily given. But devastating. His body overruled his head. He tossed the orders away and with it his resolve.

His hands found her waist, felt the smooth heat of her skin through the fabric, and then he leaned back onto the bed, drawing her down beside him. He had lived seven years for this moment. No one, not even he, could deny them this.

One kiss became dozens as he learned the tastes and textures and pleasures of her. He kissed her ears, her eyes, her brows, her nose, the point of her chin. He kissed her smiles, her sighs, her shyness, and finally her desire. He drew her even closer, hands reaching through the open sides of her gown to hold her bare, lush flesh.

She came willingly against him, the softness of her belly pressed hard upon his throbbing loins. He caught her lower down, fingers digging softly into her swelling buttocks to hold her tight as he rolled her over him and ground his lower body slowly under hers. She gasped in astonished pleasure, then caught him by the shoulders and mimicked his actions. She wrung a begrudging moan from him, and that drew her delighted laughter.

He did not ask where she had learned to tease a man, for he knew that she, like he, was merely following the dictates of her heart. He laughed then too, a joyous sound he had never before loosed.

The laughter stopped as their kisses returned, deeper, stronger, sharper, aided by tongues and teeth and eagerness.

He rolled her onto her back, following her body with his so that they did not break contact. He stroked her slowly from shoulder to thigh and back, reveling in the incredible sweet feel of his lady wife. Then he loosed the ribbons and pushed the gown away and met the heated skin of her breasts, satin smooth, with the caress of his lips and tongue.

When he lifted his head, her eyes remained shut tight against the wonder of her feelings. She arched under him when he tugged at her nipples and licked her belly. She dove fingers through his hair and cradled his head as he plied her with all the passion and joy of his too-full heart.

He paused only once, long enough to rise and douse the candle, at her request, and then divest himself of his clothing before stretching out over her again.

He lost himself in her sweet body, found the answer to every question his heart had posed, took her down with him into sweet, dark oblivion, where desire resides and love is forged. He loved her until they were both wet and shaking, and laughing and weeping.

He looked into her shadowed face, saw her lips parted in her first ecstasy of feeling, and knew he would never forget it. His gallant, brave, beautiful wife, worth to him more than forty thousand a year, worth every drop of blood in his veins. Like liquid fire his release pulsed out of him, sealing the bargain forever.

He cursed silently as he felt his way along the wall back the way he had come. If things were other than they were, if *he* were other than he was, this night might have had a very different end. But he knew there was now only one ending. She must never discover his secret. He was willing to do anything, *anything* to prevent that.

He felt the sudden damp caress of a sea breeze on his bare left cheek as he turned a corner. He tasted salt, sharp and cool, in the wind, and knew he had reached the terrace that overlooked the cliffs on which the villa was built.

So easy. A step up onto the low wall and then lean into the wind. The sheer drop off the precipice onto the rocks and surf below would end his unnecessary life.

If he were a man, one who still felt pain and anguish and regret, he would do it. But he had no humanity to prompt the emotional turmoil required of such despair.

He moved on the way he had come, in secret and silence, under the cover of all-forgiving darkness.

Della braced herself as she threw open the deep green shutters of her room. She inhaled smells of the garden blooming bright below her in surprised delight, and then stepped out onto the stone balcony with an ironwork balustrade into a morning drenched in sunshine. The night before the villa had seemed a vision of the inferno. In the morning light it was a dream of earthly paradise. Roses and bougainvillaea nodded on trellises. Pot of geraniums splashed color against paving stones.

On either side and below her, the multilevel red tile roofs of the villa sat atop stucco walls tinted soft, earthy shades. The sunlight spilling through the slats of the departing clouds made the air soft and warm and fragrant. It seemed as if overnight spring had pounced upon the neck of winter.

She made her way carefully from the delicate ironwork balcony that led from her room, down onto the terrace that overlooked a hillside olive grove. Now she could fully appreciate the climb made by the traveling coach. The promontory offered a panorama of the surrounding countryside to the east and the white sand forming a pearly necklace around the curving sweep of the azure sea coast to the west.

"Oh, you're awake, then, my lady."

"As you see, Sarah." Della turned toward the woman who had entered the terrace from the main house.

The woman's expression was doubtful. "You might have sent for me if you wished to rise and leave your room. You've not been well, my lady."

"But I feel perfectly fine," Della assured her. "How long did I sleep?"

"The clock twice around," Sarah answered.

"So much as that?" A frown formed between Della's dark brows at the thought that she had lost an entire day. How embarrassing. "Our host must be quite put out with us."

"I couldn't say, my lady, as I've seen no sign of him since that first night. I can report the servants run wild here, for they do." She nodded in confirmation of her speech. "Can scarcely be found to do a job when most needed. Not a one will allow as they know a word of good Protestant English, though they spend time enough lurking about eavesdropping: We should leave this place today."

"I cannot, not yet." Della favored her with a brilliant smile. "I have many things to consider first."

"Well then, I will leave you to ponder on them. Take this until I can fetch you a proper wrap." Sarah slid from her shoulders her alpaca wool shawl.

"Oh, no, it's much too warm for that," Della replied. As if to demonstrate her point, she pushed back the lace cuffs of her long-sleeved rose-colored morning gown. "Is it not a most beautiful day?"

"It is. But I still don't like the looks of you, my lady. You're peaked. Come inside and have a bit of breakfast."

"I will, in a moment. Do go on without me."

Della turned away toward the low wall fencing the rocky precipice that led abruptly down toward the sea. She hoped Sarah would take the hint and leave her to her thoughts, for they were many. To her relief, the woman did.

She had slept two nights and a day! No wonder she felt so refreshed and at her ease. The trepidations of the last months seemed, miraculously, to have vanished.

She had not risen immediately upon waking, as Sarah had supposed. She had lain a long time behind her shuttered twilight world, thinking. It was no longer possible to accept the elaborate tissue of implausible connections that she had held together these past months by sheer willpower. The realities that her beleaguered mind had been incapable of understanding when she arrived there two nights earlier were now perfectly apparent.

The *signore* of the Villa de Toscana was not her husband. Nor was he a faceless demon. He was a pathetic, maimed, ailing creature.

She could remember clearly now that the right side of his face and both eyes had been wrapped in bandages, leaving only his mouth, wreathed in a black beard, and left cheek bare. Poor man, he must be horribly disfigured as well as blind. That did not make him a fiend.

She pressed her palms to her blushing face. Dear Lord! She had run screaming from him like the truest twit.

With the cobwebs lifted from her mind she could even explain away her mistaken belief that her Italian host had called her by name. She was certain now he had said only *bella,* "beautiful." After all, he was Italian, and *bella* was a common enough appellation for a gallant to apply to a woman.

She was highly ashamed that she had allowed her own anxieties and fears to overtake her good sense. In truth, she had not been herself since the news of Rafe's death reached her.

"Rafe is dead."

Spoken aloud in the brilliant light of this gorgeous day, the thought struck her with the power of its reality.

Rafe was dead.

She had never before uttered the words. Even when Lord Kearney told her he had been with Rafe at the last, she had not completely and unalterably believed him. There seemed something held back, something unspoken.

"But now," she whispered to the breeze that brought the scents of the sea up from the coast for her pleasure.

Now she could begin to look upon her last months as a form of hysteria where she had seen and heard only what she wanted to. Rafe was not here. Nor had he engineered an illogical plot to lure her to Italy. Fatigue and a near-mad desire to believe the impossible had driven her to make this journey that could have no real destination.

She would put those maddening sorrows behind her and seek a rational method with which to live in the present.

She walked slowly about the terrace, her gaze ranging back and forth over the gardens and the sea far below. Rafe had spoken fondly of his time in Italy. Looking out over the hills of olive and vine, of effulgent sunlight and soft blue shadows, she could understand his delight in the beauty of it.

The thought struck her that there was no great need to return at once to England. No one waited for her there. Her cousins had made their bow into society. Clarette had delighted her with the written news of her engagement to her erstwhile lieutenant, Mr. Hockaday. No, there was no need to go home just yet.

She spun around slowly, absorbing the soothing heat on her upturned face. What better place to heal in spirit and lose her sadness than on the sun-drenched coast of Italy? Yes, she would rent a place of her own nearby. Perhaps her host could advise her.

"My host!" How would she ever make amends for her invasion of his home and her horrid behavior?

She understood now why he had advertised for a nursing companion. Though she was curious to learn why letters had come to Heallford Hall, she could believe that there was some rational, unsinister explanation. Whatever the case, she had taken the position under false pretenses. Certainly she must replace herself in that capacity. In the meanwhile, there must be some other way in which she could be useful.

She turned back to gaze at the house. For all its air of ancient beauty, the villa was little more than a ruin. Viewed up close, one could not miss the fact that however engagingly romantic it might strike the eye, the façade was crumbling. The paving stones of the piazza were broken and uneven where tufts of grass had pushed through between the individual stones. The garden near the door had run to weed, and the rose arbors at the back of the house were weighed down by unchecked and dead canes. The estate was very much in need of a firm hand and definitive eye.

Della smiled. She might not be good in a sickroom, but she had managed her father's residences for years which boasted an accumulated number of fifty-seven servants. The gardens needed weeding, the flagstones a good scrubbing. It was nothing short of shocking the way the man himself had been neglected by his servants. A pauper or beggar was better kept. The least she could do was offer to organize his household in exchange for room and board until she found a place to settle into on her own.

Resolute in her plan, she turned toward the house in search of the tea and toast she smelled wafting from the open doorway. After that she would put on her best dress and beg an interview with her host.

Sixteen

Scotland, November 10, 1815

Quinlan sat back in his chair in a private dining room of the
Crown and Thistle Coaching Inn near Edinburgh and listened
to the flurry and bustle that accompanied the noisy arrival of
yet another shooting party up from London. All men this time
by the sounds of their stomping boots and hearty laughter. Aristocrats all, by the sound of their voices.

"I say, 'pother, old fellow, have a care with my trunk!"

Definitely, this was a party of fops. The polished, unnatural
tones and effected lisps leaking through the chatter provoked
his smile. Even his more formal speech had softened under the
relentless burr of the Lowland Scots surrounding him. But that,
nor they, were not his concern.

Quinlan took a long draw on his cigar. For the past two and
a half months he had been squirreled away at the Highland
Scottish estate of an absent friend, Lord Bannock, writing and
bemoaning his lack of success. His writing had gone from poor
to nonexistent. Giving up the struggle, he had applied himself
these past three weeks to reading and rereading his favorite
authors while making unfavorable comparisons with his own
efforts.

It was only with the arrival of the first snow last week that
he thought to bestir himself from his self-imposed exile and
moved south into this Edinburgh coaching inn.

If not for Lady Heallford, there might be no bright spot in his life.

He had in his pocket proof that his anonymous letters to her had been a success. He had deliberately spun out the suspense for her, believing that too abrupt an approach would have put her off the game. For six weeks he had posted the same letter before dropping his bait, the miniature of her. She had snapped at it like a Scottish salmon after a bog fly. She should have reached Italy, and Rafe, by now. He wished them well.

"Egad! The fellow won't mind," came the boisterous rejoinder just outside the door of Quinlan's parlor. "Tipped a coin or two for his trouble, he can jolly well drink his whisky in the common room."

The door was thrust open on the high girlish laugh of the intruder. "See here, fellow," he began to address the room at large. "There are English gentlemen who've need of this parlor. Be good enough to remove yourself at once."

"Since when do you qualify as a gentleman, Ashford?"

The fellow started, his face growing red with affront as he followed the direction of Quinlan's voice to find him sprawled comfortably on his chair. When he recognized him, he snatched his hat from his head, revealing a fringe of light brown hair. "I say! It's you, Lord Kearney!"

"None other," Quinlan replied amiably, though in fact he was at once thoroughly amused. If Ashford led the party, then the birds could breathe a sigh of relief. None of his party could likely load a musket. If one could judge by his puce riding coat and daffodil riding breeches, Ashford was in Scotland solely to sport the latest in lord-of-the-manor fashion.

Never one to feel obliged by sociability's sake, but disposed of a sudden curiosity about life in town, Quinlan said offhandedly, "Care to join me for a drink, Ashford?"

"Damned if we won't!"

"Precisely one of you may join me."

"Really?" The rotund man just a shade this side of forty did a double-take toward the hallway, saying over his shoulder, "No room here after all. 'Tis the common room for us. Be along in a toddle after a piss."

He stepped inside the room with comic alacrity and stopped just short of rubbing his hands together in glee. "Nice of you, surely, Lord Kearney. Didn't know you saw the acquaintance as particular."

Quinlan merely nodded at this blatant bid for intimacy. Ashford's wide, flat mouth and bulging eyes, as well as his toady qualities, put one in mind of any number of unfavorable amphibian comparisons. "Do help yourself to whisky. You seem in need."

"Indeed." A theatrical critic and fellow playwright, Sir Beaufort Ashford considered himself a wag and Quinlan to be his greatest rival and roadblock to fame.

Ashford moved to the sideboard, where he quickly poured and then ingested a large glass of the local malt whisky. He filled it a second time before taking a chair.

"What's the news of town?" Quinlan prompted.

True to form, the fellow wasted no time in launching into his opinions of London, specifically its theatrical scene. For the next quarter hour he dissected the year's offerings, stopping periodically to refill his glass.

"Other than my success in the spring, Drury Lane theater's gone stale. Revivals are all the rage," he said, as he began to wind down. "No new fellow can get so much as a patronage, never mind a production to fruition."

Ashford helped himself to a sip. "Of course, we all looked forward to the annual DeLacy farce. Listening to rumor, however, one might have thought we'd be deprived of it this year." He rolled his head toward Quinlan. "Pity, we all agreed. Delicious confections, your works."

"I don't believe I catch your drift," Quinlan answered, more fortified by whisky than his guest but with the harder head.

"Come, old boy. No need to dissemble between friends." Ashford fixed his competition with a sly eye. "It's been put about that you were under the hatches with your muse. That's why you're rusticating."

He leaned in close, his flushed face bearing an unsober smile. "You may tell a fellow scribe the truth. We all feel the pinch of nerves. Am I right?"

"Having never suffered from a disbelief in my abilities nor my audience's, I couldn't say," Quinlan lied smoothly.

Ashford snorted in amusement. "How, then, do you explain the rumors derived from Longstreet's public musings?"

"I cannot, not being party to them."

"Very well. Pretend you did not put him up to it! But you wouldn't be the first to use a bit of controversy to sweeten the interest of the public. Byron has made a life's work of it."

Quinlan merely shrugged.

Obviously disappointed not to have drawn Kearney's admission of contrived publicity, Ashford's expression soured. His plays had never attained the critical and popular success of Kearney's, and he was certain it was not a lack of talent but because he did not equal the viscount in looks and blunt. Ladies dragged their gentlemen to plays and ladies were ever in favor of a pleasing face. He had heard it said that the mere rumor of Kearney's expected attendance at a performance was enough to sell out the theater.

"Autumn is an awkward time to produce a new play," he began to explain in a fresh assault on Kearney's good humor, "what with the *ton* mostly in the country, shooting. Yet I'll bet enough have been lured back to town by the talk." He winked at Quinlan. "Your name's on every tongue, and you know why."

"Again, I'm afraid you have the better of me in this matter."

Ashford snorted. "Must you make me the fool for repeating to you your own *on-dits?* Very well." He used the forefinger of one hand to tick off the details on the fingers of the other "First rumor came in the height of the Season. It said there'd be no DeLacy play this year. Next we hear there's a play but no De-Lacy. Longstreet himself put it about that the unpleasantness at Waterloo had taken its toll on you. Said you were too demoralized to face an opening night audience." He winked a second time. "I suppose that's your excuse for the awkward transition in act two, scene three. Not that I think ill of you for that." For the first time, Quinlan allowed his interest in this discourse to show through his bland expression. "You've *seen* my new play?"

Ashford nodded absently. "Longstreet held a closed performance for those of his royal backers who would not be in London for the premiere next week. Must admit I was curious to see if you'd lost your touch."

A play of his was in production! While Ashford prattled on, Quinlan, let that cannon blast of news roll over him without visible reaction.

"Prinny's down to Brighton oftener than in town. Taken it into his head to oversee an extensive remodeling of the Royal Pavilion, so they say. He was most particularly interested to see what your talents had wrought."

"And?"

Ashford's answer was begrudging in tone. "You've nothing to fear, old fellow. My opinion will run in the *London Gazette* after opening night. You look fit enough to withstand it."

With envy he surreptitiously eyed Quinlan's superb lean form clothed in serviceable attire of buff breeches, dark blue riding coat, and white stock. "The tale of your suffering was spread around in order to draw sympathy for your effort, what? Afraid your audiences wouldn't take to it as with previous ones. Might as well pop down to London and see it for yourself." He paused to sample his glass, emitting a satisfied sigh after a large swallow. "Writing for Kean ain't to every taste. Passed on it myself."

"Kean stars in the production," Quinlan said quietly, as if he were talking to himself.

"There's little to alarm one in his performance," Ashford allowed, watching his companion very closely for any sign of distress. "Bit old for the part, if you ask me, and you didn't. Still, he smoothed over the more troublesome speeches. That's why he's in demand, when he ain't been imbibing too often."

Again he eyed Quinlan, the malice no longer masked within his glassy gaze. "If *Fortune's Fool* ain't quite up to your finest efforts, 'tis a respectable addition to your body of work. We should all suffer as you did, what?"

"Just so," Quinlan answered darkly as his thoughts ranged away again. What the deuce had Longstreet thought to gain by pawning off another author's work as a DeLacy play? If he had thought he would get away with it, he was sadly mistaken!

He looked around sharply to see that Ashford was draining the bottle they shared. He stood up abruptly. "As you've killed the soldier, I'll wish you a pleasant evening and good hunting."

"I say. What—" The door closed behind Quinlan so rapidly that Ashford was left gaping. "Now what did I say?"

London, November 14, 1815

Quinlan sat at the back of his darkened theater box, a playbill in one hand and a loaded pistol in the other. Behind the drawn curtain that shielded him from the curious gazes of the assembled audience, it was too dark to read. He did not require light. The title page of the handbill was burned into his mind.

Fortune's Fool by Quinlan DeLacy
A Comedy in Three Acts

There were two things in error in that. He had never written the play the handbill proposed to advertise. Nor had he agreed to lend his name to the work of another.

He had arrived in London only that afternoon to find out he was not too late to halt the treachery about to be perpetrated upon him and these unsuspecting theater-goers. The play was premiering that very evening. He had had only enough time to change and make his way to the theater before the curtain was due to go up.

Eager to see for himself this travesty perpetrated in his name, he had slipped past the arriving audience and heard their buzz of excitement over what they supposed would be another of his popular farces.

". . . waited ever so long for another DeLacy play."

"Heard Prinny's pleased . . ."

". . . rumored to be in the audience, my dear."

". . . the Regent himself!"

". . . that Longstreet's bucking for a knighthood."

"Another DeLacy success . . . who knows?"

"Not bloody likely!" Quinlan muttered, and crushed the play-bill in his fist. He had come to make certain the impostor and his villainous producer were caught in the act!

He would wait until the performance began and the audience expressed their dismay and then dissatisfaction and finally anger at the poor quality of the play. Only then would he rise from his seat and reveal his presence. Because he doubted the author could resist attending the first public performance of his work, he would then demand that Longstreet point out the fraudulent hack who had dared submit his vile efforts under the prestigious DeLacy name.

Quinlan slowly rubbed his thumb back and forth over the butt of the pistol he held. He had never felt more like committing violence on his own behalf, yet he might well turn the artistic embezzler over to his hoodwinked audience. London audiences were known to explode in public brawls and riots on less provocation. In one matter he was resolute. Longstreet was his.

He had been suspicious of the man for months. If he had not in part allowed his chagrin last August to spur him out of town so quickly, he might have learned sooner that his suspicions were not out of proportion to reality.

He could not imagine why Longstreet had thought he would get away with this. He had turned the problem over in his mind a hundred times on the trip down to London with no clear-cut answer coming to mind. Then, on the outskirts of town he had composed a possible reason though he could not quite believe even Longstreet had the audacity to pull it off.

Longstreet intended to undercut the DeLacy name while trading on it to draw an audience for his newest protegé.

The thought appalled and infuriated Quinlan. He had never credited Longstreet's character with morals. Yet he had believed the man retained a certain measure of ethics when it came to business. Yet a scheme to set one man up so that his name might be blackened while advancing that of another was nothing short of diabolical.

"He won't get away with it while I live," Quinlan muttered. "No, while *he* lives!"

As the curtain went up, a strange excitement came over him. He felt much as he had when the call to arms signaled the start of the Battle of Waterloo. The blood was pounding through his veins, his breath came and went quickly as he leaned forward in his chair to peek through the box's drapery. The gentle applause that greeted the pastoral stage set sounded to his ears like the opening reports of distant rifle shots.

At first he was too angry to even listen to the words the actors spoke. The hero was a swaggering, puffed-up lieutenant who set about seducing and then abandoning an Irish lass with the same dispatch he used in the next scene to attack his enemies. This was no play of his. He had never written a farce set in Ireland, nor had he ever written about war and soldiering . . . until he wrote his first drama. Someone had revamped his latest literary effort, turning it from a tragedy into a comedy!

"By Jove!"

The abrupt expulsion of rage drew many eyes to Quinlan's box, but he had withdrawn to conceal himself from view.

Feeling that he had been struck by a bolt of lightning, Quinlan cautiously dragged the curtain open after a moment and leaned again into the shadows to watch more closely this time.

Something strange began to happen to him as he watched and listened, riveted by the story unfolding before him. His scalp started to tingle and his mouth went dry. He began to recognize the play!

Not the actors' speeches, exactly, but the elements that went into making them. Phrases, minor characters lifted whole from other writings, these and more he acknowledged as his own.

By the time act one ended, he sat back in his chair too stunned to react. It seemed as if he were a little mad. He did not write this play, but he *might* have written it. All the elements of his style were there.

Someone had stolen his work, plagiarized bits here and snippets there. The play was nothing less than a wholesale pillage of his repertoire of writings amalgamated into a vaguely familiar theme yet new story line.

As the curtain went up on the second act, it did not occur to him to interrupt the proceedings. He was now the most eager member of the audience to witness the rest of it.

Glued to his seat, he began to try to stay one step ahead of the writer in the following act, guessing which line he would lift next. Often he guessed correctly, but occasionally he was taken by surprise by an unexpected twist to equal the amusement invoked in the audience. Those rare, breathtaking original turns of phrase made it clear this was no mere hack, but a talented writer.

The final scene of act two was such an example. In it the play returned to Ireland, where the abandoned girl, now pregnant, received a stinging disavowal of affection from her officer lover in the form of a letter. In despair, the poor girl turned to suicide but with wickedly comic results. She tried to hang herself, only to discover that the rope would not hold her weight. The river she dived into would not drag her down to drown, but deposited her on a boulder. The precipice she leapt off had a narrow ledge onto which her skirt caught. Giving up, she resolved to have the child who must want to live more than she wanted to die.

Quinlan squirmed in his seat as the curtain went down on act two. What was clear now was that the play was not aimed only at entertaining an audience. It was the most diabolically subtle and deviously clever satire of a playwright's work he had ever read or seen performed. And he was the object of the jest!

Not one speech in the script was wholly original, yet that made it all the more unnerving. It was as if the writer had been inside his head, ferreting out every weakness and conceit of his style and bringing it blatantly to light.

Quinlan's hand trembled as he massaged his sweating brow. Who could have done such a thing? Someone who knew his writings as thoroughly as he did himself. Someone who had watched him work, or heard him talk about his work. Someone with the talent to mimic style and the comedic understanding to skewer his every literary device. Someone who wanted a very public and humiliating revenge upon him.

For several seconds he pondered the possibility that Lord Byron had elected to avenge himself in this manner for Quinlan's barbed satire of him the year before.

Quinlan's cheeks stung. If so, he had been perfectly roasted.

Edmund Kean was playing with supreme confidence the part of the strutting soldier brought low by his own willful arrogance. Every pompous speech he uttered was exaggerated to sound as if it were written by an author of unexcelled eloquence. It was inconceivable that so great an actor would have stooped to enact a role written by anyone less well known than himself. *Was* Byron the author?

Driven by curiosity, Quinlan gave his mind free rein at conjecture. Upon reflection, the scurrilous letter which the Irish girl read from her lover seemed remarkably like the one he had composed for Pettigrew. Yet, that was impossible. Even if someone had put about the story of his letter writing for other soldiers, no one else knew precisely what he had written for Pettigrew, unless Errol himself had been indiscreet enough to boast of it. No, it must be unlucky coincidence. Byron's powers of imagination were more than equal to his own. Asked to write such a letter, would the contents not necessarily be alike?

Quinlan squared his shoulders. He had never doubted he had detractors, only he never suspected any would be so cruelly vindictive. His gentle satire of Byron had been as flattering as it was teasing. This was a witty vivisection.

As the third act began, it seemed as if he could now detect here and there a strain of derision in the general laughter. There must be those present who knew exactly what was occurring.

For a few moments Quinlan turned his gaze to the audience, searching for a particular luminous pale face with curly dark hair among the glittering aristocrats arraying their boxes. He did not see Byron, but that did not mean the man was not there.

Whoever the architect of the play, he knew how to please an audience. The play was winning them over to a man.

When at last the curtain came down on the final act, Quinlan sat with both hands gripping the railing, staring at the empty stage. The audience exploded into vocal and hand-clapping praise. The curtain rose immediately, allowing the various actors to accept the appreciation. The swell of applause rose again and again like waves of approval lapping at the apron of the stage. Kean's entrance was followed by a roar of enthusiasm that threatened to tumble the candles from the huge chandeliers. Finally the thunderous ovations turned to calls for the playwright.

Having waited for this moment, Quinlan stood up and stepped forward for a better view so that he might catch sight of the culprit. Though whether he intended now to congratulate or challenge him, he was not yet certain.

To his consternation, he was spotted at once by those on the main floor. Cries of "Author! Author!" filled the air, matched by applause and cheers that set the huge chandeliers tinkling anew. Bouquets flew through the air, breasting the balcony railing and landing at his feet.

His face stinging with chagrin, he acknowledged the unwarranted praise with a slight inclination of his head. He was not the playwright, but he meant to discover who was!

Then, from the corner of his eye he caught sight of a short, stout figure stepping forth from the wings onto the stage.

"Longstreet!" he muttered through clenched teeth.

To his amazement, Longstreet gazed up at him and smiled. What is more, he began applauding Quinlan, as if for all the world he had not been the power behind this pillaging of De-Lacy's career.

He turned abruptly toward the back of his box, only to have the door snatched open before he could reach it.

"Kearney, you've done it again!" came the genial greeting from the first of the gaggle of admirers who pressed in upon him.

Seventeen

"What do you mean you did not write *Fortune's Fool?*"

Horace Longstreet gazed in bland amusement across the champagne supper of grilled oysters and lobster tails laid out before him. "Of course you did, Lord Kearney. Why else would the marquee read a Quinlan DeLacy play?"

Quinlan's gray-green gaze, as forbidding as a winter gale at sea, swept over the man. "That is what I have come here to ask you."

He had lost the elusive producer in the embarrassing crush of admirers eager to impart to him their congratulations over a play he had *not* written. Without displaying outright rancor to members of the *ton,* he could only let the human tide carry him along toward the door, by which time Longstreet had disappeared.

Luckily, Longstreet had run true to form, retiring as was his habit to his club for an intimate supper with his favorites of the moment. They happened on this occasion to be actresses who both had had bit parts in the night's production.

The drive there had given Quinlan time to stoke his temper to a fine blue-white burn. He sneered as he surveyed the seducer's lair. The private chamber boasted a heavily laden table and a sky-blue-satin-draped bed half hidden behind a Chinese screen. When he was done, the man would be lucky if he would ever recover enough to use it again.

To that end, he pulled from the depths of his greatcoat the coiled horsewhip he had borrowed from his driver.

As the oiled black leather uncoiled from his hand, one of the women shrieked in a not-quite-believable display of fright.

Quinlan's hostile gaze moved from the portly manager's suddenly ashen countenance to first one and then the other of the comely brunettes flanking him. Though the actresses were undeniably attractive, he was in no mood to respond to their heavy-lidded glances.

"If you don't wish your dinner guests to be upset, I suggest you dismiss them." There was no missing the aristocratic presumption behind his suggestion.

"You heard the viscount." Horace's features stiffened in a nervous smile as he lifted both hands in an action to scatter birds. "Shoo, my little doves. Gad! Don't swill champagne, Gloria. A lady don't slurp. There'll be plenty more when we're done."

The women removed themselves reluctantly from the room, the one named Gloria pausing to cast a flirtatious wave and lingering glance in Quinlan's direction. He ignored it and moved toward his prey.

"There now, my lord, just as you wish." Horace spread a benevolent hand toward one vacated chair. "Help yourself to the turtle soup. They do it supremely well here."

"I've no appetite for soup!"

One moment Longstreet was lifting a teaspoon of soup toward his lips, the next he was caught in a throttling grasp that lifted him off his chair and up on tiptoe. It was then he knew what he had always suspected; the taller more sinewy viscount was capable of extreme physical violence.

Quinlan thrust his face close to the apoplectic producer's. "Now tell me in very simple words. Who wrote that play?"

Horace made a little choking sound before the words would come. "You did, my lord."

Quinlan tightened his grasp, pressing painfully on his victim's windpipe. "That is not the right answer."

"I—I have—" The producer's face turned an alarming shade of red. "No—other!"

Quinlan released him so abruptly, the man collapsed back into his chair, his mouth gaping like a beached fish's as his eyes rolled in his head. There he half lay panting for breath for nearly a minute.

It was only half playacting. Horace needed a few seconds to recompose himself. He had decided on his tactic months before, right after Kearney left town. He would say that as far as he knew, Kearney had written the play he produced that evening. What he had not known was that it would require he give the performance of his life to bring it off.

He straightened himself slowly, one hand held protectively to his burning throat as he tugged his waistcoat down over his paunch with the other. Only then did he dare gaze at his attacker. It did not do his courage any good to see that while DeLacy had moved several feet away, he was toying with his whip as if readying it to strike. "My lord, believe me. If there's been some mistake—"

"You made it." Quinlan's gray-green gaze flicked over the producer. "You expect me to believe you simply accepted a work and produced it without so much as requiring a line be changed?"

Horace shrugged. " 'Tis true, we have been at some difference of opinion of late."

"Impasse would be a better term."

"Yes, well then, you can see how I was eager to placate—no, alleviate any further friction between us." Horace took a hasty swig of his champagne, wincing as the bubbles scraped his raw throat.

"How did you come by the play? Don't bother to lie. I will know if you do."

Horace did not bother to contradict him. "About a month after you left town I received a package containing your new play."

The sharp snap of the whip caused by the flick of Quinlan's

wrist made him wince again. "Very well, let us say I received what purported to be a new play from you. When I read it, I was more than pleased."

"I want to see this play, the original copy."

Horace paused in reaching for his fork, eyes alert. "Why?"

"So that I can attest that it's not in my hand."

"Actually, that never occurred to me," Horace confessed with more frankness than he meant to impart. Thinking more quickly than ever before in his life, he added, "Alas, that won't be possible. I had it copied by a Fair Hand before I even read it."

He glanced at the wicked tip of the whip snaking across the floor under the power of Quinlan's restless hand. "It was smeared by water damage. Yes, I recall now. It had gotten wet in the transport. Devil of a do to dry it out. Once it was copied, we threw out the original."

Quinlan did not so much as blink. "Who copied it?"

Horace dabbed at the sweat on his upper lip with a napkin. "Possibly I have that information in my files. Yet, why question me? You can't actually believe I knew the play was an imitation."

Quinlan snorted. "I've suspected for months you were up to no good."

"Did you, indeed?" Horace chortled despite a lacerated throat. "Thought I was out to cheat you, my lord? How rich! What had I to gain by it? Nothing, I say. You may check with your solicitor in the morning. Your advance was posted with your bank within a week of the play's receipt."

"I never signed a contract."

"Your solicitor has the power to do so," Horace reminded him. "You will, I think, be pleased with the terms. The house was packed tonight. We're promised a good run."

Quinlan absorbed this news with a generous amount of skepticism. His ego was still smarting from the satirical flaying by the play. Yet, if Longstreet were telling the truth, if he had not been out to embarrass or outright dupe him, then who could have plotted to stage a sham DeLacy play in place of an authentic one?

He did not know why the mysterious redhead came to mind, but he was suddenly certain she had had a hand in this mischief. "There was a certain young woman, an Irish lass with flame-red hair, working in your office last August. Who was she?"

"Miss—er, now, let me think."

The tip of the whip licked across the platter of oysters and wrapped with vicious intent about the tail of the lobster resting on Longstreet's plate.

"Geraldine!" he cried as he leapt from his seat.

"Miss Geraldine?" Quinlan cocked a brow. "Then she was not wed?"

Horace trembled in spite of himself. "She said her man died at Waterloo."

"Who was he?"

Horace stepped hastily backward. "I do not know, my lord! I swear it!"

"How did she come to work for you?"

"She said she had been a Fair Hand in Ireland and needed money for her child. I took pity on her and hired her."

Quinlan had never known Longstreet to show pity, but he let that pass. "How long did you employ her?"

"A few months. If I may ask, how do you know her, my lord?"

Quinlan shook the whip free from the lobster and began recoiling it. "I came upon her in your offices one night. She was working on a text she did not want me to read. I saw too little of it to say if it was part of the play you staged this evening, but I would stake a great deal on the possibility that it was. Tell me again, exactly, how the play came into your hands."

"As I said before, it came in the post."

"Did you frank it yourself?"

"Of course not. My clerks do that sort of thing."

"Then you don't know with certainty that it was delivered by post. It could simply have appeared in your office."

Horace pretended to lag behind in understanding of the viscount's thoughts. It was a dangerous gambit to thrust the deed off on the actual perpetrator, but his life was in imminent danger and an absent sacrificial lamb was better than none.

He smacked his brow. "I see where you're headed, my lord, and the deduction is nothing short of brilliant!"

He nodded, rubbing his hands in anticipation of his acquittal. "Possibly the girl was lying about her lover's death. Perhaps he was some seditious Irish writer who set her in my office for purposes other than a fair wage. They may have connived together so that she could slip his work in under my nose with none the wiser. Dear Lord! My career! This could ruin me!"

Quinlan found this explanation a shade too tidy, for it completely exonerated Longstreet. "How could she have known I would not return to London before its premiere and queer her game?"

"I don't know," Horace answered honestly, for this scenario was as new to him as it was to the viscount. But he knew when to let the other fellow carry the tide.

"She made no money on it," Quinlan said after a moment. "Her lover will get no credit. How can it benefit them? Unless . . ." His expression became withering. "They intend blackmail."

"Blackmail?" Horace repeated. "Oh, yes, I see. You think that now that the play has debuted, the girl and her lover may threaten to tell the public that you accepted another's work as your own. It might fly since it's been put about that you were having difficulties completing a play." Horace judiciously omitted the fact that he was the source of the rumors. "You suspect that the rogues may hope you will offer to buy their silence in order to save your reputation. It is a thought."

As the last words flowed out of him, Horace leapt on the idea of the threat of scandal himself. Lord Kearney was a man who set great store by his name.

"Come to think of it, my lord, the scandal resulting from exposure of the counterfeit play could call into question all your writings. It could, in fact, dim your literary light forever!" he said with just the right touch of indignation.

When Kearney did not quickly agree or refute this argument, Horace looked up at the playwright and found his gaze was now vaguely unfocused. Not at all certain his lordship was following along the path he had laid out for him, he said in summary, "As we all know, once lost, a good reputation is seldom ever completely regained."

Quinlan was making conjectures of his own. Miss Geraldine had been singular in his experience, a well-read young woman who had had the audacity to stand up to him. At the time, he had marveled at the temerity that had driven her to tear her work from his hands. Now he could put a new interpretation to her actions. If she were out to dupe him, that would go a long way toward explaining her desperate behavior. It might also explain why she stood so complaisantly under his kiss.

He had been unnerved by the depths of his response to her even after he learned she carried another man's child. For weeks after, his psyche plagued him with the pleasant memory of the kisses he had forced on her. But if what he suspected now was true, then perhaps he had felt only what she had meant him to feel. She had responded instantly to his kiss, and he had been aroused just as quickly. He almost believed that he could have brought her to pleasure by kisses alone.

Quinlan tapped the butt of the whip against his palm. Perhaps she would even have let him take her on Longstreet's desktop if he had insisted. Would she have lain with him for her own sake, or merely to distract him from her lover's work?

He glanced up at the producer, who was dancing in place. Was it the result of nerves or a weak bladder? He was not convinced the flame-haired Miss Geraldine could have plotted this alone. Longstreet stood to gain by the production of the play, as well. A knighthood, if rumor did not lie. Until he spoke with the girl, he could not be certain whom to believe.

He spoke abruptly. "Where will I find her?"

Horace lifted his eyes toward heaven, hoping that an unwed

mother on the lam would not be easy quarry. "She sailed for Italy last month, my lord."

Naples, November 14, 1815

"A lovely *bambina*, Contessa! God has blessed your line."

Kathleen turned her head toward the woman's voice, but her vision would not clear. Pale light spilled down upon her like dawn viewed through dimity curtains.

"How is she?" a strong masculine voice inquired from the doorway.

"She is well, *signore*." How deferential that voice sounded, but unintelligible. It was only afterward that Kathleen realized the woman and man spoke in Italian.

"And the child?"

"A girl, born alive."

"Ha."

Even though she did not recognize the words, Kathleen understood intuitively that this last syllable contained a wealth of emotions—relief and understanding, but also resignation, disappointment, and a certain fatality. Why that should be she did not know. But then she felt only an enormous weariness. Not even the faraway wail of a newborn could keep her eyes from falling shut.

Sometime later a tall, slim silhouette of a man interposed itself to stand beside her pillow, blocking out the light. A hand touched hers and lifted it. She felt lips, warm and dry, salute the back of her hand before it was carefully lowered back onto the bedding. Then he spoke to her in English.

"You are delivered of a girl child, Contessa. I am sorry, *cara*, that it could not have been otherwise."

Kathleen licked her dry lips as she stared up into his shadowed face. "Who are you?"

"Do you not recall? It must be the laudanum." His voice held a note of amusement. "I am the man you agreed to marry."

Kathleen blinked several times before the countenance of the speaker came more clearly to view. He was tall with pale olive skin, a narrow aquiline face, and a thick shock of silver hair. He was not old, but neither was he young. The hawklike nose and mobile mouth bespoke a patrician heritage and indulgent temperament. But most of all the knowing look in his dark, hooded eyes told her this was a man in complete control of his world and that for the present she was part of it.

After a moment he went on speaking in impeccable Italian-inflected English. "We may speak more frankly in your native tongue, *mia cara.* Our agreement was that if your child was a boy, I would marry you and claim him as my heir. Alas, you have produced a girl. Charming though she is, *cara,* I cannot now wed you."

The wonder of his confession surprised the question from her. "Whyever would you have wished to do that?"

He smiled at her with gentle pity. "You will remember all in due time. But now you must sleep." He said more forcefully than before, "The babe came quickly, too quickly for the doctor to arrive. The midwife says it is God's way of keeping the butcher from your door."

He shrugged elegantly, calling her attention for the first time to the elegance of his black satin coat, the costly gold lace at his wrists and throat, and the diamond stickpin in his black silk stock. "But you are weak. You were barely recovered from the ague when the labor pains began. Sleep and rest and know that you may stay under my roof as long as you wish, you and your charming *bambina.*" He leaned forward and placed his palm over her eyes.

As if he had passed a magic wand over her, her lids fell shut and she drifted into a deep, dreamless slumber.

When next she awakened, the room was darker. A woman dressed in black bombazine stood beside the bed with a squirming, bawling bundle wrapped in white cloth.

"She must eat, Contessa," the woman said in an urgent tone. "The *signore* requires that she not cry while he is working."

Kathleen lifted her head from the pillow, only to feel great pain like a weight attached to the back of her head pull at her consciousness. Amazingly, arms reached out for her, some to pull at her shoulders to help her sit while others stacked pillows behind her to prop her up. As the light-headedness dissipated, the swaddled babe was thrust into her arms.

With a tender hand she lifted back the edge of the cloth to reveal a tiny face, pleated and red from crying. The breath of air seemed to distract her, for the babe instantly ceased crying and opened her eyes as the wrinkles of distress eased from her face.

Kathleen caught her breath at the stab of pleasure-pain that went straight to her heart at this first sight of her daughter. "Oh, she's beautiful!"

"Lots of black hair like the *signore*," the nurse said with a pleased nod.

Kathleen did not answer. The baby's dark hair and blue eyes were gifts of her father, Errol Pettigrew, the Baron Lissey.

"Now she must eat." The midwife quickly unbuttoned and rearranged Kathleen's clothing so that she might offer a breast to her babe. When she stroked the babe's cheek with her nipple, the child latched on with very little prompting and began to suckle strongly.

"She's going to be a strong child with a will of her own," the midwife commented in approval to one of the maids hovering about. "Now you go! Out!"

Only when the others were gone and the midwife had removed herself to the shadows did Kathleen lift her eyes for a moment from her child's face to look about.

She lay in a large, cavernous room whose elaborate furnishings and other ornamentation gleamed, even in the dull light of too few candles, with the extravagance of their gilding. Beyond the edge of the bed the telltale sheen of marble shone between the paths of rich carpets. This was part of a palace.

The tinkling music of a pianoforte came softly through the corridors beyond the piazza. Now she remembered. Her host was the conte Francapelli, a renowned composer of symphonies and operas.

They had met while boarding a ship from Marseille to Naples when she had, quite by accident, fainted at his feet. He had been kindness itself, offering her his stateroom in which to revive and then refusing her reluctance to accept his hospitality for the remainder of the voyage.

Perhaps it was her illness or the fact that she was much too tired after the long, desperate, lonely journey to hold her secrets from this kind Samaritan, but he had quickly cajoled out of her the entire tale of her life. He knew everything. And then he made her an offer.

He wanted, nay, needed, an heir without the entanglements of seeking a bride. She would come to Naples and live with him and be known as his English contessa. If she gave birth to a son, he would legally wed her and raise the child as his.

But she had not birthed a son. The child in her arms, more dear to her now than ever, was a girl.

She bent her head to place her lips against her child's plush, moist cheek and whisper, "I don't know what luck brought us this far, *cushla-ma-chree,* but I swear I will do whatever I must to keep you safe!"

Eighteen

Scotland, November 1815

Clad in a long-sleeved Irish poplin gown with a drawstring neck and four rows of embroidery above the hem, Clarice Rollerson lounged in a charming state of indolence upon the imperial blue satin couch in the grand saloon of Lord Mayne's country house. Her wheat-gold hair was drawn high upon her head with a deep blue ribbon from which flirtatious curls escaped to tease her cheeks and brow.

A little apart, Clarette stood staring out the velvet-draped windows. Gowned in a plain muslin gown with a tobacco-brown spencer that did nothing for her complexion and made her black hair appear as dull as wood, she followed the progress of the gentlemen trudging through high grass toward the misty woods. Musket barrels slung over arms, dogs on the leash, and beaters moving ahead ready to flush pheasant from their nests or hiding, the gentlemen were off for a morning's sport.

"I detest shooting!" Clarette declared with disgust. "I hope all the birds fly away or are killed by an early frost!"

"How cruel, dear!" Lady Gryphons, another of Lord Mayne's guests, calmly rearranged the embroidery hoop balanced on her lap. "It would quite spoil the gentlemen's holiday."

"Worse yet," concurred Lady Stanhope, "they should leave to seek sport elsewhere."

"That might be best," Clarette murmured to herself. Was it

possible that she was the only one of the party whose thoughts were twisting and flopping about like a trout on a line?

From the little she had seen of Jamie the past two weeks, he might as well have remained behind in London. As for the company she was forced to keep in the country, she would rather have been at home in Somerset, where she would at least have had the run of the stables. Protocol, she was learning, was mighty confining in "toplofty" society.

For instance, she and the other ladies had recently returned from a leisurely breakfast for ten, which was exactly half the number of guests Lord Mayne was entertaining. Now the ladies were obliged to sit around for the rest of the day. Deemed too innocent to even listen to the matrons' conversations spiced with town gossip and scandal, she and her sister were expected to paint or draw, sew or compose letters to friends less fortunate than themselves. Considering her boredom, Clarette could not imagine who that would be.

"It looks like rain. Do you suppose they will return early?" she questioned the room at large.

"Nothing shall bring Lord Gryphons in until he has bagged his partridge," his wife announced with a chuckle.

"My sister is in a sulk because the sport lures Mr. Hockaday away," Clarice teased.

"Some of us are more fortunate in our suitors." Clarette turned from the window with a frown that turned in an instant into a smile when she spied the single gentleman who had deigned to join them in the Great Saloon. "Are the hunters returned, then, Lord Mayne?"

"No, Miss Clarette." Though a gentleman of consequence, he looked slightly discomforted as he approached the corner where the two sisters were ensconced. "I did not go out with them."

"Do you not favor shooting, Lord Mayne?" Clarice asked in a rare attempt to begin a conversation.

"I confess I do not," the gentleman answered gravely, though his eyes held what in a lesser mortal might have been termed a twinkle. "But then, I am spoiled. I've had my fill on any number of occasions these last months." He crossed to take a seat on a Louis Quatorze chair nearest Clarice.

Bored with gazing out at the sights, Clarette turned her discriminating observation on Lord Mayne. In two short weeks Lord Alfred Mayne had become her sister's most persistent admirer. Older than the usual sort to run at Clarice's heels, Lord Mayne was, at eight and thirty, a man of sober expression with a touch of gray at his temples in otherwise thick dark hair that waved away in stiffly defined rows. His nose was a trifle long, his mouth a little wide, and his gray eyes set so deeply beneath jutting brows as to seem perpetually in the shade. Which was not to say he was not a handsome man, she decided. The various features worked to compliment one another more than tolerably well. Perhaps his arrogant expression did give him away as a trifle high in the instep, as Jamie had characterized this newest threat to his peace of mind.

All the better, thought Clarette. Clarice needed a firm mind to dominate her own.

Of course, there was that whispered business about his temper, which supposedly explained why he had spent the past two years biding his time in Scotland while waiting for a royal pardon to make him persona grata in London again.

The gossip that had made him a byword was one to which, naturally, she was not party. It had taken her a week of wheedling to pry the details out of Jamie. Jealousy over last night's seating at dinner, which had for the third day in a row matched their host and Clarice, had finally driven Jamie to tell her of "the wretched matter."

The result was to make Clarette revise her opinion of Lord Mayne as "dull stuff" to one that was terribly romantic. It was not every gentleman who dared duel in the shadow of Whitehall, yet again kill a member of Parliament who had insulted his late wife's name. The insult to the Crown caused by the location of the incident was clear, but there were those in sympathy. Banishment from London was deemed preferable to a stint in the Tower for the prideful Mayne.

The royal pardon had come exactly two years later, late in September yet in time for Lord Mayne to extend an invitation to the Rollersons and several other parties to shoot on his estate.

Rusticating had not harmed him, Clarette decided with a smile of mischief. In fact, his countenance suffered none of the ill effects one might have suspected on a man who had—according to Jamie—spent the first six months of widowerhood so deep in his cups that he was near insensible half the time, and completely insensible the rest. His cheeks were lean, tanned by wind and a summer spent fishing in icy mountain streams. His form, while more solid than the younger toffs about him, retained a vigor that was apparent even at rest in buff riding breeches and plain blue riding coat.

Clarette had overheard the matrons among his houseguests exclaiming behind their fans that such stamina lay behind his abiding interest in the opposite sex. It also explained why those same ladies retained a pointed interest in him. He was, it deemed to her, the very image of the new romantic ideal: a handsome, wounded, reckless lord in need of a good woman's love.

Alas, all of this seemed lost upon the object of his current interest. Clarette frowned again. Clarice tolerated, nay, favored Lord Mayne's company, she said, simply because he did not simper, stutter, or spill his tea in her presence.

As he was not a nodcock or slowtop, Clarette suspected her host was in rueful possession of the facts and tolerated her sister's tolerance. Which made for fine gossip among the ladies relegated to entertaining themselves indoors while the gentlemen did so out of it.

Clarette moved to stand before a full-length portrait of one of Lord Mayne's more colorful Lowland relatives clothed in kilt and tartan. If only Clarice would fix her feelings with Mayne, she mused, her own situation was bound to improve. Once Jamie saw that Clarice was lost to him, he would turn to her for com-

fort, and she might then freely declare how much she loved him
and always had.

She gnawed her lip. Jamie had been strangely distant since
the night at the Everharts' ball two and a half months before,
when she had maneuvered him into kissing her. She had spied
him at odd moments staring moodily at her when he thought
she was not aware of it. The devil of it was, she did not know
what she had done wrong. Not that it mattered to her. For whatever reason, Jamie had kissed her, and those kisses still sang in
her veins like champagne! She wanted him to repeat the exercise, and much more. How could he not know how she felt?
And, if he did, how could he not respond? If only the world
would simply leave them alone, she was certain he would come
to see the truth. But the world, her papa to be exact, was anything but absent.

She had succeeded twice in heading off her father in his press
for Jamie to name a wedding date. Yet these long sojourns in
the woods were bound to result in a moment when the two men
would find themselves able to converse privately. And that, she
knew, jeopardized her hopes. Twice in as many weeks Jamie
had all but accused her of not seeking hard enough to attract
the interest of another suitor. She must contrive something, and
quickly, before Jamie cried quits and she lost him forever.

She turned suddenly from the portrait she had been staring
at with unseeing eyes. "Lord Mayne, are there not Roman ruins
here and abouts?"

"You are correct, Miss Clarette. The countryside is littered
with ancient monuments. For instance, nearby is the famous
Bruce Stone, said to be where Robert Bruce, the Bruce, as some
Scots call him, stood in 1306 to begin his campaign against the
English, who were camped on the slopes of the Mulldonoch.
Seven years later, when he was done with war, he was crowned
King of Scotland."

Clarette clapped her hands. "Better and better. I know 'tis
disloyal to say so, but I much admire stories of your brave

Scotsmen." She glanced at her sister. "They make such romantic figures."

Lord Mayne smiled a little enigmatically. "Then perhaps you will allow me to show you the local sights someday."

"What is wrong with today?" Clarette blushed at her own impulsiveness, but that did not stop her. "That is, if you aren't otherwise engaged."

"No, not at present." He glanced at Clarice, and Clarette's spirits soared. "Perhaps your sister would care to join us."

"I'm certain she would." Clarette rushed over to her sister's side. "Clarice loves Scotland even more than I, don't you, dear sister?"

Puzzled by her sister's sudden predilection for things Scottish, Clarice murmured most charmingly, "Well, I don't—"

"Certainly you do. Don't be shy." Clarette grabbed her by the arm and hoisted her sister to her feet. "Clarice is ever reading Robert Burns. Do quote something for Lord Mayne."

Blushing scarlet, Clarice whispered, "Very well. 'Scots, wha hae wi' Wallace bled, Scots, wham Bruce has aften led; Welcome to your gory bed, Or to victorie.' "

Seeing Lord Mayne fix her sister with a strange look, Clarette could have hugged herself for her cleverness. It would take very little more to forward this pretty romance.

"Well done, sister!" She pushed Clarice toward the door. "We will just go and collect our bonnets and wraps and meet you in a quarter of an hour in the stables. If that is to your convenience, Lord Mayne," she added when she saw his expression of alarm at her bald attempt to orchestrate his day.

He had risen to his feet. "It would be my very great pleasure," he said formally, and offered them a correct bow. "Do dress warmly. The Scottish climes can be unpredictable this time of year."

"I certainly hope so," Clarette murmured under her breath. The devious bit of foolishness forming in her head required providing any and every excuse to cuddle.

"But you know how I detest monuments," Clarice protested

when the two sisters had glided gracefully beyond the salon door."

"You do not care for anything but gossip and gowns, that's your trouble. How do you expect to fix the affections of an eligible *parti* if you never show any gentleman's conversation a modicum of interest?"

Clarice's injured-Cupid glance would have driven any of her suitors into paroxysms of retraction. "I don't think that's entirely fair."

"Perhaps not," Clarette answered dryly as she hurried her sister up the main stairway. "Yet it is a close approximation."

To distract her sister from her mulish tendencies, she continued without pause. "At least the outing provides you with a chance to wear your new red levantine pelisse with the cream floss silk edging. Lord Mayne's colors are red and cream, did you know? He will be certain to notice. The Caledonian cap of black plush with red bands and foxtail feathers will set things off admirably. Don't forget your blond muff with the ermine tails."

Clarice brightened considerably as her thoughts turned to a subject she understood with excellent ease. "Yes, that does sound right. But what shall you wear? Oh, I've the very thing. The lemon cloth pelisse with capelets. The color will make your hair shine. You may borrow my Huntley bonnet with prince's badge. The plaid will complement the yellow, and the plume will give you a little dash. That way Lord Mayne will have twice as much to admire."

Clarette doubted the need for dash in her costume but kept silent in the smug assumption that once Lord Mayne had seen Clarice with the wind in her hair and the sun in her cheeks, he would not notice if her mushroom of a sister wore bark and moss.

Clarette considered it the best possible piece of luck that Lord Mayne chose to drive the phaeton himself, as there was not sufficient room on the high seat for three riders and a groom. The groom rode astride a hack who could not keep apace of the high-sprung huge-wheeled carriage unless the speedy equipage chose a pace far slower than its spirited team would have liked.

Bear rug firmly tucked about his guests, Lord Mayne made quick work of leaving the stables and setting off down the narrow lane that led out of the larch and pine forest onto the deceptively smoother slopes of Glen Trool.

Deceptive because the park was in reality a very wild and rugged landscape with mossy green mountain ranges in the distance through which granite peaks thrust baldly above the tree line. Fortuitously, to Clarette's mind, the groom's horse tossed a shoe on the rocky ground not long into the drive and he was forced to return to the stable for another mount. This left the earl free to drive at any speed he chose.

He drove in a brisk, spanking manner that Clarette greatly admired. It was only Clarice's repeated "ohs" of distress that caused him to again slow his pair of grays to more of a trot than a canter.

Clarette had gallantly offered to ride on the outside so that Clarice would be wedged safely between them. Secretly she had deliberately positioned Clarice against the firm body of Lord Mayne. Once under way, she kept shifting on the seat at every possible opportunity in order to force her companions closer together.

If she had not firmly believed Lord Mayne to be too old and august a person to stoop to stratagems, she might have suspected he made right turns more often than necessary. In the end she decided it was only that it was the sort of thing she might have done if she were a man.

Only occasionally did Clarice object, making Clarette shift away, and then another curve would set them sliding toward Lord Mayne's side of the carriage seat once more.

Yet even that disagreement was soon abandoned as the bewitching beauty of the day spread out before them. A rare autumn sun shone brightly between long skeins of cloud untangling from the mountaintops. The blue sky shone back as a deeper sapphire from the surface of a loch they passed.

As they crossed a bridge spanning a winding gorge, Clarette could contain her enthusiasm for the spectacular view no longer.

"Is this not glorious?" she cried into the wind as she reached up to save the bonnet which it would have snatched from her head.

"It is quite lovely in a wild sort of way, my lord," Clarice seconded.

He glanced down at the lady by his side. "Then you are not overawed by its magnitude. Some despair of the rough and wild country. Scotland can be a lonely and barren place for a soul who loves London."

"I suppose that might be so," Clarice answered, a thoughtful frown drawing her delicate brows together. "Yet I've a partiality for the country myself."

To prevent her sister from explaining this preference—Clarice hated London because it was there she was most pestered by her many admirers—Clarette leaned forward with the observation, "You're a great hand with the ribbons, Lord Mayne!"

He smiled and offered her a little nod. "Won the Camden races two years running. Keep a stable and my own jockey to run in the derby each year."

"I should love to see you race," Clarice said with the first hint of feeling. "I do so enjoy a good whipster."

Her compliment had unexpected results. Lord Mayne lost his head completely. "Would you care to hold the ribbons, Lady Clarice?"

Clarette held her breath. Her intention was to increase the earl's interest in her sister. She had not planned to put her own neck at risk in the process.

"Oh, no, I couldn't," Clarice protested of the proffered reins. "Papa says I'm cow-handed," she declared in absolute honesty.

"I should run your cattle off the road and send us all to perdition. 'Tis Clarie who's the whip hand."

"Hardly," Clarette replied, coloring in spite of herself as the earl regarded her quizzically over her sister's head. "I've had a very little practice only."

"Then you should take every opportunity." So saying, Lord Mayne handed the reins over to Clarette.

There was no moment to think. The reins were in her hands, the traces slipping between her fingers as the Rollerson groom, Nebbits, had shown her when she was only ten. A moment later the tug of the several hundred pounds of moving horseflesh made itself felt. She had never handled so high-spirited a pair. A sense of momentary panic made her saw on the reins for control.

The phaeton abruptly lurched. Clarice cried out in alarm while the earl uttered a more pungent sound of alarm.

"Ease up on the ribbons!" he admonished as his pair of grays balked and snorted under the awkward guidance of Clarette's hands.

Acutely embarrassed, Clarette attempted to hand over control to the earl, but the horses stumbled once again. Clarice cried out pitifully a second time, flung herself into the astonished embrace of the earl, and clasped both hands firmly about his neck. "Save us! Oh, please save us!"

Her sister's reaction was enough to steady Clarette's nerves. Here, indeed, was a situation worth preserving.

"I've got the right of them," she called gaily even as her struggle continued for some seconds. The carriage careened toward a lane-side boulder.

She could see the grim outline of Mayne's profile from the corner of her eye but dared not glance at him for fear she should lose control a second time. If she tore one of his grays' mouth, she should be dispatched home in disgrace while her father would be put to expensive restitution. Working the ribbons, she managed to avoid the rock as they bounced back onto the rutted path on one wheel.

"Give them their heads," Mayne admonished when he seemed satisfied that Clarette would not land them in a ditch. "They're a good, steady pair and know the lay of the land. They'll bring you safely to your destination."

Clarette smiled and nodded. Their destination did not seem nearly as important at the moment as the fact that Lord Mayne's steadying arm remained about her sister's trembling shoulders.

The contretemps lasted less than a minute, but when it was done, Clarette felt her heart thumping so heavily that she was certain all must hear it. Even so, she was quite proud of herself. It was not every day a young miss held the ribbons for a bit of prime blood.

"You will wish me to relieve you of the ribbons," Lord Mayne said in a carefully controlled voice after a minute more.

Clarette turned to him with a great smile. "If you please, my lord, I should like to drive awhile longer." She said it with more heart than she felt. If she did overset them, at least it would throw Clarice even more firmly into the earl's strong, protective arms.

Mayne eyed her coolly from the top of her bonnet to the tips of her mittens before saying, "Very well. If you will promise to go slowly and tell me immediately when you tire."

They drove on only another few seconds before Clarice began to moan.

"What is it, my dear young woman?" Lord Mayne intoned in grave concern as he bent his head toward Clarice.

"I am unwell. Unwell," Clarice repeated more faintly. "I should like—like to step down."

"Rein in!" Lord Mayne commanded.

Nineteen

Clarette was amazed and pleased by the responsiveness of the earl's team. She had overmanaged them the first time around. This time they came readily to a halt, well trained to obey the slightest confident command.

The earl jumped down from the high-perch vehicle before turning back to offer Clarice a hand. "Allow me to help, dear child. Come, give me your hand. Yes, I know it's a steep climb, but you can manage it."

"Listen to Lord Mayne," Clarette urged from the other side of Clarice. "He will not allow you to fall. That's a good girl. One foot. There, on the spoke. Now the other. See how easy?"

A moment later Clarice was deposited into Lord Mayne's arms. For a moment she hung suspended, her arms braced on his broad shoulders clothed in blue superfine while his hands easily spanned her narrow waist. It seemed to Clarette to require a great effort on his lordship's part to lower and release her sister. He had no similar trouble in helping Clarette down. She was set free before her boots firmly touched ground. Just as well she had not set her cap in *that* direction.

Clarice wailed abruptly. "I shall be sick!"

"No, you certainly won't," Clarette scolded as she put an arm about her sister's waist. Sinking spells were an acceptable weakness in a young lady of delicate temperament. Ejecting one's breakfast was not!

Clarice swallowed hard and seemed to rally with a faint smile.

4 BESTSELLING HISTORICAL ROMANCES BY YOUR FAVORITE AUTHORS CAN BE YOURS, FREE!

Kensington Choice, our newest book club now brings you historical romances by your favorite bestselling authors including Janelle Taylor, Shannon Drake, Rosanne Bittner, Jo Beverley, and Georgina Gentry, just to name a few! Each book is filled with passion, adventure and the excitement of bygone times!

To introduce you to this great new club which is part of Zebra Home Subscription Service, we'd like to send you your first 4 bestselling historical romances, absolutely free! And once you get these 4 free books to savor at home, we'll rush you the next 4 brand-new books at the lowest prices available, as soon as they are published.

The way the club works is that after your initial FREE shipment, you will get our 4 newest bestselling historical romances delivered to your doorstep each month at the preferred subscriber's rate of only $4.20 per book, a savings of up to $7.16 per month (since these titles sell in bookstores for $4.99-$5.99)! All books are sent on a 10-day free examination basis and there is no minimum number of books to buy. (A postage and handling charge of $1.50 is added to each shipment.) Plus as a regular subscriber, you'll receive our FREE monthly newsletter, *Zebra/Pinnacle Romance News*, which features author profiles, contests, subscriber benefits, book previews and more!

So start today by returning the FREE BOOK CERTIFICATE provided. We'll send you 4 FREE BOOKS with no further obligation: A FREE gift offering you hours of reading pleasure with no obligation...how can you lose?

*We have 4 FREE BOOKS for you
as your introduction to
KENSINGTON CHOICE!
To get your FREE BOOKS, worth
up to $23.96, mail the card below.*

FREE BOOK CERTIFICATE

Yes! Please send me 4 Kensington Choice (the best of Zebra and Pinnacle Books) Historical Romances without cost or obligation (worth up to $23.96). As a Kensington Choice subscriber, I will then receive 4 brand-new romances to preview each month for 10 days FREE. I can return any books I decide not to keep and owe nothing. The publisher's prices for Kensington Choice romances range from $4.99-$5.99, but as a preferred subscriber I will get these books for only $4.20 per book or $16.80 for all four titles. There is no minimum number of books to buy and I may cancel my subscription at any time. A $1.50 postage and handling charge is added to each shipment. No matter what I decide to do, my first 4 books are mine to keep, absolutely FREE!

Name _____

Address _____ Apt._____

City_____ State_____ Zip_____

Telephone (____) _____

Signature_____

(If under 18, parent or guardian must sign)

Subscription subject to acceptance. Terms and prices subject to change.

KC0197

4 FREE
Historical
Romances
are waiting
for you to
claim them!

(worth up to
$23.96)

See details
inside.....

KENSINGTON CHOICE
Zebra Home Subscription Service, Inc.
120 Brighton Road
P.O.Box 5214
Clifton, NJ 07015-5214

‖‖..ı..‖‖....ı‖ı.ı.ı.ı..ı‖.ı.ı.ı..ı‖ı..ı‖‖...ı

"You are right. I need only a moment to rest in the shade." She gave her sister an appealing glance. "The ride, the sun and wind, it is all too much."

"Of course it is, darling," Clarette agreed solicitously. "We will take care of you. Shhhh, don't cry, dearest. Lord Mayne will think we are a pair of ninnies."

"Not at all," the earl answered gallantly as he finished anchoring the carriage reins to a boulder. "How may I be of service to you?"

Clarette turned to him, genuine distress for her sister sobering her expression. "I fear she's had too much Caledonian air and sun. Perhaps if she could rest awhile in the shade of those trees." She pointed down the slope of a hillside, where a copse grew near a gurgling stream.

"But certainly, ma'am." He turned to the wilting form of Clarice as she looked up pleadingly with tear-drenched eyes of gentian blue. Trembling maidenhood had never been seen to a more heart-melting advantage. "Allow me to assist you, Lady Clarice."

"I don't know that I can manage a stroll of any distance, my lord."

"Say no more." Without asking permission, he reached down and lifted her up into his arms, balancing her slight weight high upon his chest. The pose was one an artist would have appreciated, his dark head bent toward her ethereally blond one. Stark masculine power embraced the slender elegance of beauty. The contrasts begged a painter's eye.

"Lord Mayne, you must not trouble—" Clarice began in proper protest.

"No trouble at all, Lady Clarice." He grinned, and the cocky smile transformed the severe man into someone a good deal younger and less careworn. "Beg you allow me the liberty. After all, there is your sister to stand as chaperon."

"Very right of you to point that out," Clarette answered, and began backing away from the touching scene. "Do go ahead. I shall be right behind you. I believe I must have dropped my

handkerchief by the carriage wheel as we were climbing down.
I'll—"

She noticed with a certain amount of rueful chagrin that the
earl did not even wait for her to finish before he began striding
away with his booty.

In her natural frankness, Clarette was incapable of indignation over the slight. She smiled in approval of the earl's preemp-
tive if shockingly unorthodox method of conveying her sister
to safety. There was something lighter in his stride than she had
ever noticed before. Perhaps eight and thirty was not as ancient
an age as she had opined.

She tarried several minutes by the carriage, pretending to
look for the handkerchief that was tucked into her sleeve. Finally, she glanced back over her shoulder to find her companions had reached the distant shade. In fact, Lord Mayne was
bent tenderly over her sister, who sat in the grass with her back
supported by a tree trunk.

A satisfied smile curved Clarette's mouth. All in all, it had
been a good day's work. Now there was just one more thing to
be done. As it happened, she had just been struck by an Idea!

She searched for several seconds more before she found what
she needed, a heavy rough stone twice the width of her palm.
She hated ruining a perfectly lovely vehicle, but then reminded
herself that it was being done in Cupid's service.

She gave one spoke of the wheel a whack with the stone and
then another and another until she heard the hard wood snap.
Working more quickly, she cracked two more, looking back
over her shoulder between every blow to check that no one saw
her.

It was only when she had tossed the stone away and was
wiping her hands that the enormity of what she had done struck
her. She had willfully destroyed property that did not belong to
her. Worse, she was stranding two people beside herself in a
desolate place. Perhaps her Idea was not so brilliant after all.

She cringed with guilty reflection that became a shiver as the
freshening wind carried a chill that had not been there moments

before. She looked up toward the mountain peaks and saw pur-
plish clouds heavy with rain sliding and spilling over the jagged
summits. The sun, once so strong, had disappeared behind fingers of mist. Lord Mayne had been right to caution them against
the unpredictability of the weather.

Even as she thought this, she heard the earl's voice hailing
her. She stepped out from the shadow of the carriage to find
him striding toward her. Her stomach did cartwheels, but this
contrition was much too late. The damage was done.

"We must head back. The weather's—" He stopped short,
his expression arrested by Clarette's stricken gaze. "What's
wrong, dear lady? Are you, too, ailing?" The idea was plainly
one for which he had no relish.

"No, no, not a bit." Clarette tucked her chin so that the feather
in her Scottish bonnet shaded her gaze from his steel-gray stare.
"I'm afraid, Lord Mayne, that I did not merely graze the boulder
as we thought." She stepped away from the phaeton even as she
pointed out her felonious handiwork. "The wheel is dashed."

The earl regarded the damaged wheel with consternation and
despair. "A thousand guineas," he muttered.

"At least your prime bits were spared," she offered in consolation.

That earned her a dagger glance, then the slow torture of
remaining silent while Lord Mayne carefully inspected every
inch of his horses. "Not a scratch," he pronounced in a tone of
bare tolerance when he was done.

"I am so sorry, Lord Mayne. So sorry." The last words drifted
off in a whisper of exquisite embarrassment. Perhaps she had
gone too far, dared too much. Why did she always feel the need
to heap additional coals onto a brightly burning fire?

"What shall we do?" she asked as the first drop of rain struck
her nose.

"What indeed?" The earl's grim question did not improve his
temper. He gave the damaged spokes a second probing inspection and then murmured, "Nothing for it."

He turned back to Clarette with a scowl that made her step

back. "I'm afraid you must remain here with your sister while I proceed on foot toward the house. With luck, that laggardly groom has followed us on a fresh mount and I will intercept him. If so, I'll send him back for a carriage."

"Oh, let me!" Clarette stepped toward him in genuine appeal. "I am to blame, after all. The least good I can be is as your errand runner."

"Absolutely not! You are not strong enough for so great a hike."

"Balderdash!" She lifted her skirts to show remarkably stout boots and a scandal-making glimpse of her calf. "I'm remarkably fit, I assure you. These boots have seen me through every inch of mud and stream in Somerset. Besides, I'm certain, as you say, your groom must be on his way to join us. I wouldn't be surprised to meet him a half-league down the road. He can take me up behind and we'll go together to fetch rescue."

She could guess he was struggling with the temptation of being left alone with her beautiful sister. He was a man of the world while she was a mere romantic. "There is impropriety in what you suggest."

"What impropriety can there be?" she asked innocently, delighted that he wished to be persuaded. "It would certainly seem to me less gallant were you to abandon an injured lady to the wilds of the Scottish mountainside."

"M'lord!" The hailing cry sent them both looking around.

His lordship's groom was leading his horse by the bridle across the grass slope opposite the road as if he had long ago dismounted and had been walking his creature by the loch to cool it.

"I'm sorry, my lord. Didn't realize you were ready to go back." The young man's gaze darted toward Clarette but stopped short.

The earl appeared not to notice. He smiled. "Just the fellow I need! We've come a cropper, owing my plaguey-poor handling of the reins. Going to need help."

"So it would seem, m'lord." Again the young man's eyes

darted as quick as lightning toward Clarette. This time they met hers and he turned scarlet.

With a muffled squeak of alarm Clarette realized that she might not have been as clever in her subterfuge as she had supposed. Had he seen her destroy the wheel?

"I should like a word with yer lordship," the groom began, only to flinch as the sudden swoop of wind brought with it an icy pelting of rain.

" 'Tis no time for speech! Get saddled, man!" the earl roared impatiently, and he reached up to pull the bearskin rug from the phaeton seat. "Send back a wagon and blankets! Lady Clarice has fallen ill. There's no time to waste!"

"I'll go back with him." Clarette stepped up to him as the groom mounted. "He won't know what to say and Papa will be apoplectic until he's assured that neither of his daughters has come to harm."

She reached up to the young groom, who regarded her with dismay. "Come, I won't bite. Away! We must help your master and my sister."

"Well? Why do you dawdle!" The earl made a dismissing movement with his hand. "We shall all be drenched, in any case, before you return."

Color ran high in the groom's cheeks as he reluctantly offered Clarette his hand. As he lifted her, the earl boosted her up until she could scramble up behind the stable hand.

They covered the distance back to Lord Mayne's estate in remarkable time, considering that the wind swooped down upon them like retribution, and rain lashed them unceasingly.

By the time they reached the stable yard, the weather had destroyed Clarette's bonnet and reduced her yellow pelisse to a soggy, semitransparent veil.

"Good God! Clarette!"

She recognized her father's bellow before she saw him. Heedless of the rain, he had rushed out of the house, as had many of the other male guests at their appearance. She supposed the shooting party had returned at the first sign of rain.

"Papa!" Clarette exclaimed in relief as her father reached up to help her down. Afflicted by guilt, triumph, remorse, and half a dozen other conflicting emotions, she fell into his embrace as if she could hide from her thoughts in the folds of his coat.

"There, there," her father comforted, patting her back. "Are you all right, my dear?"

"Where is Clarice?"

She turned her face from her father's chest to encounter the haggard expression of Jamie Hockaday. "Where is Clarice? Is she injured?"

Something twisted deep inside her. He had not even asked about her! "With Lord Mayne, I expect, as I left them together."

"Left her? But what is wrong?"

"The carriage broke a wheel," she answered, though she turned her face up to impart this information to her father.

The head of the stables was already shouting orders to his helpers, unnecessarily aided by the gentlemen who felt the need to be useful.

Jamie called for his horse. "I shall find them!"

"They aren't lost," Clarette said sharply. "They are merely stranded."

Jamie's brow cleared. "Cla—Lady Clarice is not injured?"

"Not a bit." She tossed her head to fling the drooping feather out of her eye. "Nor am I, thank you for inquiring."

He had the grace to look embarrassed, but he only said, " 'Tis not fitting that a lady should be left unchaperoned."

Clarette drew herself up indignantly, for he seemed to imply that she was once more in the wrong. "I doubt you will find Clarice of a similar mind!" So saying, she flounced away, though in truth she looked more like a bedraggled duckling in her sodden yellow finery.

An hour passed before there was a new contretemps in the yard which signaled the return of the rescued. Clarette had changed by then into a practical wool gown with long sleeves and even managed to dry her hair before the fire.

She had also had plenty of time to fear what should happen

to her when the groom told Lord Mayne what he had seen and then informed her father of the same.

If one could die of shame, she believed she would have done so in that hour. This was far worse than her deception over Jamie's letter. That, at least, she had not had to invent. But destroying Lord Mayne's prize phaeton, how could she explain it? She could not. The truth would make her out to be the worst sort of busybody and a brigand into the bargain. She imagined she would be sent home in disgrace.

Nor did her imagination allow her to believe that the matter would end there. She had heard enough versions of gossip during her time in London to know that the most innocent story had a way, with repeated telling, of being twisted into a rapacious scandal broth. She might even be accused of doing her father's bidding in trying to place Lord Mayne in a compromising situation so that he would be forced to wed Clarice. If that happened, pride would force Lord Mayne to repel any tender feeling he might have been forming toward her sister. And would put them all beyond the pale!

And if that occurred, her dramatic mind conjectured, she would have to do something rash to redeem them. Some sacrifice would be required. Perhaps she would fling herself in the Thames or whatever body of water she was most convenient to at the time.

As it happened, she did not need to fling herself in any direction. The party of rescuers entered the house with high, jovial voices. Instead of behaving as nobles returning from a miserable ride in the rain, they sounded rather like a centuries-old party of Scottish reivers returning from a successful raid of another clan's cattle.

Clarice was carried in her father's arms and taken right up to bed while Lord Mayne called for blankets and hot water and rounds of his best whisky for the gentlemen who had braved the elements on his behalf.

Much later, as Clarette hugged the wall of the bedroom while servants and matrons clucked and fussed over her sneezing sister, Lord Mayne came up to check on his frail guest. He spared Clarette only one sharp glance but said nothing before walking toward the bed.

Dinner was more jovial and free than before, aided by the earlier imbibed whisky and an undercurrent of anticipation that no one spoke directly to. Laughter and smiles and raucous conversation covered the conspicuous lack of animation of two of the diners. While Clarette sat as subdued as a cornered mouse, Jamie sat opposite her, continually draining his glass and shooting murderous looks at his host.

Something had occurred. Clarette could feel it in her bones, but she dared not inquire about it until after dinner, when she discovered Jamie sitting alone in the entry hall, cradling a bottle of claret in one arm while he drank from his glass with his other hand. She was moved by his plight, until she remembered with redoubled resentment that she loved him while he rejected that gift.

She approached him without the caution a wiser woman would have shown. "I hope you're happy with the fool you made of yourself this afternoon."

He swung his head toward her, a sulky scowl and the effects of too much liquor flushing his handsome features. "What do you know of Mayne?" he demanded without preliminaries.

"Little enough that is exceptional," she answered automatically. So then, Jamie was jealous. That meant Mayne must have let show a partiality for Clarice. She hid a tiny smile. Things were proceeding nicely. Now to help them along in Jamie's mind. The sooner he faced the truth, the sooner his heart could begin to mend, and she had just the needle and thread to help it along.

She sat down beside him on the horsehair-stuffed settee as closely as she dared. He looked like one of Lucifer's fallen angels, the one with the absurdly lovely mouth and curls so golden they reflected firelight. How she loved him, loved everything about him, even when he smelled of wine and self-pity, as now. She longed to lay her head against his strong shoulder and revel in the pleasure of touching him. If only he would encourage her the least bit, she would show him how much she loved him.

She brushed his sleeve with her fingers as if to remove a bit of lint. "Lord Mayne has set himself up to be in Clarice's company as often as possible without drawing undue attention."

"The old reprobate," Jamie muttered.

"I quite like him," she added maliciously, for he was so plainly in distress over Clarice while her own feelings were completely neglected. "He puts me in mind of a boulder on the moors."

Jamie snorted. "You mean because he is thick and dull and older than the hills?"

"Never. His presence has a solid reassurance about it."

"They were kissing!"

The furious whisper caused Clarette to glance around. "What did you say?"

"They were kissing!" Jamie's voice rose on the last word, causing the hounds who lay sprawled before the gothic hearth that heated the entry to lift their heads. "Burrowed under a bear rug they were when we found them, like two proper savages! Your father declared he would have words with Mayne this evening. Mayne replied that he would welcome the discussion."

He angled his body toward her, eliciting a faint gasp from her as his shoulder brushed her bodice. "Do you know what that means? He thinks to win Clarice!" His mouth distorted in pain. "If I am forced to watch and do nothing, I do believe I shall go mad!"

Clarette reached out to cup his face as he turned his anguished expression from her. "My dearest. Perhaps it is for the best—"

"Aw *God!*" Jamie sprung up away from her. "Leave me alone, do you hear?"

Clarette sprang to her feet and took a step toward him. "But I want to help you."

"Help me?" He stared at her as rage overtook his features.

The emotion was so alien to his usual nature that only his enemies in the heat of battle had ever before witnessed it. *"You* are the cause of all my misery! I wish I'd never set eyes on you! Go away! Let me be!"

Clarette stood rooted to the spot until he had passed through the archway and left her entirely and utterly alone.

Until that moment it had never actually sunk in that in losing Clarice he might come to blame and hate *her* for it.

A hard shiver shook her, and then another and another. She never cried. The hot moisture trickling down her cheeks, she assured herself, was mere fatigue.

"This is perfectly impossible!"

Too restless to sleep, Clarette lay on her side on the narrow, hard cot located in the dressing closet of the bedroom she and Clarice had been sharing. Clarice had taken a chill from her afternoon's adventure and was reduced to wheezing and coughing intermittently. On the advice of Lady Gryphons, who claimed to have great experience with the contagious qualities of "the grippe," Clarette had been relegated to the safety of the maid's bed while the Rollerson maid was bade to keep watch over her mistress from the bedside position of a drawn-up chair. Clarette was not at all certain who was making the greater sacrifice.

She turned onto her back on the lumpy, thinly filled down tick and stared at the shrouded ceiling of the windowless room as Jamie's parting words echoed through her head.

You are the cause of all my misery! I wish I'd never set eyes on you! Go away! Let me be!

"He cannot mean that," she whispered to herself. Or could he?

Of course he was miserable. She should have expected no less. After all, she conceded, he thought himself in love. It was a mistaken love, but he was not yet aware of that. Clarice's surpassing beauty had blinded him to all other considerations.

How could it not, when Lord Mayne had fallen victim to the same fever upon a few days' acquaintance? But there was a difference. If Clarice had, as Jamie claimed, been discovered in Lord Mayne's embrace and nothing more had followed than that her father requested an interview with the earl, then it must have appeared to be a mutually agreeable exercise on the part of both participants.

She flipped over onto her tummy and propped her chin in both hands. Which meant that Clarice, just as she had hoped, was not indifferent to Lord Mayne. Which meant that Jamie had lost her, no matter what.

Poor Jamie, drinking himself into oblivion because he thought *she* stood between them, when in fact Clarice herself was the injuring party. She loved, or at least her affections were inclined, elsewhere.

"If only Clarice were not so ill!" Clarette smothered her mouth with her hands, hoping no one had heard her. Poor Clarice. If she were not ill, she might have explained her true feelings for Lord Mayne to Jamie and absolved her sister of all blame.

Clarette sat straight up in bed, pulling an underarm seam as she did so, for her night rail was twisted around her like a shroud from all her tossing and turning. She ignored the rip. An Idea had formed yet again.

She did not like the thought of being hated by anyone. Jamie's enmity was unbearable. She would not be able to shut her eyes until she was certain he had relented at least a little in his anger. Perhaps if *she* explained that Clarice had encouraged Lord Mayne, he would blame her less for his present misery.

She tossed back her covers and felt around in the darkness for her slippers. As she did so, a distant clock struck twice. The muffled chatter and laughter from the gentlemen's billiard room had ceased shortly after the single clock strike. By now everyone would be abed. What more perfect time to have a private chat with Jamie?

She had never sought out a gentleman in his quarters before.

She had not been allowed in her father's bedchamber since her mother died. She was only vaguely aware of where Jamie's room might be found because she recalled overhearing one of the other guests asking him if he had a view of the famous Mull-donoch mountain. He had replied that, alas, he did not because his room was located in the east wing on the opposite side of the house. Did he sleep alone or share a chamber? She would soon discover for herself.

Twenty

"Jamie? Jamie?"

Jamie turned away from the sound of his name. It was far too late and he was far too drunk to hold discourse with anyone.

"Jamie? It *is* you!"

The fact that it was a feminine voice registered with him only dimly. Must be dreaming. How wretchedly unfair that the source of all his trouble—women—should follow him into the oblivion of his dreams.

Behind closed lids the impression of faint red from the glowing embers of his dying fire made itself known. He smiled crookedly. Always had preferred the coziness of a fireside to chilly sheets.

A hand touched his shoulder.

He shrugged it away. "Don't both—both—bother me."

Fingers fanned out across his cheek. "I'm so sorry, Jamie."

"Don't!" He swung wildly away and tumbled right into space. His fall was broken when his head hit the floor with a decided *thump*.

"Oh, Jamie, are you hurt?"

"Don' know," he murmured into the floorboards where his face was pressed. With great effort he rose on his elbows and shook his head like a dog to clear it of its whisky fog. It did not even thin. The world inside his head sloshed about.

"Poor Jamie, dear."

As arms came around him from behind, he pushed himself

up into a sitting position on the floor and bumped into a ma-
hogany furniture leg. With much difficulty his drugged lids
lifted a fraction and he saw the fuzzy outline of a chair before
him, the one he had fallen asleep on sometime before.

"Got—go t'bed," he muttered.

"Let me help you."

He did not bother to inquire as to the identity of the young
woman who was helping him to his feet. One of Mayne's maids,
no doubt. Mayne! How he hated the very idea of the man. "Blast
him to hell!"

The muttering sounded more like "Bla' shim to 'ell!" but
that did not matter. Sentiment was not lost in the lack of elo-
cution.

He was more than proud to find himself standing upright.
He could not recall exactly how he achieved the attitude until
his hand, arm thrown about slender shoulders, curved down and
encountered a soft mound just palm-size. Naturally, he squeezed
it.

"Jamie!"

He smiled lopsidedly as his hand was smacked. "Breast!" It
was the first completely comprehensible word he had spoken
since midnight. Lust invariably had that effect on him, a sudden
sobering, or at least focusing, of what faculties he had left.

He glanced down at the young woman who was acting as his
crutch. He could not see much. The top of her head reached
only to his shoulder, and the spill of long, dark hair all but
shrouded her face as she guided him, one arm around his waist,
across the room. Not that looks mattered much when Master
Tom was involved. He used the arm slung about her shoulder
to draw her in, absorbing the feel of her yielding curves against
his own leaner, harder frame. Ah, yes, quite nice and round and
tender.

One of Mayne's maids, he decided. Very gentlemanly of the
earl, sending him a consolation.

In a sudden reversal of mind he dismissed the earl's largess.
His fallen angel's face swelled with pride. As if he needed a

consolation from the man who had bested him! His heart had been dragged out by the roots and squashed beneath Beauty's boot heel!

He started in amazement at his own turn of phrase. Poetic! Nothing less! Ha! Quill would be quite proud of him, if only he knew where to find the man. He had decamped from England more than two months before without even a word of farewell! Some friend! Still, he would write it down for him—whatever it was he had just said . . . or thought or . . . or . . .

He swung his head in what he assumed was the direction of the bed, and his body canted in sympathy, nearly dragging his guide off her feet.

"Do be careful, Jamie!"

That voice! He knew that authoritarian voice. *"Maman?"* he ventured cautiously.

A quickly stifled giggle was his only answer.

When they reached the bed, he fell back against the mattress in a diagonal sprawl. After a moment he jerked to consciousness as he felt his boot being slipped off. Of course. Maids knew how to do all sorts of things, he reasoned groggily.

A minute later he gasped in alarm as his face was enveloped in cotton cloth and then he realized that she was merely trying to pull his shirt off over his head.

As he obediently lifted his arms, another thought slid by on the whisky tide of his consciousness. Why could he not see the delightful creature who was ministering to him?

It dawned on him as slowly as the beginning of any sunrise that the reason might be that his eyes were closed. He considered opening them, considered how he would feel if he were wrong about the comeliness of the plump little maid. She might be horse-faced with three hairs growing from a huge mole on her chin. No! He would not open his eyes and destroy the first pleasant moment he had had in feminine company in months.

As self-pity tugged at his lusciously masculine mouth, he sighed. He had said harsh things to Clarette. Have to make it

up to the puss! He did not really believe she was the cause of
all his trouble, but he needed someone to blame and she—

"I say!" He reached down in surprise as hands brushed his
bare stomach, tickling him.

"I need to unfasten your breeches."

As his brain lagged behind his body, which showed remarkable signs of life despite his inebriated condition, his actions
were born of the natural response of a healthy young man who
found himself alone with a woman.

Reaching down, he clasped fingers about the pair of hands
working rather clumsily at his waistband. "Not there. Here."
He pushed her hands down his placket to where his erection
bulged rather impressively.

He heard a gasp as he pried open her fingers and placed them
on his crotch. "Here's how," he said with remarkable clarity,
and attempted to show her how to stroke him.

"Oh, Jamie!"

Something familiar in that voice! No, he must be mistaken.
He asked no more of life than this moment of self-indulgence.
No faces, no names—no pledges!—just pleasure.

He turned his head toward hers and brought his hand up until
he encountered the plush of a woman's cheek. Young skin! He
plowed fingers into her heavy hair as his other arm slid firmly
around her waist to pull her down on the bed beside him.

She did not speak as his lips went blindly exploring along
her chin line, up to her cheek, and then down across its fullness
to the corner of her mouth. He heard her sudden intake of breath
as his lips met hers softly, lingered a moment, and rose. She
tasted of sunshine, a bright, clean taste that brought a smile to
his lips.

He rubbed his face into the heavy fall of her hair that spilled
across the coverlet, and he smelled the fresh scents of hand-
milled soap and heather and her. The sweet liquid urgency of
desire burst through his veins as he kissed her again, harder,
deeper, longer. With every passing second the anger and resentment and despair melted out of him to be replaced with a long-

ing so strong and right, he knew he must have felt it before. But where and when?

Eyes still closed, he concentrated on the feel of her, on the weight of his body pressing hers, of the insistent throb of his manhood hard against her thighs. But he was too woffled by liquor to hold on to the lustful urges pumping through him.

Regretfully, he turned his head to nuzzle one breast, and instead drifted off into a slumber more insistent than his passion.

Blushing from their exertions, Clarette lay still beneath Jamie's half-naked dozing body. Dear, sweet Jamie had kissed her! No, this was not *her* Jamie. This snoring man with an elbow digging into her right hip and long, hard limbs pressing her knees painfully into the bedding seemed a stranger to her.

As for her own complicity in the matter, she could not account for it!

She had done more than allow him to kiss her. She had allowed him to press her hands to his nether regions in a most shocking manner! Covering her hot face with both hands, she felt the forbidden thrill of desire disappear down the emotional drain of her conscience. She had discovered a wildness in herself. Did that make her a slut?

Seventeen years of training in decorum had never covered such contingencies of etiquette. Yet when even the simplest social act was governed by a bewildering set of perplexities, it took no effort at all for her to believe she had grossly misbehaved.

Her aunt had often blamed her for a "want of femininity." Nothing else, she had complained, would explain her niece's determination to throw over the traces of proper behavior.

Clarette bit her lip, the awakening of old pains draining even her defiance. Her aunt had stopped just short of saying that this want of femininity was tied directly to her lack of beauty. But any excuse served to make her sigh and murmur, "If only little Clarie had more style" or "A little sweetness" or, most wounding, "The least prettiness."

She did not have far to look for a comparison. Clarice was

everything she was not. The wounds went deep, so deep she had never even thought to doubt her aunt's opinion.

Clarette turned her face to Jamie's, which lay on her outstretched arm. Would he consider her actions in coming here unfeminine and unforgivable?

He moved restlessly, shifting his head from where it lay on her shoulder so that his lips puckered against the fullness of her breast.

A hard, stinging blush consumed her head to toe. "No, no, please," she whispered almost frantically as she pushed against his prickly cheek. Obedient in his half-sleep, he drew back.

Grateful, she curved a shy hand about his stubbly chin and kissed his brow. "I do love you, Jamie. I always have and always will."

Jamie heard her voice from far away, the sweet, familiar voice. He snuggled against her. Oh, she was sweet, so sweet, his sweet little Clarette. No! Not Clarette.

He turned his head on the pillow, seeking the identity of the mystery woman whose features were indistinctly outlined by the firelight. She seemed so familiar, so . . . Could it really be Clarette? No, he must be dreaming. Now, why should he dream of lying with Clarette?

Frowning, he lifted a tentative hand toward the apparition. "Why aren't you Clarice?"

Clarette's heart contracted. He thought she was her sister!

A tremor shook her diminutive frame. With little or no encouragement, she had fallen in love with all her heart and soul. She loved him so much that she had willingly denied her pride, her virtue, and her sense of right in coming here. Yet even in his dreams he could think of only Clarice!

Blinking back bitter tears, she slid away from him onto the floor, then turned and fled.

Jamie leaned against the mantel in the entry hall, ostensibly warming himself at the hearth after the morning's shoot. He had not gone in to join the others for the midday meal because his stomach was in a fidget. The thought of thick sliced ham, omelettes, stewed figs and apples, and the Scottish abomination they called porridge—which he called mortar paste—was not to be endured.

His low-crowned beaver hat with the curly brim was pulled low over his eyes to shield them from the cheeriness of the morning light. Perhaps if his hat had not been wedged so tightly on his head there might have been room for the thought that he could move away from the sunlight. But movement of any kind seemed impossible for him at that moment. He was amazed he had made it this far.

He had awakened to a headache. When combing through his curls he had found a suspicious knot on the back of his head. If he had not known better, he would have thought he had fallen off his horse or mayhap out of bed.

A footman had dressed him while he held a pouch of cracked ice to his aching brow and sipped champagne as a cure for his throbbing head. The morning hunt in frosty air had momentarily revived him, but the extensive walk had also taken its toll.

He could admit it. He had gotten a trifle foxed, or perhaps a better description would be spit-in-your-eye drunk, the night before. He had felt entitled.

A disreputable smile wreathed his face. He had also felt entitled to help himself to something even more intoxicating than wine. He had wanted Mayne's bewitching baggage of a maid. Though he had faltered in his pursuit of her, the exercise in lust had delivered back to him his sense of equilibrium where women were concerned.

He had been thinking in loops and curlicues of feelings for months. Besotted, that is what he had been. During the long, dismal months in the continental army, knowing he could die at any moment, he had penned his hopes of a future on the most shining example of English womanhood he knew, Clarice Rollerson. He had held her image up before him when he was afraid, or despairing, or tempted to debauchery. She had been his protection and banner while under the broad wings of death. She had also been a perfect blank page upon which he had writ his future when it seemed most in doubt.

Now, at last, he saw things clearly, or at least more plainly. Pent-up appetites had led him astray. Clarice was a perfectly— well, perfect vision. But one did not lust after a vision. He did not really know a single thing about her. Why, he could not quote any two sentences she had ever spoken.

Now, Clarette! He could quote her verbatim on any number of subjects. And curious though the fact was, she did stir his carnal appetite, at least in his dreams. But that was beside the point. He did not want to be leg-shackled to any lady. What he wanted, needed, was his freedom.

The solution to his temporary aberration of feeling had presented itself in his bed the night before. He was not ready to be wed, not when temptations such as Mayne's maid were readily available. He needed sex, and lots of it. Marriage could wait upon the fatigue of his middle years.

Yet he did have some plans. At the first opportunity he would importune Mayne to point out the wanton on his staff who had come so readily to his bed. He was going to take her back to London and set her up as his very own ladybird!

Now the only tangle in his plans lay in how to get Clarette to cry off the engagement. He supposed he might give her reason by squiring his "frail bark" about London in the fashion of an unencumbered bachelor. That should set up Lord Rollerson's back. If indeed he needed any further excuse to dislike him.

"Young man!"

Jamie straightened with a wince. Lifting his gaze, he found the subject of his reverie bearing down upon him from the main staircase. He had not seen Lord Rollerson during the morning shoot and assumed that discouraged by the frost, he had stayed abed.

" 'Morning, Lord Rollerson." He jerked his hat off as a gallantry and approached the stairs, appearing more pleasant than he felt.

Looking himself like a man who had just spied the culprit who had left a dead toad in his bed, Rollerson stared down at the younger man from the advantage of two stair steps.

"I will be brief, sir." His thick gray brows twitched as he glanced left and right out from under them to assay if they were alone.

With a nod of satisfaction he turned his withering glare on his companion. "I've spoken with the girl at length, but she won't hear different." He cleared his throat. "My daughter don't want you."

Jamie's expression cleared of vacuous pleasantry. "Your— Clarette?"

Rollerson nodded, his lips tucked together as if he had been offered a dose of cod liver oil. "The girl wishes to break your engagement."

"Clarette wishes to throw me over?" Jamie's heart soared. Midway its steep climb, his elation began to stall. Something must have occurred to which he was not privy. "Did she say why, my lord?"

For a jolly man, the earl was showing a remarkable capacity for sober indignation "She did. And much as I regret it, I cannot but agree that she is right. To be blunt, she says you've shown yourself, particularly last evening, to be a gentleman of uneven temper and fits of melancholy. In short, you possess a frivolous nature."

"Frivolous?" The insult implied in the word stung. "I?"

Again he nodded once. "I can't say that anything I have learned about you these last four months has done other than confirm her impression. You may be a stout companion in arms, but you don't know how to get on in company with the ladies." Rollerson looked thoroughly put out, like a schoolmaster who had discovered his best pupil cheated on an exam. "While in London you neglected Clarette shockingly for the gaming tables. You stood no more than the obligatory number of dances.

You were tardy in your appearances at the head of the evening and mighty abrupt in your departures on the heels of it. In short, you treated her as if she were a wife!"

This assessment of his failings did not impress Jamie. "Clarette never complained."

"No. And you should know, the girl defended you at every turn until last night. Admirable quality, loyalty," Rollerson pronounced as if her virtuous qualities reflected even more poorly on Jamie. "When she wanted you, I was willing to overlook your shortcomings—"

"Shortcomings?" Jamie repeated indignantly, the match touched to his wick at last.

Rollerson thrust out his chest, which in actuality accented his girth. "Do you opine, sir, that you lack shortcomings?"

"Certainly not!" Jamie shrugged impatiently. "Every man has his flaws."

"Then, sir, I say your flaws are anathema to my daughter's sensibilities."

"Clarie's sensibilities?" he bleated.

"Your echo grows tiresome, sir."

Jamie pulled himself up squarely in military fashion, for it was now a matter of pride. "I think I deserve to know what conduct of mine has brought about this sudden revulsion of feeling on her part."

"I did not inquire." Rollerson stared down at the young man who had brought his youngest child to tears before eight of the clock in the morning. "I do not, as it happens, wish to know."

Stung by yet another setdown, Jamie moved to mount the stairs. "Then I will ask her myself."

"That you will not do." Rollerson set a hand on either banister, blocking his way. "She does not wish to see you. Her hysterics were such that I could scarcely make heads or tails of her confession. Missed the morning shoot to console her."

"Clarette cried?" The idea appalled Jamie. He could not conceive of any eventually that could bring that intrepid spirit to tears. She had been a brick through the entire ordeal. An action of his had made her weep? Surely not. Perhaps he had been a trifle negligent, but she had assured him she did not mind. What had he done or said? Then he remembered.

He had shouted at Clarette. When she had tried to console him over his discovery of Clarice in Mayne's embrace, he had shouted at her and accused her of being the source of all his misery.

Guilt washed through him. No wonder she had cried off. Stinking with whisky and self-pity, he had treated her shabbily. She must have been truly crushed to seek to cry off from their plan. He would have to apologize and mend their friendship.

Steady now, a nefarious corner of his mind whispered. Did he really want to mend fences quite so soon? How would it look to Rollerson? Clarette had just voluntarily freed him from an unwanted attachment at the very moment when he wanted it most. No engagement. No wedding in the offing. As of this moment he was free to do exactly as he wished.

Despite his throbbing head and guilty joy, Jamie knew with certainty that if he did not make immediate amends to Clarette and reinstate the engagement, the man glaring down at him in righteous indignation would sooner sell his daughters to an Oriental potentate than hand either of them over in marriage in the future to the Honorable James Hockaday.

There was nothing to do. Unless he wished to marry Clarette, his gun was permanently spiked in the matter of the Rollerson girls.

As if to confirm this, Lord Rollerson said, "As we are obliged by Clarice's lingering ailment to remain here with Lord Mayne for some days yet, I hope you will have the good sense and decorum to make your excuses to our host and vacant these premises today."

"Is Clarice seriously ill?" he asked with a guilty start. By Jupiter! He had completely forgotten she had been put to bed before dinner. Perhaps he truly was cured of his infatuation.

"A touch of ague only," Rollerson replied. "Now, good day to you, sir. I don't anticipate that we shall soon meet again."

Jamie bowed briefly as the man returned up the stairs. In one short conversation his life had changed. He was free of an unwanted engagement *and* a morbid infatuation all in the same breath!

He tipped his hat back on his head and strolled toward the dining hall, for his appetite had made a miraculous recovery. "You have your freedom back, Jamie me boy!"

Part Four

"Awake, my heart, to be loved, awake, awake!"
—*Awake, My Heart, to Be Loved*, Robert Bridges

Twenty-one

Naples, January, 1816

Life in Naples resembled nothing so much as one of the opera buffa for which its native composers were renowned, Quinlan mused as he watched the streets from his carriage. Eight years of Napoleonic rule had paid off the city's debt and brought unprecedented order, but nothing could suppress the exuberance of Napoli's people. And like most foreigners, he had joined in readily with the permanent pageantry of Neapolitan life. He was in full dress for the evening's festivities, from his claret evening coat to his cream small clothes, silk stockings, and satin waistcoat. More unusually, silver lace edged his cuffs, and ruffles his neck cloth, and he wore dancing pumps with diamond buckles rather than boots.

The mild weather, even in January, permitted the city's citizenry to all but live in the streets even at night. Though it was well past nine P.M., the main thoroughfare, the Toledo, was clogged with vehicles and people of every description. Here, where wretched deprivation sat hovel by palazzo with inordinate wealth, there seemed at work a genuine sense of the ancient democratic principles sorely lacking in a place like London. From beggar to aristocrat, Neapolitans held themselves in highest regard and required very little excuse to explode in vocal phrases at one another, effusive or abusive depending on the cause. And everywhere from the nobility to the uniquely privileged underclass called the *lazzaroni,* the guiding principle of their lives was to never work for a living but only enjoy themselves.

Even the public Vetturino vehicles were drawn by three horses decked out in colorful trappings, plumes, and jingling ornaments. The night was lit by hundreds of liveried footmen bearing torches and shouting out warnings and jostling one another for prominence as they ran alongside the carriages of the gentry and nobility. These huge, heavily carved and gilded open carriages, harkening back to the *ancien régime,* were built for display instead of speed, and their occupants were duly decked in their finery for the evening's events, whatever that might be.

Nor was there a lack of pageantry in even the most solemn matters.

Quinlan gazed in bemusement at the funeral procession making its way through the piazza near the Theater of San Carlo. The body, carried on an open bier, was covered with a crimson-and-gold cloth. The professional mourners wore white gowns and masks, with family and friends marching behind. Heading the party was a black-robed priest and cross bearer. But even with death in its midst, the exuberance of the city could not be tamed.

The striking courtesan whose carriage was stalled by the traffic near his deigned to send Quinlan a coquettish glance from behind her sooty lashes. Smiling, he returned a nod. Encouraged, she touched her lips lightly twice with her fingertips, then held up five bejeweled fingers twice before making a horizontal cut in the air with her palm. He was being invited to dine with the comely woman at half past ten o'clock.

Quinlan laughed but shook his right hand, forefinger extended toward her, in the Italian sign for no. She lifted her shoulders and tossed her head, dismissing him from her view. The pantomime play was not unusual in Italy, but he knew from a prior visit that it had been raised to an art form in Naples. Had he agreed, she would have sent one of her footmen to convey her address to him. Alas, though the temptation was great, for Naples was known throughout Europe as the city of the most accomplished and beautiful courtesans, he was expected elsewhere this evening.

He had been in the city for less than three days and so was amazed yet gratified to receive an invitation to a *ricevimenti,* or reception, being hosted by Conte Paolo Francapelli, the city's most famous composer of opera since Niccolo Piccinni.

As he neared the sober gray stone palazzo belonging to Conte Francapelli, Quinlan decided to step down and brave the circus atmosphere of the street rather than spend the next half hour sitting while his carriage inched its way up the long block in the procession of carriages depositing their guests at the maestro's door.

He did not know how the composer had come to hear of his presence in the city, but he suspected that news of any English viscount's arrival in town would quickly reach the count's ear. Having accepted the invitation, he was determined to forget his fruitless search and enjoy himself.

His quest through Italy for a red-haired Irishwoman big with child had come to bear more than a passing resemblance to the quest for the proverbial needle in the haystack. He had spent several weeks each in Venice, Florence, and Rome, where he had met Irishwomen, redheads—natural and otherwise—women blossoming with child, and even one doughty soul of seven and sixty named Miss Geraldine. He had visited British embassies and expatriates, spoken with the leading arbitrators of society and the literati, in short had gone everywhere in each city where one might expect to find a British subject. He had exhausted all avenues but Naples, his last hope. Whatever the outcome of his efforts here, he would go home at the end of the month.

Inured to the carnival scene of the streets, Quinlan was nonetheless alarmed by the enormous crowd of guests filling the suffocatingly hot rooms of Conte Francapelli's palazzo. More than fifteen hundred had squeezed into a space meant to accommodate less than half that number. The frenzied pleasure seekers swarmed through the rooms, swilling wine and chattering at the top of their lungs like a thousand flocking magpies. Yet, these were no soberly clad birds. The house teemed with members of royalty, courtiers, and exalted foreigners along with the city's costliest courtesans dressed in silks and velvets, diamonds and pearls worth a king's ransom.

As widespread drunkenness seemed the order of the evening, Quinlan made his way through the first two rooms in search of the terrace at the center of the palazzo, where, as he expected, long tables were set to dispense wine and other spirits.

"Viscount Kearney, my friend!"

Quinlan paused in reaching for a glass of wine to turn toward the owner of that voice. A slender but wiry young gentleman in a blue velvet coat with brown-black hair combed straight back from his high, handsome brow was bearing down on him.

"Signore Carrare," Quinlan greeted his former Cambridge schoolmate. As an Italian cavalry officer under the French forces led by Murat, Carrare had until recently been his nominal enemy. But the war was over and Italy was again an ally.

The younger man gripped Quinlan by both shoulders and planted a kiss on each cheek before his mobile mouth broke into a broad smile. "But why have you not informed me that you were in town!"

"I did not expect to find you in Naples," Quinlan responded with genuine pleasure to see a familiar face. "Last I heard you were in Paris with your King Ferdinand."

"Pff! That!" Giacomo Carrare made a rude gesture with his hand. "Death to all politicians. Soldiers only should rule."

Quinlan again reached for a drink. "I doubt your king shares your sentiments."

Giacomo laughed. *"Il re lazzarone,* he is still a commoner in his heart. But enough of that. It must be five years since we drank wine together. We must toast the moment. Genuine Vesuvian ice," he declared, pointing at the ice chips floating in the glasses of wine. "It is said to be good fortune that the snow lies so thickly on the rim of the volcano, for they say she will not erupt while she wears a beard."

Quinlan laughed with him and then drank a toast to Naples's greatest tourist attraction, the nearby ancient ruined city of Pompeii.

"I suppose you have heard the reason for the evening?" Carrare asked with a wink of mischief.

"Is there a reason?" Quinlan asked blandly, for Carrare was an inveterate gossip who needed little encouragement.

"But certainly. We are awaiting the presentation of Conte Francapelli's English contessa. The *ricevimento* is in her honor." He smirked. "Of course, there is more than the usual interest in her."

"Indeed?" Quinlan murmured, uninterested in local gossip.

Carrare smiled salaciously as he leaned close to impart, "Because she has recently given birth."

Quinlan's interest was piqued. Francapelli's preference for the company of men was well known though deemed unremarkable in this tolerant city where artistic temperament ruled. "The lady must be singular if she has snared Francapelli's interest even temporarily away from his inclinations."

Carrare rolled his dark, liquid eyes. *"Signore!* The child is not the count's."

Quinlan's brows rose. "Then why this mummery?"

Carrare smirked. "Rumor only, you understand, says Francapelli found the lady already with child and offered to marry her on the condition she produce a son whom he could claim as his heir. Alas, she was delivered of a daughter. So, to achieve his purpose, he is putting her out to breed again."

This statement struck sparks of indignation from Quinlan's Whiggish heart. "Wretched woman. It's nothing short of bondage."

Carrare lifted both hands to disavow support of the idea. "It is but rumor. Still, Francapelli saved her from a life of shame. And it is said the choice of lover will be left to her." He winked again. "Who is to say but that you, I, and every other gentleman present were invited here as prospective bloodstock, stallions to be chosen by the mare. It is the way of the world."

The evening's festivities had lost all interest for Quinlan. He had seen enough cruelty in war to no longer accept with equanimity the more subtle forms of inhumanity society shrugged off as the "way of the world." He set his empty glass aside. "Excuse me, Carrare. I find I am more fatigued—"

"But, *amico mio!*" Carrare interrupted, his face aglow with the sight he had glimpsed beyond Quinlan's left shoulder. "There she is!"

Quinlan turned casually in the direction Carrare indicated, prepared to withhold his disdain until he could escape. But poised at the top of an open-air stairway stood a vision of beauty too compelling to ignore.

He heard the collective intake of breath of the crowd and knew that his was part of it.

"*Dio mio!* Francapelli's a genius." Carrare sighed and kissed his fingers at the vision. "Is she not the most beautiful Madonna ever?"

Quinlan simply stared, transfixed.

She wore a gown of layered emerald and sapphire silk so sheer the slim skirts shifted and shimmered on the night breeze from the bay. The play of silk and shadow, producing silhouetted glimpses of her hips and slim thighs, was as seductive as Salome's dance of the seven veils. The high-waisted gown left her flawless shoulders and neck bare. Her bodice, so cunningly cut as to appear almost nonexistent, dipped in the center to display the full cleft between the twin globes of her breasts. Insubstantial puffs of sapphire-green silk banding her upper arms were all that held the garment up. Whoever had dressed her was a genius in the art of flirtation. It seemed as if she were merely veiled in a blue-green haze that might at any moment, like fog, drift away, leaving her radiantly nude.

Yet, as flamboyant as her costume was, it was a mere setting for the woman herself. The gown's jewel coloring complimented her hint-of-gold complexion. Brushed high on her head in loose sunset-red ringlets that cascaded onto her bare shoulders, her hair put to rest a comparison with other redheads. Lit by torchlight behind her, the flame-red color incandesced.

She was, despite the carnival crush of the thousand-plus guests, a singular and unforgettable sight.

Something moved deep within Quinlan, a force never before experienced. He had wondered a dozen times each day if he had just passed her in a busy piazza without recognizing her. Now he knew he could never have missed her. He knew her as a compass needle unerringly seeks true north. He knew her in a way he did not know himself. The ennui of the last months cracked and crumbled away, exposing a longing that ached with the pulse of his blood.

I know her.

"Do you really?" Carrare declared at his elbow. "Then by all means, my friend, you must introduce me."

Quinlan had not realized he had spoken his thoughts aloud. He simply walked away from Carrare, not looking back when the man called after him.

"My heart is doing fair to a jig in my chest," Kathleen whispered to the man on whose arm her trembling fingers rested. "I had not expected so many."

"Cara," Paolo Francapelli chided, "did you think I would not honor you as your beauty requires?" As he withheld her descent to gauge her appearance upon his guests, the tall, severe figure whose shock of silver hair was the only color in his unrelieved black attire nodded regally at the assembly, and they in turn began to applaud.

"Look at all those faces turned up toward you, *cara!*" he whispered confidentially to her. "They are at your feet, where they belong. Tonight all Napoli is yours. Tomorrow and every day after, you must remember this night. You are Venus arising from her shell. They are your vassals to be favored or discarded at your whim. You are my English contessa, *donna bella!*"

Kathleen blushed but did not decry her host's effusive praise.

She had learned during the past weeks that while the Irish had a gift for blarney, the Italian soul was so romantic as to make her feel as if she had fallen into the honey pot. Voluptuous in their praise, they were equally volatile in their rage. For once she felt herself to be a very subdued spirit among those of wild extravagance.

"Come, let us show them what true magnificence is."

As he stepped down, Kathleen teetered for a moment, uncertain of her balance. Her slippers were Venetian with high spool heels, unlike anything she had ever before worn. Yet with the firm anchor of the count's arm she quickly regained her poise. In many other ways as well, she reflected, Francapelli had become a firm anchor on which she could depend.

She could not quite believe the bargain she had struck with the count. Though his original offer of marriage was rescinded, his generosity was by no means a one-day wonder. He had extended the offer of his protection to herself and Grainne, which allowed them to live under his roof as long as they wished. In return, he asked only that she run his household and act as his hostess on those social occasions requiring a woman's touch.

He had already explained to her with surpassing delicacy that he was not "endowed with the feelings" that would predispose him to bed her, for she was so "fundamentally female a creature." For the pleasures of the flesh he had a lover, a young sculptor by the name of Angelo Garzanti.

Kathleen had been quietly shocked but not, as she might have supposed she should be, disgusted. The count had been too kind, too generous, too good to her for her to feel anything other than gratitude for his friendship and the desire to repay his benevolence.

He had, however, stunned her by suggesting in the most discreet and flattering terms imaginable that she, too, take a lover. There was more. If she should in the future come to have a son without an offer of marriage, he would renew his own offer to give her child his name and his title. He freely admitted that a son to claim as his own was all that he needed to complete his happiness.

Kathleen supposed she might have given him false hope in the matter. But with the honesty that was her nature, she had told the truth, that he should not depend upon the latter arrangement. She had quite had her fill of romantic interludes. To make herself feel less obligated and more valuable, she had offered instead to translate into English the libretto of the opera he was composing on commission for the Duke of Devonshire.

As she looked out over the handsome, glittering crowd, she doubted that she would ever again be "endowed with the feelings" required for her to bed another man.

She pushed that thought aside. For the moment she had more than she could ever have expected because life was secure for her darling Grainne.

When the count paused halfway down the stairway and turned to bow over the hand of his "English contessa," Kathleen offered him a deep curtsy in return. Yet her winsome smile was provoked by thoughts of her daughter.

She had named her Grainne, which was Gaelic for Grace, after her mother. That is what her daughter had become for her, an instance of grace in return for months of uncertainty and regret. Love for her daughter so filled her mind and heart that her former yearnings for romantic love had nearly been forgotten.

She breathed in a trembling breath of relief as she rose and turned again to descend to the main floor. It was at that moment that an entirely new sort of disaster presented itself.

She saw him long before she should have.

The crowd rushing up to meet her quickly eclipsed her view of the room. Just as quickly, the count's footmen formed a buttress wall to hold them off. Before they did, she glimpsed among the crowd a claret coat and the beautiful face above it. It occurred so quickly, she doubted she would have recognized anyone less striking.

But Quinlan De Lacy was not a man who passed unnoticed.

He was as golden, as beautiful, as mesmerizing as she remembered.

A wave of dizziness swept over her as bitter regret. She wanted to cry and run away. How unfair! How could he have caught on to Longstreet's plot so quickly? Had Longstreet betrayed her? She had thought the producer too wily to ever set his own neck in the noose. Yet nothing else would seem to explain why DeLacy would be in Naples at this reception.

"What is wrong?" Francapelli placed his hand over hers, where it lay on his arm. "You are trembling!

Kathleen looked up into his concerned face with sorrow. "I regret . . ." She turned a little into his shoulder to shield her words. "There is someone here, an Englishman, who could discredit me before your company."

Francapelli drew back, his hooded eyes searching her face. "You fear this person?"

Kathleen shook her head. "Only that he may embarrass you."

"Do you think I would allow that, *cara?*" His hawkish features were smiling, but the glint in his dark eyes was that of a formidable foe. "No one annoys my guests."

Without looking up, he made a gesture with his hand. Seconds later a footman appeared with a glass of wine for her. "Now, this is what you shall do," Francapelli said in a murmur as he pressed the wine into her hand.

As he continued to whisper rapidly, ignoring the frustrated chatter of their guests, Kathleen began to smile. For the first time in months she no longer had to fight her battles alone. She had an ally, a very powerful and knowledgeable ally who would not be daunted by the English Viscount Kearney.

The line of footmen parted and the introductions began. The faces of those pressing eagerly forward to be the first to seek an introduction swirled and blended into indistinguishable identities. They meant nothing to her. She was waiting for only one introduction. It came amazingly soon. She had consumed no more than a sip of wine before the voice she could never forget rang in her ears.

"Buona sera, Contessa."

She forced herself to look up into the face of the man whom she had loved madly for so long.

Ecru silk hair shot with gold swirled about his sensitively molded features. His haunting eyes shone with rare clarity, the sea-glass green unclouded this once by temper or dark thoughts but possessed of some warmer and more stimulating emotion. Her gaze slipped to his smile. She stared at the triumph sketched there, too fascinated to look away. She knew only too well that his wide, tender-lipped mouth could be mocking, even cruel, in its smirk of humor. But oh, it revealed its full sensuality in a kiss. Unlike Errol's vanity and bullying, DeLacy's beauty was his greatest weapon, she realized anew. It tempted a woman whether she wanted it to or not—particularly if not.

With elation and despair she knew that her feelings had not subsided. She felt cold and too warm by turns, felt her pulse beating in her throat and her fingertips. The spasm of delight running through her, this madness in her blood, was that of a woman in love. He was staring at her as a man looks at a woman he desires. He was reaching out for her hand. With very little encouragement she knew she might do whatever he wanted her to. She was no longer frightened of being unmasked as a fake. She was afraid, but only of what might happen next.

Francapelli's discreet cough saved her. Her trembling knees unlocked and she went down in a collapse that was very like the real thing.

"What would you have had me do, *cara?* " Francapelli's voice was all patient amusement.

"I did not expect you to invite him to dine!" Kathleen paused in her pacing of her private chamber. Francapelli himself had carried her fainting form up to her room, but not before she heard him invite Viscount Kearney to dine with him the following evening. "What possessed you to do it?"

Francapelli shrugged, hugely enjoying this, the first fit of temper she had ever displayed before him. What fire, what passion! Her sapphire and emerald skirts swirled about her legs like a tempest-tossed sea as she resumed pacing. This venting of her emotions was good for her. He had been worried about her. No woman so young and without a lover should be so serene. She was not serene now, and he had the Englishman to thank for it. He did not fault her for her extreme response to the man, he fully understood it. *Dio!* The man was perfection!

"What better way to judge his mood, *cara,* than in a private tête-à-tête?"

"I can tell you his mood." Kathleen heard her voice swelling with emotion, but she could not stop it. " 'Tis thunderous. He will expose me for a fraud and then . . . then . . ." She sputtered off in an excess of feeling, but the lie would carry her only so far. DeLacy had not been angry. He had looked like he wanted to haul her off to the nearest bed. And heaven help her, she had wanted to go.

"Then what?" Francapelli sighed elegantly. *"Cara,* you worry needlessly. You do not even know what he knows. As for exposing you, he can tell me nothing you had not already confessed to me. You are in Italy. You need never go back to England. What difference is it to me that you wrote a play under another's name? It has been done before."

"Has it?" Kathleen's eyes narrowed in doubt. "When?"

"Deceit is always rampant in the arts. Sometimes an idea, sometimes a form, sometimes a melody. Why do you think I do not show my work until it is complete? So that no other composer will steal my themes."

Kathleen's mouth firmed in humor. "Then you should be having second thoughts about housing a person of my character beneath your roof."

He lifted one imperious black brow. "Do you compose music?"

Kathleen shook her head with a smile.

"So then there is no danger for me, yes?"

She laughed.

"There, that is better." He nodded in approval. "You are meant to laugh."

"And you are free to believe only what best pleases you, *signore,* because your power and wealth give you such freedom."

He chuckled at her impertinence. "And you, *cara,* are out of your shell at last. My compliments. Venus has a temper. You should be painted in that dress with this high color in your cheeks. Now, this Englishman." He stroked his chin with a thumb. "There are methods of dealing with him if it will make your life easier."

Kathleen gasped. "Oh, no, you mustn't do anything to him."

"Do?" He looked at his hands. "What could I do to the fellow? No, only what pleases you. I will make your excuses at dinner tomorrow."

"No." Kathleen nodded in approval of her own thought. "I may be a *blatherskite* and a *gom,* but I've never been a coward. I must face him."

"What is a *blatherskite* and *gom?*" the count inquired politely.

Kathleen offered him her first easy smile of the evening. "It's Gaelic for a chatterbox and a fool. I've been both of late. You are right, of course. The viscount's appearance here tonight may have nothing to do with the play I wrote for Longstreet. I was told Lord Kearney left England last August to court his muse in foreign climes. As to that, he may not yet have returned to England."

"Then he may not even know you wrote a play under his name."

"Exactly!" Kathleen expelled an audible sigh. Though she had never thought to see DeLacy again, she could not help being glad that the meeting had come that night, when she was on the arm of a powerful, handsome man and dressed more beautifully than she could ever have imagined.

As for the idea of seeing him again, it was too much to pass up. For, incredibly, she had not been able to dismiss the daydream she had entertained for a year and a half, that she might one day sit with him as his equal and discuss the world and literature, and his own work. Now, in this place and at this moment, she *was* his equal. And that was a very heady thought.

She glanced again at Francapelli, even though it made her blush. "Let Lord Kearney come to dine tomorrow."

"You need not do anything that distresses you." Francapelli let the thought dangle before adding, "There is, after all, the child to think of."

"Yes, Grainne." Kathleen rubbed her brow impatiently. "I do not so much care for myself, but for Grainne's sake I must try to reason with Lord Kearney."

Francapelli gave her a long, searching look. "You had better think this over very carefully, *cara*. It is not Grainne who stands in danger, I think. Is there, perchance, something you have not told me?"

Kathleen looked up to spy the knowing expression on his face. Were her feelings so transparent? Jesus, Joseph, and Mary! She would not stand a chance against DeLacy.

"You know the worst, how I came to be with child by a nobleman who promised to wed and then rejected me. You know I went to London with nothing but my father's last text—"

"Which you wrote," the count inserted.

"Yes. You see, I have been utterly frank with you." Kathleen measured her next words carefully. "You know that I was hired by Lord Kearney's agent and producer to complete a play his lordship could not. In return, I received passage to Italy."

"Is that all?"

"What else could there be?" she countered. Except my feelings, she amended in thought. She had not lied to the count, only omitted that she had met Lord Kearney, but that did not seem to matter.

"You did not tell me you knew Lord Kearney."

Kathleen shot her host a glance. "You must explain to me this sorcery that allows you to read minds."

Francapelli laughed. "When a woman looks at a man as you

did tonight, I need no magical powers to speculate that there is more in this than you are telling me."

"Do not speculate on that account. I have had my fill of romance."

"Have you? I held the impression you have not yet been properly loved. Ah, but I am getting old."

The tragic tone made Kathleen laugh again. "I know no man less infirm than you, *signore*. You are most handsome and virile."

He struck a pose for her in profile. "Do you really think so, *cara*? The chin, it does not yet sag? The nose does not grow out of proportion?"

"You should commission a bust, *signore,* that you might preserve your features for posterity."

He smiled at her. "I have given the commission to Angelo only this week. Then, you do approve?"

"I—" The sound of a distant wail brought Kathleen to her feet. "Oh, goodness. Grainne must be famished. I must go, *signore.*"

The count shook his head in gentle confusion. "It isn't proper, a noble lady suckling her babe."

"So you have told me," Kathleen called back over her shoulder as she headed in the direction of her child's lusty cry. "But you know that I am no lady!"

"I know you are a magnificent creature on the brink of love," he answered under his breath.

His appreciation of her finer points was aesthetic. The viscount's had been nothing short of rampantly carnal. He had watched in fascination as the Englishman struggled to master his inclination to snatch her up and make off with her when she succumbed to a faint at his feet. Had they been alone, he suspected the viscount would have made love to her right then and there on the terrazzo floor.

Francapelli chuckled. "Ah, passion, how it does betray one's best efforts."

He could, of course, simply inform the English viscount of

Kathleen's true feelings toward him, but he rather thought the Englishman needed the emotional exercise of chasing her.

Kathleen's very unwillingness to succumb to her emotions where the lovely viscount was concerned meant that the younger man would be put through his paces which, no doubt, would be a novelty for so virile and wealthy a man. "Ah, *cara mia,* he shall be so good for you."

Twenty-two

"Ah, there you are," Francapelli greeted his tardy hostess warmly. "We were about to go in to dine without you."

"I beg your pardon, Conte." Kathleen dropped into a respectful curtsy inside the door that belled her slim sea-green crepe skirts about her. She did not address either man in the room as she said, "Grainne was fretful today. I did not want to leave her until she had fallen asleep."

"Grainne is your daughter?"

She lifted her head and met DeLacy's gaze evenly. "Yes, my lord. She is the joy of my life."

Quinlan smiled at the cool bravery in her eyes, apparent even at a distance. She must have guessed why he was in Naples. Yet she had come down to join them when he would have staked a hefty sum on the bet that she would have found an excuse to hide away. It was a good thing he had not gambled. To his delight, she was proving as unpredictable as she had been in London. "I should like to meet your daughter."

She raised blazing eyes to his and saw an answering flicker of challenge in his cool gaze. "She is asleep, my lord."

Her swift expression of alarm surprised Quinlan. What was it about the child she feared him seeing? Good God! He hoped it was not, after all, a ringer for Longstreet! "Then perhaps another time?"

"Perhaps," Kathleen answered grudgingly. She looked away from his beautiful face, resenting his request to glimpse her new life. Though he would never know it, she had fought hard to win free of the feelings she had constructed for him on too many long, lonely nights. Now he had, by his mere appearance in Naples, thrown her emotions into fresh turmoil. She did not want to look at him, to admire his immaculate tailoring, his superb physicality, his grace and strength. She did not want to remember his kiss or the feel of his hands on her. She wanted to hate or despise or resent him for those things. Failing that, she had wanted only to be left alone. But that was impossible. So all that was left her was her pride and a show of spirit he would not soon forget. As for her pulse, she was certain it would slow with a little wine.

She glanced at Francapelli for help. "Shall we go in?"

"Of course." The count's expression was mischievous as he turned to his guest. "Would you escort the contessa in to dine, Viscount?"

"That isn't necessary," Kathleen countered in a tone that drew her host's speaking glance. *Coward,* it said.

"But it will be my pleasure." Quinlan moved forward to intercept her as she crossed to the middle of the room, giving himself over to an inspection of her as he did so.

The downtrodden mien of the improvised Irish Fair Hand had again disappeared behind the skillful modiste's touch. He noted her gown of the exact color of her eyes, and wondered in envy if Francapelli had chosen it. Though cut low across the shoulders, the neckline was square and tight, revealing the shape of rather than her breasts themselves. Her hair was down, confined at the nape with a large black satin bow much like those used to hold a gentleman's peruke half a century earlier, and pulled forward over one shoulder in a torrent of curls. The sight of that burning tangle disturbed him more than he expected.

Her only jewelry was a thin silver chain around her neck, but the locket or bauble attached was lost behind the neckline of her bodice. Had they been alone, he was certain he would have dared to delve in and pluck it out, if only to see the anger rise in her fine green eyes. Despite her first challenging glance, she was refusing to look at him as he approached. "Contessa?"

Kathleen stared at the masculine hand reaching out to her. She offered hers unresistingly but did not raise her gaze to his. He bent over her hand and she felt the touch of warm, dry lips even through the thin fabric of her glove. She knew she should not close her eyes at his touch, but she could not help it. "No!" she whispered fiercely, and opened them.

"No, Contessa?" She jerked guilty eyes to meet his smiling ones. "Does my salutation offend you?"

"Of course not, my lord."

"DeLacy, surely," he answered confidentially as he tucked her hand into the crook of his arm. "After all we have shared."

"You know the contessa?" Francapelli inquired in mock surprise as he, stood in the doorway that opened into the dining hall.

Kathleen wished to kick Francapelli as she preceded him into the room, but it was too late. His wicked glance meant he intended to amuse himself at her expense.

"Did the contessa not tell you?" Quinlan inquired as he surveyed the long table set with only three places. "We have met, though not formally." He glanced down at the woman walking defiantly by his side, and patted the hand she rested reluctantly on his arm. "We once shared a producer in Drury Lane. But in point of fact, I do not recollect that she ever gave her name."

"Ah, but this must be remedied." Francapelli's gaze warmed as it lit on Kathleen's stubborn expression. "My dearest, allow me to introduce Lord Kearney to you. *Signore,* the most fortunate find in my recent travels, the contessa Hermione."

The ridiculous name drew a gasp from Kathleen and put a quirk in Quinlan's smile.

"Hermione?" Quinlan repeated. "Is that not the name of the queen in Shakespeare's *A Winter's Tale?*"

"It is!" Francapelli agreed in pleasant surprise as he moved to his place at the head of the table. "Your Duke of Devonshire suggested it to me as a possible inspiration for my opera for him. The contessa has been translating it for me. Do you know the tale?"

"Of course," Quinlan answered smoothly, wondering how one might inquire if "the contessa" was his wife or his mistress. "As I recall, the play was derived from a story called 'Pandosto.' "

"Then you know it was your Shakespeare's invention that Hermione not die as in the original telling."

Quinlan cast a speculative glance at Kathleen. "She is merely spirited away from her lord's realm until he comes to fully appreciate what he nearly lost."

"It is a telling I much prefer. Ah, but I am Neapolitan." Francapelli's laughter was as elegant and understated as the rest of him. "I find a woman of such passion and courage too intriguing to murder."

Quinlan noticed the count's gaze lingered fondly on his "Hermione." What was there between them? Despite Carrare's gossip, he could not reconcile the tender glances between them with the cold, selfish interests of a nobleman who had brought a penniless unwed mother under his roof in order to serve as brood mare for his prospective heir. Had rumor erred on the point of Francapelli playing seducer to his would-be mistress? The thought slipped an unexpected stab of jealousy under his ribs.

Quinlan's attention moved back to Kathleen. "It would seem your virtues have quite won the count, Contessa. Yet, I should swear an oath that you were accounted by Mr. Longstreet to be a Miss Geraldine from Ireland."

"So that is what he told you," Kathleen replied. If he thought to discredit her with the count, he was doomed to disappointment. "His account of you was that you were a difficult, temperamental artist who on the occasion of our meeting had just stomped out, leaving his office smelling of sulphur and brimstone."

Quinlan's lips twitched. So she was rallying her wits. Good, he had no desire to trample the feelings of the frightened woman who had fainted at his feet the night before. He would much rather match wits with the intrepid young women who had hoodwinked him in London. "You must tell me your impression of the fellow. I found him unscrupulous, avaricious, and not above the occasional false dealing."

"Such hard words, my lord. 'Tis quite amazing you dealt with him at all," Kathleen answered, and heaved a secret sigh of relief as she took her chair in the low-ceilinged open-air room.

"Not at all. Our host will, I believe, agree that the opera world is like that of the stage, which resembles nothing as much as a battleground."

Francapelli inclined his head in agreement as he took his seat at the head of the table. "When one engages in a battle, one chooses for one's comrades those who are best equipped to carry the day."

"Exactly." Quinlan acknowledged the count's words but did not move from Kathleen's side. "Men of Longstreet's ilk have their uses. It is when their interests outweigh all others that even a nobleman such as I must look to my back. But allow me." He deliberately swept a hand along the back of Kathleen's chair, his curved fingers brushing her bare shoulders as he adjusted it. "The fellow left one of his knives in my back but recently."

Kathleen ignored this invitation to engage directly in the matter between them. She was much more interested in the reason he was behaving as if he could scarcely keep his hands off her.

He bent to her, silky lips parted as if half given over to the inclination to lean forward and kiss her. "Are you now comfortable?"

"Yes. Thank you." Kathleen abruptly turned her head away. She did not trust her feelings, or him. She suspected that underneath the attraction he was seething.

Quinlan took his seat between them, but he was not done teasing her. "I believe, Contessa, when last I saw you you were transcribing a play for Longstreet. Now, what was the author's name?"

"I don't recall."

"Do you not?" he asked as he reached for his glass of wine. "A pity." He seemed to study the clarity of the wine as he said, "I should like very much to converse with him."

"Umm, 'tis a pity," Kathleen murmured tightly, and reached for the silver ladle to serve herself from the tureen held by a footman. So he thought to play her like a mouse between his cat's paws, did he? She should have liked to serve him a bop on the crown with the heavy ladle for the insult. Instead, she frowned with a concentration that should have curdled her asparagus soup.

"Have you been recently in London, my lord?" Francapelli inquired suddenly, drawing the startled glances of both his guests.

"Not recently." Suspicion furrowed Quinlan's brow. "Why do you ask?"

"The contessa's expression puts me in mind of the year I spent in your country." He smiled over the rim of his wine. *"O Dio mio!* But dreadful winters!"

An embarrassed warmth crept through Kathleen. "Surely there are many more pleasant things about which we might converse than English winters."

"Indeed, there are." A rare glance of intense interest shone in Quinlan's expression. "I've just finished a new play."

"But that is delightful," Francapelli declared heartily. "Tell us about it."

Quinlan smiled, but there was a glint in his eye as he turned to Kathleen, who was not even looking at him "It's a comedy of sorts, Contessa. A satire of war and warriors."

"I see," she said faintly, refusing to acknowledge him with a glance.

"I have called it *Fortune's Fool.*"

She did glance up then at his blandly smiling face, and at the charm of his smile, but it was to wish him to the devil. So he did know! And he thought he was there to shatter her newfound, barely won life.

"Tell us more," Francapelli encouraged.

Quinlan turned to the man whose timbre of amusement was less contained than before. It suddenly occurred to him that Francapelli might have had a part in the fraudulent play. If he believed Longstreet innocent, then Miss Geraldine needed another co-conspirator. Who better than a famous composer and librettist?

"The play premiered in London this November past. A shame you missed it, Conte. The critics were quite vocal in their opinions of it."

Kathleen gripped her soup spoon, barely able to keep from inquiring directly whether the reviews were good or bad. "I trust you were well served by the actors."

Quinlan swung his head toward her. "I was—surprised, Contessa. In fact, I confess that sitting in the playwright's box listening to the cast recite their speeches, I could scarce believe I had writ them. For you see, I had intended it to be a drama. A tale of the horror of war. Having spent an hour or two upon the battlefield in the 'Grays,' I felt imminently qualified. Yet the cast made of it a wicked satire that quite skewered my pretensions to tragedy."

"But you are too modest, my lord," Francapelli answered, picking up the thread of conversation. "I was in London when news of Napoleon's defeat reached the city. Such rejoicing! A great victory. People talked for weeks of the fateful charge of the 2nd Dragoons."

"It is true. I made the ride." Quinlan's expression remained bland. "But there was very little victory in it. Many fine men fell in battle that day. Among them were two great friends, Lord Heallford and Major Pettigrew."

Kathleen sprang to her feet with a small cry as the contents of her soup bowl splashed into her lap.

"*Dio!* Have you scalded yourself?"

"No, no." Kathleen dabbed at the soup stain on her skirts with her napkin. "It is nothing. Only please excuse me. I must change."

The two men had risen as she did. Quinlan moved quickly to offer her his arm. "Allow me to escort you to the door."

Kathleen looked up into his gray-green eyes, expecting the triumph of his discovery, but she could read no hint of mockery there. He could not know what Errol Pettigrew meant to her. And yet he knew something. It was there in his piercing gaze.

Quinlan held her arm too tightly for her to take it back without a struggle, and he knew she did not want it to come to that. Ah, but she was magnificent! The starveling look was gone from her cheeks. Her face was a trifle fuller than before, the chin not quite so sharp. Her figure was a shade more lush and provocatively mature. Something in her expression—for her features were too pert for true beauty of the conventional variety—lifted her out the realm of pure lustful design. "I hope you will rejoin us soon, Contessa. I so look forward to continuing our conversation."

"I don't know." Kathleen glanced past him to where the count stood, watching them. "There is my child to see to."

"But certainly you have a nurse for such things."

Kathleen blushed. "I prefer to look after her myself."

"Such dedication is charming. Yet I trust I will see you again."

She lifted her hand from his arm. "I can make no promises."

"Ah, but that is something on which I must insist." He said the last so softly that she read the threat in his eyes rather than heard it in his voice.

"Very well. In an hour, perhaps." She turned deliberately to the count and offered him a brief curtsy before slipping out of the doorway.

The two gentlemen spent the remainder of the meal conversing politely of their mutual interests, music and literature. Francapelli did not miss how often the viscount's attention strayed to the closed door through which Kathleen had disappeared. It really was too naughty of her to quit the field just when things were becoming interesting. Ah, well, he would have to stir the pot himself. If Kathleen flew at him later for what he was about to do, he would remind her that she might have stayed and prevented it.

When the port had been poured, Francapelli lifted his glass in a toast. "To my contessa. She is quite beautiful, is she not?"

"Indeed," Quinlan remarked-in the drawl he reserved for conversations he did not wish to have.

"The man who wins her will gain a rare prize."

Quinlan considered that statement before saying, "Forgive my lack of understanding, Conte, but I thought she was yours."

Francapelli's voice was as civil as his expression was observant. "The contessa is my guest, *signore,* just as you are. She has my hospitality and protection as long as they shall be required."

Quinlan smiled with equal barbed civility. "How generous of you."

"Generous, yes. But even generosity has its usefulness." Francapelli saw his statement did nothing to ease Kearney's irritation, which pleased him no end. "The contessa's wit is as useful as her considerable beauty. As I have said, she is helping in the translation of the libretto for my next opera. She reads and writes Greek as well as Latin. But then, you know this."

"No," Quinlan admitted, "but then, we are nearly strangers."

"Is that so?" Francapelli allowed his expression to at last reflect how much he was enjoying himself. "I was under the impression from the way you stare at her that you knew her very well."

Something in the count's tone drew Quinlan up short of his first response. He stared at the Italian nobleman for a while before saying, "We formed a slight acquaintance in London last summer but I assure you the child is not mine."

The count laughed at the presumption. "That much anyone could ascertain by looking at the babe. Grainne is raven-haired with the bluest eyes. So then, your gazes are ones of regret that you do not know her mother as well as you would like."

"You presume a great deal." It was impossible to judge by his expression what the count knew or suspected, if anything.

"Signore! I may not share it, but I understand the inclination. She has a rare loveliness, less flamboyant than beauty. Yet she is a wounded bird, *signore*. She has come to roost beneath my roof, to heal and regain her strength. I will protect her in every way until she is ready." He gave a philosophical shrug. "When she is, she is free to fly away."

Quinlan did not believe that offhanded manner. "Does she know she can leave?"

"That the cage door is open? But of course."

"Yet," Quinlan drawled as his gaze roamed significantly over the wealth displayed in the room, "it is a gilded cage."

"She is not a fool nor avaricious, *signore*. She will go where her heart dictates. Alas, she has learned in the most difficult way possible that there are many pitfalls for a woman who flaunts convention and follows her inclinations. I think she will be much more circumspect in the future."

"You may be correct. And yet she cannot complain of her present circumstances." Quinlan wondered at the bitterness in his tone, but he could not master it. "Mistresses seldom fare as well. I would imagine her last keeper did not house her in a style half so elegant."

"You do not know, then?"

"Know what?"

"That she is no courtesan. She is—how do you English have it—ah, yes, an impoverished gentlelady. Her father was a man of letters like yourself. But then, you must at least know this?"

"No." Quinlan hoped his surprise did not show.

"Forgive the question, my friend, but what do you know about her beyond the fact you desire her—and that she wrote a play?"

"She wrote—"

Francapelli could not pretend not to notice the transfixed expression on Kearney's face. It startled him out of his humor. "Do not tell me you did *not* suspect the author was she?"

"I—did not," Quinlan answered simply, uncertain that he believed it was possible even now. He leveled his gaze at the Italian. "I rather thought it might be you."

"But this is too delicious!" Francapelli crowed in new insight. "You think because she is a woman she is not capable of such wit and skill? *Signore,* at last I believe you do not know her at all."

"The play is much more than a skillful effort." Quinlan caught himself on the edge of an admission that still shocked him. "It is a good, nay, I will say splendid satire of my former work. How could she, a stranger to me, gain the competency required?" He shook his head in doubt.

Francapelli shrugged. "She does not confide everything to me, *signore.* A woman's heart is full of secrets. Perhaps you have the key to unlock what I cannot."

Quinlan stared into the tawny red depths of his port. "She wrote the play," he murmured.

A man of infinite patience as well as tact, Francapelli allowed the young English noble to wrestle with demons he could only guess at. And yet it was not without its rewards. The composer was a connoisseur of beautiful things. The fascinating play of shock and desire and chagrin brought into focus the rare beauty of the man. He could not, Francapelli decided, have chosen a better partner for his contessa if he had spent a year seeking one. Yet the English seemed to him a fainthearted people when it came to passion. Too often they walked away from what they most wanted. Kearney struck him as a man whose pride might just get in the way of his passion. It was up to him to make Kathleen an irresistible challenge.

"Though she may feel I betray her, I will tell you what I know of her." He was gratified by the swift attention Quinlan gave his offer of indiscretion. The man's face was a study in curiosity. "She is no wanton. She was seduced and abandoned by one of your English nobles. The scoundrel promised to wed her but rescinded his offer after she told him she carried his child. The details you must ask her."

Quinlan did not answer this time. Something clicked into his brain—the look on her face before she rushed away from the table. No, surely not! Impossible. Absurd! Too wild a coincidence! Yet, Hockaday had speculated—no! Not possible.

"You have been fairly warned," Francapelli continued. "She has much reason to arm her heart against all men. She believed a roué. Possibly she will never again trust herself to recognize love."

He reached for a candied fig from the silver epergne. "Which is not to say she will not eventually sink into a life of wanton and meaningless pleasure. She is young, and nature has given her the body of a voluptuary." He paused to judge whether his guest was following his bread-crumb trail of thoughts. He had never seen a man less inclined to show his emotions, and that was the best sign of all.

"It is often the fate of the failed romantic to use debauchery as a weapon against the very emotions that broke her faith in love. But I do not tell you these things to fan your desire for her. No, with your face and form you just might succeed in ruining her entirely. No, that is the tragedy of wounded innocence, *signore*. I am thinking of writing an operetta to it. Of course, it must have a happy ending."

"Of course."

"Life does not always offer such things in real life. Alas, the yearning keeps me in business."

Quinlan regarded Francapelli with new respect. "You are a very astute man."

"We artists share that understanding of the human heart even if we do not share in the foibles of love's snare. So then, I must ask you, why are you here? It is not the play. The play you could have discredited with a letter to the London *Times* and handbills in the streets. You came to find Signorina Geraldine. Why?"

"Is that her real name, Geraldine?"

Francapelli laughed indulgently and shook his head. "You did not know so much as that? The impetuousness of youth! She is Kathleen Geraldine late of County Kildare."

"Geraldine?" The name struck Quinlan as familiar. "I know Rufus Geraldine of Kildare, a poet."

Francapelli nodded. "Her father."

"His daughter," Quinlan said slowly, reminded of the letters of mutual admiration he had exchanged with the poet. "Perhaps he wrote the play."

"That would be impossible, since he is dead." Francapelli lifted his arms in defeat of the matter. "She is alone in the world. She has done what she must to survive and make a life for her child. My admiration for her is unbounded. I will not have her hurt. So again, aside from the matter of the play, why are you pursuing her?"

Quinlan shook his head. His feelings had nothing to do with the play, or, rather, the rights and money attached to it. What he had not been able to get out of his mind was the thoroughness with which the author of *Fortune's Fool* had crawled—sight unseen—into his psyche and mined his imagination for his—or her—own creations.

"If you are wondering how she knew you so well when you know her not at all, why do you not ask her?"

Realizing he had given away more of his thoughts than he intended, he stood up abruptly. "You will have to forgive me, Conte Francapelli. I recollect I have another appointment for which I am late. Give my regrets to the contessa."

The count stood and nodded regally. "She will regret your desertion."

Quinlan gave him a hard look. "Rather, it is a parting only, Conte. I should be more than happy to make it up to her. Does she, perchance, ride?"

"I am certain a carriage ride would be enjoyable for her. Tomorrow at three."

"Then, until three tomorrow. *Addio.*"

The moon lit the city, sliding white and silent from the amphitheater formed by the surrounding hills down to Corso and into the dark liquid surface of the Bay of Naples. Here and there the velvety darkness was pricked by the warm, golden flare of a footman's torch which picked out a bit of color or glitter from the cover of the night. The hour was late and the night surprisingly cold after the heat of the day. It had driven vendor and beggar, even the greater portion of the *lazzaroni,* indoors. Yet the solitude suited Quinlan as he made his way home. His conversation with Conte Francapelli had given him much to think about. His thoughts were scintillating.

He had found the author of *Fortune's Fool.*

"Kathleen Geraldine," he mumbled to himself for the dozenth time as he hunched his shoulders against the chill.

He could not possibly have guessed it from their brief acquaintance in London. Yet he had sensed from the first that she was more than what she seemed.

So the russet-haired waif in the worn bonnet was capable of penning witty satire to rival his own!

The idea of a woman composing prose did not amaze him, though he had often lamented the fact that he did not know personally any truly gifted females. Certainly any child of Rufus Geraldine's would have had access to a fine education. Yet her competency answered only a part of the puzzle.

The author of *Fortune's Fool* had done more than write a good play. She had mastered the DeLacy style, in places poked fun at it, and most amazingly of all, accomplished what he had not been able to do—tell a story of war's cowardice and bravery in a way that made people twitter and then bellow with telling laughter. Her characters were recognizable. Now he knew why.

Her swaggering but stalwart hero had been modeled on Errol Pettigrew. She gave that away by fleeing Francapelli's table the moment he mentioned Pettigrew's name. She had used her own life as fodder for her play. The young Irishwoman seduced and abandoned by the hero who spurned her in a letter from the battlefield was Kathleen herself.

But how and where had they met?

Quinlan climbed the stairs to his rented rooms in a *pensione* off the Chiaia. When he had lit a candle he began rifling through his papers. The item he sought was mashed into a corner of his portmanteau, all but forgotten. It was the letter Della Heallford had written to the erstwhile Professor Giorgiolani accepting the · position in Porto Venere and signed Kathleen Geraldine. "An Irish relation and cousin to Lady Heallford" she had written in the text. Kathleen was Lady Heallford's cousin.

The last piece fell into place. Pettigrew must have met Kathleen at her cousin's wedding, a ceremony he had been expected to attend himself but could not. Rueful humor twisted his lips. Had they met, he might well have been Pettigrew's rival for her attention.

He found the text of *Fortune's Fool* quickly enough, a bonus he had pried out of Longstreet before he left London. For the next hour he reread it slowly and carefully, slowing even more when he came to the passage in the second act where the Irish lass receives a letter from her lover in which he spurns her.

He had been too stunned by the performance itself to absorb the details of the speeches. Now the phrases of the letter leapt off the page at him.

No self-respecting woman would find herself so compromised . . . can in no way permit you to connect my name, my consequence . . . generous nature opportuned upon by your treacherous wiles . . . suspect to my regret that other men must in like favor with you . . .

Kathleen Geraldine was, it seemed, many things he had not even suspected, including a plagiarist. *He* had written those words.

Quinlan closed his eyes. He could so easily imagine now how a young, unwed mother-to-be must have felt to receive from her lover so scathing a rejection. But where were all his fine feelings when he had sat down to write the letter? Drowned by brandy and the self-righteous suspicion that he addressed a slut!

Oh, he had been a fine fellow, telling himself that perhaps the woman didn't even exist. Dear Lord! Knowing that it was Kathleen who had received his brutal epistle, his effort seemed the cruelest form of cowardice. No wonder the character in her play had attempted to murder herself not once but three times. The buffoonery of the efforts did not mitigate them, only made them more poignant.

Had Kathleen Geraldine been moved to that extreme of desperation?

The irony of it was, had he told the tale in his usual droll style, the players would have been drawn as little more than caricatures of virtues and vices, the very essence of farce. Poor, naive Irish lass, dazzled by the pompous swaggering cockscomb of a dragoon officer, is seduced and abandoned only to be saved at the last minute by the revelation that she is the cousin of an English countess, wife to the dragoon's fellow officer and friend, and therefore worthy of his hand in marriage.

But Kathleen's story had not come around in the final act. Her father had died. With Errol's death, she was left utterly alone in the world to carry and care for a child who did not bear its father's name as protection. Forced by treachery of others to do what she must to survive. Courageous through tribulations. Queen Hermione, indeed.

He thought of his pretentious behavior in moving to the slums of Lambeth. He had wanted to learn about the poor by living among them. Yet he had never lived with them or even as they did. His valet had brought him whatever he desired. It had been nothing but an egotistical illusion. He had not gone hungry or cold, or in fear of the future.

No wonder she could write about what he would not. She had lived what he had not.

He sat quietly, stiffly, until the self-vilification faded and with it the shame and the remorse, until there was only one desire burning in him: to know her as she knew him.

He could still remember their first encounter in Longstreet's hallway. Her face had been turned up with softly parted lips, and the wonder of surprise and delight was in her wide green eyes. She *knew* him, spoke his name. That recognition had caused him to tarry, had tempted him to speak to her, but he knew he was too angry. Whatever he might have uttered would have obliterated her awe and her rapture.

No woman before or since had ever looked at him with quite that unguarded acknowledgment of desire discovered. Without artifice or design, she had offered him something less than adoration and much more than mere lewd invitation. Had he not known it to be impossible, he would have said hers was the glance of love.

Nothing he had discovered tonight answered the question, how had she come to know so much about him? She would have had to make a study of his work to pull so broadly and correctly from his text to place in hers. Had she made such a study of him? Did she suspect he had written that letter, or was it only unhappy coincidence?

"Kathleen Geraldine." Saying her name aloud made him smile. He had thought of her each day for five months without being able to put a name to her face. Now he could.

He could still recall the stinging embarrassment he had felt watching her play. It seemed as if she had climbed inside him, roamed through all the secret private corridors of his mind, and ransacked them for bits of wit and parody she could skewer. He had felt he was being publicly flayed. He now knew it was less than he deserved.

Everything he had learned this night augmented his desire for her. He wanted to know her in ways he had never before imagined. He wanted to know the woman behind the verdant green gaze and brilliant red tresses. He wanted her to be real, not some pretty reflection of his own ego to be possessed and displayed for the admiration and envy of other men. He wanted to know her thoughts and ideas as well as her feelings. He wanted to learn her strengths and her courage. He wanted her to think and live—no, thrive. He would help her. For with her talent she must write more plays!

He ached for her, not with callous self-interest, but with the certain need that he would never be whole again until he knew her as well as she knew himself. He wanted to take her to bed, but he would wait until he had gained her confidence. Only then would he take her, slowly, lovingly, replacing every hurt he had done her with joy. He would learn what made her heart beat and then make himself as necessary to her as that.

Twenty-three

London, January 15, 1816

Though by nature a man not given to reflection, Jamie could not help but muse on the vagaries of life from the comfort of his new copper tub. For instance, now that it had gotten around that he had come into his majority, shopkeepers and merchants of every sort were clamoring to offer him a plethora of items formerly beyond the touch of a young blood of modest means. Even better, they did not require the down payment he was accustomed to advancing—both buyer and seller being aware that the first payment would be the last many a gentleman felt obliged to make until the dunners arrived.

The tub, a French import with porcelain interior and gilded rim, curved high in back to prop him up at a relaxing angle. He leaned back and with a negligent hand waved to his new valet.

"More warm water, Fletcher. This new mode of bathing has my patronage. I intend to encourage among my friends the virtues of a good soak."

"Very well, sir." The beak-nosed man of indeterminable age made a small bow.

"Then you may bring me one of that batch of cigars I purchased this morning."

"Very good, sir." Again a deferential bow.

Jamie scowled. "Do cease that plaguey bowing and scraping.

Such obsequious attention makes me feel as if I should remove Aunt Elberta's silver to a safer place."

"How droll, sir," the man replied without a hint of mirth.

Jamie glanced sharply at the gaunt creature in navy tailcoat, white small clothes, and powdered peruke who was serving him. Fletcher was his aunt's idea, as was his livery. She said that now that he had come into his inheritance, he needed a man of more consequence than Simpkin could manage.

"Doing it a bit brown," Jamie grumbled. He felt as if he were being served by a runaway page from a French opera.

Slipping lower in the rewarmed waters, he kneed aside the bar of soap that had slipped off the rim. It was French-milled, a gift from Lord Rollerson before their relationship had become estranged.

Jamie scowled as he picked up the gelatinous mass. The attendant luxuries of his new life were not the only things occupying his mind these last weeks.

Upon reflection, it did not seem fair that he should come out of the matter of his broken engagement so well. Not when, after word reached London of the dissolution of their engagement, Clarette had immediately become the subject of gossip and just as quickly been labeled a "jilt."

How unfair life could be. She had only tried to help him. Still, the more he protested that his unnamed transgressions were fully as vile as necessary to turn the affections of a constant young lady, the more intractable the speculation became.

In the end he had decided that if he made a spectacle of himself while in town, rumor might turn in her favor.

He smiled, but it was a little less jaunty than usual. He had cut a swath so wide and deep through the gaming hells of ill repute that none would doubt why Clarette had cried off.

Except they did doubt it.

The rumors continued to spread, and every embellishment added another adjective of villainy to Clarette's name. They called her "hard," "unfeeling," "merciless," and "overproud," all for having driven "that poor Hockaday fellow to run wild in his grief."

Now, at least, the matter of Clarette's reputation was in proper hands. He was quite pleased to have thought up the solution on his own. He had decided to turn the prickly matter over to his aunt Elberta. After laying before her the bare outline of their breakup, she had packed up to pay a visit to the Rollersons. Excellent thing! Aunt Elberta was a veritable Tartar among the *ton*. If she saw fit to continue the acquaintance, Clarette's reputation could not long remain in shadow.

Jamie took the cigar offered by his new valet, noting the suspicion of a yellow stripe in the man's breeches. His aunt's taste in livery needed adjustment!

Strangely, the more he tried to rid himself of thoughts of Clarette, the more he found himself thinking about her, even missing her company in some vague way. He had supposed at first that it was not unlike missing the company of one's favorite spaniel. No, that was not quite right. He missed her tart tongue and excellent wit. He was never at a loss for words in her company, and she never seemed to tire of his rattling on. He would even have liked to continue exchanging letters with her but knew that was impossible.

He had then supposed it was like missing a favorite sister, except that he had detested his sisters while growing up among them. *Tolerance* was the best adjective he could apply to their present relationship.

Recently it had come to him that he simply missed her. And the feeling had quite astonished him. She had made him feel wise and funny and quite dashing. He had actually found himself dreaming about her, quite bawdy dreams that left him feeling a little embarrassed. Of course, she had kissed him as if she were quite fond of the exercise. He could not now understand why he had not availed himself of the pleasure more often.

Suddenly the admiration in her dark eyes, which he had always thought of as childlike, looked more clearly like adoration in retrospect. Had he missed something? Had Clarette actually cared for him?

"Gosh," he murmured in a tone quite unlike his usual snappy cant. It made so much sense, he felt quite gauche. What a nod-cock! The shy puss! She had had only to hint at the truth and he would have caught on. After all, he was a subtle fellow. Yet, how could he think of approaching Clarette again, when her father stood so solidly between them?

"Lord, no!" he muttered with a suppressed shudder. Roller-son would have him booted from the door.

Jamie sighed expressively, issuing a thin bluish cloud of fragrant smoke that rose to fill the dressing room.

If only he were able to confide in Quinlan, he might receive some sanguine advice. But The Quill had left town in November—drat him—and no man of his acquaintance had received so much as a couplet from the fellow.

"Odd fish, that," Jamie remarked, then drew with savoring pleasure upon the cigarillo he had lit to accompany this experience in full immersion. The Quill was not one to decamp without a hail and farewell. Yet, rumor said he had popped into town for the debut of his new play and then escaped again without so much as a tip of his hat to anyone. When the fellow did turn up again, he supposed there would be some rare tale to explain his behavior.

Perhaps the reality in reverting to his bachelor ways had him blue-deviled. That, Jamie supposed, was because he had forgotten the full meaning of term "eligible" where the *ton* was concerned. Despite his unavailing attempts to publicly blacken his own character, he had been buried beneath invitations to "proper pursuits" as his aunt called them. That was because a handsome young man who could dance and smile, even if a bit disreputable, was ever in season.

"The bachelor's life is ever at risk, Fletcher," Jamie mused aloud. "He may think he has the world by the tail, but he's ever the fox at society's hunt: constantly targeted at teas, sought after at soirees, cornered at card parties, beset at balls, and run down at romps! 'Tis enough to ruin a man's health!"

"Yes, sir," his valet answered politely.

Jamie reached for the brandy snifter balanced on the tub's rim. What he needed was a respite from London. He longed to be in warmer climes. Italy would be sunny and warm while London was cold, wet, and dismal. He should pop over to the continent and take a look at grapevines, the major source of his new income.

"The very thing! Fletcher! Begin packing. We're off at the end of the week for sunnier climes!"

"Very good, sir," the valet answered with all the enthusiasm of a man who had been sentenced to be hanged.

"I think that's taking a rather high-handed tone," Lord Rollerson replied, his indignation apparent in his coloring.

"I should think it not censorious enough," Lady Ormsby retorted. "Consider what you've done to those sweet children."

"What *I've* done?"

Lady Ormsby tapped her cane impatiently on the parquet floor of Lord Rollerson's second-best salon. "Did you not encourage the match despite my nephew's protests that the letter had gone in error to your second daughter?"

Lord Rollerson was usually at his best in the company of handsome women of a certain age, but Lady Ormsby's sudden appearance at his home one half-hour before boded ill for his hospitable reputation. "Madame, we are scarcely acquainted. That aside, I do not care to discuss either of my daughters' personal concerns with you."

"That is quite too bad of you. I should think you would seek to secure your child's happiness. Even if, in obtaining it, you must admit to flaws in your own character."

"Flaws? My character?" Lord Rollerson snapped his mouth shut. He had never in his life insulted a lady, but the termagant glaring at him from beneath a towering bonnet of purple satin and black ruching was sorely tempting fate.

"I am prepared to amend my opinion of your position to one of overzealousness, providing you agree that you are at fault in the misalliance of your daughter and my nephew."

"I did not, at the time, consider it a misalliance. However, your nephew's subsequent shabby conduct can be described only in such terms as I refuse to utter in the presence of a lady."

"Fustian! Had you not found Jamie a perfect, unobjectionable match for your Clarette, you would not have given it your blessing. Who ordered the banns be published before the poor dear boy had uttered one word or pledge to anyone?"

Despite his resentment of her tone, Rollerson winced. "Very well. I stand corrected in that matter. But the girl had a letter!"

"She had her sister's letter, and I'm very much convinced you suspected as much."

"How dare—"

Lady Ormsby smiled serenely. It had been more than a year since she had taken part in a rousing discussion with a gentleman. "I dare very much, because there is no fool like an old fool, and you should know!" As he cast around for the proper setdown, she sailed on in her speech. "I recall as a young girl watching you rush your fences year after year at the steeplechase races in Somerset."

"You do?"

"I remember in particular the year you rode a pride bit of horseflesh named Gallow's Meat. Detestable name, but what a runner. Yet when you felt your lead pressed at the final hurdle, you rushed too quickly to the goal and ended arse over top in the mud. How many times has that flaw defeated you?"

"Enough," he muttered, pleased and annoyed that she remembered being witness to his folly. "Yet I won more than I lost."

"Which proves my point. You are not a complete fool. I suspect you are willing to learn from your mistakes."

As she offered him a sweet smile, he began to suspect she was flirting with him, but she had stung his dignity in so many tender places, he was not at all certain he should respond. Still, churlishness was not part of his nature. "Always thought Ormsby found himself a better match than he deserved."

"It remains to be seen if my nephew will be fortunate enough to do the same," she returned pleasantly.

Rollerson smiled. There was no denying the lady had style and wit and, he suspected, cherished getting her way.

"What do you propose we do?"

"Nothing. The children have been meddled with quite enough for one year. I propose that you allow me to extract Clarette from under your roof and the constant reminder that her beautiful sister has landed a splendid husband while her own chances for happiness seem quite spoiled."

"I hadn't thought of it quite like that."

"Men never do. Do you suppose she is pleased to know that she may never have the man she loves, while, in fact, her sister never wanted him?"

"That is Hockaday's fault!"

"You fault him for loving either of your daughters? How very odd. I should rather believe he, in his own way, suffers from an excess of good taste."

Oh-ho, thought Rollerson, she knew how to apply balm after her stings. "Whatever the case, he's made a hash of it."

"He's confused. He loves Clarette, only he don't know it yet."

"How do you suppose he will ever come to the correct conclusion?"

"Have you ever known a gentleman to not seek to recover something he lost, particularly if the thing he lost is attracting the attention of others?"

Not liking the sound of that one bit, Rollerson puckered up. "Perhaps you should be more specific."

"I wish to take Clarette as my companion for this next half year. As my year of mourning is officially at an end, I can make use of the company of a lively girl as I go about. I know ever so many of the right sort of people, you understand."

He smiled in relief. "That might serve as the very thing."

They were of like temperament, he reflected with suppressed amusement. His Clarice might just prove to be a bit too spirited even for the redoubtable Lady Ormsby.

"I don't doubt but that you'll rub on well enough," he answered, enjoying the irony in his choice of words. They would no doubt strike sparks.

"Rub on I shall, my lord," Lady Ormsby answered with a smug smile. "Well enough to see to business on your behalf and mine."

Clarette did not know precisely why she had been selected to serve as Lady Ormsby's new companion. Yet she was certain it was a punishment for her behavior. The fact that her benefactor was Jamie's aunt in no way mitigated the matter. According to her father, the Honorable Mr. James Hockaday had left England, perhaps for good.

She did not doubt the place to which she had been told she would be traveling with Lady Ormsby would be full of dark and cheerless spaces. To be locked in a musky country domicile with an elderly and ailing woman on her last pin was, no doubt, no more than she deserved after the consternation and embarrassment she had caused her family.

One thousand pounds for a new carriage wheel!

Her ostracism from the family bosom was occasioned, she supposed, by the fact that Clarice had become engaged to the Earl of Trool, Lord Alfred Mayne, at Christmas. Her shenanigans of the previous autumn were seen as a direct, though lamentable, reflection on the event. Though even Clarice admitted that had she not been stranded with the earl that afternoon in the shadow of Glen Trool she might never have looked so favorably on the possibility of the match, it did not alter matters in her father's eyes.

As the door to her room was opened by a maid, Clarette jumped to her feet from her bed, on which she was perched.

The woman who sailed in was no taller than Clarette but was

quite twice her width and triple her age. She wore black relieved by gray lace at the throat and cuffs, the first step in semimourning. Her bonnet cap of black satin with double borders of scalloped lace looked like a funeral daisy tied over her curls. Though she carried a cane, her gait was energetic. She walked right up to Clarette before lifting her lorgnette to give the younger woman a thorough perusal.

When she lowered it, she revealed an expression of exasperated surprise. *"You* are the chit who had my nephew stomping about and swearing against witches and toads?"

Clarette looked stricken. Jamie had cast her in the part of toady witch. "I'm very much afraid I am, ma'am."

"I don't believe it! You are the chit with the ruined reputation? Impossible!"

Clarette dipped her head, for once at a loss as to what was expected of her. "I beg your pardon, ma'am. 'Tis common knowledge my first Season was a disaster despite your nephew's attentions. The breaking of the engagement, I'm told, shall mark me a Tragedy."

Lady Ormsby's lips twitched. "You, dear child, are no Tragedy. If there was a mistake made, it was your father's. What could the man have been thinking to allow you to debut with that Incomparable, your sister? Your mama would never have allowed it. Happily, Lord Mayne has removed your sister from the fray. Now I think it's time *you* were properly introduced to society."

"I should abhor that," Clarette answered honestly. "The outcome would be the same. I shall be labeled a Disaster."

"A Disaster? A Tragedy? You give yourself a great deal too much consequence, dear. I've been witness to Disasters and Tragedies of mythic proportions. You do not squint like the Weatherly girl, nor do your teeth buck in the horsey manner of Lord Stilton's eldest. You do not limp, sniffle constantly, or possess numerous moles, spots, or excess hair. You are not deformed or possessed of any objectionable feature. In short, you do not qualify as even a minor Tragedy."

"I am plain," Clarette said with a quiver of emotion.

"Plain?" Elberta flicked her lorgnette into place with the snap of her wrist. "Plainness is no test of my skills. You are a merely badly styled." Her detailed perusal ended at Clarette's toes. "Your hair is dressed incorrectly, your carriage a disgrace, your complexion unmanaged, your style of clothing an abomination, your shoes, well, the less said the better."

"Yes, ma'am." Clarette had begun to smile in the midst of this cataloguing of her deficiencies.

Lady Ormsby dropped the lorgnette to dangle by its ribbon. "Sit, child. Now then," she said when Clarette was seated on the bed. "I shall endeavor to turn a worm into a butterfly. 'Tis easily accomplished. Yours is the harder part. You'll be required to follow my every instruction."

Despite her first impression, Clarette was beginning to feel that her internment with Lady Ormsby might not be such dull stuff after all. "If you believe yourself well equipped to the challenge, I shall endeavor to oblige."

Lady Ormsby's brows rose at the girl's pert tone. "There's nothing I like better than a challenge. I judge that you are accustomed to obeying no one. That, my girl, will change."

Clarette felt a prickle of trepidation as the older woman bent her eagle eye on her. It was a new experience for her, to be intimidated. She could not say she liked it, but she was stimulated by it. "Whatever you say, ma'am."

"Whatever I say, is it?" Lady Ormsby rapped her arm with her fingers. "Don't play the mealy-mouthed chit for my benefit. I've bested stronger wills than yours."

Suddenly Clarette knew why she was being sent away. She was to be ridden, broken, and tamed by the old curmudgeon before her. She stiffened, determined to give as good as she got. What else was there? Jamie was lost to her forever. She lifted her chin, challenge in her eye.

Lady Ormsby ignored the insolent glance as she smoothed a wrinkle in her skirt. She had known a few spirited souls in her time, herself being one of them. The girl was caught in a tug of her own warring wills from which she did not know how to extract herself. If someone clever did not soon take her in hand, she would break her wings in the struggle before she had even properly tried them. That would be a waste.

"I make you a wager, Miss Rollerson. If at the end of the next Season you have not received an honorable proposal, I shall beg your pardon and . . ." She glanced about her person for something to offer. Her gaze lit on the large square sapphire on the middle finger of her right hand. "My ring. 'Tis Persian."

Clarette's defiant smile dimmed. "I do not wish to marry anyone."

"But my wretchedly myopic nephew?" She chuckled. "Don't look stricken. It spoils your pose as Lady Defiant. One assumes that there was some finer feeling in you for him, since you accepted his proposal. I heard enough of his private ranting before he popped the question to know he once believed himself in love with your sister. What I want to know is why, then, did you allow him to become engaged to you?"

Clarette found the impression made by her mittens in her lap suddenly fascinating. "It would be difficult to explain."

"I'm an old woman. I have nothing but time. Explain away child. Wait!"

She sat down beside Clarette and patted the space beside her. Very reluctantly Clarette moved closer, only to be caught by the shoulders in a motherly embrace.

The older woman's smile was as sweet as her gaze was sharp. "Now then, you may tell me everything. Omit nothing."

Clarette recounted her tale, leaving out nothing that would have made her shine in a better light. In fact, the chance to confess felt quite good. For months she had hidden from those closest to her, and even herself at times, the true motivations for her actions.

"Shocking. Quite shocking," Lady Ormsby inserted calmly at intervals in Clarette's soliloquy, but she never once said what or who she thought was shocking.

Only at the end did Clarette pare her tale. After all, Lady

Ormsby's tolerance could be expected to extend only so far. Clarette knew if she admitted going into Jamie's room, she would be thought a strumpet. With unanticipated longing she suddenly wanted very badly to remain in the good graces of this remarkable woman who accepted so much with admirable aplomb.

When she ran out of words, Lady Ormsby permitted herself to say, "My nephew thinks he knows a great deal about the world, yet what he knows least is his heart."

"He seemed very certain to me," Clarette said under her breath. She would never, but never, forget how he had called out Clarice's name when it was she in his bed.

"What do you consider to be your greatest fault, child?"

Clarette was startled by the question. "Why, I suppose it would be that I am plagued by Ideas."

"Ideas?" Lady Ormsby chuckled. "Surely that is no cause for grief. Too few people have them, by my estimate."

"Mine are not just ideas, but Ideas, fits of inspiration that seem at the time to answer every need." Clarette sighed in new self-awareness. "It is only after I proceed upon them that they sometimes turn out to be, well, not very wise."

"I see. May I suppose my nephew has been victim to his share of these Ideas?"

"Yes, ma'am."

She nodded thoughtfully. "The trouble with very clever ideas is that they are most often wishful thinking, selfish thinking, if you follow. They don't serve because they are not meant to. You will learn to control them."

"Yes, ma'am."

"Which is not to say you may not have them." She found the thought she did not share very amusing. "In fact, I should like to know the next time you are taken by such an Idea."

Clarette smiled. "As it happens, I was having one earlier."

"Were you, child? And what was it?"

"That I should run away and disappear, thereby relieving everyone of the misery of my presence."

"I trust you've since discovered the fallacy in it?"

"My father would be inconsolable. My sister should blame herself, and I should only find myself in deeper trouble without the resources of my family to aid me."

"Excellent reasoning, child. Once you have learned to face the truth, however distasteful to you, you will be undeniable."

"It doesn't matter, really." She left unspoken the phrase *now that Jamie has gone away.*

"We'll review this conversation in a few months. Yet, first things first. You've been told that we shall be traveling?"

"Yes, ma'am."

The tragedian's tone spoke volumes. No doubt the girl thought she was being carted off to rusticate. Lady Ormsby grimaced as she shifted one shoulder slightly. "I'm afflicted with rheumatism. A sojourn in warmer climes than England provides is in order. We sail Monday a week for the Canary Islands."

Clarette's mouth fell open. "The Canary Islands?"

Lady Ormsby nodded, the possibility of a very lively winter unfolding in her thoughts. Her scapegrace nephew was not the only one who needed a new perspective on life. "From there we shall go to Italy."

Clarette gaped. "Italy?"

"You have nothing against the Neapolitans?"

"No, ma'am. I don't even know any."

"You will, child." A smug smile. "You will!"

Twenty-four

Porto Venere, January 1816

"Eight weeks! Damnation!"

The sound of a shattering bottle did not rouse the interest of anyone beneath the roof at Villa de Toscana, for it was a common occurrence these days. The master was continually drunk. If his mood was perceptibly worse with each day, so grew the tolerance of the residents. Yet few dared venture out after dark for fear of encountering him in the hallways which he haunted like a vengeful corporeal ghost.

Tonight he did not roam the villa. He lay in a stupor on his bed, resisting the urge to retch. He felt suffocated behind his bandages. He was afire from a fever within. His inflamed eye ached and ran as if he had been staring too long into the sun.

That thought drew mirthless laughter from him. He would have welcomed the burning intensity of the sun on his corneas, if he could but see.

He coughed, a dry, hacking sound. The cough was new, an indication that he was sickening. That thought enraged him. No wonder he was ill. His peace was shattered! He no longer found rest even at the bottom of a bottle.

Della still resided beneath his roof. For eight agonizing weeks she had remained. All because his blighted conscience had not allowed him to turn her out.

He could not believe his ears when, two days after her arrival, she had explained through the housekeeper that she wanted to remain in Italy for a time. Further, she sought *his* advice on a residence she might rent in the vicinity.

Furious, he had tried to frighten her away. He had had the housekeeper tell her stories of the bandits who roamed the hills and of the pirates who frequented port cities like Porto Venere. Rumors of an Englishwoman living alone and therefore easy prey would circulate quickly along the coast. She would end up robbed, raped, and/or murdered.

But Della, as he knew to his present disgust, was nothing if not stubborn. She had informed him in a letter that she would remain in Italy whether he helped her or not. She was no intrepid traveler. To his knowledge, she had never ventured farther than her family estate, or his. Heaven only knew how she had managed to reach Porto Venere without coming to harm.

And so he had relented, ungraciously. If, being a fool, she could not be persuaded by reason to go back to England, she must remain under his roof for as long as she was in Porto Venere.

Cursing under his breath, Rafe reached out to clutch the full bottle of wine left open and within easy reach on the bedside table. He took a long swallow that stung the rawness at the back of his throat and made him choke.

His was a wildly miscalculated gesture. Had he known what it would cost him to have Della constantly within reach, he would have preferred to submit himself to the punishment of the military lash. He had become a prisoner in his own home, condemned to hiding during the day and skulking in corners at night, afraid that she would learn his secret.

She had made the peaceful monastic life he had carved out for himself impossible. She invaded his waking thoughts with the cherished sound of her voice. The haunting scent of her perfume ambushed him from every corner of the villa, prodding to life the passion that had long lay dead within him.

Night after night he lay rigid with a desire he could never

again soothe. No torturer had ever invented a more subtle punishment.

And so he drank.

He sucked down a little more wine, burning and sweating and shivering in anguish against things that should not be and feverish dreams that must not be given life. Maybe the fever would kill him. Maybe that would be best.

"Then, at last," he muttered thickly, "I will have peace."

"Oh, my lady! There you are!" Sarah cried when she found Della kneeling in the kitchen garden, weeding the asparagus. "You must come in at once!"

Della lifted a hand to push back the wide brim of her straw hat. "What is wrong?"

"It's the *signore,* my lady." Sarah shook her head. "He's run mad, that he has! Roaming blindly about, smashing anything that comes under his hand. Roaring drunk, if you pardon my language, my lady. Only it ain't proper, the way they are trying to stop him."

Sarah rose to her feet, scattering vegetable matter from her skirts. "What do you mean?"

"The housekeeper has brought in two hands from the field, big strapping fellows, to deal with him. I don't know but what they will do him to death."

"We'll just see about that!" Della marched toward the house with Sarah close behind. As she did so, she stripped off her gloves and apron and finally her straw *cappállo di sòle* which she had bought in the village to protect her complexion from the heat of the sun.

Though she had not spoken directly to the *signore* since the night of her arrival, he had, to her astonishment, become her landlord. Yet, for all she saw of him, the *signore* might as well have been absent.

In return for his hospitality, she had set about reordering his villa. There were so many things to be done—gardens to be weeded, rooms to be cleaned and aired, and many small repairs needed doing that never would have been allowed to go unattended had the master not been blind. Though she found herself in opposition with the housekeeper at every turn, it served only to augment her determination. She needed to be needed, and this seemed little enough in payment for her host's generosity.

Not that he had in any way expressed his appreciation or even recognition of her activities. If not for the occasional sounds of him roaming the halls in the depths of the night, she might not have been certain he remained in residence.

She knew, also, that he was continually drunk. Once, when she had found his door unguarded, she had tried to enter after there was no answer to her knock. The room was occupied and the *signore* had thrown a crockery pitcher with surprising accuracy at her head, making her duck.

After that encounter she decided that he and his activities were none of her business. But if his servants sought to do him some injury, that was most definitely her business, if only as the defender of a helpless invalid.

The shouts and cries of the altercation met her long before she reached the top floor. She gained the open doorway to the room shuttered in gloom in time to see two young men wrestle their master to a standstill in the center of the floor.

Stretched between the two burly men, the *signore* in soiled shirt and breeches looked very much like a filthy scarecrow or Guy Fawkes doll, hooded head and all. He was taller and slimmer than she remembered, and though he was breathing hard behind his mummyish covering, he seemed in no way hurt by the ordeal.

"Release him this minute!" Della ordered in her best schoolroom Italian as she entered the room.

The housekeeper, who had been crouching by the doorway, struck a defiant pose before Della. "He's *pazzo, signora*. He must be tied down! If we do not protect ourselves, he will murder us in our beds!"

"Nonsense!" Della knew nothing about nursing and very lit-

tle about madmen, but she had seen more than a few drunkards
in her life. "He's not insane, merely drunk."

She stepped closer to the men but addressed only her host.
"I am sorry your servants felt it necessary to resort to these
tactics, *signore,*" she said succinctly to the man who smelled
powerfully of wine and neglect, "but you must see reason. You
will injure yourself or someone else if you do not calm yourself.
I wish only to be of service, but you must cooperate."

In answer, he swore viciously and thrashed out, nearly throw-
ing off the two men holding him as they buckled under his
alarming strength.

"*Aaaah!* Tie him! Tie him down!" the housekeeper cried from
her position of safety at the far end of the room.

"You will do no such thing!" Della countered quickly. When
the two men again held their charge firmly between them, she
reached out and snatched from him the half-empty wine bottle
he had been swinging like a mace with his left hand. "No more
of that! You will do as I say, do you understand me, *signore?*"

He did not answer, but neither did he swear or struggle this
time.

Satisfied with that, she turned to the men holding him. "You
may now release the *signore.*"

The young men's frightened glances passed from her to the
housekeeper and back. Clearly they were uncertain as to whom
they owed their allegiance.

The housekeeper swung around on Della, her black eyes narrow with indignation. "You have no rights here. No rights."

"I have every right!" Della responded, though she knew she
did not.

The woman's lips curled back over yellowed teeth. "What
you think to do for him, *signora?*"

"First of all, I intend to see to it that he is bathed, and given
fresh clothing and a decent meal before he retires to sleep off
his—his snoutful!"

She smiled at her recall of her father's colorful expression as
she thrust the half-empty wine bottle at the woman. "Now, take

this away with you and do not bring spirits of any kind in here again until the *signore* has regained his self-possession. When you do return, bring two charwomen with you. Bring also fresh linen, clean clothes for your master, a clean feather tick, and lots of hot water."

Her gaze swung in disdain around the room. "Do you think because he is blind the *signore* has no other senses? This room is a pigsty. It smells of the chamber pot! Cinders must be carted from the fireplace and those shutters open to allow in fresh air. Every inch of the floor must be swept and scrubbed. Further, you must burn every rag you collect from this chamber, bedding included."

The older woman regarded Della with a bright black glance that held equal parts amusement and admiration. "You do not know him, *signora*. He will fight."

"If he will persist in behaving like a spoiled child, I shall have no alternative but to treat him as such."

Della turned her head in her host's direction, hoping he would hear and understand her next words. "The petulance of spoiled boys must be ignored."

"He's had the fever these last days," the housekeeper warned. "Maybe you catch it too!"

"I do not believe you," Della answered quickly as the laborers started in fear.

The woman had voiced the challenge with too much glee for Della to take her seriously. No doubt she hoped to provoke the hysteria Della had displayed that first night. But that tired, pathetic creature had been put away for good.

Della turned coolly to her reluctant patient and said calmly. "I would urge you to cooperate, *signore*. I wish simply to make you more comfortable. If you only assist my effort, I promise to leave you in peace as quickly as possible. The decision is, of course, up to you."

For the space of three heartbeats Della thought she had reached through his liquor-induced stupor. But that was not to be. With a roar of profanity he convulsed in an effort to throw off his assailants.

She had never seen a man struggle so fiercely, as if he thought they were about to put him on the rack. His old injuries had, perhaps, made him a little mad, she decided, though madmen were not always dealt with as gingerly as she had proposed. If only he could have been made to understand that she was his ally.

Della gnawed her lip, determined to reveal no distress to the openly smirking housekeeper as the three heaved and fought and tussled for nearly a full minute. They played a wild game of pop the whip, careening into furniture and knocking over an oil lamp before he was again overpowered.

In the end she said nothing as the housekeeper directed them to tie the *signore* to the bed, tethering his one good arm and both legs to three of the massive, ornately carved bedposts. Only his maimed arm was allowed to be free. She had been to visit Bedlam once—a mistake she had never repeated—and seen there raving men and women who had been restrained for their own protection. The *signore* might be one of those men, but it wrenched her to see any person treated so brutally.

When he lay spread-eagle and strangely still, Della shook her head then squared her shoulders. She could not prevent this, but she could make him more comfortable. "We will now continue. He needs to be bathed. Remove his soiled clothing."

As the laborers reached for him, the patient flung his crippled free arm up protectively over his bandaged head and loosed a harrowing bellow that rose up from the depths of his soul, filling the dark, fetid room with the sounds of inhuman despair.

The cry so disturbed Della that she nearly relented. All that held her firm to her purpose was the desperate knowledge that this was not a wounded beast but a wounded man.

She stepped forward and placed a hand lightly on his shoulder. "Oh, please do not make this worse, *signore!* Lie easy, I beg you."

He went rigid but still, his arm still flung over his face. After a moment Della removed her hand and nodded at the doubtful laborers. "Be gentle," she said quietly.

They set about removing his shirt with their knives, slitting seams in it until they could strip the foul cloth with a single yank.

"Dio mio!" cried the men together as they jumped back and crossed themselves. The patient's torso was spotted with blistering sores. A few oozing scabs that had stuck to his shirt trickled blood and pus. "The pox!"

"You see!" You see!" the housekeeper called in malicious triumph as the laborers scurried past her out of the doorway. "He's got the pox, *signora!"*

"Lady Heallford!" Sarah cried, so forgetting herself as to call her mistress by her right name. "Come away! The pox!"

The cold touch of stone at her back halted Della's backward progress from the bed, a movement she had not been aware she had been making. Yet the sight of pustules was not what frightened her. What made her heart pitch up into her throat was a much more harmless ornament lying on his chest.

Supported by a thin gold chain, an oval gold locket embossed with the initials RH nestled in the tangled damp mat of his black chest hair.

She had given Rafe a locket very much like it as a keepsake when he left for the Peninsula War. Inside was an image of her painted when she was only eighteen. She had had his initials etched on the surface, just as his love, the note accompanying it said, was etched for all time on her heart.

Della stared at his shrouded face. Was it possible that this raving lunatic was the man she had once promised to love, honor, and obey?

Della launched herself away from the wall. "Out! Out! Both of you, leave me!"

She bore down on the housekeeper and Sarah with such purpose that the women hesitated only a moment before fleeing. She slammed the door shut on them, nearly catching Sarah's hem in the process, and then slid the crosspiece into place, bolting them out.

Breathing hard she leaned upon the polished planking, one
fist softly pounding out the rhythm of her panic, delaying the
dreaded moment when she must again face the man on the bed.

She cast her mind back to the nightmare of the evening of
her arrival. It had seemed then that the shrouded man was a
demon who had risen up from hell, but those were the mere
phantasms of an exhausted soul. They were nothing compared
to the very real possibility that had offered itself to her now.

Della pressed her hands to her face, covering her eyes with
her fingers. She could not bring herself to look again and confirm it. Not yet.

At the onset of this journey the reasons Rafe had not come
home to her had not weighed heavily with her. She had fought
too many battles against the cold rationale of others to yield to
the temptation that her point of view made no sense. Now she
trembled at the thought that her fondest wish might have been
granted at the very moment when she would willingly abandon
it.

A low moan from the bed sent her spinning in fresh alarm,
back pressed into the cool polished door. The shuttered dimness
left the heavy gothic bed in shadows so deep that only his re-
straints, torn from sheets, glowed faintly pearlescent in the
gloom.

She heard the bed creak as he tested them, jerking his booted
legs and anchored wrist. Did he think he was alone? Could he
not hear her knocking heart or her labored breathing? Could he
not smell her fear? Or did he not care? Was the madness in him
not of wine's making but a result of his wounds?

He yanked again and again, but though the wood groaned
and popped, the carved bedposts were at their broadest the cir-
cumference of Della's waist. Madmen were said to be inordi-
nately powerful, but Della suspected he would have needed the
power to uproot trees to free himself. Finally he stilled with a
loud groan of frustration and began pounding the bedding with
his free arm. Poor man, how he must be suffering.

She took an instinctive step toward him on feet silenced by satin slippers.

This he heard. His body went stiff as he lifted his head awkwardly from the mattress.

"Who's there?" he challenged in Italian.

"It is only I," she answered in kind, hesitating to identify herself.

He grunted, his head and body slumping back into the bed.

As she drew near the bed, she found herself studying his boots, anything to delay the moment when she must once more gaze at the golden oval hanging around his neck. The boots were Wellingtons, and though scarred and long unpolished, the quality of the leather was easily discernible.

Unbidden came the memory of Rafe once telling her that a soldier's pride could be measured by the care he took with his gear. Polished boots, a well-honed sword, and tightly sewn shiny brass buttons were more than tedious work. They represented a care for the very things upon which his life might depend.

This could not be Rafe, she told herself. Rafe had been a very proud man. A rare disloyal thought struck her. Both their lives had suffered because of his pride.

She paused an arm's span away from the bed, but her gaze was not as brave as her feet. It skipped sideways away from the man and alit upon his left boot which was missing its heel. Did that explain his limp?

"Help me," he said suddenly, again in Italian.

Her gaze twitched upward over the occupant of the bed. The long, heavy muscles of his thighs were taut beneath the grimy contours of his breeches, as if he were readying to test his strength once more against his bindings. Yet he remained no more than a shadowy presence in the depths of the bed. To see him properly, she needed light.

She moved toward the windows and lifted the sash to push the heavy green shutters open. Midday-white light sliced at a sharp angle across the bed. Blinking against the glare, she turned back to see that he had again lifted his free arm to shield his face.

Frowning, she cautiously approached him. Why should he have done that? Blind as he must be, the light could not have caused it. Was he ashamed of his appearance? Or did he have something to hide?

With that thought to bolster her, she studied him more freely, still avoiding the risky area of his throat where the locket lay. She had no fear of his particular illness. She had lived through an epidemic of smallpox as a child, and was immune. Though dirty and erupting in pox blisters, his upper body was that of a man in his prime. The lean torso lightly feathered in dark hair was undamaged by the wounds that had so afflicted his face and right arm. Even so, she realized that were this Rafe, she would not be able to recognize her own husband's body.

A fleeting memory came to her of their first and only night together. In response to her shyness he had doused the candle before undressing and coming to bed beside her.

She had been too overwhelmed by the sensual pleasure in which he had wrapped her, too amazed by her own body's un-expected response to his touch to recall details of his naked body. There were only memories of his tenderness and the firm, solid feel of him beneath her shy hands and then the weight of him bending over her yielding frame, the gentleness and then thrill of his passion, the pleasurable mastery of her body, and finally the strength and resilience of his vigor.

Della shook her head. This would not do. She had to know. Lifting her eyes a few scant inches, she sought out the golden locket.

It was no longer there. Only the thin gold chain spanned his throat.

Belatedly she realized that in his thrashing he must have caused it to slip off his chest. Bending low, she discovered it lying on the bed next to his left ear.

She had to press a knee on the bed to reach for it. He twitched his head toward her when he felt her weight. The hangman's mask of his swathed head came so close to hers that she felt his wine-infused breath and shivered, but she grabbed quickly at her prize.

The locket latch was broken; it fell open at her touch, revealing what she most feared, a tiny color miniature of herself.

She dropped it and scrambled off the bed, torn between the diametrically opposed desires to flee and to throw herself weeping upon this wreck of a man who lay so still he might be sleeping or dead.

"Why did I not listen?" she whispered raggedly. The truth had been there in Quinlan DeLacy's shadowed gaze when he brought her Rafe's letter.

Her gaze darted to his bandaged right arm that ended where a hand should begin. Of course! she thought a little wildly. The letter had not been from Rafe. DeLacy had written it! Had it been his way of trying to spare her what he knew? She had seen his reluctance when she questioned him about Rafe's death. The silent plea in his gaze had begged, "Do not ask me for the whole truth." Was this the whole truth?

She pressed a fist to her lips to keep back a cry of pain as her gaze swung wildly toward the man on the bed. Maybe she did not want the whole truth.

Calling herself sensible, she had in her darkest hours conjured up every contingency she could imagine that left Rafe alive, even those that hurt her most. She had imagined him lying wounded or out of his mind, or that he was being held prisoner for ransom, or that he was wounded and in hiding for fear of his life in the French countryside, unaware that the war was over. She had even faced the possibility that he might have fallen in love with a foreign beauty who had saved his life and would not now forsake her. In every case it meant he was alive. No matter the pain she endured with these thoughts, it seemed easier to bear than to believe that he was dead. But now . . .

She turned to stare out at the bright sunshine, focusing on the distant vistas until the glare made her eyes burn and run with tears. This was real—the day, the warmth, the olive trees and distant tile rooftops of a village, the red earth and flash of silver that betrayed a river snaking through the green valley.

Gradually she realized that she felt very calm. There was only the rush of her own blood humming though her veins to make her aware that she existed. Her natural confidence no longer directed her thoughts. It had betrayed her too often. The instinct of self-defense and survival had taken over.

The man behind her did not yet know who she was. Why not leave things as they were? The servants did not know her real name. Only Sarah knew her full purpose in coming here. She could go back to England, live out her year of mourning, and then begin her life anew with none to suspect that she knew the whole truth.

How young and foolish and self-deluded she had been not to realize before then that there were worse things than being a widow. Worse than widowhood would be to find herself burdened with a maimed and mentally afflicted husband. No, she had no heart for that.

Della released a tremulous sigh. The whole truth was worse than anything she had considered possible. Now that she knew it, could she live with it, with herself, if she simply went away and willingly joined the conspiracy's sham?

She crossed the room, opened the door, and then slammed it behind her with a fury that surprised even herself.

Twenty-five

"It's only the chicken pox, Sarah."

"Be you certain, my lady?"

"Perfectly." Della looked up from bathing her patient to the woman who hovered in the doorway. "I have seen the small-pox," she said softly, not wanting to be overheard. "The pustules are shaped differently. These are globular and milky. The fever is mild and he suffers only a little lung congestion. In the next days he will be discomforted by the rash, but it will soon disappear, leaving no scarring."

The bed suddenly trembled as if in laughter, drawing her gaze back to the man in breeches and bandages. She had spoken to Sarah in English. So far she had addressed him only in Italian. He had yet to speak a personal word to her, but she was certain he understood her. Was he capable of the kind of self-awareness that found amusement in her reference to scarring?

"You should not be bathing a strange gentleman, my lady. 'Tis not seemly. Where is the help you asked for?" Sarah questioned as she edged into the room.

"I could not reason with them." Della turned back to continue her gentle scrubbing of his ribs. "There is putrid fever in the next valley, the housekeeper says. The laborers fear for their lives. They will not be back for days."

"As well you might see a lesson in that," Sarah scolded. "Here, I will do that, if you insist it be done."

"Oh, no, I wouldn't dream of abandoning my patient," Della

said in a deceptively sweet voice. "I shall see to his complete care myself."

"Very well, my lady, if you insist. But I shall remain all the same. For the sake of propriety." Sarah did not miss the glint of anger in her mistress's handsome dark eyes. Something had happened, but she knew too little about the matter in total to put together the particulars. Belatedly, she realized that another alarming change had occurred. "You've released him, my lady."

"I have," Della answered matter-of-factly. "I should hate it if I had been trussed up like a chicken. Now let me concentrate on my patient."

Della saw Sarah's sharp glance out of the corner of her eye, but ignored it. No one was more astonished than she that she had returned to this room.

It had taken only the time required for water to boil, which the housekeeper fetched in, for her to realize that she could not leave him. Though he had not wanted her to know he was alive, she did now know it. She could not turn her back on that unassailable fact. She had once loved him, still loved the man he had been. She could not bear to see him in such pathetic circumstances. Though he need never be certain of who she was if she were careful, *she* knew she was his wife. When she left him, it would be into the care of someone far superior to the servants who now inhabited this villa.

She had been shocked at his state of neglect. It had taken several basins of fresh water to remove the heavy coating of grime on his upper body. She lathered now his good hand, taking a personal satisfaction in cleaning his nails and then paring them with the toilette utensils she had brought in from her room for this purpose. She had never known the intimacy of ordinary touches with Rafe. She had once daydreamed of learning him so well that she could recognize him by the shape of his hands, or even his feet. By the time she was finished drying his hand, she felt she knew it very well. It was a strong, square-palmed hand with long, lean fingers shadowed at the first knuckles by fine black hair. She unconsciously squeezed it briefly before placing it on the bed. If he noticed, he made no reaction.

Yet when she reached for his right arm, he jerked it free of her touch.

"See here, *signore*," she said sternly in Italian. "I can see that you've suffered a grievous wound, but even that must be kept clean. If you do not do so, it may eventually suffer a festering that will cost you the rest of the limb."

This news seemed to galvanize him. He swung his arm toward her and just missed smacking her in the chest. "I shall be careful, but you must be very still," she warned as she took his arm firmly in one hand and applied her scissors to the wrapping.

To her relief, the wound had not been allowed to heal unattended. She had seen many veterans of the wars against Napoleon begging on the streets of London. Often their wounds were infected or healing improperly. This wound at least had seen a doctor's care and been neatly stitched shut to heal a single smooth ridge of tissue. Oh, but what agony he must have suffered in the loss.

Instinctively she closed her fingers over the stump, saying, "Why do you wrap it? It is not hideous."

In answer, he turned his head away.

Sarah helped Della remove his boots. Sarah said nothing, but clucked her tongue in disapproval of the stench that was released. Without a word they each picked up a boot and tossed it out the window onto the veranda below. Then each took a foot to clean.

To preserve his dignity, Sarah lay a cloth over his loins before they removed his breeches. They were both surprised when he suddenly sat up and took the cloth from Della's hand. "Out!" It was the first word he had spoken, but the quiet authority in it made both women retreat to the far corner of the room while he finished his own ablutions.

The housekeeper appeared with fresh linens, but spitefully turned her back and left when Della asked for fresh clothing for her master. Settling on the covering of the sheet, Della evaded the matter.

When there was nothing left to wash but his face, Della turned to Sarah and said, "You may leave us now."

The older woman gave her a long, piercing glance, but said nothing, tactfully closing the door behind herself.

Della's hands shook as she poured clean hot water into the bowl. "At least I will know with certainty that this is Rafe," she said under her breath as she brought the bowl to the bedside.

With scissors in hand she leaned over to lift the edge of his bandage, which began under the right side of his chin. His left hand immediately snaked out and caught her wrist in a tight grip.

Della bit her lip to keep from letting him know he hurt her. "I must clean your face, *signore,* and you are most desperately in need of a shave."

"No."

"You must have been your mother's chief torment when you were a boy," she replied with a lightheartedness she did not feel. "You deserve no better than that a razor be wielded by an inexperienced hand." She shook her arm to try to release his grasp. "And if I should make a mistake, will it really matter?" She was appalled the moment the words left her mouth. How could she have said—

He laughed, a dry, husky, hollow sound, but genuine laughter nonetheless. To her amazement he released her wrist. "If I were a wiser man, I would have spared you . . . this."

Della froze as his words echoed in her thoughts. He knew who she was! He had paraphrased his last letter to her. Had he known from the beginning?

She clenched her jaw against every contingence of ugliness she could imagine that lay beneath his bandages. Snipping very carefully through the layers of linen, beginning at his chin, she peeled them back very slowly. At first she uncovered only the black forest of his months-old black beard. It was surprisingly thick and resilient, curling about and clinging to her fingers as she worked. Finally she was able to slit the bindings that held the masklike galea in place and then, as he lifted his head, she removed with infinite care the last of the wrappings from his face.

She closed her eyes briefly to steady herself and then opened them.

It was not as awful as she had imagined.

He had turned his damaged side from her. The left side of his face was achingly and unfalteringly familiar—the high, clear forehead; the markedly arched black eyebrow; the beak of a nose; and the lean cheek. The skin above his beard was unusually pale, almost translucent from lack of sunlight. His eye, closed by matted black lashes, failed to reveal its topaz depths. Gazing at his perfect left profile she might have thought him merely asleep.

Tenderly, she cupped his bearded chin and turned his face, despite his resistance, toward her.

A long red seam snaked down from his hairline on the right side, cutting through one proudly arched black brow, across the ruined sinkhole of what had been his right eye, and gouging deep into his right cheek. A doctor's stitches had left thin crosshatch marks in places where it had been necessary to pull flesh together. It was a horrible disfigurement, but not the nightmarish atrocity she had been expecting.

Something she had not expected happened. Her heart burst open, flooding her with love and pity and relief and such tenderness that she moaned against the enormity of it all. "Oh, my dear, your poor face."

Hearing her reaction, he lifted his left hand and hooked it across the right side of his face.

"No, please don't," she said in a gust of breath. She reached out and drew his protective hand away. Faintly surprised, she noticed that he flinched when she moved so that the sunlight fully struck his face. "It is a bad scar, but it is not what I—well, it is not afflicting. When it has healed a little more and the discoloring fades, it shall be—well enough."

He said nothing, but his hand closed very tightly over hers.

"You must, of course, have an eye patch. I recommend a black silk one. I've always thought there was a piratical flair about you." She heard herself babbling but could not stop. "Very dashing. Mark my words, that's what the ladies will say behind their fans."

She saw the quiver at the edge of his mouth, and it broke her heart. "Have you allowed no one else to see you?"

He did not answer, but she thought the shuddering passage of his breath through his lips was answer enough. He had not known how he looked, had never allowed anyone else to help him. Perhaps his wounds had been worse than they appeared now that they were mostly healed. Or perhaps it was impossible for him to gauge what he could not see.

"It will be fine," she assured him, though she was not at all certain what she—or what he—would do next.

She touched his good cheek and he flinched away. Then she bent over and very gently placed a kiss on his good eye.

His muscles tensed under her hand, then quivered under great duress of his self-control, and the hot splash of a tear slipped from between his lashes and under her lips.

"This is impossible!" Rafe pushed back from the dinner table with his glass of wine in hand. "I am maimed. Useless. Less than a man. What kind of husband can I be to you?"

"The usual sort, I imagine," Della answered calmly from her place opposite him. "You can continue to drink too much as Lord Farthingale does, roar at everything and everyone who displeases you just as Lord Eastling does, and generally do as you please, which seems to be the prerogative of all noble husbands."

In answer, he threw his wineglass in the direction of the fireplace. She did not flinch this time, having in the last week almost become accustomed to his frequent tantrums. Sarah, however, had been banished by him to take her meals in her room.

He had not secluded himself since the day, three weeks earlier, she had discovered who he was. Yet it might have been better if he had. It was not that he was difficult to look at. Quite the contrary. Once his rash healed, she had trimmed back his beard to a even black pelt and cut his hair so that it dipped carelessly over his right brow, shielding a good part of the scar: simple things that dramatically altered his image. The eye patch she had fashioned from a black silk petticoat gave him the distinguished if not romantic flare she promised. In short, he was still a handsome man despite his pinned right cuff. What worried and frightened her was that when he left his room for meals, or rarely to sit in the sunshine, he was always drunk.

"I cannot even cut my meat," he muttered in disgust.

"We could eat only meat pies and soups and things you can eat with your fingers."

"I am blind!"

Are you? she wondered not for the first time these last days.

He pretended to see nothing, though his left eye opened and closed normally. Yet, when he thought she did not notice, he often stared intently in her direction. When they were out in the sunlight, she had even seen him turn his head to follow her as she walked around the garden. Perhaps he could not see well, but he could see something, she would swear to it. Why was he hiding that from her? And why would he not let her touch him? The one time she had reached out to him in tenderness, threading fingers though his thick black hair, he had knocked her hand away and shouted, "Never do that again!"

Della shook her head, mastering her misgivings. He needed time. She could not begin to imagine what he must have suffered. Yet she did wish he would share it, anything of himself, with her. "Would you care to try the cheese? The housekeeper bought it this afternoon."

He said nothing for a moment, only sat staring into nothingness. "I would prefer another glass and more wine."

"You might at least try—"

"Damn you! I want wine!" So saying, he swept out his right hand and knocked his plate from the table to the floor. The clatter of silver and china bought the housekeeper in, her gaze openly derisive. She bent and began picking up the pieces.

"More wine!" Rafe cried when he realized she had entered.

"Sì, signore." With a parting glance of triumph at Della, she hurried out.

"Is this really how you intend to spend the rest of your evening?" Della asked in exasperation.

"Yes."

The word left no room for argument. Della tossed her napkin on the table and rose. "Then you shan't require my presence for that."

"At last, enlightenment."

The accusation brought her up short. "What did you say?"

"You must realize that I don't require your presence for any reason. Why are you here?" He jerked his head to the right, as if he had belatedly realized that she was no longer opposite him but heading down the right side of the table toward him. "Why do you stay? You have bearded the lion in his den. You have ferreted out all my secrets. Now that you have them, why don't you leave me in peace!"

"I—I don't know," Della said in a tight voice as she paused within an arm's length of him. She longed to reach out to him, but she did not dare. "Perhaps it's because I remember what you do not. You were once an honest, courageous, proud man."

He shot to his feet, oversetting his chair, and with uncanny accuracy grabbed her by the wrist. "Open your eyes, madame, and see what is clear even to me. I am a blind, afflicted sot!"

"You are my husband," she whispered.

"I am no husband to you!"

She dared not contradict him, but she did reach up and touch the fingers of her free hand to his coat in the region of his heart. Through the cloth she felt it beat strongly.

He jerked her in close by her wrist until the warmth of his

breath fanned her lips and the heat of his body penetrated her
silk bodice. His eyelid fell shut, and for one wild moment she
thought he would kiss her. Then his fingers tightened cruelly
around her wrist, causing the skin to burn.

His eye flew open, staring out beyond her shoulder. "What
are you wearing?"

"A rose-colored gown, my lord."

"No! The scent!"

"Roses."

"I hate roses!" He tossed her arm back at her, releasing her
so abruptly, she stumbled back. "Go and wash it off and never
wear it again in my presence."

"No." Della cradled her aching wrist in her other hand, more
insulted than hurt. "If you have no wish to be my husband, then
you can have no say in what I do or what I wear or where I
go." But her anger would carry her only so far. When he swept
out his hand again, just missing snatching at the curl that lay
against her right breast, she quickly stepped back.

"So you do fear me!" She saw him smile but it was the
coldest expression she had ever seen on his face. "You have
cause. Now leave me."

Provoking him was not wise. She knew it, but she, too, had
been pushed too far. "Not before I give you my gift."

She saw his expression change from rage to curiosity so
quickly, it was almost comical. "What gift?"

Della moved back toward her end of the table. She had hoped
he would sense her surprise on his own. She picked up the
crystal vase brimming with flowers and brought them toward
him. When she reached him, she lifted them to his face.

He lifted his head like a dog catching a scent in the wind.
"Flowers!" he scoffed after a moment.

"Not just flowers," she answered with a smile. "They are
roses from the gardens at Heallford Hall. I preserved them last
summer against your return, for I never really believed you were
dead. Not even after Lord Kearney brought your letter." There
was a suspicious quiver in her voice, but she continued. "Now

they are blooming here in Italy in celebration just for us. Do you not remember what day this is? It is our first anniversary."

She thought she saw the haughtiness drop for an instant from his face. It vanished almost at once.

In one swift, unexpected move he lashed out and knocked the gift from her hands.

Della gave a little cry as the crystal flew away from her grasping fingers and then dropped like a lead weight, shattering on the tiles and sending needle-sharp shards of glass in all directions, even into the hem of her gown.

"Leave me!"

She looked down at the shattered crystal and trampled roses, seeing not them but her heart. Then she looked up at him and saw the absolute blankness of his stare. "How could you!" she cried in an emotion-torn voice. "That was unforgivable. Such lovely roses!"

"Della!"

Sick at heart, she did not notice that the step he made toward her as she turned away had a beseeching not threatening quality to it.

"Thank God!" Rafe muttered when at last he heard the door close behind her. He could not have stood another moment of her presence without breaking his resolve to let her go. He had wanted to make her angry or frighten her, do anything that would make her quit his house and get out of his life forever. She was shredding his soul with her tenderness. Did she not understand he would not be able to keep away from her?

"Roses!" She had preserved them for him. What a pitifully sweet thing for her to do. So, she had not thought he was dead, even after . . .

He had wondered whether Quinlan was to be trusted. He had set him an awful task. Now he knew his letter had been delivered. And yet she had continued to believe he was alive.

Bitterness cut the beauty from his smile. Once her unwavering loyalty would have meant everything to him. Now it was only a troubling obstacle to be overcome. Somehow, incredibly, she had found him. He suspected Quinlan's hand in that. The lie he had been forced by friendship to carry out would not have abided easily with him. Yet even that did not matter. Della must go. He would not burden her with his afflictions. He did not want her to play nursemaid, wasting her life while she led him by the hand, cutting his meat, and pouring his wine.

How valiantly she tried to ignore his ugliness while her beauty danced like a flame in and out of his distorted vision.

She did not know that he could see her.

Sometimes, when the light was just right, she appeared like a dream, whole and perfect for his view. But she must never know. He would not take her beauty and squander it. He would be ruthless in order to do her a kindness.

But sometimes, as when the scent of roses warmed with the spiciness of her own skin's fragrance wound itself about him, the absurd desire moved within him to clasp her to him and beg her to stay with him.

His hand flexed into a fist. Absurd. Ridiculous. Impossible.

He bent down and felt among the glass shards for roses until he had found and picked up every one of them. She must go. Tonight. Her abiding presence would make sticking to his conviction impossible.

"Impossible!" he muttered as he breathed deeply of the fragile, bruised blossoms.

Twenty-six

He waited until he was certain she was in bed.

He waited until he had drunk a good deal more.

He waited until the night was so deep that he could no longer see the tantalizing silhouettes of things that had come to haunt his waking hours.

He waited until he was once more what he had been for months, a blind shadow lurching like the hint of a nightmare at the vision of other mortals.

He waited until he was a wraith, a ghost of things past, an insubstantial reminder of what could never be.

The room smelled of roses.

One set of shutters lay open to a black sky quilted with starlight.

He moved to stand beside her bed as he had done nearly every night during the past two months. While she slept he stood guard against his own desire.

He scattered a few rose petals very carefully about her sleeping form. The remainder he had pressed between the leaves of a book to keep as comfort for the rest of his blighted life.

When she awoke she could make of the gesture what she liked. He hoped this sign of his presence in her room while she slept so trustingly would disturb her and prime her urge to flee.

He had been wrong to think he had lost his humanity on the

battlefield. He had been wrong to think he could bear to have her beneath his roof and not be with her. He was much too painfully aware of life in her presence.

She made him want things. She made him want to touch, to hold, to laugh. She made him want a future, one in which he would kiss her mouth and watch their children swell her belly. She made him want life with all its painful yearnings, happiness, and sorrows. Drink could not kill those impulses, though he had tried mightily to drown them. The desire to live throbbed like a canker in the region of his heart.

He felt what he could not see, her eyes opening with alert attention to the presence of another.

She did not move or speak for so long, he began to wonder if his senses were deceiving him. Only her slightly quickened breath disclosed that she no longer slept. He wondered what she was thinking. He could smell her, the roses, and the cool spice of apprehension. He did not detect the odor of fear, yet he caught the sharp tang of sweat. Then he realized that it was his own.

"Why are you here?"

The sound of her voice made him want to weep. "To tell you that I have arranged for a coach to fetch you and your companion in the morning."

"You're sending me away?"

Fool! It had been a mistake to come here! "Yes."

He sensed her struggle with the urge to argue or plead. Her pride held her in good stead. "Where is this coach taking me?"

"Anywhere you'd like." He took a step back from the bed as she sat up, panicked beyond reason by the shadow she presented to his returning sight. "At the harbor you can board the sloop back to Marseille. From there you should undertake to travel by private coach to Paris and then to London."

More silence. Why was she so silent? Della had never been at a loss for words. He wanted to grab and shake her, to force her to utter the panic and sorrow and despair locked up inside him.

"I don't know that I'm ready to leave Italy."

How young she sounded, and uncertain. Perhaps the silence was better.

"I should like to see Florence, perhaps even Naples." Her voice was strangely hesitant, as if she were substituting each word for another thought.

"Whatever pleases you, as long as you are gone from here tomorrow."

More silence. He began to shake. Could she see his vibrating silhouette in the darkness? Dear God! Why had he come here?

"If that is all," he said in a tone of dismissal, and took a step backward.

"No."

The word halted him. If only she would cry or shout at him, he could roar in rage at her and they would both find a kind of cathartic release from this immobilizing pain.

Della bit her lip. Her cheeks were stiff with dried tears from the fit of weeping she had given in to after quitting the dining hall. A great crack had opened inside her with the shattering of that crystal vase, and from it leaked in precious droplets her belief in herself and in him.

One could not love enough for two. Once she had fearlessly held the world at bay because she believed he loved her. Without that . . .

He was sending her away. It was the only rational thing to do. They both knew that. She did not belong here. He was no longer the man she had loved for twelve long years.

She could escape the truth. If she walked away, he would never come after her to cast doubt on whatever happiness she might find away from there. Better than a parliamentary divorce was this offer to live a perfect lie.

"Well?" he asked sharply.

"You made me a promise. I can bear everything but a broken promise."

"What?" He sounded fully as surprised as she by her words. "If you mean the marriage contract, consider it null and void."

"That is nothing to me!" Her voice was suddenly fierce. "I mean your private promise. I have it right here." She reached under her pillow and pulled out the well-worn letter that smelled of rose perfume and her body's oils. She held it out to him, though she doubted he could see it. "This is your promise to me."

"What is it?" he asked suspiciously.

She opened the paper. Though it was too dark to see, she did not need to read the lines, she could recite them by heart.

Sweet wife,

You are right to wonder at my silence, for it would seem to bear ominous tidings. Be assured, the fault is not yours, gentlest of hearts. The disquiet that burdens my soul and reduces me to silence is of my own making.

Tonight, as I prepare for battle, I feel the breath of mortality upon me and believe I shall not long be among the living. Let me then be quick to the purpose before my courage fails me.

Despite all evidence to the contrary, believe this to be true. In all my wretched life I have loved none but you!

Too brief our union! Too long the years of separation! Have I left it unsaid too long? Have I forfeited our chance for happiness? The possibility distracts me from all purpose, and I am ashamed. I beg you forgive the folly of a man too proud for his own good.

Do not be sad for me. Seek your full portion of happiness with another, dearest one, with my blessing. Yet believe: Had I lived, you should never have regretted wedding me.

" 'Had I lived, you should never have regretted wedding me,' " she repeated slowly, letting the sound of her voice fill the quiet, velvety darkness.

Rafe held his breath. He could not answer that.

"I believed those words. I still do," she added.

"I lied." His voice sounded strangled, disembodied.

"I do not believe you. You have shared little enough of your feelings with me, yet you never lie. You could not have set down those words had you not meant them."

"Meant them? I never even wrote them." Yes! That was the antidote. He was fighting for his life, for her life. "Lord Kearney composed the piece for me. He is good, is he not? A man with sentimental phrases for all occasions."

Della searched the darkness until she found him, a tall shadow sharper than the surrounding night. "Lord Kearney swore to me these words came from you."

He heard in her voice a plea to spare her illusions, but he made an impatient gesture. "You are easily fooled."

"Am I?"

"You believed I lived because you wanted to believe. That is not steadfastness and loyalty. That is selfish, childish fancy!" He spat out the words at her, furious that she had not let him slip away. "You've never listened to reason! Not from your family and friends! Not even from me!"

Silence. Heartbeats. The scent of roses.

"If I did not listen to them, it is because I believed you . . . cared for me." *As I love you,* she left unspoken.

Rafe swallowed bitter memory. "One cannot live in the past. That way lies madness."

"You—-you've lost your nerve!"

He jerked as if she had struck him.

"Yes, I call you coward. If you were dead, I could forgive you. But this?" She rose up on her knees on the bed. "This hiding away is the action of a small boy who's skinned his knee and doesn't want anyone to see his tears of self-pity! 'Tis unworthy of you. The man I married would not have put me to such grief as I have known these last months."

"The man you married is dead!" As that cannonade echoed through the room, a swallow swooped passed the window, its delta shadow sailing briefly across the starlit floor.

He heard the bed creak as she shifted. "Have your feelings truly changed?"

The pitiful question left him precious little room to maneuver. "Only one portion of that letter expressed my true feelings. 'Seek your full portion of happiness with another, dearest one, with my blessing.' "

"That is what you want? That I should marry another?"

"Yes."

The word burned like acid in Della's mind. She had fought everyone in her life; now she was matched against the man she loved. She had no heart for it. In the calm rational center of herself she had faced a stark truth weeks before. She knew she could walk away and, no matter the present pain, there would begin a healing. But not for Rafe. If she left him, she would be abandoning him to this living death he had chosen for himself. "How will you live?"

"By charity."

Della sighed. "Then you will need an allowance."

"I need nothing from you. The house is Kearney's. He's deeded it to me for my lifetime. I do not want your dowry. I will not touch it if you are so foolish as to send it."

"I see." It took everything not to cry. "Then you have everything you need."

"Everything I want."

"Yes, of course." In a small voice she asked, "Then why are you still standing there?"

"Damn you!" He swore low and viciously. "Do you want to hear it from me?" His silhouette loomed suddenly before the open window, betraying the billow of shirtsleeves and tight breeches hugging lean hips. "Do you need to hear that I crave the touch of your silky-soft skin to assuage my revulsion of my own frightful countenance?"

"It is not fright—"

His arm swung out, repelling her words. "Do you need to know that my palms itch to touch you? Both palms!" He lifted his handless arm as if he could see it. "Strange, isn't it, to want to touch with what is not there? Even my phantom hand seeks to touch your beauty." He held it out toward the bed. "Does that not please you?"

"Don't be—"

"Be what? Indelicate? Truthful?"

"Bitter," she whispered.

"Why not? You drive me mad and yet you would have me be all kindness to my tormentor."

Della scrambled to the foot of the bed. "I don't mean to torment you." She reached out a hand to him. "I want—"

"Don't!" He jerked back as if he thought his only avenue of escape might lie through the window. "Don't even think it. You don't know what you want. I was never real to you. You dreamed me up, Della. I can count on my remaining hand the number of months we spent together these past twelve years and have fingers left over! Do you hear me? You do not know who I am."

"You are my husband."

He groaned. A knife through his heart would have been easier to bear than this simple defense. "I would be your damnation."

"Show me."

"What?"

"I want to taste the sulphur of damnation on your lips. Singe my soul and let me embrace your hell so that I may understand it."

He blinked. For an instant she came into perfect focus, a shapely feminine silhouette kneeling in a scanty night rail. "I have not said I am indifferent." How odd his voice sounded in his ears, abashed, subdued. "I am a man, after all, if only the wreck of one."

"So then, you cannot do it?"

He knew at once where her thoughts had gone. She was thinking of their wedding night, when he had tried to resist her and failed.

Part of him, the part that did not wish her at the devil, admired her ability to maneuver in a fight. She was a formidable foe in a battle he wanted desperately to lose. No, he must win!

"You will get nothing but my lust. Any man can empty his seed into a comely woman."

"I did not ask for that. Only a kiss."

He took a warning step toward the bed. "You will get what I give you!"

It infuriated him that she slipped off the bed to meet him as he moved in on her. It rankled his male pride that she so confidently threw her arms around his neck before he even embraced her. It lit the fuse of his anger that she tilted her mouth to his with the smug assurance of victory.

He caught her about her waist with his right arm and took her chin in the fingers of his left hand. He squeezed her jaw cruelly as his mouth sought hers. This was no lover's kiss. He ground his mouth, open and wet, insultingly against her.

She gasped and tried to pull free, but he was not nearly ready to let her go. This was what she had asked for. He tugged at her lower lip with his teeth, then nipped and sucked at it. Then he thrust his tongue deep into her mouth, plundering its silky, wet warmth with rapacious force. She fought him, pushing and beating fists on his shoulders, wanting her freedom. She had asked for a view of his hell, and he did not want to disappoint her.

He lifted her enough to force her backward to the bed, and then he pushed her away so quickly that she fell with a cry onto the mattress. He moved forward quickly to trap her legs between his knees. He pushed his hand into the middle of her chest to pin her as he lifted her gown with his stump.

She was breathing hard and making little sounds of protest, but she was not screaming at him or begging him to stop. And that is what he wanted; it was all that would stop him.

He lifted his hand from her chest, running it with a slow, loving caress down her rib cage to her naked waist, which he had exposed, and then ever so fleetingly, over the swell of her bare hip. She felt like silk and velvet and his last wish on earth.

He bent and kissed her navel, tasted salt from the tears on

her cheeks, and wondered even as he backed away from her why he thought this was a battle he could win.

"I cannot fight you any longer!" His breath was dragged, distorted by emotions over which he no longer had perfect control. He swung around, arms splayed against his own passions. "I hate you for this!"

"I love you too," she whispered.

She dared too much for a man shaken out of his self-possession.

Once more he was leaning over her, his mouth against hers. This time no anger fueled his kiss, only a fatalistic surrender to the inevitable as she wrapped her arms tightly about his neck.

He kissed her long and slowly, savoring every nuance of the senses he brought to bear in the darkness. He stroked her swollen lips with his tongue and gently sucked the sweetness from her mouth. For only the second time in his life he tasted pure desire and knew he must possess it or die.

Her response was immediate and surprising. She clung to him and kissed whatever part of him she could reach, the side of his hand holding her face to his, the silk of his beard, the furrowed scar in his right cheek. She struggled with his clothing and buffeted his frustrated curses with caresses that made her bolder and him more frantic.

He made love to her as though he were fighting a battle. He moaned and groaned and held her too tightly. His thrusts were like blows and yet it could not last. The rhythm of outrage altered quite of its own accord to match his dry gasps of tears. One moment he was grinding against her, the next he was carrying her along. His curses changed to whispers of need and desire and sorrow and pleasure and pleas for forgiveness.

She went with him, caught in the same flood of emotions where the dark, whirling sea of love and sorrow, desire and regret, surged and blended and raced out over the edge of the world.

As he poured his seed into her, she broke open her heart to receive his gift of love.

"We will live to regret this," he said in a quieter moment.

She put a hand to his mouth. "We will not."

He pulled her too tightly against him. "Promise me!"

She turned onto her side, bringing their bodies once more into harmonious alignment. "I promise."

They had had too little time together for memory to outweigh the wonder of each other as they found new ways to seal their oath.

Twenty-seven

Quinlan paced the length of the palazzo's anteroom with an impatient stride. He knew the exact number of black and white marble lozenges that paved the length of the eighty-foot gallery because he had strolled it often during the past four weeks. Today alone he had measured the distance three times in the past hour. There were few things in life he detested more than waiting. To his consternation, he had discovered that tardiness was Kathleen Geraldine's greatest fault.

He had discovered other things as well. She was a brilliant conversationalist who with great skill could debate the merits of Chaucer or Swift, as well as Dante, Byron, and Shelley. Her insights into his own work intrigued and flattered him. She often turned passionate when engaged in debate, yet she never hinted at anything other than scholarly interest in him. Then again, when he held forth on some topic, the rapture in her unwavering green gaze was enough to stir his emotions long into the night. She was as enamored of him as he of her. Why would she not admit it?

He could not decide whether it was his own eagerness to be with her or the fact that she so plainly did not harbor an equal eagerness to be with him that fueled his growing impatience with her. She never, he noticed, kept Francapelli waiting. He envied the uncomplicated attachment between them. The count often served as buffer and distraction between their own more restrained relationship. But Francapelli was away today, gone to Milan to audition sopranos for his new opera.

"This is preposterous!" Quinlan looked up the long, wide staircase unfurling from the second floor and made a decision. He was tired of playing the oh-so-patient swain who should feel that his life was complete because his ladylove had deigned to glance his way. He was weary of the attempt to win her trust. He wanted to show her how much he cared.

"Care be damned!" he muttered as he began his ascent. Despite his resolve, his chivalry was shriveling under the blazing heat of emotions no longer quite in his control.

It was delicious! Outrageous! When the truth was out, he would become fair sport for his gentlemen friends. So be it. A woman whom he had scarcely kissed had stolen his heart. To him, of all people, had come love.

Love was an entirely new experience for him. He was not at all certain how to behave under its impetus. Yet he knew something had to be done.

He did not know precisely where Kathleen's rooms lay, but he had watched her descend from the left branch of the stairway often enough to suspect they lay in that direction.

In the end it was quite easy to find her. The sounds of a woman's teasing voice and gentle laughter drew him down the airy hallway to the open doors at the end of the passage.

They were alone. Mother and child sat in a high-backed chair bathed in the exquisite light of the Italian afternoon pouring through the archway of the veranda. Kathleen's fiery hair was tied back from her face with a simple ribbon at the nape. Her pale blue gown was unfastened in the back and hung from her shoulders, exposing one fully rounded breast. Pressed to her flesh was a head full of loosely hooked sooty curls.

As Quinlan paused in the doorway, he saw one tiny pink hand reach up and clutch greedily at the summit of her mother's full breast while the suckling sounds of contentment came softly to him on the breeze.

". . . you are, *bella bambina!*" he heard Kathleen say in a lilting voice as she bent to kiss the dark head. "Always and forever, *cushla-ma-chree.*"

Once he would have laughed at this prosaic tableau of domestic bliss. Certainly, Kathleen's behavior would be considered *de trop* by the *ton*. But an unexpected wistfulness held his amusement in check. He would have denied it if asked, but the sight of motherly nurturing touched him.

He could not say his own mother had held him in so intimate an embrace. In fact, he was certain she had not. Like most aristocratic children, he had been given to a wet nurse at birth. As much as he could recall, no person had ever cradled him as compassionately as Kathleen held her daughter, cooing to her in an eclectic mixture of English, Irish, and even Italian.

He felt a little guilty spying on them, but he could not bring himself to go away. His gaze moved to Kathleen's profile and lingered. Its gentle contours had become as familiar as his own. A companion to his thoughts and torment of his dreams, she was never long out of his mind. He did not yet know precisely what he was going to do about his feelings for her. But he had a very good idea that whatever it was, it would infinitely complicate his life.

She looked up suddenly and smiled. "Ah, Viscount." Her face was flush, but not from embarrassment. Her gaze was softened by an expression he had never before seen there. But it was not for him.

"We had an engagement, Contessa."

"Did we? I'd forgotten."

It struck him in that tender place containing his ego that she was not sorry or concerned that she had forgotten their outing.

He came uninvited onto the terrace lavishly adorned with flowers and small potted trees. "I am not accustomed to upsets and disruptions in my plans," he said with an incivility for which he could not account. Usually he behaved most pleasantly when he was most annoyed.

"That is because you are an aristocrat," she responded without heat. "You expect upsets and disruptions to be borne by those who must alter their lives to please you." She looked down at her child and cooed softly before saying, "In this place, Grainne rules the day."

He swallowed an arrogant rebuttal to her setdown. She liked to point out that he was a lord while she was mere gentry, and Irish at that. Why did it never seem to occur to her that his lofty position should influence her to curb her opinions? If her pride of place were laid down alongside his highborn arrogance, he did not doubt arrogance would fall short.

"There is still time to enjoy the festival at the harbor."

"I must decline." She smiled at some private thought. If only she had smiled at him, he would have been mollified. "Grainne is teething and that has made her fretful."

Quinlan gazed at the head of black curls nestled against the full curve of her mother's breast, and envied the tot. "She seems perfectly fine to me. We need not be gone long." He put the full persuasion of his seductive voice into the next words. "I have a surprise for you."

She lifted eyes to his, a bemused expression on her face that had nothing to do with his presence. "What did you say?"

Indignation flared his nostrils. She was so wrapped up in the child in her arms that he might have been a fly for all the attention she gave him. It seemed he had found his competition.

Curious, he moved in close to her chair to inspect his rival for her affections. Wrapped in a shawl so fine it seemed little more than spiderwebbing was the infant of unremarkable size. "So that is she."

Kathleen lifted her daughter upright and turned her to face him. "Is she not the most beautiful child in the world?"

"So you might believe, madame," he said blandly.

The babe had a squarish face, rounded at the corners, blue eyes the size of sovereigns, and a pursed pink mouth. His brows rose imperiously. He could not have picked her out from a dozen others of similar coloring.

But then she hiccuped, which widened her eyes and produced

a great gurgling smile, and Quinlan felt his heart jump. "What a taking little thing! I do believe she likes me!"

"Wind," Kathleen countered calmly, and lifted a napkin to tap at her child's milk-marbled lips. Grainne yawned so widely it closed her eyes. When they opened, she discovered her fist dancing before her face. Mouth opening like a fish after a worm, she lunged forward, making sucking noises as she tried to jam it knuckles-first into her mouth.

"Are you still hungry, *acushla!*" Kathleen resettled her child and brushed her milky nipple against the babe's cheek. Grainne turned her head automatically toward her mother's breast and latched on.

Quinlan tried to pretend that conversing while she nursed her child was an everyday occurrence in both their lives. In fact, this was the first time he had ever been allowed to set eyes on Kathleen's daughter. But when, after only a few sucks Grainne released her hold with a sigh of contentment and closed her eyes, Quinlan found himself staring at her mother's bare breast tipped by a long, dusty pink nipple.

The sight aroused him, powerfully and wonderfully. It also reminded him of how little their relationship had progressed these past weeks. The pearly luster of her skin begged his caress, yet he had never touched her. He had not even kissed her since he found her again.

With the exacting honesty that made his wit his greatest weapon, he realized that here he stood in full rut while she treated him with the calm indifference of a brother, no, a eunuch.

He was accustomed to charming women, to bringing them to swoons by the power of his words alone and to ecstasy with the mastery of his touch. This could not continue.

He was sleeping badly and writing long into the night just to keep thoughts of her at bay. In consequence, he had finished one play and begun another. Frustration might be stimulating his muse, but, he noted with droll self-awareness, it was cutting up his peace of mind and ruining the line of his breeches!

He had never been denied anything he wanted as badly as he wanted her. He did not mean to be gainsaid, even by a babe.

As if she could divine his seething thoughts, Kathleen looked up, her eyes wide with a question he knew only one way to answer. He bent over and kissed her.

Her lips were soft and moist, her breath warm and sweet in his mouth. His lids fell shut. He seldom closed his eyes when he kissed a woman. Always the connoisseur, he judged by a woman's expression if and how much she was responding. But with Kathleen he was more caught up in his own reactions.

One kiss and he was erect with need. One kiss and his belly quivered. One kiss and he could have taken her then and there on the floor. It was not the fact of his arousal, but the nature of the desire that took him aback.

He felt a strange sensation flow over him as he lifted his mouth from hers and found himself afloat in the green sea of her gaze. Desire gazed back at him, and the wonder was that he knew his longing matched hers. The covetous urge to hold and secure redoubled. He did not want only to take her to bed, but to take her away from every possible distraction. He wanted to make love to her until every memory before that moment was erased. Then he would tell her how much and how deeply he loved her.

His gaze lowered to her naked breast with his hand following, but the gesture was never completed. He spied pinned in the lining of her gown a gentleman's ring. The Lissey baronial crest was unmistakable.

She looked down in the direction of his gaze, then reached to quickly pull her bodice closed. With a deliberate lack of emotion she said, "So now you know everything."

"You might have confided in me before." Her refusal to answer did not silence him this time. "I should have advised you that possession of the Lissey baronial ring would be considered by his peers as proof of his alliance with you. Grainne's marked dark looks should seal your claim to part of Pettigrew's personal estate. After all, he died without wife or other issue."

She looked up at him in absolute resolution. "I thought of that. I doubted they'd have a use for Lord Pettigrew's pregnant mistress. Yet I feared they might try to take my child from me once it was born. There'd have been none to take my side against them."

"You may trust me always to take your part. If you wish, I will write them in your behalf." It was an extraordinary thing to witness the sudden leap of gratitude in her gaze and in response to feel so utterly struck by the very emotion he had once dismissed.

He wanted to kiss her again, but she stood up abruptly. "I've no need of their charity now. Please hold Grainne."

It seemed to him that the dozing babe was thrust at him with all the ceremony of passing a sack of meal. Taken aback, he found himself in awkward possession of a squirming bundle in swaddling. His hands seemed too large for the task, his arms too long and angular. The hard planes of his masculine chest offered a poor substitute for the generous bolster of her mother's ripe bosom. He glanced at her in appeal for help. "I know nothing about nurslings. I've never even held a babe before."

Kathleen flicked a glance at him as she pulled her bodice back up on her shoulders. "Don't drop her. That is all that is required."

"Exactly." With much trepidation Quinlan finally managed to maneuver the babe's head in the crook of his right elbow and then tucked his left hand under her bottom for support. With a broad smile he looked across at Kathleen, expecting praise, but he was disappointed.

Her gaze was cool and mocking. "I think I will join you after all. If you will excuse me, I must dress."

"What of Grainne?" he called in alarm, for she was walking away.

When she turned back, her gaze held a twinkle of mischief of the Old Sod. "Ah, well, I'll be ringing for the maid. You may hold the babe till then. That is, if you've no better thing to occupy you."

He might know nothing of babies, but he did have the presence of mind to know no man would get far with a mother whose child he did not praise. "Certainly. She's no trouble. I shall be more than content in Grainne's company, if you trust her to my care."

"Trust has nothing to do with it," she said philosophically. "If you are not to her liking, she will cry."

Too often, Quinlan mused in irritation, she managed to put him in the wrong. "Ten minutes, Contessa. I will wait only ten minutes more."

"That should be sufficient," she answered, and disappeared through the open door.

Far from mollified, Quinlan peered down into the small face tucked in his arm. Black lashes fanned twin crescents on her cheeks. Her nose seemed merely a hint of what a real nose should be. But the mark of Errol Pettigrew was unmistakable. Only her mouth, deep pink and lips pursed, reminded him of her mother.

"You and I are not as much strangers as your mother may suppose, little one," he murmured with a rueful smile. "I knew your papa well. He was a wicked wastrel, yet he made a fine friend. When you are older, I shall tell you how he saved my life at Waterloo. But first we must strike a bargain. We both seek your mother's affection. If she will have me, what say we share?"

Grainne opened dream-weighted eyes at the unfamiliar sound of his voice. He was not at all certain she awakened enough to see him, but the smile that twitched into being on the uneven pulleys of her plump cheeks nourished his conceit that she did.

Each time she went out into the city, Kathleen drank in with awe the permanent spectacle that was Naples. Nearly any excuse served for a feast day. Today was one such occasion, and so she concentrated on its delightful distractions with single-minded vigilance. Any excuse served to keep her mind off the seductively handsome man by her side who, by a single kiss, had offered a challenge she was not certain she dared meet.

They had arrived late in the day, when the Corso was a sea of divertissements. She stood awhile where a wooden stage had been erected and laughed at Pulcinella, who was having a quarrel with a monkey. Early on she listened to a peddler extolling the virtues of his nostrums, said to cure everything from baldness and infertility to constipation and gout. She studiously admired jugglers and mimes, dancers and street singers. As afternoon passed into evening, she lost herself in a perusal of stalls selling locally manufactured silk stockings, soap, tortoiseshell snuffboxes, marble tables, and ornamental furniture. She gave in to raptures over Naples's finest artworks; porcelain and *presepio,* the elaborately carved, painted, and gilded Nativity displays long famous throughout Europe.

Later they wandered through farmers' stalls, where she gazed wonderingly at the polished vegetables, raisins, melons, and figs piled high in the attractive displays demanded by Neopolitan shoppers. Fish were displayed on layers of green leaves. Rock lobster, oysters, clams, and small mussels each had their own baskets. In butchers' stalls, quarters of beef, veal, and mutton were strung up; their unfatty parts, heavily gilded, made her gape. In others, long paternosters of gilded sausages were held up by red ribbons, and capons had little red flags stuck in their rumps.

At dusk she admired the people, who were dressed in bright colors of scarlet and royal blue, in velvets and satins, gold lace and feathers and jewels, more jewels than might be found at a reception at Whitehall. Dressed for the carnival that would last well into the night, some wore masks and others nearly nothing at all. Priests and nuns, lawyers in black cloaks, provided a study in contrasts with the flocks of footmen in full livery mixing among the crowds who paraded along the seashore. Splendidly decorated carriages pulled by as many as six and eight horses each sought to outdazzle her with their presentation. In the bay, boats had formed a parallel parade to rival the one onshore.

And yet, when the sun had set and the night revelry began, the spectacle of Naples was no match for the man beside her. The mere impatient flicker of a finger was enough to draw her undivided attention. She suspected she could draw his hands, so often had she gazed at them during the last few hours in order to keep from looking directly at him.

Torches were lit to hold back the encroaching night. Each time they passed under one, the glow illuminated DeLacy's profile and gilded his light brown hair. Each time he spoke she was caught with the exquisite beauty of his voice. When they accidentally touched, she wanted to weep in frustration. Resistance was hopeless. She ached with the yearning of pure desire each time she gazed at him. He had kissed her once that day. When would he do so again?

For nearly a month she had made every attempt to match his cool mockery and sophisticated reserve. Though she suspected it was only a veneer for his blatant sexuality, he kept such an icy control over himself, she did not know what to make of his marked yet reserved attention. The suspense was driving her to distraction. She cried nearly every time he took leave of her, always unkissed. She thought about him constantly when he was away, and when she was with him she was miserable. How could he be so calm, so indifferent, so maddeningly attractive? It was all so very unfair.

Only two days ago Francapelli had thrown up his hands in disgust with the situation. Only the English, he exclaimed, would tie up their feelings in a mass of aching confusion in order to avoid a little healthy lust!

Francapelli had suggested she seduce DeLacy and then allow the future to take care of itself. "What will be, will be," he had said with a carefree confidence she could not afford to share. There was Grainne and her future to consider. But as important were her own feelings.

She had fallen in love with Quinlan DeLacy when his character was only words in a book and his face mere lines on a page. How much more potent was the man himself! Familiarity had not turned the color of his eyes ordinary. His perfect façade did not wither or wear thin with repeated viewing. She found his company more stimulating than any imaginary conversation she had ever invented. She could not be nonchalant in her actions toward him. The longing went far deeper than mere lust and infatuation. Her attraction to Lord Pettigrew had been only a fraction of what she felt for the man walking beside her. Better to suffer in silence. If he spurned her advances, she would die.

As they reached the end of the pier, a sumptuously decorated barge lit by a dozen torches and rowed by four strong men moved in close to shore before them. Amid the velvet squabs at the boat's center lounged a dark-eyed young woman gowned in a wrapping of tissue gold. Her long, heavy dark hair had been artfully arranged with flowers to enhance her languid pose. Her face was impassive, her gaze indifferent. Yet when she spied Quinlan she lifted both hands to her bodice and divided it to her waist, giving him an unrestricted view of her considerable charms. Then she offered him a slow, seductive smile that transformed her from a cool, lovely work of art into a sultry flesh-and-blood beauty as she sailed on past.

"What a beautiful lady," Kathleen declared without resentment, though she did not miss the dilated interest in Quinlan's eyes. "I confess I am struck constantly by the sloe-eyed beauty of the city's people. If I were told it was a crime to be ill-favored in Naples, I should believe it."

Quinlan regarded her with a skeptic's amusement. "Naples is notorious for its abundance of charming, willing young virgins and equally attractive, biddable young men.".

The pleasure on her face dimmed a little along with her smile. Had he been sampling those charms when he was not with her? "So I have heard."

"Heard only, Contessa? This is Naples. Here people are expected to freely partake of all that is presented to them, especially one another. I would have thought Francapelli would have apprised you of the city's reputation, particularly its more notorious one."

Kathleen licked her lips self-consciously. His lazy, lidded gaze had never been quite so amused. "Why should you suppose that?"

He did not alter a line of his expression, yet she was aware of a sudden alertness within him before he leaned forward and placed his mouth on hers. His actions drew catcalls and ribald oaths from the citizens who noticed, but there was no room for embarrassment in her.

This was no gallant's salute, but a sensual offering of lip and tongue. The glamour of his slow, sensuous kiss stunned her senses. Yet even as she reached out to touch him, he leaned back, his mouth shining with the gloss of hers. The frisson when their gazes met curled her toes inside her slippers. Never but never had she been kissed like this. But why here, why now?

"Why did you do that?"

He laughed softly and brushed his thumb across her lower lip. "You seemed to require kissing."

Kathleen glanced away from his lavish smile, her cheeks stinging. He wanted her! The lust that made other men appear foolish or distasteful polished to perfection his chiseled face and made tempests of his eyes. She felt she could bask in that glow of his desire all her life.

His hand moved and touched her face again, this time to draw back a strand of hair that the breeze had raked onto her cheek. His finger remained to trace a circle on her cheek. "Come with me."

She frowned "Come where?"

His eyes held with new intensity to her own. "To my bed."

She meant to smile, but suddenly she was bordering on tears. She looked away, staring at the torchlight reflected off the bay. Oh, what was a woman supposed to do when she had fallen in love with a man like him?

The shouts had not caught their attention, for the day had been full of noise and bands and haggling cries. But suddenly they were stunned by an explosion and then the night was shattered by a shower of tiny firelit stars.

Kathleen glanced up, dazzled by her first sight of fireworks.

The crowd roared and sighed, offered a smattering of applause, yet the sounds of its approval were cut short. Something ugly and dangerous hissed through the knot of people to her left. Exclamations in Italian followed by a piercing cry.

Even as she jerked her gaze away from the darkening heavens, an eerie momentary hush fell, puckering her skin with apprehension. She glanced toward Quinlan, but he was no longer beside her. Two men to her left had drawn knives with blades that glinted wickedly in the torchlight. One man lunged toward the other as the silence was shattered by a half-dozen shrieks punctuated by the hiss of new rockets climbing the sky.

She had never witnessed a riot, but she knew instantly what was about to happen. Panic swept the crowd like a wildfire whipped up by the winds. Little knots of scuffling broke out at the fringes of the original fray. Against the glare of fireworks, every detail of the nightmare unfolding was kindled or silhouetted. Frightened or irate, people shifted and surged toward and away from the altercations, screaming and pushing and shoving. Zigzag streaks of fire lit the night as more rockets were launched and burst into patterns against the darkened sky.

Suddenly she was firmly gripped from behind, an arm about her waist. "Come! Quickly! This way."

Quinlan swung her around, and then with a firm grip on her wrist began pulling her along behind him. His stride was quick and purposeful, but not panicked. Sensing his authority amid the general chaos, the crowd fell away before him, aided by the occasional stiff-armed shove on his part.

Shaken and trembling, Kathleen ran and stumbled to keep up, angling her body to squeeze through the passage he provided but which quickly closed in his wake. Someone stepped on her foot. She lost a shoe. Yet he did not let her fall or falter, and gradually elation outdistanced her first fears. She sensed she could not be harmed as long as she was with him. Buoyed by that irrational confidence, she went sailing along behind him like a kite attached by his string.

Once away from the harbor, he did not slow their pace but wove a path in and out of a warren of narrow, winding streets that opened into little strangely empty piazzas.

When at last he paused in a deserted cobblestone square and turned to her with smiling eyes and laughing mouth, she was laughing and shaking as well. For a moment there was only the two of them in the world, and it was enough.

He gave her wrist a tug and she tumbled into his waiting arms. No attempt was made to seduce or beguile her. She tasted passion pure and bracing on his lips. When he set her back on her heels she knew the despair of a truth no longer denied. She was foolish enough to gamble her future again on her love for this man.

He stepped back toward the narrow staircase of the building behind him but held out his hand. "Come with me.

Kathleen blinked and cast a doubtful gaze about the unfamiliar piazza. "Where are we?"

He turned back to her. "The *pensione* where I have rooms."

Kathleen looked up at him, a flutter of apprehension vying with the vast aching throb of her love for him. "What about Grainne?"

"I will send word to the palazzo." He looked down at her with tenderness and pity. "You know she will be well cared for."

She stared at him with a flush feeling of triumph marred only by a trace of disappointment. It seemed this was the only sure method to rid herself once and for all of this witless yearning, to ease this wretched desire for him. "If this is your wish, I will come with you."

"No." He shook his head. "Come with me because you cannot stay away, or don't come at all."

Because she could not stay away. His words contained a challenge, a dare, a warning, and an escape. Pettigrew had offered her no escape from her foolish passion. But Quinlan DeLacy was another man. He would not force her, take away the decision or the responsibility for the next hour.

She knew she should go, should flee with her heart intact.

She held out her hand.

Twenty-eight

He took the wine from her hand and set it aside. "Are you feeling better?"

Kathleen nodded. "I cannot account for it. I was not so afraid in the street. But now . . ." She held out her still-trembling hands before her. " 'Tis such a foolish thing to happen, collapsing on the stairs."

Quinlan checked the impulse to suggest that it was not only the riot but her decision to come with him that had frightened her into a half-swoon. Her lips were still a trifle pale and her cheeks matched her white gown. " 'Tis an excess of spirit only, Contessa."

She gazed across at him, her mouth a little tight. "I'm not a contessa. I'm plain Kathleen Geraldine."

Shadows cast by the candlelight danced in his light eyes. "Never plain, Caitlin."

"Why do you call me that?"

"Is that not Irish for Kathleen?"

"Aye, it is. But none but my father ever called me by it."

"If you don't wish me to—"

"No." Embarrassment spread her smile. "I like it fine."

He almost felt sorry for her. She had been quaking by the time they reached his quarters on the third floor. Though he had wanted so much to pick her up and carry her straight to his bed, he had not lost all his finesse in the frenzy of first love. She needed time to recover her self-possession. Instead, he had spread the sea of pillows from his exotically styled Turkish bed onto the floor before the open doors that led to a small balcony. This is where they sat drinking wine.

"More wine?"

"No, thank you. I cannot drink much of it without becoming quite giddy."

That might be useful, Quinlan thought, but contented himself with a long sip of his own. She was like a violin whose strings were too tight. When he glanced over, he noticed she was fidgeting with the set of tiny ribbons that held closed her bodice. "Are you too warm?"

"Oh, no." She dropped her hand guiltily.

"Afraid?" he suggested as he leaned closer and braced himself with an arm.

"I—well, I suppose." Her smile flickered uncertainly.

He touched a knuckle to her cheek, amazed anyone could be so soft. "You are free to leave."

She looked down at her lap and shook her head.

Quinlan frowned. This was not the Kathleen Geraldine he knew. She seemed ready to make some sacrifice, but that was not at all what he wanted. He wanted her passion, as eagerly offered as taken.

His hand moved to smoothe the silky skin along her jawline. "I have news. I am leaving Italy shortly."

Her chin bumped his fingers as her head swung toward him. The alarm in her gaze was quite gratifying. Yet all she said was "Ah."

He skimmed fingers down her throat to where her pulse beat a little rapidly. "I've finished a new play. I should like you to read it before I take it to London."

"Certainly." What had happened to her voice? It sounded caught in her chest. Or perhaps it was just that she had turned away from him again. "If you'd like me to look at it now—"

"No." He lifted his hand away from her. Sweet, silly creature. He had not brought her there to play editor. "Now I want you to look at me."

For a moment she did not move at all. In the distance beyond her shoulder he saw Naples shimmering, bound by golden necklaces of fire produced by the masses of torchbearers threading through the streets.

"Caitlin?"

When she turned and met his eyes he wondered if she knew that her destiny was written in her vivid gaze. It had been there from the first day, that sudden recognition of each other. He had felt the frisson, had responded to the attraction at once more subtle and direct than mere lust. Her gaze, as now, was for him alone. Another time he would make her reveal its origin.

"What do you suppose are the chances for love in one's lifetime?"

The question took Kathleen by surprise. It was the kind of philosophical question she had once dreamed of debating with him. But now it seemed a trap. What did he expect in answer? The tender amusement in his green eyes was not helpful. She wanted to amaze him, to astonish him with her wit. But her irreverent Irish humor had gone wandering away down the pike. "I cannot say."

"Indeed?" He tugged at the ribbon at her nape holding her hair in place. "Have you never been in love?"

He was so close, she could smell the tart, fruity wine on his breath. She had little doubt that he was as aware of her every breath. After all, he had brought her there to seduce. Why, then, should he care whether or not she had ever been in love?

Pride. Of course! She had heard Francapelli's friends chatting about feats of seduction when they assumed her thoughts were otherwise occupied. It must be a male trait. Men liked to keep scores and records, like bankers and accountants. No doubt, he wanted to know about Grainne's father. But her answer served her feelings for him. "Yes."

He tossed her ribbon away, and reaching up with both hands shook her hair loose so it formed a tangled veil of curls about her shoulders and back. "And was it wonderful?"

"It was . . . unexpected and . . ."

He hooked a curl with his forefinger and tested its resilience. "And?"

"Difficult."

He leaned in close to her and kissed the curl lying on the summit of her shoulder. "And?"

"Unpredictable."

"Love in your lexicon sounds like an ill wind."

"That too, I suppose."

"Strange." He shifted his head to lay his cheek against hers, and she felt the pleasant scratch of his hours' old beard. How nicely he smelled, like sunshine. "Did none of your finer feelings come into it, Caitlin?"

"Of course." She swallowed as his hand found her waist and Then slid up to lie just below the fullness of her left breast. "But the joy and tenderness are inconsequential to the randomness of the choice."

He brushed dry lips against her ear to whisper, "Then you regret your choice in matters of love?"

Kathleen turned her cheek away from his. She tried to concentrate on her thoughts, but all she could think of was that he was going away, to London.

His lips strayed down from her ear to the side of her neck, leaving the faint impression of his breath on her skin. "Yes?"

She closed her eyes against the gentleness of his touch. What had he asked her? Oh, yes, choices. "I do not think we choose to love, only to accept or deny the fact of it."

His hand moved up to frame the underside of her breast as he buried his face in the side of her neck. "How curiously you speak of love. Young ladies usually speak of it as something that can be won by posies and poetry or a graceful showing on the dance floor."

"Young ladies of your acquaintance do not share my experience," she said with quiet dignity.

For a moment longer there was the heat of his lips and breath and hand on her, and the chill of forewarned loss.

Then he lifted his head to look at her. "How do you think of love?"

She met his gaze behind a veil of graceful privacy. "As a treachery in the blood."

"Ah." Quinlan wanted to kiss away the tremble of her lower lip, to assuage every hurt she had ever known. "Has the experience of love ruined your life?"

"Yes. And no." Her sudden smile pleased him. "To be truthful, I cannot say no. I have Grainne."

He pulled her toward him by the waist and lifted his other arm to bring her within the circle of his embrace. When her head lay still if not easily against his shoulder, he smiled. "Aren't you curious?"

"About what?"

"About how I would answer that question."

"Yes, of course."

He chuckled. "Your enthusiasm overwhelms me. I will answer anyway. I am known among my friends to be invulnerable to the emotion people call love. I have always suspected that the word was a mere repository for every kind of sentiment men and women attach to the fleeting yearnings that come with desire. At best it seemed a very selfish and self-serving emotion."

She tried to lift her head, but his hand held it anchored to his shoulder. His smiled absently as he inhaled the fragrance of her hair, something he had wanted to do for months. She smelled of lemons and softer scents of femininity.

How warm he was, and solid. She felt she could sink right down into his warmth and strength, hand over if only for the night her burden of loneliness. But she resisted the urge. If she softened even for an instant, the world would be too difficult a place to bear when he was gone. She had come with him to exorcise her demons, not surrender to them. She clutched at straws. "You do not believe in love?"

"Rather, call me an agnostic. For you see, I've never before been in love."

"Oh."

This time he did not stop her when she lifted her head to look at him. His smile, so near she had only to stretch her neck to kiss him, was achingly tender. As she gazed into his face with its fine features and seductive gaze, she wondered how she was supposed to survive after this night with him.

Forcing herself away from the temptation of his mouth, she sat up. She would not give in so easily to love a second time. This time she would keep a little of her own self tucked away. In a bargain, something was gained and lost on both sides.

"I've come here tonight because I want to be with you," she said with an honesty that set her cheeks aflame. "But this night, 'tis all I have to offer you."

Quinlan knew what she was doing, and he admired her for it. Integrity was one of her most endearing qualities, though he wished at times that it were not quite so pompous a virtue. "Have I asked for more?"

"No, but I thought you should know that I won't be, can't be, your mistress."

"I see." He lay a finger on the first ribbon in the row on her bodice. "Is there anything else I should know."

"Yes." She looked down at his hand, fingers knotting into the loops of the ribbon to pull them free. "I am no longer unblemished."

It took three heartbeats for Quinlan to catch her exact meaning. "Ah." The ribbon slipped free of its knot. "The rigors of motherhood."

She nodded her head. "I thought you should know."

He placed a hand over her right breast, fingers resting on the bare swell above her neckline. "I am a man of some experience. That being the case, do you not think your fears are misplaced?"

"I did not think of that." She glanced up shyly at him, able to believe to a too-generous degree the number of women who must have willingly spread themselves beneath him. *"Oh!"* His thumb had found her nipple beneath the thin muslin of her gown.

"Come to bed with me, Caitlin. Let me show you how you deserve to be loved. Let me pleasure you. Let me show you the pleasure that can be shared."

She longed to push back the lock of hair that fell across his brow, to touch him lovingly and be held lovingly. But that was all. Why did men demand this surrender that was more pain than pleasure? "What if you cannot please me?"

Had she not, Quinlan wondered, ever been touched by passion? Gazing into her eyes, into green currents shadowed by doubt, he wanted very much that she should learn that lesson from him.

He reached up and snared her chin with his fingers and leaned in close to lay his lips on hers. He dragged his slightly open lips back and forth across hers until they began to tingle and then he moved away from that tempting surface to kiss her cheekbones and then her eyelids. There was no need to rush, no hurry. He had time. He had nothing but time, and he wanted to make it right for her.

Finally he brought his mouth back to hers and licked first her upper lip and then her lower. He felt her shiver, her fingers reach out for and tighten on his arms, and knew she was fighting some latent sense of fear. Had Pettigrew coaxed her to complacency only to violate that trust with violence?

Kathleen shuddered as he pulled her closer. She shivered as he lifted her upper lip with the tip of his tongue and slid it behind. The rough swipe of it along her teeth and sensitive lining made her moan.

He withdrew slightly and was pleased that she continued to lean toward him, eyes closed and lips raised in offering. He touched her kiss-drenched lips with a finger. "Now then, tell me you feel nothing."

She opened her eyes. "I feel afire inside," she whispered, abashed.

He laughed in relief. "Come here."

He settled her across his lap, her head cradled in the crook of his left arm. He bent his head and kissed her again. His fingers trailed over her cheek, caressed her brow, smoothing through the fine hair at her temples, curved about her head, played in the swirls of her ear and then came back to her cheek.

All the while he kissed her softly, gently, with just the surface of his lips. And then he pressed a finger at the corner of her mouth, breaking the seal of her closed lips, and he kissed her more deeply. He found the open seam and plied it with his tongue until she was sighing and her lips opened wider. He stroked her hidden tongue with the tip of his, coaxing and encouraging it to participation. He taught her slowly, patiently, how to respond until her tongue slipped out to lick his upper lip. He held still until she did it again. And then he sucked hers into his mouth. He tugged and stroked the tip of her tongue with a mating rhythm until she was sighing and kneading his shoulders with her hands.

Kathleen did not feel him loosening her gown, nor did she realize that he had found the way through her chemise and stays until his palm, shockingly warm, closed over her naked breast.

She shivered, liking his touch, so different from the grabbing, pinching—no! She would not remember. Think only of now, she told herself, only of this one perfect night, when she held and was held by the only man she would ever love.

She turned into his caress and pressed her hot face into his sleeve, wishing she knew how to offer back a little of the pleasant feeling he gave her.

"Caitlin?" he whispered teasingly into her hair.

"What?" she murmured into the crease between his sleeve and armpit.

His fingers formed over and tenderly tugged her exposed nipple. She moaned and squirmed against him. "Am I hurting you, love?"

How, solicitous he sounded and not the least amused. She rolled her head on his arm in denial.

"Then why, *acushla,* are you hiding?" Reluctantly she turned her head to gaze up at him, her eyes wide and her cheeks colored the pale glare of candlelight russet. "That's better."

He kissed her hard and briefly before he lifted her up. She realized why he did this as her gown slipped from her shoulders to her waist. She reached for it, but his hands were in her way, drawing her up by the waist onto her knees before him.

He had a magician's skill with clothing, she decided in faint panic as her gown and undergarments slipped from her hips to pool about her knees. For a moment she knelt before him in the starlight, her arms crossed self-consciously but not effectively before her.

He reached up and gently but firmly pried her arms apart to hang by her sides. He saw her eyes close and her expression tighten. Did she expect he would be unkind, or was this a reflection of some remembered pain? Her vulnerability touched and amazed him. She had a great deal of spirit. She had been betrayed by her lover, had endured her father's death shortly thereafter, been left penniless to bear and raise her bastard child, and never once had she quailed before him, yet this was somehow more difficult for her. He put his arms around her to hide her nakedness from herself. He felt her shake, heard the tiny moan of self-pity she would have denied, and fell in love with her all over again.

His hand never leaving her body, he shifted her down on the pillows. His hand caressed ever so slowly, lovingly, down her front, lifting the fullness of a breast, stroking her flank, riding the inner curve at her waist, then brushing a salute over the slight mound of her belly before delving into the flaming curls below. And then he lifted his hand away.

Her mouth twisted with an emotion he could not guess at, but then her eyes opened and she lay staring up at him, still and childlike, not daring to speak.

"You are exquisite, Caitlin." He bent toward her, his hair brushing her cheek as he kissed her softly.

He rose and quickly stripped off his clothing, ruthlessly shoving shirt and jacket off together with his breeches to follow.

Kathleen watched, astonished by his sleek-muscled beauty

shining in the starlight. How fitting that his face should not be the best part of him. And then he stepped from his breeches.

Her gasp caught at his thoughts and twitched his head toward her. "Have you never seen a man before?"

She leaned up on an elbow, her expression flattened by the lack of light. "I did not look."

The simple statement told him more than she knew.

He stood back into the meager light falling through the window. "Then look your fill, Caitlin."

She did, and when she was done she said, " 'Tis wondrous proud, my lord."

" 'Tis wondrous impressed by your beauty, Contessa."

She smiled and then lifted her arms to him.

He looked down at her a moment longer and then joined her on the pillows.

He worked her beautifully with his hands and mouth. He kissed her everywhere, finding and plying just the right places. With the pressure of his fingers he teased and then retreated so that her whole body shuddered in need and desire. She had not expected, had not thought—she had no words, no realm of comparison for the sensations coursing through her like a swarm of bees in flight. What he was doing to her was magic, surely nothing less than his own special brand of magic.

"Enough, love?"

She opened lust-drugged eyes and whispered, "What?"

He laughed in satisfaction. "Never mind. Just enjoy. This is for you, my love. Take all you want of it. My gift to you."

Kathleen wanted to believe him. Staring up into his gorgeous face with its lean lines and lips glistening with the sheen of his loving, she wondered how many women had capitulated to the tempest in his eyes.

"Do you want me, Caitlin? You must say so. I will not force you."

"I—do."

He shook his head slightly. "That is resignation. Do not be

afraid of the passion you feel. You are its mistress, it will obey you. What is your desire?"

She looked up at him and wondered if, like him, her soul was reflected in her eyes. "That you make love to me."

"I will make love *with* you."

She smiled. "Yes."

"Yes?" he teased, smiling down into the clear green sea of her eyes.

The distraction of his beauty was no longer a veil for the man beneath, this man whom she had fallen in love with long before she knew him as flesh and blood. And now, now she knew she would never love another the same. No matter what.

"Oh, yes."

He dipped his head and applied himself to suckling first one then the other of her full, swollen breasts, tasting the proof of her recent motherhood, until she was arching under him in an unconscious attempt to offer what he was loving so thoroughly.

He came into her carefully, lifting and wrapping her legs about his hips as he entered her inch by precious inch. She was sleek and ready, hot and yielding, and he sank into her with the perfect expression of his need. She said nothing, but clung to him, nails pressing crescent shapes into his shoulder blades. When he filled her completely, he wrapped his arms tightly around her and buried his head in her hair. And then he began moving against her.

Kathleen kept her eyes tightly shut and her arms locked around him, and waited. But her body was wiser than her memory. This was different. She began to move with him, pressing up to meet his thrusts again and again. His breath came harshly in her ear, and her own came in gasps until she began to shudder and he shuddered, and she smiled.

Much later, she still held him, held on as if she could keep him with her for the rest of life. He had tricked her! This was worse than before. Oh, life was unfair!

Quinlan heard the sob she could not hide. He lifted up to

look at her, smoothing perspiration—or was it tears—from her cheek. "Why the sudden sadness, love?"

"I don't want the moment to end." She sounded bereft as she clutched at his shoulders. "I don't even want to breathe."

He understood far better than she could imagine. If she had just discovered her first bliss, he had just discovered the treachery of her first love. "Then you are not disappointed, Caitlin?"

She gazed up at him with passion-darkened eyes. " 'Tis somewhat difficult to describe my feelings, my lord. Yet they were not unpleasant."

"You've a remarkable capacity for understatement." He kissed the tip of her nose, then rolled his hip against her thigh so that the evidence of his renewing arousal came to her attention. "Now then, you will not be so reluctant to submit a second time?"

" 'Twas never a reluctance, my lord." She was surprised to hear her own laughter. " 'Twas more a—hesitation before the unknown."

"How well you put it. But you, for me, were the unknown as well."

She shook her head, suddenly serious again. "Don't tease me. You've bedded dozens."

He caught her face between his hands. "But never you, Caitlin." He spread a possessive hand across her breast and then smoothed a damp curl back from her nipple. *"We've* never been lovers. This is new and wondrous and precious to both of us."

They made love again, and the glory of it was with them and in them, skin to skin, until all his doubts and her past memories were mere shadows of things being forgotten.

Twenty-nine

Kathleen stroked shy fingers over the back of his hand as she leaned upon his chest. Candlelight exaggerated the fact that his skin was darker than hers and lightly fuzzed with golden hair. Most surprising, the knuckles were flecked with small white scars. "How does a viscount come to have so battered a hand," she asked in genuine interest.

"Every officer who wields a sword bears scars." He yawned and stretched under her and the silk comforter he had pulled up over them on the bed. "The fewer the number, the better the pupil."

He said it lightly, but her gaze came up to his and remained. "Were you wounded at Waterloo, my lord?"

"I was," he answered carefully. It was the middle of the night, but Kathleen was nothing if not unpredictable. After dozing only an hour, she had awakened with an enormous appetite which he had attempted to sate with more wine, figs, cold chicken, and grapes taken from the *pensione's* kitchen.

"I ask because I have wondered how it was for Lord Pettigrew to die in battle." She looked away to pluck one of the grapes remaining on the dish balanced on the bed beside them.

"He died a quick and honorable death. He had just saved my life." Her glance was so penetrating, he needed to know its source. "Did you love him very much?"

She shook her head, surprising him. "I did not ever love him. In the end I did not even like him."

"Because he forced himself on you?"

She bit her lip. " 'Twas my own silly fault for believing the blathering of a man who saw me for the silly girl I was."

"Men can be cruel when lust drives them," he said quietly.

"Then I think he must have made a fine soldier, for he could not be turned away once set to his purpose."

"He was your first lover?"

Again her glance arrowed through him. "He was my only lover. The once. Pity, isn't it, how one slip can be enough?"

"It is regrettable." Had he not, after all, taken the painful memory from her? "May I ask again why you keep his ring?"

Kathleen nodded. "You've the right. Now." Her smile was a little sadder than before, almost embarrassed. "It's a reminder of a mistake I hoped never to repeat." She lifted a challenge with her gaze. "What else do you wish to know?"

Quinlan had wished for more time, but he knew that if he ducked this moment, she would remember it later and doubt his motives ever after. He wanted her trust. He had to risk telling her the truth.

He brushed a hand across her cheek, wanting yet knowing he could not forever spare her this. "I doubt there's little you can tell me I don't already knew about the character of Errol Pettigrew"

Kathleen's cheeks flamed. "You knew about me? About the babe?"

"And the letter he sent you. I wrote it." She went so still, he wondered if this was how Lot had felt when he discovered his wife had become a pillar of salt. But she was not salt. She rose from his chest, uncaring now that she bared herself to the waist for his view. "You wrote the letter." It was not a question.

"I wrote many letters for soldiers. It was what I did to pass the time. They called me The Quill."

"I don't believe it!" she whispered, the color stricken from her lovely face. She made a soft strangling sound and edged back off the bed. Before he could guess what she was doing, she had snatched up her gown and was digging about in the bodice. She came up with a ragged piece of paper.

Tossing her gown away, she came back to the bed but did not climb back on it. She held out the missive. "Did you write this?"

He took it from her though there was no need. He opened it, scanned it with a wince, and then looked up. "I did."

She looked as hurt as if he struck her. Then she grabbed up the quilt, baring him even as she covered herself. "How could you write something so vile?"

He kept his voice low as he sat up and casually reached for a pillow to cover his half-aroused state. "When he told us—"

"Us?" she whispered in a horrible voice.

"He told several friends he'd gotten a woman with child. He wouldn't say who you were." The look of incredulity on her face chastened him. "When he asked me to write a letter jilting her, I agreed."

"Why?"

He lowered his gaze. "It was pure arrogance on my part. I was intrigued by the dramatic possibilities." He lifted his eyes as she made a movement of denial. "That is no excuse, I know. I was puffed up by my own consequence and self-importance. It was a game to me to wonder how a pregnant young woman might react to the news of her abandonment."

"I hope *Fortune's Fool* enlightened you," she suggested so sweetly, he blushed.

"Lord, yes!" Her character had tried three times to kill herself. "Did you—"

"No. 'Twould have been cowardly not to see the matter through." Her voice lost none of it frostiness as she added, "Yet it made for good drama, do you not agree?"

His admiration of her redoubled. "Your play was a scathing indictment of my own ineptitude and willful blindness. You exposed the letter as nothing more than what it was, a vile attempt to destroy whatever tender feelings a woman might have held toward her seducer."

"You achieved that part amazingly well."

He saw her lower lip quiver, and something twisted in his gut. He had never before felt this connection with another. In hurting her, he was hurting himself. He longed to spare them both. but he knew she needed honesty from him even if he might lose her because of it.

"What I did was loathsome. If it is any consolation to you, I had drunk myself to numbness before I wrote it."

"I thought so!" she whispered in fury. "Though I thought it was Lord Pettigrew's guilty drunkenness that crabbed the handwriting. So then, did you show it to Lord Pettigrew and share a laugh at the poor little slut's expense?"

Quinlan's expression lost a little of its humility. "If anyone else dared call you a slut, I should strike him or her for it."

"Oh, I see. You will take the high ground with my character now that you have unburdened your conscience. Well, who was it who discredited me with accusations of my treacherous wiles, lack of character, and too-free favors with other men?"

He spread his arms wide in surrender. "I offer no defense of my despicable part in your humiliation. When I learned the letter had been sent, I knew I would live to regret my part in it. I would have sought you out immediately to offer you my protection if I had known who you were. Be assured my conscience has never stopped troubling me."

"Oh, I am certain I should feel better for that."

He ignored her sarcasm. She had every right to that and much more. He had always liked her best when angry. At this moment, wrapped in his blanket with her glorious red hair tumbling in curls over her shoulders and back, she was magnificent! He had found his mate.

He smiled at her. "Isn't it ironic? I might never have known who you were if you had not written a play."

She jerked in surprise. "You recognized my plight as part of the tale of *Fortune's Fool?*

"No," he admitted begrudgingly. "I wish I were that astute.

But I felt the author's rage and anger and knew it was personally directed at me. Then, after the night when Francapelli—"

"Conte Francapelli gave me away to you?" Her hauteur crumbled. "Is there no end to men's treachery?"

In a steady, unemotional voice, he continued. "Francapelli told me only that you were the author of *Fortune's Fool* and that I should meet his opposition if I did not treat you well. I pieced the rest of it together. I suspect you are Cordelia Lytham's cousin. I surmise you met Pettigrew at her wedding to Lord Heallford." His gaze warmed as he lingered on the shapely thigh and calf exposed by the parted blanket. "It should have been me who met you there."

"I see. And when were you planning to tell me all this?"

He smiled his most charming smile. "In about a hundred years."

She did not smile back. "And what did you think before you knew I wrote the play? Who did you think wrote it?"

"I suspected your new lover wrote *Fortune's Fool*. I presumed that he had placed you in Longstreet's office in order to pass his work off as my own."

"Oh, so you thought me a brazen bit of muslin fit to spread herself for your friend but too stupid to compose prose."

He rose from the bed. He saw her eyes lower for an instant to his blooming flesh, but ignored the stain of embarrassment it caused. To hell with her outraged sensibilities. "I swear I could shake you for that."

"That's right. Intimidate what you cannot defend against." But it was she who was backing up. "Lord Pettigrew used such tactics."

He paused. "Did he hurt you?"

"He seduced me against my will." She flung her hair out of her eyes. "I suppose I might have cried rape, but I feared it would have spoiled Cousin Della's wedding for naught. In the end I was no more eager for the deed to be discovered than he."

"Then you are Lady Heallford's cousin?"

She stuck out her chin, refusing to answer, but that was answer enough.

He spread his arms wide in surrender. "You have every right to detest Lord Pettigrew and my part in his deceit."

"How kind of you, my lord, to give credence to my grief." Her tone set his teeth on edge. "But it was not so much Lord Pettigrew's character I despise. I knew him for a devil, but I was beguiled and so I got what I deserved."

"Your honesty astounds me."

"It is your low opinion of my character that allows for the astonishment," she said with all the hauteur of a genuine contessa. Lord, he did love her!

"Though you may not credit it, you're better off free of Pettigrew. He'd have made you a very bad husband."

"Is marriage what you think I wanted? I did not! 'Twas the lowest day of my life when the Gypsy Titania told me I was bearing Lord Pettigrew's child. I disliked him for spoiling my virtue, but, ashamed as I am to admit it, I was relieved when I read his name among the dead. Then came the letter."

Her eyes were dark with hurt and accusation. "That changed everything, don't you see? I would rather Grainne have had a dead hero than a coward and a cad for a father."

That appalling fact—which had never before occurred to him—stunned Quinlan. He, not Errol, had ruined her last illusion of love. He was deeply ashamed.

He took a step toward her, a hand held out. "That's all behind us now. I want to marry you, Caitlin."

She snorted in derision. "That is cruel."

"It's the truth. I swear to you that I love you."

She glared at him, and for the first time he knew what it was to be held in contempt. "Did you not say this very night that you had never been in love? No one—not even I—would expect you to knowingly take a friend's soiled piece to wife. Was it curiosity? No, I don't want to know." She lifted a hand to cover her eyes and sighed. "I'm past caring, I am. I hope you've learned what you wanted to know."

"I've learned I love you."

"Random sentiment," she quoted. "The feeling will pass."

"You won't forget me so easily, Caitlin."

She lowered her hand, and the look in her eyes made his belly quiver. "I won't be forgetting you at all, and that's the damnable part of it."

"Where are you going?" he asked as she began dressing.

"I'll not be telling you for all the gold in Russia."

"Oh, that's right. Play the wronged Irish maid. It isn't a part you pull off well." When she looked up, he placed a fist on each hip, daring her to dismiss his blatant desire for her. "You carry Pettigrew's letter and ring around like emblems of mortification or a scarlet letter. You're damned proud of your misery. A little too proud to be completely believable!"

She was so angry, she flew at him, all fists and feet.

He was surprised to learn that she could hit very hard for a woman of her size. She broke his lip and left what were certain to be more than a few bruises on his face before she wore herself out and slipped to the floor before him.

He went down on his knees beside her at once, but when he tried to embrace her, she thrust out her arm to fend him off.

"Let me be! Please!"

"Cai—Kathleen. Tell me what I can do to make it up to you?"

"Nothing." She lifted her head and held her curtain of fire-bright hair back from her face with a hand. "You've done quite enough. I must go home. Grainne will expect me when she awakes."

"I will go with you."

"No." She struggled to her feet, trying unsuccessfully to keep him from helping her. "If you would do me a favor, then promise me you will leave me alone."

"I cannot promise that. Why should I?"

She gave him a bleak look. "You won't ever get under my skirts again. No matter what I've done here tonight."

He smiled at the venom in her tone. She was good and truly frightened of the passion they had mutually aroused and shared.

"I don't believe you. What will you do, lock yourself away in a convent?"

"Yes!"

He smiled and tasted blood from his broken lip. "No, you won't. You will go away and lick your wounds and then you will start to think about me and tonight and what we've shared. And you will begin to make excuses for my unforgivable lapse in writing that disgusting letter. You will do it because you have a good, kind, forgiving heart, and more, because you love me."

She lifted her chin when the last bow was closed over her bodice. "I've wrapped my arms around a snake for the last time."

"You will wrap your arms and legs around me again, and I will love you until we are both wet and weak and sated."

Something happened. The lines of defiance and rage and righteousness broke apart in her expression, leaving him staring at the very real desperation inside her. It frightened him. He did not want to break her spirit.

"I won't touch you again until our wedding day if you will it, but I mean to wed you, and soon."

"Never!"

He relented. "I can see that you're ready to go. I will agree that this is good-bye between us only for now. You are free to go where you please and live as you please, if I cannot convince you otherwise. You will make a charming old maid and I will make a reprobate bachelor. When in later years I am too deep in my cups, I will prose on about a green-eyed Irish lass I knew too briefly. I will say she was the only love of my life."

She did not answer. She did not even look at him again. She simply unhooked Pettigrew's ring from her bodice and laid it on his table, and then she walked out his door.

He stood watching from his window until he was certain she was taken up by a *vetturino,* and then he picked up Pettigrew's ring and flung it as hard and as far as his anger could propel it.

"I will marry her."

He was filled with a mixture of longing, incredulity, and relief to have said the words aloud. It was extraordinary to admit it, and magnificent too. He did not at the moment care how many obstacles lay between them. After what had passed between them tonight, he knew she would sooner or later give in.

"I will marry her," he said in a deep, resonating voice that Longstreet would never, to his regret, ever hear reverberate through the Drury Lane Theatre.

Part Five

The Postscript

"Jove and my stars be praised! Here is yet a post-script."

Twelfth Night, William Shakespeare

Thirty

Porto Venere, April 2, 1816

"Where are you going?" Rafe inquired as his wife slid out of his bed to the accompanying rustle of her dressing gown.

"Not far." Della went to the window and threw open the shutters to the sunny morning. The sight beyond the window never failed to astonish her. Yet today that remarkable clarity of air and sunshine would serve a more prosaic purpose than to seduce the senses. "The morning light is best here. It should enhance your vision."

Rafe grumbled something profane under his breath. "You know my opinion of your experiments."

Della turned from the window, her expressly feminine figure outlined starkly against the brilliance of the day by which she was framed. "They are not experiments but exercises. Therefore, you should indulge me. Now then, tell me what you see."

Rafe sat up a little higher in bed, drawing the bedclothes for modesty's sake up to his waist. Tilting his head to one side, he frowned at the figure before the open window. "I see your silhouette."

"Good. Now tell me what else you see."

He squinted, for his vision was not, as she supposed, at its best upon awakening. "Three fingers."

"Try again."

Rafe frowned heavily. "I do not like these games."

"I suppose I shall grow accustomed to your morning grumpiness," she mused aloud. "Wives must accustom themselves to all sorts of new experiences."

He grunted noncommittally.

"How many fingers now, darling?"

"Three."

Della lowered her two fingers. "Very good. You see, you are improving."

Rafe pushed an impatient hand through his hair. "That is a matter of opinion."

"It seems, at times, as if you do not wish to see at all," she murmured.

"I have grown accustomed to blindness."

Refusing to be drawn by his contrary mood, she braced her hands on the sill, leaned out into the beauty of the spring day, and inhaled the spicy scent of wisteria from the blooming vines that encircled the window. He had seen her fingers! What matter if he saw two or three? It was not a math quiz, she mused. Yet she suspected that he was holding back on her.

She pulled loose the knot that held her robe closed and shimmied the silk off her shoulders until she was bare to the waist. Turning in profile to the light, she asked, her voice pitched low and sultry, "What do you see now, my lord?

Alerted by her tone, Rafe turned his head toward her and his black brows suddenly arched. "Good Lord, Della!" he cried, startled out of his complacency with laughter. "Cover yourself before one of the servants sees you!"

"Yes, my lord." Smiling a secret smile, Della rewrapped her dressing gown. If he could recognize the silhouette of her breasts, then his sight was not as dismal as he led her to suppose! During the past few weeks Rafe had changed in many ways. He no longer drank heavily, nor did he hide away. But that had deeply worried her. Byron, it was said, took the cure for alcoholism regularly, but it never lasted. To her relief, Rafe had never once become intoxicated since the night he had made love to her. He was no longer drowning his emotions, yet he was still brooding, his thoughts as dark and indecipherable as they had been when he hid behind that hood of bandages.

For instance, he had not once come to her bed at night. Yet he did not turn her away when, as the night before, she came to share his. In the darkness he made love to her as if it were the first, passionately, tenderly, with infinite care. Yet she sensed him pulling away into himself each time their lovemaking was over. He seemed afraid to remain open to her, to anyone. He strolled the grounds of the villa, but he would not venture into town and certainly not expose himself to strangers. She had done all she could to restore his belief in himself, but it was patently obvious he needed more.

She was a great believer in doing rather than brooding. He needed a shove out of the nest. It remained to be seen how far she could push him.

When she spoke again, all trace of her frustration with him was absent. "I should go and prepare for the day."

"I would rather you remain with me."

As she approached, Rafe enjoyed the view of his wife silhouetted against the bright blue sky and felt his heart swell with the enormity of his love for her. Sometimes, like now, things came miraculously into focus. Her features, the thrust of her bosom, and flare of her hips beneath the silk all were distinct. Equally apparent in such moments was the tantalizing possibility that their chance for happiness had not passed them by. When he could reach out and touch her and she smiled at him as though he possessed all she would ever require of life, he could believe in new beginnings. But that vision of a rosy future was much like his vision. It was not reliable and it faded as quickly as his sight when his eye tired. He must not allow maudlin yearnings to ruin her life. He could accept the moment, live fully in it, and yet he understood there would be a time after.

Until these last weeks he had thought he knew the full extent of his love for her by his willingness to counterfeit his own death for the sake of her future happiness. Now he knew his love for her would always surprise him, as would the knowledge of the sacrifices he was still prepared to make for her.

Della gazed down at him with a smile. How handsome he looked. Hair tousled and his features still sleep-softened, he seemed less careworn than she had ever known him to be. How rarely the ease of laughter filled his face and stretched his mouth nestled in his glossy black beard. When he was smiling, as now, he was a heady and rousing sight.

"I wish you could see how handsome you are."

Rafe smiled ruefully. "You see beauty in this battered body because you are besotted."

"I don't deny it." She bent to kiss his cheek. "Your color is so much better. Walking has helped it and your appetite."

When she bent lower to kiss his mouth, he turned to offer his bearded cheek. "What is this false modesty? May I not kiss my own husband in the full light of day?"

"You needn't offer me flattery."

She sat down on the edge of the bed. The eye patch he wore made him more inscrutable than ever. "You think my kisses are simple flattery?"

He flinched as she placed her palm on his bare chest. "I am content that you come to me at night."

"I come to your bed because you do not come to mine."

Rafe looked away from her, a faint flush climbing his unscarred cheek. "I do not want you to feel obligated. Or that bedding your husband is a duty you must perform."

The thought struck Della that they seemed to take a step backward for every two steps of forward progress their relationship made. For an usually discerning man, her husband could be remarkably obtuse when it came to assigning motives to her actions. She lightly raked her fingers through the fine black hair feathering his chest from nipple to nipple. "Do I seem to be doing my duty when I am in your bed?"

"No," he admitted as he turned back to her. "You are quite—spectacular."

Della basked in his reluctant smile. "I like that description. So then—"

"So then?" How wary he sounded, as if she had offered him tainted cheese.

"Are you daring me to make love to you here and now?"

"Certainly not!" The thought had not crossed Rafe's mind until she gave it voice, but then, it was all he could imagine.

"Certainly not?" She rose up on her knees. "How can you deny a woman who behaves so 'spectacularly'?"

"It was not a challenge," he answered defensively, but she was once more tugging at the knot that held her robe closed.

As the garment slid off her, she bent over him, her body flowing over the contours of his like water over rock, covering the worn, battered places, filling with her soothing cascade the dark crevices of his thoughts, seeking out all the sharp disappointments and rough grief with her embracing balm until they merged seamlessly into one each other, his rigidity enveloped in her clinging wetness, and they forgot for a moment that there was a morning and a future or anything beyond this coalescence.

"You are a wanton creature," Rafe said in admiration when he had caught his breath.

"Only for you." Della curled tightly against him, abashed by her own daring. "Only because of you."

"Della, what am I going to do with you?"

"Love me?"

"Yes, there is that," he said carefully. "You miss London, don't you?"

"Oh, yes." She sat up with a pleased smile, for he had brought up the subject uppermost in her mind. " 'Tis nearly April. I should like to begin preparations for our return to England. I miss Heallford Hall and my garden. It's time to mulch the roses and clear out winter's debris."

"Then by all means you should go home."

"*We* should go home."

He moved his hand to cup her face. "I am never going back."

Della swallowed her amazement. "Do you love Italy so very much?"

"There is nothing in England for me."

Della tried not to hear the undercurrent in his voice that was absent only when he was whispering words of passionate longing in her ear. "I see. You will want me to close Heallford Hall and let your house in London before I return."

"No. I never intended to hold you here. Your life is in England, and that is where you should live. You may visit me as the need strikes you. Perhaps winter with me. Many of the *ton* winter here."

The absurdity of the idea did not keep her from wishing to follow his line of reasoning before she cut it to pieces with the shears of her righteous indignation. "What do you suppose, in the meanwhile, I should tell my friends and family?"

"Whatever you choose." He paused, wanting to comfort the fresh hurt he heard in her voice. "You may find being a widow has many rewards."

Della gasped softly and sat up to look at him. "You mean everyone else is to continue believing that you are dead?"

"It would be best."

"Not for me."

He turned his head to her. "Most especially for you, Della. We must be reasonable. Though you are too kindhearted to admit it even to yourself, I should be looked upon by the *ton* as little more than a freak-show creature. I should be pitied and the subject of secret glances and sadly shaken heads. I will not have it."

"London won't be the same if you are not there beside me."

"Bumping into furniture and treading on toes?" he continued, painting the picture that gave him nightmares. "You won't be able to take me to a dinner party or a ball. I will be the subject of snubs and patronizing remarks. At first you will make excuses for my errors and then you will suffer in silence, and lastly you will begin to despise the minor humiliations I cause you."

"You paint a lovely picture of me as a ninny. I refuse the judgment. Besides, you are becoming quite dexterous with your left hand, now that you practice."

"I can't sign my own name or cut my meat at dinner."

"Time will mend the first, and what matter who wields the knife?"

"I will not be the subject of gossip!"

"Then you should not have been born." That, she was pleased to note, momentarily silenced him. "You've never been unexceptional, Rafe. All your life you have had but to enter a room to cause comment. Your bearing, your looks—and they are not detracted from by your wounding—your rank and personality; all these things and more have always made it impossible for people to ignore you.

"Do you imagine speculation would have been half so high about our marriage had you been short, stout, and ill favored, or had I a wandering eye and clubfoot? No, people were jealous of our genuine happiness in each other. My father called it the height of arrogance that I did not pretend to give consideration to the stupid and greedy and conceited. To be sure, there were many gentlemen who would have found favor with the size of my dowry. Countless mamas and their well-dowered daughters may never forgive you for not flattering their egos with your attention or offering them passionate glances nor testing their virtue by luring them into secluded gardens. What they could not forgive was our devotion to each other. As to that, nothing has changed."

"Except that I do not want to be stared at and discussed."

Then you must contrive not to call attention to the small differences."

"The lack of a hand is not minor. I cannot greet a friend with a handshake or kiss a lady's hand."

"I do not find the latter a handicap." She smiled at his startled glance. "It is a small joke, Rafe."

"You believe you are again ready to face public scrutiny, but I know I am not."

"How can you be so certain of that?"

"I know."

"No, you speculate, you assume, you cannot know unless you go out into the world and experience the truth. Therefore we should experiment." She braced herself before saying, "That is why I have invited my cousin Clarette and Lady Ormsby to visit us."

Rafe sat up so quickly, he almost overset his wife. "You've done what?"

"There's no need to shout," she responded, but the anger suffusing his face made it seem doubtful she should have expected any other kind of reaction. "Let me explain. Among the letters forwarded here from England was a missive from my cousin, Clarette Rollerson. She is playing companion to Lady Ormsby. You may know her, for she is Mr. James Hockaday's aunt. They are presently in Florence and plan to journey to Naples shortly."

"You told them I'm alive?"

"No." Her enthusiasm faltered. "I thought to make it a wonderful surprise."

Rafe threw back the covers and stood up, modesty forgotten before her betrayal. "You had no right!"

"What you do mean?" Della's curious gaze dipped and then rose, her face flushing with this new image of her mysterious husband. "Because the house is Lord Kearney's? He won't mind."

"I mind." Rafe placed a fist on each hip, giving her a full frontal display.

"Well, that's quite inhospitable of you." Della could scarcely keep her mind on the argument. "They shall be very little trouble, I assure you. Two women and their small entourage." The thread of her thought dwindled as anger—or her repeated glances—stirred a response from his manhood. "You—you'll scarcely know they're here except at mealtimes."

"I will not see them."

She lifted her gaze to his face. "Of course you will, darling. How else can they be certain you are alive?"

"I cannot believe how you have dared meddle in my life!"

"This is *our* life!"

"Not for long. I want you to pack and leave. You may go with your cousin and her lady friend, but you must be gone by the end of the week."

Della gasped, too stunned for a moment to find her voice. He could not be turning her out like an unsatisfactory maid who would not be given a reference. She climbed out of the bed, a fist poised on each of her bare hips. "You are the most disagreeable person I've ever known."

"As you are the most meddlesome!" Rafe scarcely said the words before she turned away. "Where are you going?"

"To pack."

"For England?" He scooped up her robe and offered it to her.

She snatched it from him, her color heightened by the fact that she had nearly left his room unclothed. "Since my guests are not welcome here, I shall take rooms in town until they arrive. I've been invited by my cousin's chaperon to journey with them to Naples to attend the opera."

She paused in the doorway, her face swollen with hurt pride and consternation. "I am done asking, Rafe. Done cajoling, wheedling, and begging. It is plain as a pike that you do not wish to abandon your melancholy while it is equally clear to me that we should both drive each other to grief if I stay. I will not return here until you can convince me otherwise."

She turned and walked out.

"You are not in mourning, Lady Heallford," Lady Ormsby pronounced without preamble when she had been helped from her private carriage by a footman. She gave Della's splendid walking gown of Hessian blue with military trim a thorough perusal through her lorgnette. "And what can you be thinking of to stand unattended in a public yard? There is an explanation, I assume."

Della offered the formidable older woman dressed in the gray of semimourning a smile of welcome. "There is, Lady Ormsby. My companion, Mrs. Dixby, remains behind to finish my packing."

The ladies were momentarily drowned out by the sounds of a second traveling coach as it came barreling into the yard of the public inn in Porto Venere. Upon the moment of its stopping, four young gentlemen dressed in the latest Parisian fashions alit from within, amid much chatter and good-spirited laughter.

Della recovered first. "But where is Clarette?"

"Here I am!" Clarette stood in the doorway of Lady Ormsby's coach. She wore a traveling gown of deep red which, on a girl so young, would have shocked London society but seemed quite in keeping with Italian life. She had plucked her heavy brows and held her head with new authority. But that was not the most dramatic change. Clarette had cut her hair. Minus the dragging of its length, her dark hair had found a natural wave. When brushed up high, as today, and confined by a demi-turban to match her gown, her dark tresses draped around her head and face in softly becoming ringlets.

"Cousin Della!" Clarette cried in delight as she stepped down. "You look wonderful. So much better than—than before."

Della gave her cousin a hug. "That is because I am so much happier."

"Are you?" Clarette gazed critically into her cousin's bright, dark eyes. "Yes, you do seem happier and younger than before."

"One would have to be insensible not to be cheered by the Mediterranean clime," Lady Ormsby added with a particular glance at Della. "No doubt you've found the Italians an especially stimulating people."

"Among other things," Della murmured.

As they approached the inn, Clarette was quickly surrounded by all four young Italian gentlemen.

"Who are they?" Della asked in faint alarm.

"Well you may ask," Elberta Ormsby answered dryly. "The girl has abandoned me for the gay life of a younger set."

"Indeed?" Della answered in surprise. She could not help but wonder at the older woman's leniency. After all, Clarette was still shy of eighteen. Perhaps it was something in the air or the water that made morals more relaxed there than in England.

"Are you certain your papa would approve?" Della asked when Clarette reappeared from within the circle of admirers after only a few moments, her high color having changed her face from pleasant to quite fetching.

"They are harmless," Clarette confided with a giggle. "Lady Ormsby can confirm we met quite respectably in Florence. Would you believe it, when it was time to leave the city, they pledged their utter devotion to me? To prove it, they are determined to follow me all the way to Naples."

"Theatrics! Sheer theatrics," Lady Ormsby pronounced. "Was I not acquainted with the father of two of them, and were the Italian highways not notoriously full of brigands, I should not have allowed the escort."

Clarette smiled mischievously. "I confess I find it all rather thrilling. And as any sensible girl knows, four swains are better than one, for they spend so much time keeping tabs on one another that I am never in danger of being left alone with any one of them."

This bit of coquettish logic out of the mouth of her once-unworldly relative astonished Della. Only last summer Clarette had despaired of ever stepping out from under her exquisite sister's shadow. Now she trailed her own entourage.

"But we are here to attend you," Clarette said warmly, as if the true purpose of her visit had slipped her mind. "You never said in your letter why you are in Italy."

Della smiled a little more brightly. "It is a tedious story. Do come out of the noise and dust. When you have refreshed yourselves, I will explain everything over dinner."

* * *

"What a perfectly beastly time you've had of it, my dear," Lady Ormsby pronounced when Della had apprised her of the bare details of the past two months. "To learn that the husband you had thought dead all these months is alive and living in seclusion in a foreign country! It is nothing short of a miracle that you have survived with your wits intact."

Lady Ormsby, Clarette, and Della shared a meal of meat and cheese and pasta on the inn's terrace which overlooked the sea-green waters of Porto Venere. In the distance the last burnt-orange sliver of the sun extinguished itself on the horizon, plummeting the terrace into deep purple hues. Immediately, torches were lit to chase away the night.

"I do not understand why he did not at least write you," Clarette complained on her cousin's behalf.

"Lord Heallford was gravely wounded at Waterloo, nearly died," Della answered, coming naturally to Rafe's defense when in fact his actions had been nothing short of indefensible. "Some wounds take more time to heal than others. He is still recuperating."

"And yet now, when you have found him, 'tis monstrously unkind of the earl to send you away," Clarette countered, still capable of speaking her mind despite the disapproval of others. "How will you bear up when you know people will again be talking and whispering behind your back?"

"I suspect he is some addled in the wits," Lady Ormsby announced with appalling candor. "Still, it would behoove the pair of you to return to England and show yourselves. There was enough talk in the years prior to your marriage to set the stage for fresh scandal if you return from Italy alone."

"She is right," Clarette exclaimed. "The most innocent matter may be gotten tail-end-around and result in a most wretched business. The *ton* has labeled me a jilt!"

Glad for the segué into a new topic, Della turned her sympathetic gaze on her younger cousin. "I was much saddened to hear of your break with Mr. Hockaday. I trust your feelings are recovered?"

"But certainly," Clarette answered, yet her eyes cast shadows of doubt on her sunny tones. She glanced toward her entourage, who were sharing wine and cheese at another table. "I'm most delightfully diverted these days. I scarcely can remember the silly contretemps of last summer."

"That may be," Della said quietly. "Yet I know what it is to love steadfastly even past hope."

"But Lord Heallford always loved you," Clarette replied with a wistfulness that at once gave away her real feelings. "He even married you."

"Yes, he did. But sentiment can alter," Della offered quietly.

"It is not unusual for couples to grow apart," Lady Ormsby observed. "Some never grow together in the first place. Yet I imagine that a man as proud as Lord Heallford should be ready to honor his pledge. 'Tis said a point of honor explains the Duke of Wellington's own unhappy marriage. Heallford must be made to think of what is best for you."

Della shook her head. "I can't think of only myself when it puts Lord Heallford's happiness at risk. If I remain, we will both be miserable. If I go, at least his feelings will be spared."

" 'Tis a miserable business, loving," Lady Ormsby at last chimed in. "My generation took a more pragmatic view. Marriages merged dynasties and fortunes or sealed political alliances. Love was left for the more ephemeral realm of courtiers and trysting."

"Men are beastly!" Clarette declared.

"Yes, and wonderful, and frustrating, and a great cause of self-pity among our sex. Now then, Lady Heallford, you will dry your tears and come with us to Naples. There you shall wear your prettiest gown to the opera and conduct yourself so beautifully that all the Neapolitan gentlemen shall fall instantly in love with you."

"What good will that do her?" Clarette asked.

Lady Ormsby looked suddenly quite cross. "Where is my shawl? Go and fetch it at once."

"Very well." Clarette glanced regretfully at Della, well aware that she was about to be, once again, left out of the best part of a conversation.

"Now then," Lady Ormsby continued when Clarette was gone. "There is only one remedy for a woman in your situation. You must take a lover!"

"What?" Della voiced in amazement.

"Yes, a handsome Italian lover. I must admit, I am much impressed by the Italians. They are ever so much more attentive and ardent than English gentlemen. You must shamelessly flaunt your affair. That should bring Lord Heallford to the mark. There's nothing more humiliating for a husband than to think he has lost control of his wife. Then again, if he is that rare ilk who truly loves you, he won't be able to tolerate the thought of you in the arms of another. He'll set forth to skewer the fellow. Or, I suppose, having lost his saber hand, he will use his pistol. In the meanwhile, you will have the satisfaction of a very pretty dalliance. Remember, when choosing a lover, form surpasses wit. A proud cock is better than proud words."

Della was too taken aback by this bawdy advice to readily answer. Instead, she stared at the lengthening shadow of the tall gentleman who entered the terrace to the accompaniment of a torchbearer.

"Oh, my," Della whispered, and rose slowly to her feet.

The gentleman was her husband.

He was dressed for travel in a chocolate frock coat, buff leather breeches, and boots. A low-crowned beaver hat was canted rakishly over his patched eye, and his stock was looped simply around his neck. The tense set of his broad shoulders told her his mood—which was one of determination brooking no argument—and she smiled as her eyes followed the long, lean lines of his strong body. This was the man she had fallen in love with. The harshly attractive features outlined by torchlight were the same she had always loved. His wounded eye and cheek, cast for the moment in shadow, would not disturb any sensibilities or frighten any child.

Her heart jumped into her throat. She did not need to guess why or what had brought him there. He was dressed for a long journey, if need be. He was there, he was beautiful, and he was hers.

Still, she waited in an agony of suspense as he questioned the innkeeper, who then pointed to her table. She saw him look in her general direction but knew the shadows were too deep for all but the sharpest eyes to penetrate. Yet he turned quickly and came striding toward her as if he had two sharp eyes instead of one unreliable one to guide him.

"Excuse me, Lady Ormsby," Della said, leaving the table even as she spoke.

"Who is that gentleman accosting Cousin Della?" Clarette inquired as she emerged from the inn with Lady Ormsby's paisley shawl.

"That, I suspect though I've never met him, is her husband the older woman replied as she squinted through her lorgnette.

"Lord Heallford?" Clarette's eyes widened as she took in the details of the mysterious gentleman who had taken her cousin roughly by the arm. "He looks more like a pirate."

"Yes, indeed," Lady Ormsby answered in satisfaction. "I do believe he's come to make off with her."

"Should we allow that?"

"My dear child, of course we should!"

Thirty-one

Rafe stared down in relief at the wife he feared might have gotten away from him. He meant to greet her with words both profound and emotionally stimulating. Instead, with his relief came the feeling of chagrin that he need not have worried that she would leave the vicinity so precipitously. He need not have turned his house on its ear as he rushed to prepare for the road, need not have strided into a public place with no care for decorum or appearances. She was not, after all, alone. And he wanted very much to be alone with her.

Annoyed to have an audience for his loverlike protestations, he merely held out his arm to her and said in a high-handed tone, "Come with me."

"I don't believe I care to," she answered in her most contrary voice. "If you have something to say, you may say it here."

With less mastery of his temper than he supposed, he caught her by the arm, the muscle working in his left cheek. "Come with me now, madame, or I shall haul you out in a manner guaranteed to embarrass us both!"

The authoritarian ring in his voice, absent since the day of their marriage, was back.

Della quite liked the sound of it, but she was not about to give him the satisfaction of admitting it. "Very well, if you will release me. Else the innkeeper will think I'm being taken hostage by a brigand."

He released her but remained so close by her side that Della suspected he expected she might try to escape. She could only guess at the volatility of the emotions that had shaken him free of his self-imposed exile. She had no intention of placating him, but adding new tremors to further unseat his self-possession.

Their way lit by his torchbearer, she accompanied him into the coaching yard, pleased to see that his vehicle was fully fitted for travel with two outriders and her trunk strapped on top. When she glanced sideways and up at him, she saw temper had brought his black brows together over his nose and drawn down the corners of his mouth. He was no doubt feeling a little foolish and castigating himself for the effort. But it did her pride a world of good to view this tangible evidence of the lengths to which he was prepared to pursue her.

He jerked open the coach door and barked, "Get out."

To Della's amazement, Sarah Dixby appeared in the breech, her color high as she climbed down. "My lady," she said in an abashed voice as Rafe pointed a finger toward the inn.

"Get in!" he ordered as Sarah left them.

"Are you abducting me?" Della inquired in mock affront.

She saw a muscle jump in his cheek. "You will go nowhere against your will," he said between clenched teeth.

"Very well." Della lifted the bottom of her gown and entered the coach with all the dignity she could muster.

Once inside, she pushed far back into one corner of the carriage and crossed her arms before her chest. A heady brew of elation and antagonism laced her emotions, making her breath a little fast and her hands tremble.

"What do you want?" she began ungraciously when he had entered and closed the door behind himself.

He settled on the bench opposite her, his knees spread wide in a subtle display of imposing authority over the confines of the interior, and removed his hat. "I want you to listen to me, Della."

"Very well." Oh, but she sounded spiteful when all she wanted to do was hug him for coming after her. Yet she sensed that now that he was embarked on this business, he would not thank her for circumventing it.

"I've been thinking about all you said this morning." His voice was heavy with import as he reached to turn up the lamp. Golden light flared to fill the interior, casting jaundice hues upon both their faces. "There was some truth in your charges, Though you will admit you were near hysteria."

"I admit no such thing," Della answered firmly. "I was unquestionably provoked."

His gaze flickered up over her. "I suppose I am something of a difficult man."

"You are nothing short of arduous, my lord. Stubborn, inflexible, formidable, and enigmatic would serve to describe you as well!"

His lips twitched. "Why, then, have you put up with me?"

"I have asked myself that question many times."

"And your answer?"

But she was no longer willing to offer him solace and reassurances when he gave her nothing in return. "I am no longer certain."

"Della!" he said in warning.

"Yes?"

He lifted his hand in a conciliatory gesture that failed in mid-action. "Never mind."

Della bolted upright. "I detest that habit of yours most of all. It is a cowardly thing to do, to leave a woman in doubt at every encounter. Perhaps you are right. Perhaps I will get over you, given the time. I am nearly persuaded to try."

He shook his head slowly. "You know that is not what I want!"

"I never know what you want. Is it always black-is-white with you? It was cruel to suggest I go back to England alone. I will make no excuses for your character this time."

"I did not expect that you would." He looked suddenly tired and weary. How worried he must have been while making his preparations. Did he really think that one grand argument would be enough to erase all her years of loving him? How foolish men could be.

"I suppose you came here for a reason," she said calmly, and settled back on her seat. "I will listen."

"I should imagine every word your father spoke to you just before he walked you down the aisle has come back to condemn me in your eyes. You looked, even on our wedding day, as if you were being sentenced to a life in purgatory."

"I looked as if I could not wait to be away from everyone who would not leave me in peace. I was terrified that you might have overheard him, be insulted, and leave me."

He looked astonished. "Why did you think that?"

"Because I was waiting for you to say you loved me."

Della held her breath. She had not meant to put the matter so baldly between them, not when he was so careful to avoid it. But there it was, the crux of her fear.

"And now?" he asked softly. "What brought you to Porto Venere?"

A month ago, a week ago, she might have told him. Now she knew she would never say the words again unless he said them first. "How can I know what to answer when you've never said—when it's obvious you cannot express your feelings."

"You have them in my actions toward you."

"I know your passion, not your heart. Once I thought I could endure anything as long as I was with you. But I've discovered I was wrong. 'Tis not enough to be only your nursemaid and mistress. Do you think I long to wake up each morning on tiptoe until your mood has been gauged? I came to find my husband and all that implies."

"What does that imply?"

"A husband should be a friend, a lover, a confidant, a father to my children. He must be willing to share the good and bad. But there must be good, Rafe. If I do not cheer you, and you cannot be easy in my company, then I see no reason to be wed."

"Many of London's most fashionable couples barely exchange a word when they chance to meet in public or private. My parents were such people."

Della shook her head. "Such an alliance would be worse than death to me. I would rather be alone. I have my pride."

"Pride can be a damnable burden," he said, as he reached for one of her hands, curled into a fist in her lap. " 'Twas pride made me withhold my truest feelings when we wed." He enfolded her fist within his and held on tightly. "And fear that you would eventually conquer your feelings for me."

Della stared at their joined hands. "You thought I would stop loving you?"

"Did not every other person in our lives believe the same? I cannot rationally explain the tortured thoughts that made me believe that as long as I held a part of myself from you, it would, ultimately, make our parting easier."

Tears started in Della's eyes. "I don't understand such thinking. You always had my unconditional love. From the first. For twelve years."

"I know. It frightened me, the capacity you had for absolute belief in me. I've never understood it."

"I see."

"No, you don't, you sweet, lovely girl. You cannot. I had never before had anyone care for or believe in me as you did."

"Untrue. You had many friends, good friends, friends who would do anything for you."

"You're thinking of Quinlan."

She looked up at him. "I confess I have long been jealous of your friendship with Lord Kearney. You look surprised. You should not be. He has had claim to more of your time, your confidences, thoughts, and feelings, more of *you* than I have ever had."

"For all that, he could never get as close to me as you do with a mere glance. When I am near you, I feel how easy it would be to allow you to sink right down through me, right into my bones."

"If you can admit to such feelings, how could you think sending me away would be anything less than agony for me?"

"Perhaps I was afraid to listen. I was trying to be selfless."

"Your brand of selflessness would make us both miserable forever!"

Her waspish tone tugged a smile onto his face.

"Very well. I am finished with being noble. I came to tell you that if you still wish it—and it is a miracle to me every day that it should be so—I will go with you to London, whatever you ask of me."

"Why?" she asked suspiciously. "I do not want your resignation or pity."

"Then I suppose I should say something to make you stay."

"I can't imagine what it could be."

"I love you."

"Don't—oh, dear God, don't say it for effect!"

"Then let me say it looking at you, holding you, feeling your love flowing back into me."

She stared up at him, such pain and longing in her lovely dark eyes that something cracked inside him, and this time the cracking became deep fissures, cleaving the stoniness around his heart so that it dropped away, completely exposing the most tender and neediest part of him.

He took her carefully in his arms, balancing her hips on his long knees and then he kissed her so softly it seemed he dreamed the touch. Until he smelled the scent of roses rising on her skin and knew she was more real than anything else he would ever know. "I love you," he whispered against her lips.

Della had told herself so often that those three little words meant very little in the grand scheme of things that she could not at first credit that he had spoken them, and then she began to tremble and shake and cry.

He comforted her, holding her hard against his chest and reveling in the protectiveness he felt to have her soft and vulnerable in his arms. "If I had known this is all it takes to best you in an argument, I should have used my love for you against you much sooner."

She pushed against him then, sitting up and wiping away a tear. "Do not tease me."

"I am not teasing, well, only a very little. I do love you, Della. The feeling quite stuns me. It seems so enormous beside every other consideration."

She lifted her hand and turned his face so that the lantern light fell full across his good eye. "This is not some misplaced sense of pity or loyalty, or out of duty, or shame, or sympathy, or defeat?"

"Not even selfishness. Yet, if you need time to think about it, I will let you go, even now."

She knew what that offer cost him. It was there in the strained lines of his face. "I am free, am I?"

"If you wish."

She looped both arms around his neck. "I don't wish it."

"Lord, Della! How will we live?"

"By your wits?" she suggested archly, though she had enough money to settle five *tonnish* families comfortably. "No, we shall grow roses. We shall breed the most beautiful hybrid Europe has ever seen."

He kissed her again, this time longer and harder than before. "I will breed you a bloodred rose and shall name it Lady Della."

Her eyes misted with tears, but she held them bravely back. "You are very certain of yourself."

"I have never been more afraid in my life."

"Why now?"

"It seems I must become a respectable gentleman."

"You may erect monuments to your consequence if it improves your humor, but you would seem to possess quite too much pride as it is. What did you intend to do when the war was over?"

"Write my memoirs of my experiences in the military."

"An excellent idea. Now that Napoleon is defeated a second time, there should be a great market for such memoirs."

He held up his stump as silent refutation.

"You may dictate it to me until your left-handed style improves."

"The exercise would make captives of both of us."

"Anything that ties you to me will be a welcome task. What else did you plan?"

"I considered that I might take my seat in Parliament. Or take over full management of your properties. It seemed the least I could do in return for the income it will bring us."

"You may still do those things."

"Manage properties, perhaps, but who would be impressed by a blind man in Parliament who cannot see the smirks or piteous looks of his colleagues?"

"Why must you be so contrary?"

He smiled. "I am sorry. If I am reluctant to admit to the possibility of happiness, it is because I do not want to give either of us false hope. I could as easily awaken one day to find myself completely and irrevocably blind."

"That's preposterous. Things can go on just as they are or improve. We will go to Milan and see all the specialists. Now one thing more. You must vow not to fight me at every turn in the future."

Rafe chuckled. "You ask a great deal. May we not be like other husbands and wives who bicker over inconsequentials?"

"I suppose. But only inconsequentials. You are free to disapprove of my new bonnets, the size of my modiste bills, and the passion I have for squab—which I shall endeavor to have indulged at every meal. I will deplore your penny-pinching habits and your tobacco smoke and your choice of waistcoats."

"I have very good taste in waistcoats."

"Do you indeed? I foresee a great number of debates on that subject!"

He smiled. "I love you."

"I know."

He kissed her as though in doing it might save both their lives. The anger and fear and love and joy running though him made the blood pound in his ears. "Promise you will never stop loving me."

"It is beyond my ability to stop loving you."

"Are you certain?"

"Aren't you?"

He smiled with the sudden knowledge that she had handed him the answer. "I am."

Thirty-two

Naples, April 1816

"Good to see you, Quill! Dash it all, if you ain't a pleasant sight for a wandering pilgrim."

"Hockaday!" Having adapted readily to the effusive Neapolitan style, Quinlan briefly hugged the younger man as he stepped off the gangway of the packet boat at the Bay of Naples.

"How does it feel to be a landowner?" Quinlan inquired a little later when they had repaired to an outdoor café to drink wine.

"Marvelous." Jamie cocked his soft-brimmed hat back from his brow and smiled. "Never thought I'd be so well set up. Not like you, of course, but more than comfortable." He frowned thoughtfully as he tasted the wine he had ordered. Now that he was a vintner, he had been striving to improve his palate. He could now tell the difference between a claret, a burgundy, and a Bordeaux.

"You did not say in your note what brings you to Naples."

"A summons from Aunt Elberta." Jamie sighed. "Seems she's been touring the Mediterranean with Clarette Rollerson, of all people." He colored under Quinlan's kindling smile but moved quickly on to the next topic. "While vineyards ain't in her style, opera is. Francapelli's a particular favorite of hers. She made his acquaintance while he was in London last year. Sent her an invitation to sit in his box at the premiere of his latest effort. She needed an escort. That's me. Hate opera, all those screeching voices and dragging at catguts with bows."

Quinlan laughed at this prosaic description of Francapelli's efforts. "Strange, isn't it, how small our world is when you actually think about it? Your aunt showing up for a premiere of an opera which brings you here to me. I doubt there's any member of the *ton* whose connection we could not make through a mutual acquaintance, and that would include mistresses and indigent relatives living abroad."

"I suppose you're right. What of it?"

"I was just reflecting recently upon the probability of things we might otherwise feel compelled to call fate."

"This ain't going to be a deep discussion, is it?" Jamie inquired suspiciously. "Me guts ain't settled from the sea voyage."

Quinlan laughed. "It's a small world, Jamie. I would wager you had already met the mother of your children before you were five."

"Strange you should mention that." He looked odd until Quinlan realized that Hockaday was blushing. "You know what you once said about me missing my gooseberry tart when it was gone?"

Quinlan raised quizzical brows. "What? Oh, yes, the Rollerson chit."

"Miss Clarette Rollerson to you."

"Sits the wind in that quarter?"

Jamie's sigh was decidedly dejected. "Lord, yes. That a coil! Her father will hang me if I so much as shadow the door. Clarette no doubt wishes me at the devil and, the trouble is, I haven't been able to think of much else than her since last fall. Thought leaving London would break the connection, but it hasn't. Turned down an invitation last night from the most beautiful creature I'd ever seen because she was no higher than my heart."

"I suppose you're being no more vague than usual but, humor me, Jamie old fellow. What are you talking about?"

"Not what, who. Clarette. She comes to right here." He indicated a spot just above his heart.

"So then, you're in love?"

" 'Fraid so."

"It must be catching," Quinlan murmured.

"What?" Amazed laughter burst from Jamie. "Not you? You can't be in love. You said it was impossible."

Quinlan's lips twitched. "I did not say it was impossible for me to love. Only that it had not yet occurred. Now it has."

Jamie decided not to argue the point. "Who is she?"

"A contessa."

"Here in Naples?"

"I met her here, yes, but she's Irish."

"An Irish contessa?"

"Don't strain yourself. It will be explained in due time."

"I see. Well then, if your life is sorted out, what do you propose I do about Clarette?"

"Don't write her," Quinlan said darkly.

"Oh, no. I've had my fill of written declarations. Though Clarette is extraordinarily good at letters. I think I was half in love with her through her letters, but I was determined to ask for Clarice's hand, only, well—" He shook his head. "Ever notice how confusing emotions can be?"

"Constantly."

"I've decided to tell Clarette face-to-face all that I've been thinking about. And that is, a man could do a lot worse than to have her to wife."

"Don't tell her quite like that."

"No, of course not. Still, Clarette's one for plain talk. Kept me from making the mistake of marrying her sister."

"Extraordinary creature," Quinlan observed mildly.

"Yes. Just. Exactly. Only I don't know that she'll have me. Not after all that's occurred." Jamie's second dejected sigh was heartfelt. "If she won't have me, that's an end to it."

Quinlan laughed. "Women, my friend, are most vulnerable

when they are most adamantly opposed to a matter. She will have you just as the contessa will have me. You will see."

"Most vulnerable when most adamant." Jamie filed away this valuable bit of information on the female psyche for later reflection.

"I've heard from Rafe."

"No!" Amazement in Jamie's voice had a wide range, Quinlan decided. "How is he?"

"Reconciled with his wife."

"But how?"

Quinlan smiled. "I've been playing Cupid."

"This I must hear."

San Carlo was an elegant theater built by the order of Charles III, for whom it was named. It was more like a huge salon than a theater, for people wore full evening dress and milled about visiting one another's boxes throughout the performance. They paused only for the most popular arias or duets. Six tiers of boxes, one hundred and forty-four in all, held from ten to twelve people each in comfort. Armchairs were the only seats, but each box was hung with colorful silk drapery and such decorations as were agreeable to the taste of the owner. The front of each box was faced with a mirror to reflect the theater's illumination. Light came from the pillars between boxes which were decorated with large statues of gilded genies who held aloft candles of prodigious size.

Reflected and multiplied again and again throughout the building, the effect was one of enchantment, at least so it seemed to Clarette Rollerson, who had never before attended any opera. Trailing several minutes behind Lady Ormsby's carriage, she was escorted by her four young Italian swains who had followed her to Naples.

Feeling quite elegant in a sumptuous gown of deep sapphire, she wore her hair caught in a gold net studded in pearls. Heads turned as they made their way to their box, and not for the first time in her travels Clarette knew what it was to be admired. Only one thing more was needed to make the moment perfect, she mused in a prevalent minor key, and that was if Jamie Hockaday could see her. But, of course, that was impossible. He was still in London, pining away for loss of her sister.

They entered Francapelli's box to be momentarily blinded by the brilliance of the theater. Clarette stumbled into the gentleman ahead of her. As she was steadied from behind by four pairs of solicitous hands, the gentleman blundered into turned and she found herself looking up into the cherubic countenance of the very man she had been reflecting upon.

Jamie's searching gaze moved in approval over her deeply décolletaged gown before it came to a stunned standstill on her face. "Clarette!"

He saw her start in recognition, then deliberately turn her back to him, sailing away on not one but two masculine arms.

He had arrived at his aunt Elberta's *pensione* only to learn that Clarette had left by earlier escort to a pre-opera soirée. Annoyed that his aunt had not only allowed her to escape before he could speak privately with her, but had sent her off with four young Italian gentlemen, he had fidgeted with his watch fob in the carriage until it broke in half and he was forced to pocket it. Now she had cut him dead, like any presumptuous upstart. It was all too much!

"Most vulnerable!" he muttered as he prepared for a battle he did not want to lose. He headed after her, treading on several patrons' toes as he did so.

He did not find it an easy task to breech the wall of gallants who quickly surrounded her at the far end of the box. In fact, he was forced to grab the shoulder of one with an abrupt "See here!" to be given even a glimpse of her.

The young man swung around, every haughty line of his classic Roman face a challenge. But Jamie was not interested in any contest of wills other than one with Clarette.

"Cousin Clarette," he said in a overloud voice.

He saw her wince, and then she turned fully to him, her face as pink as a rosebud. Otherwise, she seemed fully composed. "Why, if it isn't young Jamie Hockaday," she said in a ringing voice that was as artificial as it was insulting "My, how you've changed. I didn't recognize you, dear boy."

Jamie frowned. "What's all this, then, Puss?" he muttered, and shot dark glances at each of his four rivals.

"La!" she declared in that tone he knew she had borrowed from his aunt Elberta. "You must meet my new suitors. This is Marco, Giovanni, Domenico, and Vittorio. Gentlemen, my cousin and erstwhile fiancé, Mr. Jamie Hockaday."

"First names?" Jamie responded in disapproval, ignoring the hands thrust toward him in greeting.

"Shame on you," she answered gaily, and rapped his sleeve with her closed fan. "We are not so formal here in Naples. Why, the Neapolitan clime is positively ripe with informality. Can you not feel it!"

Jamie's mouth tightened. "Claptrap! You sound like a— a . . ." It suddenly occurred to him that she was staring at him in a manner that betrayed how very much she would like to slap his face. Of course! He was embarrassing her.

He blushed. "I beg your pardon." He reached out with both hands and shook two at a time. "Now then, Clarette, I should like you to grant me the favor of an interview, a *private* interview."

"Not now." She tossed her head. "Perhaps later." She glanced up at him through her lashes like the most practiced of coquettes. "Perhaps."

She looked wonderful, he decided as she turned back to the other gentlemen, who openly smirked at this dismal of a potential rival. Why had she never worn that shade of blue before? And her eyes! They appeared enormous beneath the masses of dark curls clustered about her face. She might never be declared a great beauty, but she was no longer a plain pudding. His gooseberry tart had turned into quite a charmer.

Jamie made himself sit patiently through the act, barely glancing more than once every minute in her direction. But when he chanced to see the fellow named Vittorio lean so close that her curls brushed the tip of his nose as she turned her head away, he rose to his feet feeling that he had had quite enough of his own good behavior.

He stepped hastily between them and took Clarette by the arm, drawing her to her feet. "We must talk. Now!"

The scraping back of four chairs was alarming. Clarette glanced around and said, "Dear me, gentlemen! 'Tis only my cousin. We will be right back." She touched Vittorio, who looked most offended, on the sleeve. "Be a dear and hold my fan." His expression melted into obedience as she passed him her ornament. Lifting her arm free of her cousin's grasp, she said pleasantly, "Come, Jamie. We shall speak in the hallway."

Once in the dark hallway, however, she turned on him with a mutinous glance. "Really, Jamie! You are behaving ever so oddly."

"Oddly?" Insulted to be the one accused of bad behavior when he was about to castigate her for the same, he roared, "How am I being odd?"

She put a warning finger to her lips as she moved a few steps farther away from the entrance to the box.

But Jamie was too confused by the unexpected changes in her to be quelled. "You sound and look like any other silly goose whose only interest is in collecting the hearts of as many gentlemen as possible."

Clarette opened her mouth to protest, and then snapped it shut on the thought. Plain speaking had never gotten her anywhere with him before. Instead, she tossed her head and said in a careless fashion, "Why, Mr. Hockaday, I can't think what you mean."

"Oh, gawd!" he groaned. "Aunt Elberta has turned you into a—a London flirt!"

She glanced at him in injury. "I don't see that it's any business of yours what I've turned into."

He took a step toward her, glad to note that some things had not changed. She still reached only to chest level. "You don't, do you? You will. Why did you jilt me?"

It was not a question she anticipated. "I didn't jilt you. I simply ended our engagement, as I promised I would."

"But why?" His gaze veered toward the curtain that led to the maestro's box. "So you could flirt up half of Europe?"

With the lift of one shoulder, she half turned away, exposing him to a three-quarter profile that Aunt Elberta had assured her gentlemen could not resist. "I thought you'd thank me, but I can see there's no pleasing you." She let her lashes flutter downward. "But then, there never was."

"Not true," Jamie answered untruthfully. "I was confused, that's all."

"Confused?" She glanced up at him over her shoulder, secretly admiring his claret evening coat and cream waistcoat. He always looked splendid. Oh, why did she still feel so much love for him, when he had made it painfully clear he did not want her? "Confused about what?"

"About whom I loved and what I wanted." He raked an impatient hand through his hair and then, quite surprising himself, took her by the shoulders. " 'Tis just this way, Puss. It took me a little time to sort Jack from Jill. What with the war. The deaths. The fear. The perfect vision. Clarice, like a talisman against the night."

Clarette held still under the warm persuasion of his hands. He had never before touched her without prompting. What could it mean? She looked up into his blue eyes, dark with shadows in the dimness, and felt her heart leap in anticipation. "What do you want now?"

Jamie grinned. This was a question about which he no longer had any confusion. "I want you, Puss."

He kissed her with his whole heart, kissed her with a purpose forged from the crucible of months of confusion and mistaken loyalties and misconstrued feelings.

And, miracle of miracles, she kissed him back, rising up on tiptoe to grip his shoulders. For once he did not care that in doing so she wrinkled the seams of his coat and pulled it sadly out of line.

When they both could think again, he held her close and sighed in relief when she melted against him.

"You do still love me, don't you?" he whispered into the crown of her hair.

She lifted her face from his coat front and looked up at him, her smile so wide, it seemed to fill her face. "Of course I do. What else did you think?"

He kissed her again, and when he was done his grin was twice as cocky as before. "I just wanted to be certain."

"You always were a bit obtuse when it came to handling females," she observed in a breathless voice.

Jamie was not at all certain what "obtuse" meant, but if it had anything to do with reluctance and confusion, he had suffered the affliction. "Thing is, Puss, why didn't you tell me right off how it was with you?"

"How could I? You were so wrapped up in Clarice that you never heard a complete sentence I spoke if she was in the room. Besides, a lady can't run at a gentleman's head. It was up to you to notice the signals."

"Were there signals?" He looked as perplexed as ever. "Dash it! Didn't see them."

She gazed up into his angelic face framed by the most lovely golden curls and imagined that all their children would look like him. "You will have to approach Papa again. You've a prodigious black mark in his book, you realize."

"Can't blame him," Jamie answered as new anxieties cut up

his speech pattern. "Will tough it out. Got to. For your sake. Owe him his pound of flesh."

Clarette reached up and curved an arm around his neck. "Jamie darling, do hush and kiss me again."

He did. And she decided before passion swept every other thought out of her head that her papa could be handled before Jamie's second marriage offer, for she had just had a wonderful Idea!

Thirty-three

"This is nothing less than Draconian," Kathleen declared in disgust. "I cannot abandon Grainne to a stranger just because you require a hostess for the evening."

"Severe times call for severe measures," Francapelli answered, though he was paying more attention to the fall of lace at his cuffs than to the young woman pacing like a caged lioness before him." I have engaged someone of redoubtable character to care for your child tonight. Grainne is in perfectly capable hands."

"I won't go," she tossed over her shoulder as she paced away from him. "You cannot expect me to face a crowd of strangers when I am worried about my daughter's welfare."

"Most certainly I can." He lifted a heavy-lidded gaze to her. Her evening gown, styled to complement his own preference for ebony, was composed of black silk and silver lace. Her mane of brilliant curls had been left down and entwined with silver ribbons to frame shoulders bared by the neckline of her gown. "You will dazzle all eyes."

Her dagger gaze did not deter him. "Have I not been an extremely generous host?"

"Yes, of course," she answered with a warming smile as she came toward him. "You've been remarkably indulgent. But—"

"No buts!" he interrupted. "Tonight is very important to me. I ask only that you keep your promise and preside over the company in my opera box tonight."

"Perhaps I could face the rest," she mused aloud, her pacing resumed, "if only Lord Kearney weren't expected to be there as well."

Francapelli shrugged. "You must face and slay your dragons or you will never be free of the past."

Kathleen paused abruptly, her legs tangling in the backwash of silver and black. "You are right. I am being foolish. After all, I should have expected to see him again eventually. Yet, why has he returned from England so quickly!"

"That you will have to ask him yourself. You will be pleased, now, to get your wrap? We shall be late."

She started, surprised at her own lapse into reverie of a night six weeks old. "Of course."

When she had gone, a chuckle escaped Francapelli. He had not asked her why she was suddenly more concerned about seeing Lord Kearney than in her child's welfare. That was because he knew Grainne had nothing to do with Kathleen's reluctance to go out in public that evening.

Even though she had not said a word, he knew what had occurred while he was away six weeks earlier. Naples was, along with the rest, a city of gossips. He knew that she and Kearney had become lovers. He knew that she had gone to Lord Kearney's rooms, knew how long she had stayed, what she had eaten and drunk, and how angry she had been when she left. They had had a lover's quarrel, which was a better indication of how things would turn out than either of them had imagined at the time. Such passionate temperaments needed expression both physical and emotional.

Francapelli sighed philosophically. He was going to lose her. Kearney would take her away and he would return to his masculine life without children and the spark of feminine beauty. At least she was going to love. That was worth the sacrifice.

He paused at the end of the hall to pat the bust of himself which Angelo had delivered only that morning. He smiled. He really was quite a handsome fellow. "Ah, *amore!*"

* * *

Kathleen returned to Francapelli's palazzo residence even as the orchestra struck up the theme of act three. She had pleaded a headache, yet had been amazed when Francapelli suggested that she go right home. His opera was going to be a great success. He could spare her.

As she climbed the stairs to her rooms, she could no longer suppress her keen disappointment that Lord Kearney had not, as expected—no, feared—appeared during the performance.

When she had learned from Francapelli that Quinlan had returned to Naples a few days before, she had told herself that she should be grateful that he had not attempted to contact her. She had told herself that he was only honoring her request that he never again come near her.

She did not want him to come near her, she mused wearily as she paused to rub her aching temples when she reached the second floor. She had wanted him to leave Naples. She had wanted him to leave Italy. She had wanted countries and oceans between them. She had wanted . . .

"Oh, damn!" She wanted to see him that night. She turned toward her rooms, every step weighted by regret.

It was a sobering lesson to learn that one could quite spoil one's life by reacting in a very normal fashion. She had every right to dislike Quinlan DeLacy for the rest of her life. He had admitted as much the night they had made love. He had done a horrible, unforgivable thing in writing that venomous letter. He could not defend it. She could not love any man capable of so cruel an action.

"And yet I do."

Kathleen paused in the shadows cast by moonlight shining beyond the archway that led onto the terrace that separated her rooms from the other wing of the house. She did love him. Not in spite of what he had done but because he had been honest enough to admit what he had done. If he had not told her, she would never have known about his part in the letter. He might have spared his own character and her revulsion of feeling toward him. After all, she had just shown him how much she

cared for him by sharing his bed. Yet, he had felt honor bound
to tell her the truth. How could she not admire his courage?

She wandered out on the balcony tiled in moonlight, slipping
out her fringed shawl so that the night breeze could pass sweetly
over her bare shoulders. Quinlan had been right about her. She
had begun to forgive him once the blaze of her anger subsided.
She wanted to see the good in him, wanted to make excuses,
wanted to believe that if he had not written the note, Pettigrew
would have, and the effect would have been the same. Quinlan
was, in the end, merely the messenger. She wanted to believe
he had trusted in their feelings, his and hers, enough to burden
them with the disclosure.

Most of all, she wanted to believe that they had a future. But
since he had not come that night, she no longer felt so certain
of anything.

She spied the open doorway to Grainne's room and turned
in alarm. The servants knew to keep the doors and windows
shut against the noxious night air. She moved quickly across
the terrace toward the offending breach, only to pause short of
the door.

She saw him before she recognized him.

He was slumped in the high-backed chair drawn up before
the open doorway, his legs sprawled out before him, his elbows
braced on the wooden chair arms, and forearms folded across
the blanketed bundle with black curls resting against his chest.
Beside him on the floor was a half-empty bottle and a used
diaper. His head was canted to one side, as if he were dozing,
but the slant of moonlight falling across his face revealed that
his eyes were open. As she met that avid gaze, it went through
her like a spark.

Kathleen felt herself blush from bosom to cheek, but she did
not look away. Pale light polished his features to artistic perfection. He looked splendid. And she did love him, and hate
him a little for leaving her so long in doubt, and wished con-
trarily that she did not feel either emotion. Oh, why, she won-

dered a little wildly as the silence between them strung out,
were feelings such ungovernable things?

Quinlan smiled leisurely at the woman standing on the terrace. Even at night her fiery hair possessed the capacity to dazzle. Her shoulders were bare and so was her throat. He would
give her diamonds, he decided, and sapphires and rubies and,
oh, whatever caught her eye. But she must recant quickly or he
would be driven to kidnap her.

Relenting because the silence was more intolerable than con-
frontation, Kathleen asked in a hollow voice, "What are you
doing here?"

"Did Francapelli not tell you?" He straightened a fraction
and adjusted the babe in his arms. "When I arrived earlier in
the evening, Francapelli said that you were in need of a caretaker
for Grainne." He lightly patted with one broad hand the child
sleeping peacefully on his chest. "I volunteered."

Kathleen accepted this news with astonishing calm. "It seems
that Conte Francapelli is not to be trusted on any account."

"Do not blame him. I asked that he not tell you, for I knew
you would refuse me and he needed you at his side tonight.
Was the opera a success?"

She nodded. "I should think you will hear the bravos carried
on the air at any moment."

"Good." His gaze moved over her like the stroke of a warm
hand, making her shoulders twitch. "You look . . . exquisite."

She let her shawl trail behind her as she slowly approached
him. "I hear you've been to London."

"I have. I came here tonight to tell you that I took your
translation of Francapelli's opera with me." He saw her hesitate.
"Longstreet was impressed. He would like you to transpose the
libretto into a play for the fall season. He bought my play as
well. We're both going to be embarrassingly well known next
season."

"I don't believe you," Kathleen answered, giving speech to
her thoughts.

"Why not?"

"It seems too convenient. How could you have traveled to London and back in so short a period of time?"

"When one is wealthy and an aristocrat, as you so enjoy pointing out, one can order the world to accommodate itself to one's needs. I hired a sloop to carry me to Marseille, where I hired a private coach to carry me across France. By changing teams of horses periodically, we made amazing time. I did the reverse to return here. So you see, there was plenty of time for me to see Longstreet, to have him read both our plays and draw up the appropriate contacts."

She shook her head, suspecting his hand in the machinations. "Why are you doing this?"

He did not move, but she felt him reach out to her across the moon-slated darkness. "Because I wanted to make certain that you had a very compelling reason to return with me to London."

She took a step closer to him, impelled by a need stronger than reason. How trustingly her daughter slept on his broad chest. She could remember what it felt like and longed to repeat the action. "To be a playwright?"

"To be whatever you wish." He held out a hand to her. "I have your contract in my pocket. You shall find that you can live quite comfortably on what Longstreet is offering."

She took his hand, startled and then thrilled by the warmth of the hard fingers he wrapped tightly about hers. "I am amazed he made an offer for an unwritten work"

"You have a profitable history, Miss Geraldine. While, alas, *Fortune's Fool* will remain known as my work, we both know the real author is quite talented in her own right. While it is not my top-grossing play, it did remarkably well. I thank you for the revenue.

She blushed as he drew her in between his spread legs. "And will we share in the profit of this new play?"

He crossed his ankles behind her, trapping her within the embrace of his legs. "Only if you agree to my terms."

She leaned forward and braced a hand on the tall chair back. "What terms would those be?"

He released her and lifted a hand to her face hovering above his. "To become the next Countess of Kearney. As your husband, I will be entitled to whatever moneys are earned by my wife."

"I see. Then this is a bribe you offer your competition."

"Nay, a bargain. The contract is yours, unencumbered." He brushed his thumb slowly back and forth over her lower lip. "Yet I hope you will feel obliged to share with me."

Kathleen smiled for the first time. "Why should I wish to feel obligated to you?"

"Not obligated. Obliged." He hooked a hand behind her head and drew her inexorably down toward him. "The word has many colorations. It implies favor." He kissed her lightly. "Indulgence." Another kiss. "And compulsion." The third kiss was longer and deeper. "I want you to feel compelled to agree to share everything with me." This time he stared into her eyes only inches from his. "Because you love me."

"You are a fool!" she said roughly, but she did not pull away.

He laughed and brushed his cheek against hers. "What man in love isn't?"

She shook her head, reveling in the smell of him, so wonderful, so pleasant, so different from any other scent she had ever known. She knew he was a proud man. She had not suspected he was so reckless as to seriously entertain marrying a woman like her. It frightened and thrilled her.

"There are drawbacks to this arrangement," he said, as he lifted his head to nibble her left ear.

"I should think so," she sighed.

"I will give you a child every year."

"Yes," she said, as a sensation of acute anticipation sped up her spine.

"And that will keep you from town."

She began to smile.

"I will be very jealous. Francapelli seemed to think that's because there's a bit of Italian in my background."

"Really?" Tears found their way under her eyelids.

"And I will want to love you when you are too old for such things to be seemly." He found her mouth and kissed her under the canopy of her hair, which enveloped them as she leaned over him.

When she lifted away, he was smiling. "And you will allow it because you do not wish to hurt my feelings."

Kathleen smiled through her tears. "I do believe you're quite right."

He stroked a thumb across her damp cheek. "Then marry me, Caitlin. Be as brave as your love."

She touched her child's dark head. "What about Grainne?" Quinlan kissed the top of the babe's head and then her mother's lips again. "She'll be mine. I offer her my name, my house, my love, just as I do you."

Kathleen brushed the tears from her eyes with the back of one hand, then reached down to touch his face. There was laughter on his lips and in his eyes. And she marveled at it and at him. "You're a beautiful madman."

"Then a beautiful mad pledge it will be."

She kissed him quickly, still shy though feeling braver with every moment. "I love you," she said against his mouth.

He grinned and kissed her harder. "Did you ever doubt it?"

ROMANCE FROM JANELLE TAYLOR

ROMANCE FROM FERN MICHAELS

YOU WON'T WANT TO READ
JUST ONE—KATHERINE STONE